100 Miles to Destiny

a Novel on Running

by

Willis B. McCarthy

June 2007

Rose, I hope you find inspiration in the following pages. Get well soon and embrace the journey.

Willis

© 2006 by Willis B. McCarthy
Registration Number TXu1-311-034

ISBN 978-0-9787535-0-4

Hignell Book Printing, Winnipeg, Manitoba, Canada R3G 2B4

Cover Art by Ron Chironna, New York, NY

Copy Editing by Yvonne Sullivan

Cover Design and Text Format by Michelle Wilkinson

Printed in Canada

DEDICATION

For Adrian and Arianna,

You have given me

raison d'être

et

joie de vivre

MAP BY SCOTT SIMPKIN

THE TRAIL OF THE
WESTERN STATES ENDURANCE RUN

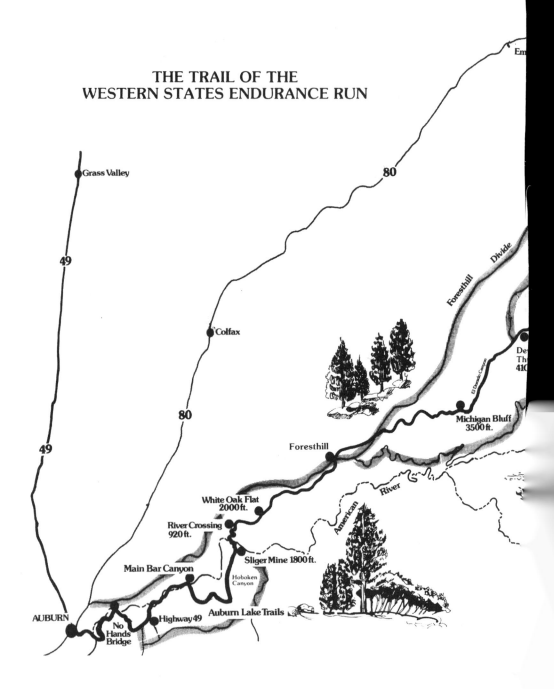

Soda Springs

Truckee

80

Donner Lake

89

Cougar Rock

Hodgson's Cabin
7200 ft.

SQUAW VALLEY

Granite Chief

Red Star Ridge

Emigrant
Monument

Robinson Flat
6200 ft.

Deep
Canyon
No. 1

Fork of
merican River

Duncan
Canyon
6000 ft.

LAKE
TAHOE

hance

DUSTY
CONECK

French Meadows
Reservoir

anyon
ft

River

American

ALTITUDE PROFILE MAP

*The altitude profile map below provides a basic outline of the terrain covered in the 100 miles.
Nothing aids a runner more in the actual race, however, then first-hand experience with the course. It is
highly recommended that, if possible, prosepective participants in the Western States Endurance Run
acquaint themselves with the trail beforehand, especially those portions which will be traveled in the
dark. If you plan to pre-run any portion of the trail, please read item 9 of "The Trail" section of the
brochure (page 8-9).*

Squaw Valley
Emigrant Pass
Hodgson's Cabin
Foresthill Divide
Red Star Ridge
Duncan Canyon
Robinson Flat
Cavanaugh Ridge
Deep Canyon
Last Chance
North Middle Fork of American River
Devil Thumb
El Dorado Canyon
Michigan Bluff
Volcano Canyon
Foresthill
Todd Valley
White Oak Flat
Greenwood Crossing (ford)
Middle Fork American River
Pointed Rocks Ranch
No Hands Bridge
Auburn

Total Altitude Gain: 17,040 feet
Total Altitude Loss: 21,970 feet
Net Altitude Loss, Squaw Valley to Auburn: 4,930 feet
Emigrant Pass to No Hands Bridge 8,180 feet Difference in Altitude

NO NATURAL WATER
FOR 16 MILES.

— 9,000
— 8,000
— 7,000
— 6,000
— 5,000
— 4,000
— 3,000
— 2,000
— 1,000
— 0

0   10   20   30   40   50   60   70   80   90   100

— Miles —

PROFILE BY AINSLEIGH

PREFACE

I have a great story to tell – a story of passion, a story of the human experience.

In the year of our Lord one thousand nine hundred eighty-four, three hundred seventy men and women assembled at the base of Squaw Valley near Lake Tahoe to participate in an inaugural 100 Mile Endurance Run World Championship. I was one of the participants. The 1984 race, the eighth edition of the Western States Trail Run, spawned the idea of this novel.

This is a story of the human spirit, the challenge of being the best in the world and the sacrifices accepted by athletes to achieve their ultimate goal. Each individual depicted in the novel is fictitious, yet I have attempted to create descriptions that are predicated upon my experiences as an American who has lived and worked overseas. Engaging in conversations with individuals who represent a range of personalities from various backgrounds, I have discovered much about the nationalities portrayed. For the sake of brevity I have used composite characterization and in advance, I apologize for the generalizations made in this text. Certainly, being an American has its limitations and my intent is not to stereotype. Instead, I intend to elucidate the diversity that exists between runners from different countries whom compete against one another on a global stage.

Despite the characters' diverse upbringings, they are connected by a common bond and a unique set of circumstances – an Olympic race of 100 miles. The race requires them not only to battle each other, but also to combat the elements that nature mounts against them. Each athlete represents a country, culture and lifestyle that molds the individual into one of his nation's best. They have been recognized for their achievement. Yet recognition in itself is not the sole reason why athletes sustain their efforts to become world-class runners.

An African philosopher once said, "Happiness is not a final destination at which one arrives; instead, it is the manner in which one has traveled." For these men, their personal journey revolves around two measures of running: distance traveled and the time taken to finish.

Whether race or workout, standards are set according to the measurements of distance and time, and man will always attempt to surpass standards.

This book describes athletes who train far beyond normal parameters to establish records that most people would think humanly impossible. They compete on an international level attempting to reap the benefits of such undertakings. Dreaming of glory, Olympic gold and national recognition, they arrive at the 23rd Olympiad to run the race of a lifetime. Unfortunately, not all will achieve their goal. Two thousand years ago Saint Paul wrote, "All runners at the stadium are trying to win, but only one will get the prize." Accordingly, there can only be one winner. As in life, long distance running can dole out some painful lessons – both physical and emotional.

No question, work ethic plays an essential role in running and the satisfaction of the daily regimen of distance training will be extolled in the following pages. Saint Paul continues, "(Athletes) at the games go into strict training; they do this just to win a wreath that will wither, but we do it for a wreath that will never wither." Even two millennia ago Paul knew the importance of training, plus how fleeting success can be. In my view, "iron" such as medals, trophies, cups, plaques and yes, even belt buckles may tarnish over time, but the memories of the races, and most principally, the people you meet, last a life-time.

The race itself represents the culmination of a way of life. When preparing for a race of this magnitude, of this significance, other facets in a person's life are usually ignored or put on hold in order not to conflict with race preparation. In part, this book is dedicated to those who have pursued excellence on a purely amateur level, receiving little or no financial gain; especially courageous are those souls who have dared toe the line of an endurance run, knowing their finest moment to be simply (or exceedingly difficult) crossing a finish line 100 miles distant. One final comment regarding races of this distance: the race encapsulates one's life - highs and lows, elation and despair, satisfaction and frustration. Personal experience has bared witness to such a roller coaster ride of emotion since I have run, jogged, walked and most importantly, experienced fully such races repeatedly over the past twenty-five years.

Lastly, there are a couple of items worth mentioning about this novel: 1) Sixteen Eastern Block countries, the Soviet Union included, did boycott the 1984 Summer Olympiad, rendering the games somewhat incomplete. 2) There has never been and most likely will never be an Olympic one hundred mile endurance run. However, if politics never interfered with athletics, and a 100 Mile Olympic Endurance Run were staged, the race would be rife with possibilities.

Enjoy the read.

A poem by the author presenting the remarkable experience of running, competing and finishing endurance runs of 100 miles:

Liminal Pain to Finish Line

Gun fires into darkness before dawn.
Pierces the silence.
Race commences.   (Old Dominion)
Stars twinkle above,
fireflies glow in nearby meadow.
Hills of Northern Virginia, a silhouette,
trigger historical thought.
Pace is swift, our first ascent.
Adrenaline rushes, endorphins flow,
running is effortless.
A new day begins.

Crimson dawn over Tahoe Basin.
Crest at 9000 feet.   (Western States)
Stop, turn – spectacular panorama.
Magnificent lake, Sierra splendor.
Unforgettable.
Long descent,
running is pure.
Aid station at ten miles.
Replenish what nature has taken.
Feeling fine, I can run forever.
Home field advantage.
Christ, it's good to be alive.

First river crossing – knee deep and cold.
Continental Divide provides   (Leadville)
breath-taking vistas – the Colorado Rockies.
Major climb - 3000 feet vertical.
Little oxygen - breath taken
12,600 feet above sea level.
Another long descent,
half way point arrives.
Blisters evident under damp socks.
Blood seeps through fabric.
Muscles sore, aching back.
Eat and drink.
Glance at my watch.
I've run for ten hours.
Stand to continue,
Finish line beckons.

Sunset over Alta,
Light filters through trees.   (Wasatch Front)
Twilight's orange hues, violets
fade to black.
Canopy of stars.
Another major climb,
Wasatch Mountains relentless,
the struggle ongoing.
Pray for next aid station,
hypoglycemia, exhaustion imminent.
Flashlight up ahead,
another runner disappears,
enshroud in darkness.
No longer a test of stamina,
instead a test of will.
Tenacity befriends me,
the race consumes me.

Muscles numb, maintain focus,
mental toughness critical.   (Angeles Crest)
Traverse last major climb.
San Gabriel Mountains behind me,
only a speed bump remains.
Cross a creek bed,
wet feet - again.
Single track trail ends,
jeep road to the finish line.
Adrenaline rushes, endorphins flow.
Running effortlessly.
Rose Bowl appears – the finish.

100 miles run, less than one day.
Belt buckle to sleep with, tangible award.
Sterling performance, ethereal reward.

PROLOGUE

The two hominids peered over a rocky crag that overlooked a deep basin within the Savannah of East Africa. The sun's rays beamed upon them this cloudless summer morning, causing their eyes to focus keenly on what lay in the distance. Subsisting on paltry amounts of insects and tubers they had scavenged the past few days, their mouths were parched and their stomachs empty. The two young males espied a moderate-sized drinking hole. From their vantage point the lake appeared relatively close and because of their recent consumption of meager rations, the proximity of the lake looked even closer. They were beyond thirst and hunger.

The two juveniles smiled at one another, baring stained teeth and knowing the prospect of their good fortune. Fresh water and the possibility of fresh meat excited them both immensely. The two could hardly restrain themselves from jumping and gesticulating wildly at the thought of quenching their thirst and filling their gut. And yet standing on this outcrop of rock, caution overtook them simultaneously from elation to acute awareness of potential hazards that may lurk in or near the water. Scanning the basin for larger predators that would threaten their safety; they could only see zebra, gazelle and in the shallows, birds preening themselves. This was an auspicious morning.

Challenging both daily to survive on whatever nature would dole out, the Savannah had been unforgiving to these two lost souls. Unlike the lush, rich rainforests of Central Africa where monkeys and apes found plenty of provender and languished in the shade of magnificent tropical trees, the Savannah was testing man's ability to exist in harsh, arid surroundings. Lacking prehensile toes and longer forearms, he was not relegated to an arboreal existence. Instead, man stood upright, moved with lithe quickness and agility, landing flat on his feet. Foremost, man had learned to run in his quest to survive. Man had become a cursorial beast. He had endurance and strength, plus a solid frame to ward-off predators if not overwhelmed. His brain and fingers allowed him the capacity to build crude tools and weapons to assist in the survival in this dry desolate land. Man was being shaped by the sheer nature of the ascetic, East African plains. Lacking an abundance of water and food, man had to improvise, use his superior intellect, and manage with what God and nature had provided.

Each juvenile had departed a populous tribe when the dominant male felt threatened by the presence of other males. These two in particular had seemed to undermine the authority of the alpha male of their respective groups. Consequently, through confrontation and intimidation the younger, more docile males had been persuaded to depart. Solely by chance, the two had met while collecting articles of food and promptly found safety and solace in one another's company. Two moons had passed since that fateful day, each eventually forgetting the sanctuary and confines of the parental group.

Kneeling quietly, they eyed the water with eagerness knowing the potential for sustenance was close at hand. The lake appeared to grow bigger, ever closer with each passing moment when the larger, more robust male glanced at his friend. The smaller one returned a smile, knowing the distance to be a formidable challenge. There was little primitive communication between them.

It could have been 50,000 years before the birth of Christ or 100,000 years before, regardless, for the first time in the history of man, one human being would pit himself against another in a race. Not a race for survival, but instead, a race to see who could move the fastest over a given distance. For these two adolescent males, it simply meant who could arrive at the water hole first. Man would not compete by throwing sticks or stones, or grappling with one another; those games would come later.
The first true test of man's competitive zeal would be a foot race.

It was straightforward, even primal, when the robust male leaped over the rocky crag followed in close pursuit by his companion. Their calloused feet moved swiftly and adroitly over the stone-laden, sandy soil. They were no longer looking at water or animals in the distance; their focus was on the ground rushing beneath their feet, arms and legs pumping in harmony as gravity assisted them down the mountain. They were in flight.

The larger male had quickly opened a ten meter lead on his opponent, but there was a great deal of distance remaining. The smaller male was moving well over the terrain close behind. In control and pacing himself, he had not permitted his friend to increase the margin. He was maintaining contact. At about the halfway mark the robust male began to feel the first effects of oxygen debt. His breathing had become labored, his chest tightened, muscles were becoming flaccid. This felt different when compared to escaping from a predator when adrenaline would course through his blood vessels. He thought he should be able to run farther, harder, but he was slowing down and there was little he could do to stave off his fellow competitor. The lesser male felt tired too, but in a different way. He could cope with fatigue better. Breathing rapidly, running relaxed and efficiently, the smaller male began to close the distance. This male's musculature and cardiovascular system were slightly different than his opponent. While nature had not granted the young man bulk and speed, She had blessed him with stamina and the brains to pace himself for the long run. And since this race had surpassed the distance of a sprint and was fast approaching a distance event, the diminutive one held an advantage. Momentarily, he thought of himself as a hunter chasing a prey animal to exhaustion without stone or spear. He would capture his prey very soon. The competitive fervor grew exponentially between these two as they approached the base of the hill.

Anatomically, there were other subtle differences between the two individuals. The lesser male had more muscle fiber that was red in color, the larger male had a greater number of white muscle fiber. The white muscle fiber permitted speed and explosiveness, the red fiber allowed for stamina and endurance. Both muscle groups were being tested simultaneously. Blood was being pumped vigorously to the limbs carrying needed oxygen and sugars for the working muscles, yet something more significant presented another problem. Lactic acid and carbon dioxide, the waste products of their metabolism, were building-up much more rapidly than could be removed. Anerobic threshold was fast approaching and both their arms and legs had begun to feel heavy and overworked. Their youth and inexperience was beginning to show as their muscles began to bind, causing the two competitors to inexorably slow down.

When the two young men reached flat ground, they both glanced forward to witness the scampering of zebra, gazelle and birds taking flight to escape the sudden onslaught of predation. They were abreast of one another, neither giving an inch nor conceding defeat. What once appeared from the rocky crag as a near-by water hole had abruptly become far too distant, especially for the more muscular male, but despite his lack of stamina, he possessed will-power and obstinacy. He refused to quit.

Each could feel the other's presence, drawing energy from one another. Like two magnets being pulled toward one another, these two were being pulled toward an objective. The two hominids were inextricably immersed in their own world, their own competitive fire, when the shimmering sunlight reflected from the surface of the murky pool caught their attention. There were five hundred meters of earth remaining to negotiate before one or the other would reach the water, and they were dead even at this point.

.

Chapter 1 - Squaw Valley, California
4 August 1984

*O*nce upon a time in the West . . .

They mill about a well-lit staging area, resembling men from a refugee camp of a war-torn country more than world class athletes. Thin, gaunt faces appear to glow from lights that surround them as they weakly exchange perfunctory handshakes. They offer their best wishes, demonstrating camaraderie and sportsmanship. Each man, in his own world, contemplates what lies ahead, what will be endured and ultimately, knowing that beyond his physical and emotional limits, he will find the man he is destined to become.

Shadows dance across the grounds and walls of an adjacent building. A man blows into Scottish bagpipes filling the air with discordant sounds and for some, perchance, tocsin notes. A Christian runner observes a shining star in the east and quotes a passage from the book of Revelations. *"For he overcomes, I will give the morning star."* Islamic runners kneel on tapestries, face eastward and recite incantations from the Qur'an. Their repetitive prayer is a reflection of their lives and faith. *"In the name of Allah, the most gracious, the most merciful. All praise and thanks are Allah's, the Lord of the Alamin . . ."*

"Good morning everybody and welcome to Squaw Valley, the site of the start of the inaugural, first-ever ultramarathon held during an Olympic games. I'm Brandon Davis, and I will be reporting live from points along the one hundred mile course throughout the day and night." A television camera with a bright spotlight transmits the broadcaster's enthusiastic face. "That's right, you heard me correctly. One hundred miles of trail separate these athletes from the finish line which is southwest from here in the small foothill community of Auburn, California. They will run, jog, walk or even crawl to get to the finish line, so I am told. Nathan Washington is a two-time winner of the Western States Trail Run – the same course these men will follow today. What's going through your mind, Mr. Washington - are you ready to run?"

The cameraman adjusts the view on a taller, slender man with a medium build. His reddish-brown hair is parted in the middle and his tawny mustache is trimmed, but extends well below his lips. A clean gray singlet is tucked neatly inside his running shorts with the red bold letters USA etched directly above his assigned number, 620. The man appears calm and resolute as he begins his reply.

"Well, hopefully no one will be reduced to a crawl . . . that gets kind of messy if you know what I mean." Both men crack a smile. "Certainly, I'm anxious to get started and ready as I'll ever be." Washington instinctively rubs both sides of his fu-man-chu.

"What chances do you give yourself to win, Nathan?"

"As good as anyone's. There are many runners here who have impressive credentials; anyone of them can win this race." Washington pauses, "I've got a shot." Pointing at one of the runners passing by he exclaims, "There's a contender, Juan-Pablo 'Bad *##' Badillo. J. P., come here for a second." The camera refocuses on a smaller runner with short-cropped black hair. He is of darker complexion. The two men exchange a handshake and a hug.

"Er . . . you two must know each other. What do you think your chances are, Mr. Badillo, in today's race?" Davis sees a confused face above the man's spotless white uniform. A small Mexican flag is centered on his singlet directly above his assigned bib number, 557. "You do speak English?"

His stilted accent sounds comical. "Sorry, I no speak English very good, can you please repeat question for me?" Washington initially restrains himself. Both men attempt to displace their tension with humor and laugh heartily. "Of course I can speak English and quite well I might add. Yeah, my chances are good, if I can beat this guy." He nudges Washington with an elbow. "Ther're a lot of great runners here, and any know they can win. Nathan and I have talked about this several times over the past year. At this point, it's anyone's guess, and obviously anyone's race."

A voice over an intercom announces, "Two minutes till race time."

Nathan looks over at his compadre and says, "About that time J. P." Badillo nods approvingly and squirts some fluid from a water bottle into his mouth.

Davis acknowledges their departure. "Best of luck, gentlemen. Well, we're just moments away from the start of the race. Everyone has assembled at the starting line, awaiting the commands from the race director, Norman Sproul. We'll have a chance to speak with Mr. Sproul later. It is an amazing story how the Los Angeles Games came to Squaw Valley. A story we will soon share."

The camera pivots toward the starting line ready to record an Olympic moment. Some of the athletes nervously jump up and down, others continue to stretch attempting to stay loose, and others remain completely still in meditation. Final preparations complete, they keenly concentrate on the starter's commands.

"One minute to start . . ." Silence descends on the staging area. There is an intense calm in the early morning's twilight when the race director declares, "Gentlemen, take your mark . . ." For one long second no one moves.

The shotgun blast shatters the still, cool, Sierra morning air. A great horned owl escapes in silent flight, a mule deer scampers from the sudden discharge and a solitary mountain lion glances over his shoulder undaunted by the echoes of distant gunfire. At this very instant in time 162 athletes representing the nations of the world, who have congregated at the Squaw Valley Olympic Village, begin their assault of 100 miles over the rugged, mountainous terrain of the western Sierra Nevada. The media's luminous spotlights have lit-up the staging area and initially blind the runners as they begin their sojourn. Spectators converge on the starting line with their cameras to witness the commencement of an inaugural Olympic race. Incandescent flashes fire as the commentator attempts to capture the unique beginning of a truly international event.

"That's no typical starter's gun Mr. Sproul. Why a shotgun?"

Race Director Norman Sproul offers a broad smile. "It's a tradition we started a few years ago and we've continued with the practice of a twelve gauge to start our race. It sure grabs your attention, doesn't it?" Sproul holds the gun with its barrel resting on his right forearm. The smell of burnt sulfur and salt peter lingers.

Brandon Davis' ears are still ringing. "Yes, you certainly caught mine."

The time is six o'clock ante meridian, Saturday the 4th of August 1984. The morning is clear, the eastern sky crimson with wisps of clouds, and the planet Mercury known as the morning star is visible in the twilight on this very special day. To the west, few notice a large gibbous moon setting behind the peaks surrounding Squaw Valley. The first seventy-five meters are flat, crossing tiled brick; then the runners step on dirt, which will be followed by a steady ascent of nearly four and one-half miles, an ascent that will take each runner from the base elevation at Squaw Valley, 6200 feet, to Emigrant Pass, altitude 8800 feet. This will be the first of many climbs the runners will negotiate to reach the finish line at Placer High School in Auburn, California – 100 miles away.

The first climb is the longest and most arduous, yet few feel apprehension and restraint since the inception of the race was but moments ago. Adrenaline is abundant in these intrepid runners, and it is extremely difficult to hold back and pace oneself during the early going. The veterans of such runs are cognizant this race will not be won in the first climb or the first twenty-six miles or even the first 100 kilometers. Consequently, these individuals approach the race with caution. Patience will be a necessity during the course of the event if they are to succeed.

Only a handful of the participants are familiar with a foot race of 100 miles. All have competed in marathons and fifty kilometer endurance runs. Many have experienced the metric measure of 100 kilometers in European races or other 100 kilometer events worldwide. However, the distance of this race is a quantum leap further, testing the mettle and resolve of all participants, especially those who have never run 100 miles. And there are limitations. A time limit of twenty-four hours is allotted to complete the grueling trek. The time element is staggering when an athlete considers the number of hours he will be moving forward just to merit the title of official finisher, medal recipient or Olympic champion. Certain faces are familiar, most are anonymous. Many have been victorious at shorter distances, running in less competitive races. Now each individual confronts the challenges of distance, nature's parameters, keen competition, and personal limitations. Athletes will have to contend with the opposition, both external and internal, in their own way. Currently, all are moving well up a moderate grade on a jeep trail. There are ninety-nine miles remaining and the runners have already begun to separate, some moving more swiftly than others.

The blast of the shotgun is not heard 400 miles south in the city of Los Angeles where the host city has welcomed the world to the site of the XXIII Olympiad. Despite international media coverage, most Americans take little interest in the start of an endurance running event. Opting to sleep through the start of the race, they are sure to catch replays, plus updates later during the day. In other parts of the world, fascination and greater interest exist as millions are poised by their televisions and radios to hear the onset of the race. This is the first ultramarathon in modern Olympic history, generating much attention, interest and undoubtedly, some consternation.

"This is a miracle. Just ten years after the inception of the Western States Trail Run, we are witnessing the development of a sport that has grown exponentially." Norm Sproul sports a white, long sleeve T-shirt depicting unique artwork silk-screened on it. The words '100 MILES ONE DAY' are printed on the left sleeve. His silver belt buckle has the same words engraved. He is a well educated man, an eloquent speaker and presently, his exuberance is evident. "We cannot believe how far our sport and, er . . . our race has grown!" Sproul purposely uses first person plural vernacular, knowing that numerous individuals have been involved in this grandest enterprise to put this race together. He likes the idea of many people taking ownership in the international event. "This is truly a monumental undertaking."

*   *   *

Members of the International Olympic Committee (IOC), who had hoped to disallow such an extreme event, had legitimate concerns regarding safety and regulations. In marathons, which consist of a standard 26.2 miles, officials had witnessed some near-death incidents of athletes who had wandered to close to the edge of human stamina. Increasing the distance nearly four fold would surely increase the number of casualties, perhaps even causing fatalities. In response, the United States Olympic

Committee (USOC) assured the participating countries that the athletes would be monitored meticulously during the entire event and that regulations would be implemented to ensure their safety.

Many of the countries had begun to prepare their ultra-athletes three years earlier when the USOC announced the addition of a novel Olympic event in Los Angeles. The committee disseminated specific information about the nature of the course, calling the race a true test of human endurance – "The Ultimate Challenge." Logistics of the race seemed clear enough: 100 miles of single trek/jeep trails, some gravel and asphalt road. 17,000 feet of vertical ascents and 22,000 feet of descents covering the expanse of the rugged Sierra Nevada Mountains west of Lake Tahoe. Temperatures could range between freezing in the higher altitudes to well over 100° Fahrenheit during the day at lower elevations. Athletes and coaches were warned about the potential risks of altitude sickness, dehydration, hyperthermia, kidney failure and even necrosis of muscle tissue. Countries were appraised of all pertinent information and encouraged to prepare their athletes accordingly. As in any Olympic endeavor, athletes and coaches knew that preparation would be paramount to the success of each runner.

"Mr. Sproul, how did this all come about? I mean, how did you and your, er . . ." Brandon Davis struggles to find the right word . . . "associates get to putting-on an Olympic event of this caliber?"

"Unbelievable to say the least." He shakes his head disbelieving his own words. "Our foundation petitioned the USOC in January of '81 to consider this race as an Olympic event, since the home country is permitted to implement new types of competition. We cited numerous reasons, the most important being the growth of ultramarathons worldwide. At first the USOC countered with the implementation of a 100 kilometer run as kind of a buffer distance. But we convinced them otherwise."

Logistics concerning race management and the coordination of such an extreme event were unprecedented in Olympic history. The USOC called upon a group of individuals who had brought ultrarunning to the forefront of endurance athletics. The Western States Trail had been used for nearly thirty years as the site of an endurance horse race. More recently, over the past ten years, runners had tested their stamina and athleticism at conquering the same distance - 100 miles on foot. The management of the endurance run was eager to transport the burgeoning national event to the world stage. The XXIII Olympic Games would serve that purpose. In fact, when the USOC announced the addition of the 100 mile event, two race directors had petitioned to have their course used during the games.

The Squaw Valley course won the rights to the Olympic race by a slim margin, just ahead of another course that traversed the San Gabriel Mountains near Los Angeles. That decision was based on three parts: 1) The Squaw Valley Race had been in existence much longer. 2) The race management had more resources at their disposal. And 3), most importantly, funding of the event had been insured by Levi Strauss, a textile company that had sponsored the Western States Trail Run in recent years.   .

Thereafter, race director Norman Sproul mobilized his army of volunteers to equip the necessary aid stations/checkpoints, thereby also establishing the mandatory communication and timing systems required to monitor the progress of each runner. In addition, he enlisted medical staff who could assist an athlete in case of an emergency. Sproul is a man in his mid-forties who has not only finished the event, but directed the race the past three years. As a result of his expertise, plus his thoroughness, he is confident he will do the job superbly, orchestrating an event unparalleled in the history of the modern Olympics.

"Buffer distance, what do you mean by that?" Davis points the microphone at the clean-shaven face of the race director.

"Simply put, it's a distance not as long and not as grueling. Plus, the IOC liked the idea of a metric distance; you know Brandon, international units and all that hogwash. However, we were steadfast in our convictions. In the U. S. we always do things bigger and better; you know what I mean." Sproul chuckles and then clears his throat. "Well, regardless, they bit - hook, line and sinker." He takes a deep breath of alpine air and then continues, "So here we are on a cool Sierra morning and we're underway."

Rules and regulations concerning the run would be strictly enforced by race personnel to ensure equity and impartiality during the race. Aid stations with a variety of foods and beverages would be available to all participants at designated checkpoints along the course. Athletes would be entitled to have personal items such as clothing, medication and flashlights stowed at the checkpoints. Otherwise, they would be required to carry whatever items they reasoned necessary to complete the run on their person. Additionally, random checkpoints would be set-up in order to ensure that each runner remained on trail throughout the entire event.

Four of the aid stations were designated as mandatory "medical checkpoints" where each athlete would be required to weigh-in, plus submit to a cursory examination assessing vital signs for potential health risks. Simple and distinct rules regarding weight, pulse and blood pressure would be monitored carefully. Medical personnel had the prerogative to detain or even disqualify an athlete if a physician or nurse deemed it necessary to temporarily or permanently remove an athlete due to the consequences of extreme weight loss, rapid pulse, elevated blood pressure or hyperthermia.

This rule provoked the most controversy. Coaches and athletes felt that certain individuals would be catered to, thus receiving special treatment. The USOC knew favoritism could be avoided by placing staff whom represented a variety of nationalities at each of the checkpoints. And the United States, especially California, had an ample reservoir of diversity from which to select. Additionally, coaches and other Olympic officials would be welcome to observe the operations of the checkpoints, thereby creating a spirit of cooperation rather than alienation.

But ultimately, the responsibility for the health and safety of each runner had to be placed solely upon the individual entered in the race. An athlete would be required to drink adequate fluids, eat the necessary foodstuffs and monitor himself throughout the endurance event. He would be entitled to some assistance at the aid stations, plus all the emotional support offered by race personnel; otherwise, the individual would be completely on his own. The consequence of not following the explicit instructions as stated by the race committee could result in disqualification.

*   *   *

A group of Africans have taken the early lead. Two Kenyans, two runners from Ethiopia, another from Tanzania, one from Burundi and an Egyptian have opened a two hundred meter lead over the remainder of the field in just two short miles. Their pace, to say the least, is ambitious. They have run two miles in fourteen and a half minutes. Seemingly a jog for these gazelles, the front runners appear to run effortlessly, smooth and efficient as they negotiate the first moderate climb. The jeep trail is wide so they can run in pairs or abreast of one another. Little conversation takes place since each individual does not wish to waste energy on idle conversation. The remainder of the pack has already begun to spread-out beneath them. The majority of the runners know the importance of running to their own ability and pace themselves accordingly during the initial phases of the race. Their strategy evident, most are content to let the front pack "break" the trail since so much time and distance remain.

The time is 6:15, the ambient Sierra temperature a cool 55° F when the front runners approach 7000 feet. At the Olympic Village in Los Angeles, athletes are content to rest before the first day of track and field competition. Sleeping quietly or awaking passively at this early hour, they will soon mentally prepare, envisioning success in their respective areas of expertise. Many events such as swimming and gymnastics have already taken place. Dreams fulfilled or lost, or perhaps, postponed. Yet for the 162 ultramarathoners their day has already begun and they are engaged against their most formidable enemy. The enemy is not jogging contentedly in front or behind each runner. Instead, after two miles, altitude has caused some to breathe deeply attempting to cope with thinner air and more specifically, the scant amounts of oxygen contained within.

The arid air is replete with the scent of coniferous resin. Stands of pine, spruce and cedar grow in places that defy the construction of a world class ski resort. It is ironic to think just twenty-four years ago at the 1960 Winter Olympics, downhill skiers approached reckless speeds of eighty miles per hour on these same slopes. At present, that trend has changed.

9

Runners, some swifter than others, are running eight or even ten minutes per mile in the opposite direction. The trail meanders up the side of the mountain crossing occasional creek beds, where snowmelt and natural springs create ripples of water descending the mountain. Nearly all the runners have eclipsed the 7000 foot level. Morale is high, the day young and the sun begins to brighten their sojourn as they continue a serpentine ascent of the mountain.

Runners will negotiate a section of the Sierra Nevada that had been crossed for centuries. Native Americans knew of the Great Lake found in the middle of the mountains. They ventured to its pristine shoreline for spiritual cleansing and meditation. It was truly a remarkable landmark, worthy of the sacrifice to reach its blessed, crystalline waters. Later, much later, during the nineteenth century, the trail was used as a pony express route connecting Reno, Nevada with Gold Towns of the California foothills. Numerous boomtowns grew prolifically, then as quickly as they had appeared, vanished with little trace when the gold mines' reservoirs became depleted. Names like Last Chance, Devil's Thumb and Michigan Bluff were once known in the Mother Lode as gold-bearing regions where exploiting the precious, yellow metal was common practice. At present, little remains of those boomtown days, except for a few hardy communities of loggers, tourism operators and of course, the obstinate gold miner who knows there's one more vein that will turn a profit.

Race Director Norman Sproul continues to speak about the logistics of the race. "Athletes have been given ample instruction of what to expect today and what to do during the course of the day. 'Drink fluids, eat solid foods, run within your limits,' they have been told repeatedly. We hope they heed to our warnings, plus use the wisdom of our experience to their best advantage. There's a short prayer athletes should recite today: 'God, grant me the resolve to finish what I start today. Give me the strength to change what I can, the patience to accept what I cannot and the wisdom to know the difference.' This mantra has its applications to our race."

"I can see that clearly." Davis nods, having heard the Franciscan prayer. "Obviously Norm, you know a lot about this race. What do you think each man will come to learn regarding your warnings and instructions?"

Sproul's reply is succinct. "Each will learn to determine his own limitations, that's for sure . . . or pay the price trying."

Chapter 2 – The Escarpment

The first aid station, known as the Escarpment, is an insignificant stop where volunteers pour water and electrolyte fluids into small plastic bottles carried by the runners. All stop to replenish their supply of the precious liquid, knowing the next stop is nearly eight miles ahead. The course leaves the wide dirt road and abruptly changes direction and slope, moving up a very steep, single trail where runners can use their hands to efficiently climb the precipice. And many employ the technique, water bottle in one hand, grasping a boulder with the other, pulling themselves upward.

One athlete's foot slips on a loose rock, his hand clings to his water bottle, as his right knee genuflects touching the ground. He looks up momentarily, pausing briefly to see the runners ahead and reflects upon how Jesus Christ must have felt when He tripped and fell for the first time, carrying the cross of humanity on his back. He had visited the Via Dolorosa in Jerusalem many times, seeing the marble wall plaques dedicated to the Son of Man whom had walked the same path to his own demise for what Christians believed to be his destiny.

"That was true sacrifice – the ultimate sacrifice," Joshua Kostinski contemplates. "Odd," Kostinski thinks, "Christianity." He shakes his head at the notion since he was raised in Israel - as a Jew. Apologizing to a runner below, Kostinski hikes with adeptness, not wishing to sacrifice time with another mistake on this portion of trail. He is an experienced trail runner who has run races throughout Western Europe and North America, including many collegiate races in the United States where he ran cross country and track.

*   *   *

During the nineteenth century European Jews escaped the violence of constant pogroms where prejudice and persecution had incited their emigration to Palestine. Joshua's great grandparents had witnessed the persecution of neighboring Jews in their community all too often. Feeling threatened living in Krakow, Poland they decided to move to Palestine where others had sought religious asylum and the hope of starting a new life. His ancestors brought about the ambitious plans of changing the face of Israel from a neglected wasteland to a productive, agricultural society. Kostinki's story is one that typifies many Israelis.

Growing-up on a kibbutz near Safed in northern Israel overlooking the Sea of Galilee, he had learned quickly to take responsibility when assigned tasks. His formative years were spent, like all other youth of the kibbutz, learning to contribute to the greater good of their society. His entire existence evolved from the communal lifestyle of giving unselfishly. He ate, slept, worked, played, attended classes and above all, learned to be Israeli while living there. The kibbutz was the epitome of collective living, each person performing duties that enhanced the overall welfare of the community. He was similar to most of the other children: Growing, developing and maturing into a fine young individual. And like other children he had become dependable, intelligent, articulate and showed promise in a number of subjects. Yet Joshua had one attribute that set him apart from the remainder of the children. He could run. No matter what race he entered, he was always competitive – even when running against more experienced athletes. If not winning outright, he seemed to find himself near the front consistently, often to the surprise of the older participants. The boy showed real promise.

His family's native language, Polish, had long been lost in the century plus that separated Joshua's great grandparents from his present generation. Many languages suffered similar fates as people assimilated into the new and developing country. As more nationalities immigrated to Israel, Hebrew, the language of the Old Testament, was chosen as the national language. Additionally, English was taught in schools knowing the magnitude and importance of the United States affecting world affairs. Joshua Kostinski became fluent in both languages.

Upon completing secondary school and three years military service to the State of Israel, he moved to the United States to continue his formal education. Joshua had relatives living in upstate New York near Albany and was invited to stay with his surrogate family for a time. He enrolled at the local state university and decided to study economics with long-term goals in mind of improving his nation's state of financial affairs. As a young man who witnessed an irresolute economy requiring much foreign assistance; he accepted his role as a student of economics. Pondering further, he also knew a miracle would be a requisite to bring Israel from an economic dependent state to an independent nation establishing its own source of internal revenue. Four hostile neighboring countries required ninety percent of its national budget to secure Israel's borders from external Islamic states.

Yet there had been numerous miracles at the conclusion of the Second World War that had brought about the existence of a sovereign Israel. Joshua Kostinski knew he was a young man who could have a positive impact in his country and consequently, he had grown-up very quickly. Witnessing hardship and war in his homeland, and anti-Semitism in the United States, he had learned to assimilate well into different environments. Despite the burden of responsibility he felt on his shoulders, there was an avenue to pure freedom, liberating Joshua from the gravity of the Middle East. Running could set him free, perhaps for only a brief time, but this time became essential to his well-being.

His cross country team was a welcome reprieve from the daily grind of classes, pressure and stress associated with college life. With his personal and team's success combined, running became even more rewarding. During a four year, collegiate career under the tutelage of his coach, he had changed from "a kid with a lot of raw talent" to a national class runner. The potential for greatness was inherent in this young man's blood.

Many clubs had attempted to enlist Josh as a member of their training group and he truly wanted to take advantage of the regimen offered by a club. One in particular in Boston appeared enticing. There were numerous runners congregating there with the hope of building an American enclave of distance runners. He would be a welcome addition to this group of national class runners who wanted to continue their training beyond college. Thereafter, Kostinski enrolled at Boston College to pursue his Master's Degree in Business Administration and to continue his training with the enclave. Joshua Kostinski improved, improved to a point of qualifying for the U. S. Olympic trials in the marathon for the 1980 Olympics, slated to be held in Moscow. Josh knew if he could make the U. S. Olympic team, he would be a shoe-in to make his native country's Olympic squad. Unfortunately, that was never to be.

*   *   *

Beads of perspiration dissipate over his bronze skin when he reaches the top of the escarpment. The sky blue insignia of the Star of David clings to his chest as his belief in God holds steadfast to his soul. Looking at his foot placement Joshua sees yellow alpine flowers seemingly emerge from rock. *"God touches this place,"* he whispers in Hebrew. Ardent brown eyes glance ahead to see several runners moving well. The twenty-nine year old Israeli unconscientiously slaps the dirt from his right knee and resumes running. Estimating his position is near the front, he does not wish to relinquish a single place. Josh cannot see the insignias on the front of the different, brightly colored uniforms. There is another Israeli runner out there – somewhere. He dares not turn around, either, to see the competitors behind. "Is it important, anyways?" he considers. "There are over 155 kilometers remaining and an unknown amount of time." The man from Judea runs-on, moving easily along the trail.

The seven African runners continue to pull away exuding confidence and determination. They have all followed the Kenyan philosophy of distance running for years. Their teams have subscribed to a catalogue of commandments that include training regimen, diet, camaraderie, focus and purpose. Not limited to a simple design of workouts, their edicts reflect a lifestyle in which athletes commit themselves to be world class runners. Born and raised in the Third World, they have not had the distractions other children have had growing-up in more "developed" conditions. There are few games, if any, a child can be given. Luxuries are for the very rich; necessities that sustain life are given priority. Not all children go to school in Africa, but those who do must find their own transportation. And for most children the means of arriving to school punctually are by foot, then returning home by the same mode of transport. Children at a very early age learn the most efficient way of travel is to run, and run they do through all their formative years.

Unfortunately, African runners have had to contend with other peripheral issues that have systematically undermined their progress. Civil wars, apartheid, pestilence, famine and widespread corruption have

15

created hardships beyond explanation that athletes from industrialized countries cannot begin to understand. Yet these men toe the line aspiring to greatness that their governments recognize and reward. They have come to the United States to prove they are worthy of the challenge to run 100 miles and win gold.

The Squaw Valley, High Altitude Center is approaching on their right where ski lift towers appear to rise above a solid rocky substrate. The Africans arrive at an alpine meadow 8000 feet above sea level, experiencing no duress.

Akira Okuda sees the black athletes well ahead of his current position as he leads the second pack of runners on a single track trail. His breathing already laborious, his heart seems to pound between his ears. *"Much too early to push the pace,"* he thinks. Akira steps aside permitting a couple of runners to pass. He breathes deeply and sighs, knowing he should not feel fatigue or heaviness at this point on the course. The quizzical look on his face underscores the issues facing the devout Buddhist from Hokkaido, Japan. The five kilometers he has completed have left Okuda breathless. Slowing his pace to six minutes a kilometer is disquieting enough, having runners pass him is disheartening. He attempts to relax as he has done in the past. The transcendental state eludes him. There are too many obstacles, trail ribbons to look for, changes in direction. Despite previewing the course over the past several weeks, he feels uncomfortable in this setting; his body and mind are not one. He slows his breathing, optimistic that his mentality and outlook will change as the race progresses.

*   *   *

Akira was schooled in the traditional Japanese setting where work ethic, discipline, and honor are inculcated values passed from generation to generation. Like the bonsai that has been nurtured and manicured by his family for over a century, so has his family's history been cared for. His ancestors, as his Grandmother had informed him, were Samurai. Duty and honor were of supreme importance to this class of nobility. And this same sense of purpose and responsibility was instilled in his youth for as long as

16

he can remember. His experiences in Japanese schools were harsh by Western standards. School six days a week with additional tutorial lessons, he was a capable student who showed promise in writing and composition. He accepted his education with diligence and vigor. Okuda is proud of his heritage. A country that had been decimated by war forty years ago has been reconstructed into an industrialized nation that is one of the world's economic leaders. This has served notice that the Japanese people are among the most industrious and resourceful people on the globe.

Akira has been coached well. His coach imbued the importance of mind and body entwined harmoniously; yielding a fierce competitor that would take his body to the limits of utter exhaustion. Awards, other accolades and public recognition are of secondary importance. An individual strives for inner peace to find fulfillment and ultimately, happiness. Akira had found that inner peace, plus success through running. Finishing in the top five places in his native country's Fukuoka and Osaka Marathons, plus top ten finishes at Boston, New York and San Francisco have given him confidence to run well over 26.2 miles.

Engaged in his first 100 mile endurance run, Okuda tries to quell the doubt creeping into his mind. Suspended around his neck a miniature Buddhist talisman dangles. He touches it for a moment hoping to draw power from its meaning and significance. Knowing that inner strength can only come from within, he searches internally for an energy that exists there. He reduces his pace for a time. Other runners continue to pass. This is a portentous start for the thirty-one year old from the Land of the Rising Sun.

The crimson sky changes from lavender to bright orange to a soft blue where a few puffy clouds cling to the horizon. The sunrise above the alpine peaks that surround Lake Tahoe is the beginning of another glorious, picturesque summer day. The weather is sure to be ideal for water skiing, swimming and fishing on the lake. However, like the Olympians occupied in their first ascent of the mountainous terrain, temperatures will also climb creating conditions far less than perfect. Sipping water from their plastic bottles all the way up the mountain, runners continue to hydrate well, heeding to the advice of the medical staff.

At a trail briefing the day before the event, the race director reiterated the need to take-in adequate fluids from the inception of the race, all the way to the finish. Most of the runners have learned to hydrate well, even the day before the competition, knowing working muscles that do not have adequate stores of water, minerals and food soon become depleted and begin to break down. These athletes have done their homework and have prepared physically, mentally and physiologically.

* * *

Over the past ten years ultramarathoning has become popular as more individuals challenge their bodies, minds and souls beyond the marathon distance. National and World Championships at the fifty and one hundred kilometer distances are staged annually in many parts of the world. Famous races throughout the world attract world class athletes as well as chronic joggers. In South Africa thousands of runners participate in the annual Comrades Marathon running fifty-four miles from Durbin to St. Pietersburg. In England the oldest ultramarathon, London to Brighton, continues to attract runners from all walks of life. The inaugural fifty-two mile race was held back in the latter part of the nineteenth century. Italy boasts two ultras - both 100 kilometers in length. La Passatore is a race run over the Tuscan Hills surrounding Firenze and Torino – St. Vincent is run through the wine producing region of Piemonte.

The United States has taken the extreme even further. Besides the John F. Kennedy fifty mile endurance run in Maryland and the American River fifty miler in California, 100 mile endurance runs are springing-up throughout the United States. Old Dominion in Virginia attracts East Coast runners to challenge themselves to running 100 miles in the George Washington National Forest near the Shenandoah River. Leadville, Colorado is in its incipient years of staging a quality event that challenges runners to "Race Across the Sky," completing "The Highest 100 Miler in the World" near the Continental Divide. East of Salt Lake City in the Wasatch Front Range, a course is designed specifically to be "The Toughest Hundred Miles of Heaven and Hell" an athlete can endure. And in California two races have emerged in the forefront of 100 mile endurance events. The San Gabriel Mountains above the city of Los Angeles host the Angeles Crest 100 Mile Endurance Run. Lastly, the Western States Trail Run has set the standard and is unparalleled in popularity among the 100 mile endurance runs worldwide. It was only befitting that the Western States Trail be chosen as a site for the endurance event of the twenty-third Olympiad.

*　　　　　*　　　　　*

Juan-Pablo Chacarito Badillo is one of the runners to pass Akira Okuda on a flat section near Squaw Valley's High Altitude Resort. Running strong and confident, he is a local favorite among Reno's running community. He had finished third on this very course two years ago and had won Angeles Crest the year before. A resident of the United States living in Reno, Nevada, he is proud of his Mexican heritage. Badillo enjoys the prosperity of living in America, but never aspires to become a U. S. citizen. He has often visited his family in the Mexican State of Chihuahua where his ancestors have practiced distance running for centuries. His boyish face defies his thirty-seven years. Semblances of Native American and Hispanic ancestry indicate his roots as his short black hair and tan skin become dampened with sweat. His mind deeply focused on the task at hand, he maintains contact with a runner directly in front of him.

Badillo had married a young American woman, and together they had opened a small restaurant in Sparks, Nevada. Their modest establishment had proven to be a successful operation as his running career waned. Too many business commitments had caused this highly competitive runner to regress into a five–mile-a-day-jogger. "Jogger," that was a term he personally detested. He had put his running career on hold while his family and business had taken flight.

Eight years earlier in Montreal, Quebec he had represented Mexico admirably, finishing in the top twenty in the Olympic marathon. Running just over two hours, seventeen minutes in the heat and humidity on a

Canadian summer afternoon, he had proven to his people and himself, he was a world class runner.

With his wife, Susan, a growing family, plus commitments with work, his training declined. Precious seconds lost became minutes lost and the Mexican faded into obscurity. Badillo convinced his wife to move from Los Angeles to the "Biggest Little City in the World:" Reno, Nevada. Two years later on one of his five mile "sanity" jogs he met a Colombian immigrant who was training for the San Francisco City Marathon. Instantly, a friendship kindled. Speaking Spanish, they talked of their homes and relatives so far away. However, both felt privileged to be living in America where living conditions are much more favorable. Badillo felt the profound desire to train once again, perhaps one last time. Juan-Pablo, or J. P. as his friends call him, conferred with his wife about another attempt at Olympic gold. Extra help was hired for the restaurant when Badillo made his decision to train seriously. That was two and a half years ago. He had leaped from the marathon distance to ultras when he heard of the USOC's decision to implement a 100 mile endurance run in the 1984 Olympics. With the Olympic 100 mile course literally in his backyard the Mexican native considered this his final opportunity to procure Olympic glory. He would not disappoint his country, family or himself.

Juan-Pablo is in the middle of a small pack of runners arriving at the base of Emigrant Pass less than a half mile from the summit. A small Mexican flag silk-screened on the front of his white singlet depicts a Golden Eagle with its talons securely embedded in a venomous snake. There is no question, with an intense look of determination; Badillo rides an eagle's wing, soaring to victory.

The East Africans have nearly reached the summit of Emigrant Pass, 8800 feet above sea level. A steep rocky trail leads them upwards as they are reduced to walking the final two hundred meters before cresting the pass. They are possessed by the heat of the moment; caught-up in the competitive fervor that drives athletes to Olympic titles or exhaustion. Much remains to be seen if these athletic zealots can hold the pace over the next ninety-five miles. The Africans smile when a few spirited hikers applaud their efforts to be first over the initial phase of the race.

A commentator and cameraman have established a remote on the summit. He sensationalizes the event as the camera records the runners' progress. "Good morning and welcome to Emigrant Pass, California." A rocky crag pierces the sky directly behind the reporter. "The front runners have just arrived after completing the first four and a half miles of the race. They waste no time moving down the slope, continuing their hundred mile Olympic journey." The reporter glances at his watch. "The leaders have run for forty minutes and at present look fresh, composed and confident. We'll just have to wait and see if the current leaders can hold their pace . . . and the lead."

Unnoticed are several individuals from the race committee busily recording bib numbers as the first athletes begin a gentle descent into the Granite Chief Wilderness, moving southwestward towards a finish line far distant from the visible peaks that surround them. At 6:45 am the view of the sunrise over Lake Tahoe is spectacular. Sunlight reflecting off the shimmering surface of the lake yields a brilliant panorama beyond compare. The hikers themselves are caught-up in this moment of heroic proportions as they look down the trail and greet the next group of Olympian. They applaud incessantly.

Eammon Horgan glares at his chronometer as he swallows another drink from his water bottle. "It's six, fuckin' forty-five and I'm still climbing," he mutters. Arguably, the most vulnerable runner in the race, the athlete from Cork, Ireland has only three years of marathoning experience and is the youngest athlete in the race. His personal best of two hours nineteen minutes at the London Marathon qualified Horgan for the Irish national team. More importantly, his second place finish at the London to Brighton race a year earlier put him in this Olympic event and his young legs are feeling remarkably good at this juncture. At age twenty-five his ruddy complexion is accentuated by the blood running through the vessels in his face. His red hair of medium length is kept above his sky blue eyes by a green, white and orange headband. When Horgan crests the summit he notices an American runner who pauses, looks eastward and points, beckoning other runners to turn for only a moment.

"Take a look, man – the view is awesome."

Lake Tahoe is a spectacle to behold.

Horgan recognizes the American whose reputation precedes him. As he turns to glimpse the view, he is taken by the magnificence of the vista. The stunning panoramic scene of a ball of hot glowing gas that etches a streamer of light across the lake; set against the backdrop of mountains is breathtaking. "My God," he murmurs, "we have nothing that resembles this in Ireland."

The feeling is contagious as others take an instant to turn and award themselves the view after clearing the first major climb of the day. Horgan sees the American cross himself quickly before moving down a gentle slope on the other side of Emigrant Pass. He quips, "Yeah, awesome," mimicking the accent of the yank. The young Irishman wishes to speak to the man who won the most famous race of this distance one year before. "Nathan Washington, Western States Champion . . ." he had read in a published running journal, ". . . is the heavy favorite to win this Olympic race." Certainly there will be time for dialogue later. He decides to trail the American . . . for a time.

Known to be impatient and audacious, Horgan not only runs against the elements nature has presented, he is also running against the sage counsel bestowed by his coach, a former Olympian who had run the marathon at the Tokyo games in 1964. His coach had attempted to impart his wisdom with one aphorism: "Discretion is the better part of valor." At this point, the Irishman has ignored his coach's advice and is running on the heels of a two time winner of one hundred mile trail events. Horgan's thoughts approach conceit. He reflects upon how easy the pace feels, loping down a gentle grade over a single trek trail just five miles into the race. "Christ," he thinks, "this is easier than a workout – I can run like this all day." Not as familiar with the course as some of the other runners, Horgan asks the American just in front, "How far to the next checkpoint?"

A voice behind replies, another accent recognized, "We're five miles out, Mate. How're you feeling?" An Australian runner has moved right in sync with the American and the Irishman. His name is David Conor and the Aussie is right where he wants to be.

The American recognizes the voices and replies, "I'm doing great on this fine morning. How's California treating you guys?"

The quick thinking Irishman in his youthful brogue boastfully points-out, "I'll let you know in fifteen hours." A time many purport will win the race.

Both the Australian and the American chortle to themselves. To brandish that statement this early in the race is foolish to say the least. Minor climbs are approaching; the conversation quickly wanes as the men prepare for series of short pulls they are about to face. In front of them the Africans continue to blaze a trail leading the race by over five minutes. Behind them, a string of Olympians are strewn along a mile portion of trail, moving well ahead of the twenty-four hour pace requirement.

*   *   *

The race committee, to avoid athletes running on the course for an inordinate number of hours, imposed mandatory cut-off times to which participants would have to adhere. Each major check-point was assigned a cut-off time prorated against finishing the race in twenty-four hours. These times were to be strictly enforced by race personnel. An athlete who could not depart a check-point before the allotted time given to complete that section of the trail would be disqualified.

All 100 mile endurance runs enforce this rule to assist race personnel in tracking runners throughout an event. In other endurance runs more generous cut-off times are permitted to allow amateur athletes the extra time to finish. These ordinary people challenge their stamina and resilience by accomplishing the extraordinary feat of ultimately reaching the finish line. Considered by many to be the toughest 100 miler in the world, the Wasatch run in Utah allots thirty-six hours for completion. On the other end of the spectrum, Old Dominion in Virginia allows only twenty-eight hours. The race committee thought of providing more time to athletes. But after deliberation, the consensus was to limit the event to twenty-four hours, since these athletes were not mere amateurs, but Olympians.

*   *   *

David Conor's navy blue cap is dampened with sweat, under which his sandy shoulder length hair is neatly tucked. At the race's commencement he had started near the rear of the pack and then slowly worked his way through the field of competitors during the climb to Emigrant Pass. In his present position and condition, the man from Down-Under is feeling quite stoked.

Born and raised in Melbourne, Australia, his experience is similar to other athletes who have dared challenge their bodies and minds to the sport of long distance running. While growing-up Conor had participated in cross country and track during his school years. Academically, he seemed to always prepare for exams; First "O" Level, then "A" Level exams, finally earning his admission to medical school. He has been running competitively since he can remember. Cricket had been too boring, soccer was somewhat rewarding, rugby – completely out of the question, but running . . . running set him apart athletically, plus set him free emotionally. He could have the worst day at school or work, but a run would always cure the pains of the day. At university, Conor studied medicine, initially wishing to establish a practice in the branch of pediatrics.

Running had changed his outlook greatly. He had developed a keen interest in comparing cardio-vascular systems of athletes with non-athletes. Specifically, analyzing blood lipids found in athletes. David Conor had studied the disproportionate levels of high density lipoproteins in training athletes as opposed to high levels of low density lipoproteins in non-athletes. He was one of the first physicians to categorically prove the benefits of exercise. On the other hand, as a practicing medical doctor, Conor knows there is little evidence to support the anatomical and physiological benefits of participating in endurance events, such as the one in which he is currently immersed.

Conor had run well at the 100 kilometer Australian national championships the year before, qualifying for the national Team. With the advent of a 100 mile Olympic event, the temptation was too much to resist. He had to give this race a try. When the Australian Institute of Sport

24

granted a stipend for living expenses, he took a leave of absence from his practice and laboratory and moved to Queensland the year before to train in the heat and humidity of the tropics. He would enter this race in the best condition of his life. So time and training have passed quickly and here, just two runners ahead, is the overwhelming favorite; the American who had proven himself over this distance and more importantly, over this course.

The Aussie sucks air deep into his lungs like bellows fueling a fire. The navy blue uniform, with the Southern Cross' constellation imprinted, sticks to his chest. He is running well within his limits. The trail has turned marshy in places where natural springs bubble forth on the western slopes of the Sierra Nevada. Conor attempts to avoid the muddy sections, not wanting to carry excess weight on the bottom of his shoes. Underbrush slaps against his legs as he negotiates the roller coaster ride this section of trail offers. He swigs the last remnants of dilute electrolyte fluid from his bottle. The aid station is still over two miles away. "No worries," he ruminates, "urine clear, sweat cooling the body." Conor mentions, "I'm looking fat."

The American overhears and replies, "We all are."

Chapter 3 – Hodgson's Cabin

Hodgson's Cabin is located on a creek bed near a landmark called Lyon's Ridge, ten and a half miles from the starting line. It serves as the site for the first major check-point of the race. The day prior to the race a dozen volunteers had transported the necessary provisions to care for the runners. They had awakened at sunrise to prepare the smorgasbord for the arrival of their clientele. Three portable tables have been arranged with a variety of beverages, food stuffs and medicinal items that the runners will use at their own discretion. Water, electrolyte replacement fluids and cola drinks are sitting in small paper cups among plates of bananas, orange slices, candy, cookies, pretzels, potato chips. Ibuprofen, aspirin, band-aids and salve are placed on one of the tables for athletes who require medical assistance. Two nurses and a paramedic are on duty in case of an emergency. However, no one anticipates an emergency, not this early in the race. Perhaps a runner will require the taping of a blister, or aspirin to reduce some minor inflammation.

When the frontrunners come through a small thicket of aspen, the smiling, altruistic faces of volunteers greet them. The East Africans waste no time in having their bottles filled as they hastily gulp the beverages available. One Kenyan jovially places an orange slice in his mouth with the peel covering his lips signaling his comrade to inspect his new dentine. The competitors laugh momentarily, enjoying a brief respite from the keen competition which began only one hour, twenty-five minutes before. Each selects a couple of food items before departing, and with a last swig of drink they vanish into a stand of lodge pole pines. A voice a hundred meters away declares, "Incoming runners".

Five minutes after the frontrunners departed the Hodgson's Cabin checkpoint, Juan-Pablo Badillo leads a small group of runners into the checkpoint. He can see the small rustic cabin in a woodland patch to his right, with a stream flowing adjacent to the structure. J. P. sees in full view the runners who have already arrived, hastily moving about taking care of their business. Many of the athletes, ostensibly anxious, do not wish to waste time at the aid stations. Not that Badillo would lollygag, but he knows that precious energy is wasted with nervous actions. So he approaches the aid station relaxed, knowing that much time and distance remain.

Their hands simultaneously reach for the same cup: one black, one white, one is Jamaican, the other's Russian. The Jamaican smiles politely, not wishing to contest the contents of the paper cup. "Excuse me, Man". The Russian remains stoic, grasping another and quaffing its contents in one swift gulp. Conrad Creary looks across the table to see the orange glow on the volunteer's face. The sun, directly behind him, has risen above the tree line. His long shadow casts across the table as he gobbles a few pretzels and a piece of chocolate. When he bends to retie his shoe he notices a runner's knee that has been scraped badly. "An ugly spill," he thinks, seeing a medic administer first aid to the wound. Not sure of his position in the early going, Creary estimates he is certainly in the top twenty-five runners and feels confident at this point. Glancing at his watch he notes the time, 7:30. He observes the Russian preparing to leave the aid station and after securely tying his shoes, he asks for his water bottle.

An attendant who recognizes the uniform hands him the filled bottle and quips, "Cool runnings, J A."

The Jamaican recognizes the words and thinks the young woman has visited Jamaica at some time or maybe she was a Peace Corps volunteer. Creary grins at the young woman. "Thanks, irie," he replies.

Creary will stay with the Russian for a while. There's something about his opponent's demeanor that entices Conrad to tag along, to maintain contact. Apparently, he will have to augment his tempo slightly, but he knows without risk, there can be no reward.

*   *   *

Conrad Creary represents the island nation of Jamaica with all its beauty and turmoil. His background is like that of many other Caribbean children from lower income status. He had attended typical public schools in Kingston that were overcrowded, under-staffed and poorly funded. Raised primarily by his grandmother, for whom he had the deepest admiration and respect, he had matured into a polite young man. His parents had both worked innumerable hours during his formative years. His mother worked days as a clerk at a local store, plus subsidized the household's income by tailoring and altering clothing. His father, whom he would see only on weekends, worked in the bauxite mines in the country's interior. Conrad never thought it odd that his grandmother carried out the parenting responsibilities. At the age of eighteen he completed his "O" Level Examinations with above average marks and joined the Jamaican Defense Force.

The JDF had enlisted some of their men on a cross country team to which Conrad signed-on immediately. Despite limited athletic success in school he excelled under the regimen and discipline provided by the military. In one year he had improved to third man on the team; after two years he was the best runner in the JDF and winning virtually all races he entered. At a half marathon in Kingston he ran one hour seven minutes. Six months later he ran his first marathon on the west coast of his native land near Montego Bay and finished third, losing only to two foreign runners from the United States. More impressive than his finishing place was his time of two hours twenty-five minutes in the heat and humidity of the subtropics. Later, in his third year with the JDF, Creary entered a forty-five mile trans-island run and won handily in five hours forty-five minutes, beating the next competitor by over a half-hour. All his personal bests, attained before his twenty-second birthday, demonstrated a potential that merited special consideration.

His superior officer, a captain in the force, observed the progress and contacted a faculty member whom he knew personally at the University of Texas, El Paso. Upon learning of the young Jamaican the head coach of the track and field program promptly initiated contact. What captured the coach's attention was that Creary was not another sprinter, but instead, a distance runner with an impressive list of credentials. When granted admission to the university he made the conscious decision to excel equally in academics and athletics. Not to take full advantage of the scholarship and opportunity would be a total loss.

Conrad had truly felt blessed by the hand of God. Baptized an Anglican at birth, he was raised to obey the Ten Commandments. His grandmother had overseen his Christian upbringing as an integral part of a youth's development. When Conrad arrived at UTEP he enrolled in the Criminal Justice Department with the intent of continuing his career in the military or law enforcement upon graduation.

Many Jamaicans would have delighted in staying in the U. S. indefinitely since many wished to pursue the American dream of the "three V's:" a video cassette player, a Volvo and most importantly, a visa. Instead, Creary's four years in the United States had left him quite homesick, especially since the young woman to whom he had promised his love lived so far away. He had married Julia upon his return to Jamaica.

The man in front of Creary is shorter, has a much smaller frame and moves lithely along the footpath. His pallor is pinkish from the blood rushing to his working limbs; perspiration flows as the morning begins to warm-up. The Jamaican can hear steps behind as other runners keep pace.

Their running styles are as diverse as their backgrounds. The Russian could pass for a refugee from a labor camp; the Jamaican with his brown skin, has much more muscle definition and could pass as a welterweight boxer. Twelve miles in, the running is pure along this flat section of trail under a canopy of coniferous trees. Breathing controlled, avoiding obstacles, each mind and body synchronized. Creary lifts his legs slightly higher and swings his arms a bit more. The Russian keeps his feet lower to the ground, his arms and shoulders relaxed. Both coordinate their bodies fluently as they proceed to a steep grade where they quickly alter their technique to "power walking." Both are world class runners who have won international races in their respective hemispheres. Brought together by an act of fate and circumstance, they are pushing each other to overtake a myopic runner, who most probably, ran too fast, too early.

Yuri Boroshkov appears haggard and much older than his age of thirty-four years. He is practically bald, adding to his geriatric façade, and what remains of his blond hair is combed behind his pronounced ears. Nevertheless, he is as fit as any athlete in the Olympics, if not more so. A world class marathoner and ultramarathoner, he was the 100 Kilometer World Champion the year prior. And despite never having participated in an event of this distance, his plethora of experience provides an advantage beyond what other athletes may comprehend.

*   *   *

A product of the Great Red Machine, Dr. Yuri Boroshkov is one of the nineteen million communists in the Soviet Union. Born and raised in Leningrad, schooled in Moscow, he has a brilliant mind. As a tenured physicist at the Leningrad Polytechnic State University, he has observed Mother Russia decline in the sciences and technology. Never granted a visa to the United States before these Olympics, Dr. Boroshkov has traveled extensively throughout Western Europe. He has witnessed first hand what collaboration between different countries can accomplish when channels of communication remain open. Yuri has spent years of futility attempting to convince his Party to open-up and communicate with the West. His efforts have proven fruitless thus far as the Soviet government further alienates itself from the remainder of the world's scientific community. Through running he has been able to travel, albeit, under the close supervision of Party members who permit little interaction between rival teams. In fact, an act of fate brought the Eastern Block teams to this XXXIII Olympiad.

Initially, sixteen countries had prepared to boycott the Los Angeles Games under the guise of U. S. involvement in Central America. Many "westerners" perceived the boycott ploy to be in retaliation to the U. S. led boycott of the 1980 Olympics that were held in Moscow. In 1980 the United States and its allies threatened to boycott the Moscow Olympics unless Soviet military intervention into Afghanistan was withdrawn. The Communists scoffed at such a far-fetched proposal and then offered one of their own. If the U. S. would withdraw its military personnel from Central America, an agreement could be reached regarding Afghanistan. The U. S. could not allow its national security to be compromised and the Soviet government took the same stand. Consequently, the Red Army remained in Afghanistan, U. S. troops remained in Central America and American athletes remained home. Sixty countries boycotted the Moscow games of 1980. Unfortunately, the 1980 Olympic boycott proved to be a worthless,

Cold War tactic. Casualties continued to mount, not only in Afghanistan, but in Central America as well. All the while, thousands of athletes stayed home, their governments not permitting participation. They were given an opportunity to compete in surrogate games, but most declined in their own silent protest. Years of hard work and sacrifice apparently went for naught - casualties of an Olympic boycott.

Four years later, a Soviet-backed, Eastern Block boycott appeared imminent. But in the early part of 1984, a new leader emerged within the Communist Party. An individual with vision and charisma who could earn the support of the Politburo and the people appeared to be gaining momentum in the infrastructure of the Soviet government. In the spring of 1984 he was appointed Secretary of the Communist Party – the highest ranking government official in Russia. He hoped to implement policies that would slowly and consistently gain the Soviet Union a more favorable appearance to the remainder of the world. These tactics would open up the Soviet Union, make her better, stronger. He entitled this spirit of communication and openness with the West - "Glastnost." Boycotting the 1984 Olympic Games would undermine his authority and his policy of détente. He quelled any fervor that remained with conservatives to boycott the games and acknowledged the Soviet team's participation. There would be no Eastern Block boycott. Eight years had passed since Montreal when the two "superpowers" had last battled each other on an Olympic stage. East and West reunited; the world is being treated to a truly global event.

Boroshkov knows he is near the front - certainly in the top twenty. He leads a group of runners from the canopy of the forest into the morning sunlight. Yuri feels the warmth against his back as much as he hears the runners breathing and their foot steps behind. He has been running well for an hour, fifty-five minutes and covered nearly fourteen miles of trail. The soft humus soil of the forest floor has given away to the rocky granite trail of the Sierra Nevada. Cougar Rock is just ahead. The Russian squirts fluids into his mouth and commences to "power walk" the steep embankment to one of the "flagship" landmarks of the course.

The last runner departs the Hodgson's Cabin aid station. He is Haitian, born in the poorest country in the Western Hemisphere. Lucky to have procured private funding, he is one of the few athletes from the western region of Hispaniola. His corrupt government refused to provide adequate funding for the Haitian team. Chewing on a piece of banana he acknowledges the efforts of one of the attendants. *"Thank you, much. You are very kind."* His French is refreshingly melodic.

God willing, he will finish this race. The first ten miles have gone well.

Many of the participants have decided not to risk the initial urge to push themselves, opting instead to relax, enjoy the morning and savor the moment. They are thrilled to be representing their countries with little intent on winning or "medaling." There is much camaraderie among these athletes in the back of the pack. There are conversations among those who speak a common language. Customary questions and answers are exchanged almost continuously.

"Where are you from?"
"Have you run this race before?"
"Have you run a 100 miler?"
"What training have you done in preparation?"
"How much weekly mileage have you completed?
"We're ahead of the twenty-four hour cut-off, aren't we?"
"Would you have some toilet paper I could use?

The answers are as varied as the questions, yet one common theme persists. The runners have logged hundreds of miles, varied their workouts, entered numerous races and use biodegradable toilet paper. All the athletes appear to have prepared sufficiently.

There are no casualties to report thus far when the final Olympian checks-out, leaving the volunteers to their final duty: cleaning-up after the 160 plus runners who have passed this way. Certainly, the sylvan owner of Hodgson's Cabin would not want to find garbage strewn about his place.

A HAM operator communicates that all runners who started the race over two hours ago are accounted for and proceeding along the Western States Trail.

Chapter 4 – Red Star Ridge

Like the marathon, there is no qualifying standard for the 100 mile event. The race committee strongly suggested that all participants, at the minimum, complete one fifty mile or hundred kilometer training run or race to acclimatize their bodies for a long, sustained effort. Many acknowledged the suggestion by running several long runs prior to the Los Angeles Olympics. Many of the runners have qualified by winning their nation's 100 kilometer championship.

One runner who needs no warning about preparation is the British long distance veteran, Nigel Preverett. Approaching his forty-fifth birthday he is a sentimental favorite among the European running community. Having competed in marathons and ultramarathons for twenty years, he is the oldest and most experienced athlete in the race. A three time Olympian who ran marathons in Mexico City, Munich and Montreal, he failed to qualify for the British Olympic team that traveled to Moscow. Preverett moved-up the ladder of distance running when he competed in South Africa's Comrades Marathon in 1981, finishing tenth overall. He covered the 54 mile "uphill" course in six hours thirty minutes. More impressive was how he accomplished this fine performance. Running conservatively early and then increasing his cadence, he passed numerous runners toward the end of the race. Nigel had run negative splits – running the second half of the course faster than he had run the first half. A year later he proved to himself and the British Olympic Committee he was not ready to retire and that he belonged in this race by posting a third place finish at London to Brighton – a fifty-two mile race in southern England. Losing only to the Italian, Pavin, and a young Irish lad whom he had never heard of prior to the race, the middle-aged veteran had performed splendidly. Preverett is delighted to be representing his Queen and country once again in an international event.

At the moment, the man who lives and trains near the industrial port city of Manchester, is not running well. Somewhere near the middle of the pack he comes to the realization that he is not having the best day of his protracted career. Too many individuals are running better than his abilities can muster on this particular morning. "Perhaps," Nigel contemplates, "too much time has passed, too many races run and I'm just a wee bit past my prime. Best enjoy the day – Carpe Diem!" The tall strapping Englishman whose gray hair underscores his years of experience laughs at the idea.

A voice from behind interrupts his train of thought, quietly requesting permission to pass in an oriental language he cannot comprehend. Preverett needs not understand the words; from the tone he recognizes what the competitor wants. Thus, acting in good sportsmanship, he steps aside, conceding his position to the faster runner. The athletes exchange a nod when the Korean runner moves ahead.

Nigel reaches a series of short switchbacks that takes him to a ridge over-looking a deep canyon lying to the southwest. The vast expanse of land is covered with secondary coniferous growth, mostly fir and cedar. An alpine lake is visible in the distance. The trail is dusty; scrub brush slaps against his shuffling limbs. Nigel pauses to sip fluids from his bottle and momentarily thinks of the father he had never known.

*   *   *

"What would Dad think of his boy who had accomplished so much through running and not through military service?" he had reflected many times. The father, who had fought valiantly in the Second World War and died attempting to protect his country from the imminent invasion of a superior Nazi force, was a mystery. As a Royal Air Force major he was an exceptional combat pilot who had scored numerous confirmed kills. Despite not remembering much of his early childhood, Preverett is proud of his father's war record. At times, even straining to recollect the faintest memories, Nigel often attempts to recall a glimpse of his remote past.

He was simply too young when his mother and older sister had received the distressing news that his father, Major James Preverett, had paid the ultimate price of a country at war. Over the years there had been numerous stories of courage, valor and bravery; Dogfights between Messerschmitts and Spitfires above Northern France and the body of water

34

that separated England from the Continent. But all the stories were told second hand, from other pilots who had experienced The War, not from the one person he had sought to know. Photographs could only tell so much, with too many spaces to fill-in between the lines of a life he could never know. The only truth to his father's death was his final resting place – somewhere on the floor of the English Channel.

Unfortunately, the only vivid memory Preverett can recall is the funeral service for his Daddy. Tears dripping off his mother's cheeks as she tried to overcome the deep emotional wounds of losing a spouse; his older sister sobbing, knowing the gravity of death, and a small boy just too young and naïve to understand. He remembers an officer presenting his mother a Union Jack and uttering his condolences. "A feeble attempt to offer sympathy," he would think years later. And lastly, the black stains of mascara that had blemished a flag his mother clutched so tightly against herself.

The Union Jack on his white national uniform is drenched with sweat as he approaches fifteen miles into this, his own personal journey. He knows in his heart that his father would be beyond proud, knowing the kind of man he had sired into the world.

*   *   *

If World War I, the Great War was the War to End All Wars, then the Second World War defined the Twentieth Century. It had shaped our world, drawn new borders with new frontiers, and served warning that the nations of the world would never tolerate another megalomaniac. The impact of World War II is still ever present; an older generation will not let their offspring forget the atrocities of war. Specifically, there were ideals worth fighting and dying for. And one particular runner in the race had been told too many times that he was lucky to have been born . . .

At the moment the West German, Wolfgang Hafner, is running well. Nearly twenty-five kilometers of trail behind him, he searches in front to find the American who is the undisputed favorite. Too many different uniforms to discern the different nationalities, he trots-on, engaging the enemy within. His national uniform with the black symbolic eagle glistens with sweat. Breathing deeply, torso relaxed, he sips from his water bottle intermittently. Wolfgang recognizes he is in an event of a lifetime and plans to make the most of it. Hafner, a relatively unknown runner, has peaked for this performance. Under his quiet, unassuming exterior is an intense competitor who knows he can be a medal contender if the day belongs to him. He has neatly trimmed russet hair above his light-brown eyes, so as not to impair his vision. The West German has inherited strong Teutonic facial features from his parents, even more pronounced due to his svelte frame of sixty-eight kilograms. At the very minimum, this West German from Landsut contemplates, "*I will cross the finish line, even if I must crawl.*"

*　　　　　*　　　　　*

The German athlete Wolfgang Deiter Hafner is a world class runner. Born and raised in Bavaria, he has competed in World Championship races from half-marathon and marathon distances to fifty and 100 kilometers runs. Hafner won his county's national 100 Kilometer Championship which entitled his entry into these Olympic Games, and in particular, this 100 mile race. Yet his running experiences pale in comparison to the saga his father had endured so many years ago.

Hafner's father had been a Wehrmacht officer assigned to command an armored column in Tunisia, North Africa. Field Marshall Erwin Rommel, his commanding officer, had been replaced by a less competent commander – General Hans-Jurgen von Arnim. Rommel had given the British forces fits in North Africa for nearly two years. The Field Marshal had the uncanny ability to strike the enemy aggressively, inflicting much damage to allied forces, often resulting in numerous casualties. Then after a brief engagement, the Field Marshall and his army would simply vanish into the desert sands. He had acquired an appropriate moniker, the Desert Fox, for good reason. Arnim had taken command when Rommel, who had become ill, had been recalled to Berlin.

The American forces arrived in the winter of 1942 and the successful campaign against the British turned sour rapidly. Generals

George Patton and Omar Bradley were competent commanders. Both led by example, often near the site of engagement with the enemy and American troops responded with unquestionable loyalty and obedience for their fearless leaders. Patton and Bradley were strategists in every sense of the word. They sought-out the Nazis unlike other commanders of the Allied forces before them. Their objective was simple: Liberate North Africa.

In a major confrontation just northwest of Tunis in May of forty-three, all hell broke loose between the two opposing forces. Arnim's Fifth Panzer Division went-up against the Sherman Tanks of Bradley's 5th Army and heavy losses were reported on both sides. Colonel Hafner's gambit was to have his armored battalion spearhead an attack against the allied forces. Regiments of infantry clashed for hours, volleys of artillery and mortar fire were exchanged incessantly which yielded little progress on either front. General Arnim then ordered the retreat to Tunis for evacuation to Sicily. However, when Hafner's battalion attempted to divert itself from the action, the American Second Armored Division (also known as "Hell on Wheels") with infantry support immediately overtook their flank. A bazooka had demolished a tank adjacent to Hafner's, another armored vehicle lie crippled not fifty meters from his, and when his tank tried to escape the onslaught, a mortar shell dislodged the tracks from his tank wheels, stranding the Commanding Officer in the middle of enemy gunfire. The last thing Hafner remembered of the battle was after opening the tank's hatch in attempt to escape, the butt of an M–1 rifle struck him square on the side of his face, splitting his cheek open and breaking the Aryan nose on his face.

In an instant the war was over for Colonel Hafner and the only question was whether or not he would be executed. He awoke dazed to hear two American soldiers argue whether or not to discharge the "dirty fuckin' Kraut" with a .45 caliber Colt one of the GI's brandished. The Colonel understood very little English, but through the gibberish he understood his life was about to come to an inglorious end. He could see no other prisoners in the enemy's confines. Hafner could see columns of smoke rising into the clear blue desert sky. Knowing this vision to be his last, he bowed his head to steady himself for the inevitable. For the first time in his life the Nazi felt completely isolated and utterly abandoned.

Then a thunderous voice ordered silence and demanded, "What the hell's going-on over here? What are you two bastards arguing about? Holster that weapon soldier." Initially, he did not understand or who commanded the respect of his troops, but the two soldiers immediately stood at attention. A stern faced captain stepped in front of him and just glared at the opposing commander. The officer exclaimed, "You're damn lucky there was a Geneva Convention pact ratified colonel, or I'd shoot you myself. Damn Nazis!"

Colonel Hafner, stripped of his weapons, belt and honor; uniform sullied with blood and the desert's dust, was taken to a stockade where he was later interrogated by the same captain and another soldier fluent in German. Their objective was clear: They wanted Rommel at all costs or wanted the Field Marshal out of Africa. And when Hafner replied the truth, *"Rommel is no longer in Africa."* The captain scoffed at the remark. One thing was clear, however, after seeing the way the Americans fought, there was little doubt: They would achieve their objective. Hafner was detained in a stockade in North Africa for weeks and then later transported to Alabama where he remained a POW for the duration of the war.

Upon his release in the late spring of 1945 he returned to a homeland that had been destroyed by war. The Russians had been especially ruthless, totally destructive. Payback came for the years the Nazis had attempted to permanently occupy the Soviet Union - to overtake Mother Russia, no loyal Russian would ever allow that. Later, Hafner learned he had lost much of his family: a brother near Stalingrad, another in a U-Boat engagement in the North Atlantic, cousins in the battle of Normandy, The Black Forest, and most sadly, his beloved sister, who had been brutally raped and murdered near their home in Munich. The German officer, Colonel Hafner, once so proud of his heritage, had even contemplated suicide. Yet he had persevered and survived to tell his own son and daughter of his plight through the Second World War and more importantly, his contribution to the reconstruction of a sovereign Germany that has become a world economic leader. His son had often asked how he was injured, pointing at the scar above his cheekbone. When Wolfgang was old enough to understand, his father imparted a history lesson the young Hafner would never forget.

*   *   *

The American too, was fortunate to be in the race and even luckier to have been born. His father, a highly decorated combat officer, had been shot twice – once almost fatally. Too many war stories to recount, Nathan Washington is proud of his father's military service. Certainly, Dad was far from perfect. He drank too much, smoked habitually and never acquiesced to cautions concerning diet. Yet there was honor in his father's presence. He had served his country faithfully for twenty-two years, both in war and peacetime. Awarded numerous ribbons of distinction for valor and leadership, including one Silver Star and two Bronze Stars, Dad seemed to always command the respect of his friends and peers. And there was little difference when addressing his two sons. As for his daughter, that was an entirely different story. He had always appeared to go soft whenever his baby girl was around. Never quite knowing how to handle disciplinary issues with the opposite gender, he would defer his authority to his wife of thirty-five years.

In the early winter of 1945, his infantry company had entrenched itself in a heavily forested region of southwest Germany, aptly called the Black Forest. Captain Robert Washington had recovered from his first wound, a bullet to his right arm, and had reassumed his command. Peering through field glasses within his foxhole, the captain surveyed a rural area under a canopy of trees near enemy lines. He had observed considerable movement of armored vehicles and infantry deployment during the past two days and passed whatever intelligence he could back to his commander at headquarters. Washington predicted a serious engagement was about to commence.

His breath condensing in front of his face, he liked the view of snow covered trees. "How pristine," he thought, reminiscing about his Wyoming home. His senses always honed to the activity in the distance; he never would have predicted that his blood would soon spill again – this time on a white carpet of snow. The bullet came-out of nowhere. A sniper had worked his way around the encampment, recognized an officer in the cross hairs of his scope and pulled the trigger. The only thing that saved the American's life was his helmet. The bullet had fractured on the base of

39

the helmet's edge, deflecting most of its vicious force. The remainder of the fragments entered the neck of the Captain, and a piece or two even lodged near the base of his brain.

Three days later he awoke in a Red Cross infirmary, dazed with the worst, most severe headache imaginable. He had survived. Unfortunately, most of his company had not. Casualties were heavy at the Battle of the Bulge – for both sides.

Major Robert Washington had informed his children about the war; how his country had fought a war on two major fronts that helped secure a world of freedom and justice. Yes, there was much pride in his testimony, and Nathan had taken that pride, plus a sense of honor with him. Even with all the conflict and insurrection surrounding the Vietnam War during his formative years, Nathan Washington remained patriotic and loyal to his father and country.

* * *

Caught-up in the fervor of this monumental race, adrenaline coursing through his veins, the American approaches another checkpoint at Red Star Ridge. "Seventeen miles down, eighty-three miles to go, and feeling great," Washington thinks.

A world of possibilities lay ahead for this buoyant, twenty-nine year old from San Jose, California. He had dreamed about representing his country on a world stage and knew the rewards would be great if he could win an Olympic gold medal. "Many athletes have cashed-in on their Olympic success. Why shouldn't I?" he had queried on more than one occasion. "Endorsements on running apparel such as shoes and shorts, nutritional items such as energy and electrolyte foods and beverages - the possibilities are endless," Washington had considered. He only needed to win this race, "his race," as he had won numerous races before.

Nathan Byron Washington is an outstanding athlete, a pure runner in every sense. He had run cross country and track for four years in high school, finishing in the top ten once at the State Cross Country Championships, and later qualifying to compete in the State Track and Field Championships at the end of his senior year. Always diligent in every facet of his life, he was the best runner to graduate from his high school and graduated with academic honors as well. Upon completion of high school, he learned of a coach in Northern California whose reputation for producing national championship teams was widely known. The coach, who had his own personal history of running, followed the teachings of Arthur Lydiard - a New Zealander, who years earlier trained their national elite runners for the Commonwealth and Olympic games.

What Washington remembered of Coach Hunter was not only the arduous workouts, but his words as well. "Personal triumph sought through running . . . Manifestations of overcoming personal adversity . . . Run beyond the limitations in which you have shackled yourself . . . Develop into the best athlete and person you can possibly be." The coach had taught much more than running; he had taught life. Washington remembered the words well, plus his coach's capacity to lead men beyond what they had thought possible. He often recollected one such speech before races for the dual purpose of motivation and inspiration: "Run aggressively," his coach would often say, "take yourself to the edge of your capabilities. That is where you will find your true self, your true worth. Anything less and you've sacrificed a gift from God."

And there was no question; running was sacrifice, a love-hate relationship in which there was no escape. Nathan loved to race, compete at his best and God willing, win. He hated the brutal workouts, but understood the necessity of their implementation. Oh sure, there were "easy" days - long distance days at leisure pace when you could converse with a teammate or friend. Then there were the "hard" days in which Coach Hunter subscribed to one basic Nietzsche tenant, "What doesn't kill you always makes you stronger." Racing around a quarter mile, cinder track or a known distance on trail or road repeatedly, was at best tiring, at worst exhausting. The coach would yell splits of encouragement or discouragement depending on the times recorded. Then of course, with no rest for the weary, the next day you'd lace your shoes and commence another workout. You truly had to love the sport to excel at it. And excel Nathan did as a runner and a leader.

Awarded team captain and all-conference honors at Humboldt State University, he qualified for the U. S. Trials for the 1980 games at 10,000 meters but failed to make the American Olympic Team. He ran

41

two, sub two hour twenty minute marathon times over the next two years and had hoped to make a bid for the 1984 U. S. Olympic marathon team.

But what transpired in the spring of 1981 changed his course of action dramatically. A fellow collegiate runner from Arizona dared him to enter an endurance run that crossed the Western Sierra Nevada. Sloughing-off the idea as some kind of hoax, he first ignored the thought of running 100 miles in one day. "Bullshit," he recalled saying to his running buddy of five years. Then the race application, entitled "The Western States 100 Mile Endurance Run – 100 Miles, One Day," arrived. A worthy challenge considering the distance and terrain, he decided to steel himself for a tough race. And prepare he did. Running between 110 – 120 miles a week, incorporating the workouts he had experienced as a collegiate runner, Washington excelled at ultramarathoning. He won several shorter races including the American River 50 Mile endurance run in April of 1982, and then followed that performance with a victory at Western States in June of the same year. His time of sixteen hours, twenty-four minutes was the third best time recorded in the seven years Western States had been run. The following year he almost became the first runner to break the sixteen hour barrier, finishing the course in sixteen hours five minutes. Remarkable performance many would say, knowing that they had witnessed or shared in an athletic event unrivaled to any other. Washington, being an articulate speaker, had little difficulty conveying his thoughts at the awards ceremony.

"Incredible, what an incredible day," he commenced. "I kept thinking slow-up or blow-up, but I never blew-up. I found a zone in which there was no escape, no slowing down, and it was effortless. I have had some good races in my life; some fine performances that brought me much happiness, much personal satisfaction. But there is nothing I have experienced in my past that rivals the feelings of elation I have with this race as a two-time champion." As Nathan delivered his victory speech he glimpsed his name engraved on the Robie Cup, the perpetual trophy kept as a record of former champions. He saw the beautiful bronze trophy of a cougar standing on a rocky outcrop, awarded perennially to the winner. "My second cougar," he reflected.

Not a man who rests on his laurels, Washington added, "Unfortunately, I will not return to defend my title next year. I have secured a position on the U. S. Olympic team to represent our country in the twenty-third Olympiad, and invite you all to come and bear witness to a historical event of Olympic proportions." He simply smiled when his ardent audience applauded vigorously for several seconds. Then he concluded. "I would like to thank all the volunteers for their invaluable support; without their assistance and efforts, there would be no Western States Trail Run. My family and friends, God bless you all for being there for me." He pointed at his brother, cousin and a couple friends who joined in the ceremony. Then he crossed himself and lastly said, "I thank God Almighty for bestowing upon me a gift that is truly wonderful and giving me the kind of day I had yesterday. Christ, it was unbelievable."

"Two-time Western States Champion, has a nice ring to it, doesn't it?" Race Director Norman Sproul asked when he handed Washington the champion's award. Overcome with joy, tears evident, he received the bronze trophy, kissed the cougar and then hoisted the award above his head. Washington did not leave the stage after the presentation, instead opting to stay there and congratulate every finisher who was called to the front of the auditorium to receive their finisher's award. Nathan Washington is not only a gentleman, but also a contributor who demonstrates genuine sportsmanship.

Washington hands his water bottle to an aid station attendant while chewing on a couple of pretzels, grabs a cup of electrolyte fluids and washes the contents down his throat. "When did the lead pack leave here?" he asks an attendant patiently.

The young man glances at his watch, "Ten, maybe twelve minutes ago."

Nathan looks around, the Irish runner has moved-on, and the Australian runner is nearly ready to depart. He recognizes over his right shoulder the West German runner arriving at the aid station leading another pack. He checks his shoe laces, notices mud caked to the bottom of his soles. Kicking the excess from his shoes, he swallows a last cup of diluted coke. Washington grabs his bottle declaring, "Number 620 checking-out," and leaves Red Star Ridge in his wake.

The Africans in front continue to extend their lead. He knows it's too early to be greedy; knows he's running well within his means. The sun's rays filter through the evergreen trees as dust kicked-up by runners dances in the sunlight. The shadows of the canopy create a twilight effect and the effect is illusory. The defending Western States champion glances at his watch – 8:30. "God I feel good," he whispers.

*   *   *

Prior to the event many athletes arrived early to acclimate their bodies to altitude and acquaint themselves with the course they would run. At the Olympic Village in Squaw Valley a number of casual interactions took place among the participants. One evening in the Olympic Village a particular debate created quite raucous in the cafeteria. A Mexican runner sat next to a young Irishman, and a polite conversation escalated into lengthy discussion. The dialogue began amicably enough when the young lad, Eammon Horgan, desired a "nice dark cold one" rather than the juice or water his coach had prescribed with his meals. "Lord knows I wish I had some dark nectar to wash down this meal. My coach forbids me to drink any alcohol until the race is over."

The Mexican returned an empathetic smile. "Yeah, that's a pretty good idea since you probably don't want alcohol in your system. I always feel a little heavy, certainly not as sharp, if I drink a beer or two with my meals. So I'm staying clear of the 'amber nectar' for a while. By the way, my name's Juan-Pablo Badillo; friends call me J. P." He reached across the table to shake the Irishman's hand, "Nice to meet you."

"Horgan's mine, I mean Eammon, call me Eammon. Are you American?"

Badillo had easily recognized the Irish accent of the younger runner, offering a firm handshake. "Only in residence, I live near here, in Reno. I'm Mexican by birth and will represent my native country in these Olympic Games. So, what kind of beer would you drink with this fine meal of lasagna, bread and salad?" He chuckled a bit recognizing the lasagna to be not of the highest quality. "You mentioned dark beer."

"Ah, the best beer in the world, that's also 'Good for You' – Guinness, or a Murphy's Stout would work too."

44

Badillo laughed sharply, "Yeah, if you like medicated syrup! Mexican amber like a Dos Equis – that has a smooth finish. Or a Corona or Carta Blanca, those are fine beers too."

"Yeah, if you like drinking water," Horgan quipped brusquely.

"That's unfair! Have you no respect to compare the finest beers in North America with American brew . . . now that's water!"

"No, that's mule piss!"

They both laughed heartily at America's reputation for producing weak, overrated beer. The conversation would have probably ended there, except, Wolfgang Hafner who is nearly fluent in English overheard the gist of the conversation and decided to offer his opinion. The arrogance in his voice was almost palpable as he offered his expertise on the subject of brewing beer.

"Gentlemen, the beers of which you both discuss are fine to the taste, but none can compare to those that have been brewed for centuries under the, hmmm . . . I believe the word is *auspices*, yes auspices of our government. We enacted a Purity Law in the 16th century that states only ingredients of the finest quality can be used in the production of our national beverage. Obviously, with our scrutiny and care, German beers are the best in the world and might I add, the most delectable to the palate. Do you know of our strict Purity Law?"

"Bullshit!" The Mexican feigned a loud sneeze as the Irishman laughed. "Er, no I didn't know of such a law. When did you say it was enacted?"

"Some time during the 1500's I believe and your brewing practices have not changed much in the past 500 years. In fact I have had German beer that tasted like it was brewed in the 16th century!" The voice that interrupted the conversation was a Danish runner who disdains German arrogance. He and a Dutch athlete approached, both of whom could speak English competently.

The dialogue was beginning to intensify as more on-lookers began to take notice of the discussion taking place in the cafeteria of the Olympic village. Acting jointly, the Dutch runner added, "What we have done is taken your methods and learned to improve the process of brewing even better beer. In fact our Heineken is the leading import to this country, our host country."

Wolfgang retorted, "And explain to me; exactly what do Americans know about fine beer? I would not boast of such nonsense."

"Point taken," the Danish runner said of the admonishment. Once again everyone chuckled over their host country's inability to brew beer with a reputation that rivaled their own.

The Russian, Boroshkov sat placidly eating his dinner with his advisor when he noticed the discussion near-by. He asked his comrade, *"What is the commotion over there?"* The translator summarized the conversation and concluded by saying, *"They think the American beer tastes like 'mule piss.'"*

"No way," the Soviet runner responded, *"we reserve that right for Russian beer!"* Both men laughed audibly. Yuri had found that Czechoslovakian beer had a great taste and learned long ago to avoid his nation's poor attempts at beer brewing.

The German sneered at the Russian with renewed arrogance, "Do you wish to add something to this conversation?"

"No, not a thing," the translator quipped. He explained what had just happened and Boroshkov snickered quietly.

"We produce an excellent beer, considered one of the world's best," the Czech runner spoke slowly and clearly with a heavy Eastern Block accent. "Perhaps you have heard of Prazdroj."

Hafner, engulfed in the argument responded, "You mean Pilsner Urquell."

"No, I mean Prazdroj," the Czech countered. "We prefer our language to yours!"

When the American walked to the table with a tray of food and beverage, he put himself right in the middle of the melee. "So gentlemen, what's all the fuss about?"

Hafner cut right through the red tape and queried the American, "So Nathan, what is your favorite beer?"

Even though he had not been formally introduced to Hafner, he contemplated for a moment before announcing, "Er, Coors, I guess. Why do you ask?"

The corner of the cafeteria erupted in boo's, hisses and laughter as paper napkins struck Washington in the face. "What the hell is this all about?" He looked quizzically at Badillo, whom he had known for some time, looking for an explanation. The Mexican could only shrug his shoulders, laughing along with the others.

"Okay, point taken," the Danish runner reiterated.

The jollity continued when the Australian caught wind of the discussion and walked over to the table. Conor asked Washington, "Do you have need of some moral support, Mate."

"Sure do. It seems these 'aliens' do not appreciate American beer."

Oooh's and ahhh's ensued when Horgan added, "We didn't say that. We said we prefer drinking your water to drinking your beer." The verbal harpoon incited more comic relief.

The Australian had to empathize with the "aliens" since he felt the same about American piss. Since Conor had some strong convictions about his native K & B and Coopers, he proclaimed Australian beer to be the best in the world. Jeers followed. Chest flexed, fists on his hips, his reply was loud and terse. "Indeed!"

There was quite a gathering as the caucus increased in number and escalated in intensity with participants offering their nation's beer as the best compared to that of the rest. Several runners and their translators decided to stay-out of the argument, mostly those who were either lacking fluency in English or simply would not be bothered by such mundane matters.

Sitting near-by, the Canadian runner, Ian Jones, could not help himself and declared, "Labatt's, Molsen and Moosehead should be granted serious consideration in this discussion of world class beers, and consequently . . ."

"Moosehead? Granted serious consideration . . . from a country that sits sequestered under the armpit of the United States," Wolfgang blared. "Your beer is no better!"

Currently, Ian Jones is the North American record holder at one hundred kilometers and is considered a medal contender for the race. He bit his lip thinking, "This German is as arrogant as any man I've ever met." Since the man's tone bordered conceit Ian wished to admonish his opponent. "Such superiority has been proven wrong twice in this century, lest we forget!"

Hafner retorted, "Do not dare bring the war into this! That was forty years ago. I have heard that remark, 'Look who won the war, anyway,' too many times. If that is the only statement you can make against our Deutschland, then perhaps you should find some other country to kick while they are down, since we recovered long ago."

The American countered, "So, the war's a sensitive issue, eh? And why's that, Hafner? Hafner, isn't it?"

"Yes, call me Wolfgang. My father was in the war . . ." The German's voice became solemn, "Captured in North Africa, he was held prisoner in your country." The jovial atmosphere had suddenly gone south and was replaced by serious silence.

Washington pondered for a moment realizing the magnitude of the situation. "Funny, my Dad was stationed in North Africa too. He was a combat officer, a captain at the time, I think. What was your father's rank?"

"Colonel, he was an armored battalion commander under Rommel, until his imprisonment. I guess I am lucky to be alive," Wolfgang began to drift.

"That makes two of us," the American offered. "My Dad was shot near the war's end and survived. I guess that makes me pretty lucky too." He stared deep into the buff eyes of the German competitor feeling his pain and knowing to be on the losing side of any war would not be an easy thing to swallow.

Nigel Preverett intervened for the first time cognizant of one thing, dark English Ale was the best beer in the world, no question about that. But his smile had long since vanished replaced by a stern brow. And in his best British brogue added, "At least you both had a father who survived the war and was there to watch you grow-up. I never had the luxury."

The Danish runner walked over, pulling a blond lock of hair behind his ear and placed his hand on Preverett's shoulder. "Condolences," he whispered.

The discussion was over.

A Chinese runner has boldly surged ahead to capture the lead pack. He is shorter and slightly stockier than the leaner, defter Africans. His breathing is heavy and labored as he struggles to maintain contact. The front runners approach the descent to the twenty-five mile checkpoint at Duncan Canyon. Xian Doi permits gravity to do the work as his

48

quadriceps absorb most of the stress and pounding of running downhill. Soreness begins to swell and spread throughout his upper legs and lower back. Doi continues to free-fall switchback after switchback, swallowing dust kicked-up by the five runners leading the race. He coughs and sneezes to expel the fine powder.

An aid station attendant cries-out, "Incoming runners."

Smiles have long since vanished, replaced by a rushed seriousness that has taken the front pack. Sweat trickles down their faces. They quickly fill their water bottles with various liquids containing dissolved salts at specific concentrations designed by their respective coaches. Each runner takes a purveyed item or two for consumption.

Doi's coach approaches with initial stoicism that gradually becomes more animated. The coach already sees fatigue in the eyes of his pupil when he addresses him in Mandarin. *"You must rest briefly – even for the shortest time."* He pours cold water on the younger man's head and neck, offering encouragement and advice to his runner. *"Today you run well – as we planned. This is what we have prepared for. Stay with them . . . for as long as possible. They will help you achieve your goal."* A lingering doubt is subtly detected in the voice of the coach. Doi consumes a piece of banana and a few pretzels, then swallows a cup of electrolytes.

The Africans are departing post-haste and this conference with his immediate superior is finished. He grabs the water bottle from his coach, grimaces a feeble smile and presses on attempting the impossible - to maintain contact with runners who are simply moving faster than his gait will allow.

Chapter 5 – Duncan Canyon

It's mid-morning, a little before nine o'clock and the sun shines through a clear cerulean sky. The temperature is seventy degrees Fahrenheit as the day begins to heat-up. A light breeze causes the tips of the trees to bend ever so slightly. Few notice. Most are captivated by the departure of the first runners through the marathon point. Twenty-five miles covered, seventy-five to go. The runners' solace, to this point, is the canopy of evergreens which protects them from direct sun rays that can drain the life from the legs of a runner. The front runners have initially drawn strength from a brief exchange with their captive audience and spirits are high as they depart the Duncan Canyon aid station. As athletes who have successfully completed the first quarter of the Western States Trail, the runners once again face the remoteness and altitude of an alpine setting they must conquer independently.

A young woman hears the sound of the wind, creating the illusion of a near-by creek bed with cool water swiftly moving over cobblestones. Slivers of sunlight pierce through trees as particulate matter kicked-up by the onlookers create tiny apparitions imprinted on the retina of her pretty emerald eyes. She is not just another volunteer at an aid station assisting runners as they move through a checkpoint. Annette Edwards sports a sterling silver belt buckle that embellishes her denim shorts engraved with the words of distinction and achievement: "Award, 100 Miles, One Day, Western States Endurance Run." The figure of Hermes, the Greek Messenger of the Gods, emblazons the front of the buckle. It is a nice piece of hardware that represents months of preparation for one very important, special day. Edwards is a two-time finisher of the event and is proud to wear such a coveted trophy. She is an accomplished runner who has run a sub three hour marathon, a sub eight hour fifty mile endurance run, plus, recorded a sub twenty-four performance here to earn her first silver belt buckle. She is an attractive woman whose long blonde hair is braided into one neat ponytail that lays equidistant between her shoulder blades. Annie, as some of her closest friends call her, lobbied to have women in this Olympic event.

*   *   *

A year earlier Annette had led a suffrage movement in which a group of women petitioned the International Olympic Committee to permit a woman's division in the race. Their proposal was straightforward: "Since the 1984 games marked the inaugural year for the Women's Marathon in the modern Olympics, why not include women in this 100 mile endurance run?" The request certainly made sense to numerous female athletes who would be candidates to represent their respective countries in the 100 mile Olympic event. In fact, three months earlier twenty-seven women had finished the Western States Trail Run, many of whom eclipsed the twenty-four hour barrier.

Their proposal would have placed men and women together in the same foot race – unprecedented in Olympic history. Unfortunately, the IOC had rejected their proposal for the same reason women had been disallowed to participate in the marathon since the institution of the modern Olympics in 1896: The feminine body was not designed nor equipped to withstand the stress of arduous, long distance runs. The risk of injury was far too great to permit women to run, perhaps causing permanent bodily damage.

"Bullshit," she had thought. Her lucid thoughts persuasive, she had not been afraid to share her opinion with other female athletes and the IOC. "There have been women entering these events for the past six years," her petition had read. "The race directors of five different 100 mile events have permitted women to run along with the men, incorporating a separate division for the ladies. "Plus," she had wanted to say, but refrained, "if women can go through childbirth - labor and delivery of an infant, then running a 100 mile endurance run becomes a cake-walk by comparison." In addition, Edwards had attempted to recruit the USOC for their support of a women's division in the race, but the IOC had held steadfast to their own convictions. In this inaugural event, the petition for a women's division would not be granted. "Petition denied," the brief statement had read. "Yet it will be given serious consideration at a future date." Edwards had despised the unofficial decision, ". . . shelved for the time being."

51

"What the hell was that suppose to mean?" She had thought, "Only to assuage the strong sentiments of a few women athletes. A bunch of stuffed-shirts who sit on their butts and establish policy; what do they know of pure athletics?"

"Not this year, but maybe in the next Olympics," she ponders further. "That is if we can get some political pull. God knows, I would love to be in the mix . . . ." A voice interrupts her train of thought.

"Annie, incoming runners," her husband announces patiently. Her husband knows this strong-willed woman too well and figures she will be distracted more than once today while attending to the needs of runners.

Edwards turns to see a black runner in an olive green uniform. Taking his water bottle she queries, "What can I do for you number er, 550?"

Conrad Creary replies politely, his Jamaican tone familiar. "Half electrolytes, half water, please, Miss." He grabs an orange slice and bites hard into its pulp. Creary hardly notices the sweet juice dripping down his chin as he snatches another slice. He looks at the pretty blonde-haired girl working diligently filling his bottle. She bends ever so slightly to expose the upper part of her thigh not obscured by the scanty shorts, revealing the tiniest portion of her right cheek. Conrad smiles when the young woman approaches with the full bottle. "Thank you much," he acknowledges her efforts. He steals a glance into the attendant's green eyes and for a brief moment loses his train of thought. The sounds of runners and volunteers vanish momentarily when he instinctively reaches to take the bottle. He is smitten by the woman who is remarkably attractive with strong legs and a fine figure.

"Anything else I can do for you this fine morning?" Annette offers.

"No Miss, I'm, er . . .," Creary fights to regain his composure. "I'm fine, um . . . that's a nice buckle you have there, er . . . I best be on my way." He recovers feebly to return a smile and leaves the aid station looking for the Russian with whom he had followed into the Duncan Canyon checkpoint.

Akira Okuda has regained his vim and vigor. He has shaken the demons that had haunted his spirit the first twenty-five kilometers and the Japanese athlete has run well over the last ten kilometers. Just outside of the last checkpoint near Red Star Ridge, he departed the trail and defecated thankfully. He had wiped himself carefully and covered his waste with pine needles, twigs and dirt. Akira had momentarily touched his Buddhist talisman that is suspended from his neck and chanted briefly. He had known since the beginning of the race that constipation had prevented the requisite nutrients from being delivered to his working muscles. After passing stools his digestion has improved greatly and so has his cadence. He swallows the last bit of electrolytes in his bottle and notices his raven hair and headband, with its single red circle, emblematic of his country, are soaked with sweat. Unconcerned with dehydration since his urine remains clear, he presses on. Okuda is hustling along the trail in an attempt to catch the leaders. Less than a half mile from the marathon point, his confidence is bolstered with each runner he passes on the dusty downhill switchbacks leading to Duncan Canyon.

His coiled black chest hair is readily seen under the soaked singlet with the Star of David etched upon it. Joshua Kostinski's progress has been solid and steady over the first twenty-five miles of the course. His coach appears from the sidelines with a broad smile and a nod of encouragement. The two men stand next to one of the tables filled with food and beverage items.

"How're you doing, buddy? Anything I can get you? You're looking great!"

Kostinski has heard that phrase too often during his running career – "You're looking great." You could feel like shit, look like shit and be running like shit and yet, the words of encouragement would be repeated all too often. "I sure as hell better look good, Coach," he counters, "I'm only a quarter way through the race. How far am I behind? What place, give or take?" The Israeli bites into a graham cracker lathered with peanut butter.

"You're in good shape Josh. They're about fifteen minutes ahead and you've gotta' be in the top twenty," the coach replies smiling, "give or take."

"The Africans?" His speech impaired by the chewy food stuff.

"Yeah and a Chinese runner as well . . . But, I doubt he'll last much longer. He looks pretty much spent already." His coach continues,

"Keep moving, something tells me you'll be in the thick of it before too long. Have you been eating and drinking enough?" Despite not having run an endurance run of this length, the coach has done his homework and knows the importance of taking in ample fluids and food.

Kostinski nods and returns a firm smile. Handing his coach an empty water bottle he requests, "Please see that I get a fresh refill; the usual, okay, Coach." He steals an orange slice and a half banana then sits a spell to remove a pebble from his shoe. Kostinski presses and prods on different points of his foot, especially his toes; Notices his socks are already heavily soiled with trail dust. He recognizes there is some chafing, a few sore spots, but nothing serious, yet. He brushes some of the powder from his socks and dons his shoe, carefully tying his laces with a double knot. Joshua glances at his chronometer - the time is almost 0900 hours when he sees his coach approach with his bottle, plus a handful of pretzels. Immediately, he stands to take the bottle and pretzels acknowledging his superior's efforts. He is glad to see the familiar face of his college coach; his presence a welcome addition to the surroundings. He entrusts his mentor to be his assistant or "crew" throughout the run and his coach obliges happily. "Thanks Coach, I'll need a fresh pair of socks at the next checkpoint. There is a stream crossing in about two miles."

"You've got it, buddy." The coach had acknowledged to Josh, on more than one occasion that he was the first athlete he had trained to this level of international competition. The coach, like the athlete, is elated to be a part of the Olympic movement. "Try to stay with the Canadian, Josh, he appears ready to head-out." The coach motions to the trailhead. "Good-luck!" He easily recognizes the North American 100 kilometer champion, and knows if his charge keeps contact with this particular competitor, good things can happen.

As Kostinski departs chomping on the pretzels, he waves and grimaces a bit. His muscles have stiffened a little during the short rest. The coach further contemplates watching his "boy" take leave. "Bad things can happen, too. In fact, there are a hell of a lot of bad things that can happen during a race of this distance; much more bad than good when one really thinks about it." The coach instinctively peeks at his watch. "Christ it's nine o'clock and the kid's right on target." He sees Joshua file in behind the white and red uniform of the Canadian runner where the trail narrows to a single track. Watching him disappear as other runners join the queue, he contemplates, "Just maybe he's a got a shot." Another wide smile ensues.

The trail leads to the second major climb of the course - the climb to the fifty kilometer checkpoint at a place called Robinson Flat.

Chapter 6 – Robinson Flat

A frenetic pace circulates the aid station. Final preparations are nearly complete as numerous volunteers await the front runners who have finished nearly one-third of the race. The time is 10:00 with an ambient temperature of 75° Fahrenheit. The chief medical director, an experienced physician who has coordinated the medical checkpoints of previous Western States Runs, gazes upward at the coniferous trees to see daylight streaming through.

Returning his attention to the television camera situated directly in front of him, " . . . at this point the runners will arrive here after climbing nearly 1500 vertical feet over a trail distance of approximately three miles. Many have begun to feel the stress and fatigue of running the first thirty miles of trail and will have need of assistance. Our job is to give aid to any runner who requires medical attention."

The commentator, Brandon Davis, a charismatic man and a veteran broadcaster, facilitates the interview that is being broadcast worldwide. "What do you mean by give aid, and to what limits will you provide medical assistance?" Davis holds a microphone under the angular chin of the man opposite him.

The doctor has removed his spectacles and is cleaning the dust from them with a clean white handkerchief. He contemplates the question momentarily. "All athletes are required to submit to a mandatory weigh-in and must maintain their body weight throughout the event. We'll offer them food and fluids, as well as anti-inflamatories such as aspirin or ibuprofen, er . . . I mean Motrin. Furthermore, athletes who wish to have minor abrasions and/or blisters treated can find help at the aid stations. As far as our limitations . . . we are not permitted to physically assist runners. Nor are we allowed to administer intravenous treatments, unless there is a dire need, such as a runner's medical condition becoming life threatening. Of course, any athlete relegated to an IV treatment of fluids or medication will be automatically dismissed from the race."

"Do you expect many disqualifications based on medical emergencies?" The broadcaster inquires hoping to bring a certain dramatic appeal to the mundane dialogue the doctor is delivering. Davis shakes his head. "I mean running 100 miles must punish these guys."

"Absolutely not," the medical director emphasizes. "These 'guys' are world class athletes who must have prepared exceptionally well for the event. Those who have not will soon succumb to nature's pressures of altitude, heat and ultimately, exhaustion. I expect some may not make the cut-off times and will be summarily dismissed from the competition. Or more often, a runner will simply withdraw because he realizes that the day doesn't belong to him."

Once again the doc peers up into the canopy and rubs his delicate right hand through his graying hair. He is a cardiovascular surgeon who has completed a number of marathons and knows from personal experience the damage running 26.2 miles can cause the human body. Running four times that distance may be good for the mind, but running distances of 100 miles will certainly take their toll. Perhaps not immediately, but in the long term . . . "We'll certainly know more later," he contemplates.

Cognizant that temperatures will surely exceed 100° Fahrenheit later in the day, he adds pensively, "I just pray these men remember to drink enough fluids throughout the course of the day."

"And how will the athletes know if there drinking enough, Doctor? What criteria will they use to judge 'adequate fluid intake?'" The announcer applies the phrase he heard the day before at the trail briefing.

"The runners wear a wristband that has their pre-race weight, pulse and blood pressure recorded. We require that they maintain their weight within three percent of what is recorded on the wristband. Some latitude will be given, but if we observe an athlete experiencing difficulty due to heat and/or dehydration, he will be obliged to rest and drink before returning to the race. That is why all four medical checkpoints have mandatory weigh-ins. The checkpoints give us an opportunity to monitor each runner, ensuring their safety throughout the day and night."

"Interesting." The commentator nods in approval. "But are there other ways an athlete can monitor his weight and fluid intake between the medical checkpoints?"

The doctor is becoming annoyed with the interview and wishes to carry out some final details before the first African runners arrive. He concludes by repeating, "The purpose of the medical check, plus the weigh-in, is to help indicate whether or not runners are eating and drinking enough and that will ultimately ensure the safety of each runner." Then speaking very methodically into the microphone, "Of course there is a much easier way athletes are capable of determining whether their 'fluid intake is adequate.'"

"Oh, how do they check their 'fluid intake,' Doctor?"

"Well, each athlete is quite capable of looking at his stream of urine. If it's yellow or darker they know to drink more. If it's clear they know they're drinking enough."

The announcer clears his throat knowing that the doctor, on national television, has just spoken of athletes looking at their piss. "And . . . er . . . the runners know to do that; I mean look at their urine?"

"Oh yes, of course . . . and obviously men have a distinct advantage over women when checking 'adequate fluid intake.'" He grins unabashed knowing he has caught the commentator totally off-guard with the remark. "I must be off as I've some things to attend to."

"Well, um . . . thanks doctor for your time and information. Your commentary has certainly been, uh . . . insightful." He shakes the doctor's hand briefly, then the camera witnesses the doctor disappear into the medical tent that had been erected earlier that morning. "That was Dr. Chad Logan, Chief Medical Director for the Western States Trail Run. I am sure we'll hear more from Dr. Logan before this day is done."

Brandon Davis has been a network employee for nine years and has served as a correspondent for a variety of athletic events. But no competition he has covered during his tenure has gone twenty-four hours continuously. This is a novel undertaking for the experienced sportscaster. There would be no question that this Olympic event could help promote his career significantly, giving him more national airtime than any other event. He will use the assignment to enhance his career and perhaps, at the next Olympic Games in Seoul, he will find himself sitting in the network center as a coordinator of coverage, rather than his current position of an event commentator. His demeanor is casual, yet professional, when he signs-off from this segment of the broadcast.

"This is Brandon Davis reporting live from Robinson Flat, approximately thirty miles southwest of Squaw Valley in the Sierra

Nevada. We will return to our network studio in Los Angeles after these important messages from our sponsors."

*   *   *

A half a world away in a small town surrounded by cherry trees south of Turin, Italy, a middle-aged woman sits in a rocking chair knitting a blanket for one of her grand children. She crosses herself for the umpteenth time as she intently stares at the television and awaits the translation from the Italian announcer. She has a rosary made of rosewood around her neck and occasionally clenches one of the tiny beads with her left hand. The American network has given only summaries of the race in which her son is participating. The coverage appears to have more emphasis on the track and field trials; plus, some equestrian performances have been televised. The mother has no idea where he is or how he's doing. She only hopes he is safe and running well.

"*Mamma, how's our son doing? Have you heard anything?*" her husband asks. The Pavin's have raised a good son and a very talented runner. Neither ever imagined their boy, now twenty-eight years old and the Italian National 100 Kilometer Champion, would be entered in event unlike any other found on the European continent.

"*No, Albino, nothing yet. There are some Africans approaching the fifty kilometer point, but I have heard nothing of Girolamo.*"

The older husband, who wishes he could have traveled to the United States to support their son, places his hand on his wife's shoulder and squeezes gently. Albino's doctor strongly discouraged travel at this time due to the weekly treatments. "*I am sure he is doing fine, much too early to tell at this time.*" He looks outside and sees the sun beginning to set toward the western horizon. The Alps are in plain view. The elder Pavin calculates in his mind, "*It is 10:30 in California. Please God, take care of our son, watch over him, guide him – Our Father who art in heaven . . .*" He whispers.

The eighteen karat gold crucifix falls outside his azure uniform just above the Italian insignia that adorns his singlet. He is breathing heavily as he ascends a relatively steep grade. Sweat is streaming down his face. The intensity on his face mirrors both the runners in front and behind. He attempts to run, but the altitude and the slope prevent him from improving his pace. Additionally, the stream crossing four kilometers behind has left his shoes and socks damp, not helping the climb whatsoever. He, like many of the other runners, is relegated to a "power walk" or a jog-walk at best. Yet Girolamo Pavin is holding his position. No runners pass as he makes steady progress to the next checkpoint. He glances at his watch; it's almost 10:30. The aid station must be close. Seeing a flat section of trail ahead, Pavin swallows the last bit of liquid in his plastic bottle. He lifts his knees and begins to run.

*   *   *

Pavin grew-up in a small town in a zone aptly named the Valley of Cherries. There are more cherry trees cultivated in this hilly region of Piemonte than any other deciduous tree. Early spring always brings cherry blossoms that appear to blanket the hills as snow would during the winter months. He and his brother harvested the crop on the family's property and then would sell the cherries during the early summer at the local open market. Girolamo learned at an early age to work together and contribute to the livelihood of the family. His father, Albino, is proud of his boys, loves his wife dearly and worked diligently to support his family. He is a good father.

Albino, who had been an avid amateur runner, would occasionally take his wife and four sons to regional races in Piemonte. At one such race he asked his boys, *"Carlo, Stefano, Lamo, there is a two kilometer fun race for children; do you wish to run?"* His wife who held the baby Roberto only smiled, knowing Carlo would never agree to run. He was not the athletic type. On the other hand, their son Stefano was an excellent soccer player whose passion for the game was evident in his style of play. Girolamo too, enjoyed soccer, but lacked the quickness and skill to develop into a great player. His older brother could literally dribble circles around him when given the opportunity, which often embarrassed little Lamo to the point of frustration. However, distance running; that was different. The younger Girolamo possessed a keen competitiveness and an innate ability to carry a pace beyond the normal threshold of pain.

"*Sure Papa, I will run,*" Girolamo replied confidently.

"*And you Stefano, do you wish to participate? Or will your younger brother be the only runner to carry the name of our family?*"

"*Of course I will run, Papa. There is no way that little cretinous brother of mine will carry our family's honor in front of me! I'll get my soccer shoes and run in those.*"

"*Lamo, do you want to wear your soccer shoes?*" his father asked patiently.

"*No Papa, I will wear these,*" Girolamo replied innocently, as only a twelve year old could. Both looked down simultaneously to see a well-worn pair of tennis shoes.

His father thought of his son's need for a new pair - very soon. "*Be sure to re-tie them Lamo. You do not want them to fall-off during the race.*"

"*Okay, Papa.*" He grinned showing the gap between his two front teeth.

It was a small race, maybe thirty kids ranging in age from ten to fifteen years. Girolamo lined-up directly behind his older brother as the race director called the children to the line. The director summarized the one kilometer course briefly. Pointing at a barn on a knoll a distance from the start, he stated clearly that they would run two laps around the area and mentioned there would be only two commands to start the run.

"*Runners take your mark,*" the race director declared and the crack of the pistol sent the young runners scurrying toward the knoll. Girolamo initially tried to stay with his brother, but was immediately bumped by other runners and lost contact.

Many near-sighted runners sprinted from the start to find themselves struggling up the hill to the barn and a few of the more patient runners found themselves passing runners as they climbed to the crest of the knoll. Little Lamo was one of those. When he approached the starting line after one revolution, he heard is father screaming words of encouragement, but had difficulty understanding. Something about ten or tenth he comprehended. It was the second climb that paid the most dividends. Many runners were fading fast and the younger Pavin found something inside that the others lacked: The stamina to pursue and the desire to win. He passed several runners on the way to the top of the knoll, the last being his fifteen year old brother. The long downhill back to the finish was a breeze. Despite not catching two older competitive runners, his third place finish was an accomplishment considering the time. His father looked at his chronometer: 7:10 for two kilometers with two climbs, not bad he thought . . . for a twelve year old. Stefano finished five seconds behind his younger brother looking somewhat embarrassed. Girolamo just beamed knowing that for the first time in his life he had beaten his older brother at something.

Albino embraced his children proudly before walking to the starting line of his race. *"Stefano, take your brother over there to get some water."* He pointed to some large plastic jugs sitting on a table adjacent to the staging area of the race. *"Lamo, hold my warm-ups for me, please."* Albino Pavin looked at his younger son and his smile enveloped the boy.

*   *   *

"I am standing at an altitude of nearly 7000 feet on ridge called Robinson Flat in the Sierra Nevada thirty miles southwest of Squaw Valley. The atmosphere is festive to say the least." The camera focuses on a good-looking man, tan complexion with an athletic build. Bruce Springteen's, "Born in the USA," is blaring in the background. Brandon Davis smilcs when speaking into the microphone and his audience easily senses the exhilaration. "There must be 2000 people here to witness, encourage and yes, even assist these athletes as they race across the mountains. The first medical checkpoint of the run is directly behind me as we await the arrival of the lead pack. Certainly, in a battle of wills, these athletes began their quest of a hundred miles this morning at six o'clock. And with the exception of an aid station or two along the way, they have been moving continuously. Truly a remarkable event considering no event of this distance and duration has ever been attempted in the modern Olympic era. We are only moments away . . ."

"Number 542 - Yosef Ethiopia." The portable broadcast system announces. "From er, Ethiopia." Much applause ensues despite the coincidence. The trail has been cordoned-off with bright yellow ribbon to lead the runners into the checkpoint and more importantly, to keep the spectators from interfering with the progress of the runners.

Brandon Davis is confused by the announcement. "The guy is from Ethiopia and his name is Ethiopia?" he queries his staff. Davis looks over to see a scrawny man standing on one of three scales. It's 10:30 when the lead runner checks in. His coffee-brown skin is already covered with white salt crystals and the intensity in his dark eyes is nearly tangible - The eyes of a competitor whose mission goes well beyond this checkpoint. There is purpose behind this man's façade.

"Yosef Ethiopia is from the province of Eritrea that lies within the borders of Ethiopia in East Africa." Davis is aware of the internal struggles that exist in many nations worldwide. "Eritrea is a war ravaged province that has attempted to gain its independence from Ethiopia since the conclusion of the Second World War. It's surprising to have a participant from Eritrea."

"Strange," Davis thinks, "his last name is the same as the country in which his province wishes to claim its independence. No wonder I was confused," he muses. The veteran commentator returns his attention to the race. "The Ethiopian must have pulled-away from his fellow Africans on the climb to this checkpoint." Another camera focuses on the runner who is having his wristband checked by the medical staff that compares vital information recorded on the band the day before.

Davis wishes to interview the man who is winning the race, but knows race policy forbids interviews during the run. The race committee was adamant about that stipulation. Observing the energy at Robinson Flat he concurs with the policy. There is enough confusion at the checkpoints without cameras and crew interfering. Three minutes later the first Kenyan arrives, and when Davis announces the arrival of Stephen Komen, he contemplates, "This guy looks a hell of a lot worse than the first guy."

Before the stream crossing, Yosef had removed his shoes and never stopped to replace them. Like running in his native country, he had completed the last three miles of uphill trail in his bare feet carrying his running shoes. A fresh pair of socks awaits in his drop bag, so he quickly dons the socks and shoes and leaves the aid station post-haste. The next section of trail welcomes the participants to a rocky path of cobblestones and boulders that will certainly impede their progress. Ethiopia knows the shoes will provide much needed support, protection and cushion.

"Number 542 checking-out." Another voice announces the departure of Ethiopia.

A few minutes later another athlete removes a white cap from his drop bag, squirts water onto the brim and places it crookedly on his bald head. The cool water drips down his neck onto his shoulders. He draws air deep into his lungs and this, coupled with the water produce a soothing effect. His interpreter and crew, a Russian doctor who has been assigned by the KGB to assist this particular runner, hands him a piece of energy bar. *"Is there anything you have need of, Comrade Boroshkov?"*

"Yes doctor, I have need of three travel visas for my wife and daughters." A cynical smile follows. *"However, in the interim you can fetch me some water, orange slices and two aspirin. Incidentally, three or four kilometers back on the trail I saw a large brown bear scampering away, most likely frightened from the intruders invading his land."* He reflects on the propitious site, then bites down on the energy bar and drinks some electrolyte solution.

"Yes Yuri, perhaps the bear is a good omen of things to come." The man leaves to fill the water bottle with the prescribed electrolytes. The interpreter knows his charge well; knows Boroshkov to be cynical of the machinations within the Soviet government, but nevertheless remains loyal to Mother Russia.

*　　　　*　　　　*

A year earlier Yuri Boroshkov had applied for three travel visas when the Soviet Olympic Committee awarded him entry into the event. He had hoped that his tenure as a university professor, plus his current affiliation with the Communist Party would merit the privilege of traveling with his family outside the Soviet Union. As an active party member and loyal partisan of the communist regime, he had been optimistic that the Visa Bureau would make an exception to the policy of not allowing families to travel outside their border. Unfortunately, Yuri had also been advocate of open communication with the West, especially concerning the fields of science and medicine. This had drawn some unwarranted suspicion regarding his motives of wishing to travel with his family.

"   . . . *My intent is not to defect to the West,*" he explained, attempting to persuade the government official at the visa bureau to approve his application. "*I only wish to take my family outside the frontier and share with them some global experiences and obviously, have their support during the Los Angeles Olympics. I do not even speak English . . . Why should I defect?*" Looking stoically at the bureaucrat seated directly in front of him, he thought, "*Stupid fucking pencil pusher, this man has no clue who I am or what this application is about.*"

The elderly official scrutinized the file, and then peered above his bifocals. "*Yes professor, you do not speak English, but your wife, Yelizaveta, appears to be quite versed in the English language . . . according to our records. And perhaps, you have ulterior motives not mentioned in your visa application. I will, however, take your application to my superior for his perusal of the document. Our agency will have an official response to you . . . soon, Professor Boroshkov. That is all.*" The meeting was over.

After his family's visa application had been reviewed by the appropriate government agency, the application had been returned, "*Regretfully denied.*" There would be no exception, no travel visas issued. His wife and daughters would stay in Russia and once again, as he had traveled so many times before, he would make his first visit to the United States – alone.

Boroshkov glances over his shoulder and sees a woman holding the hand of a little girl outside the restricted area. "*No doubt waiting for her husband,*" he ponders for a second or two. The chocolate energy bar tastes sweet. The orange that the doctor has handed him is quite sour by comparison. He stands and winces, feeling soreness in his quadriceps and calves. Boroshkov sees another woman bending and gently kissing her man . . . "*Lucky bastard,*" Yuri mutters. "*That is the kind of support I need - right here, right now.*" He walks toward the station's exit as his muscles loosen a bit and then waves at the attendant recording the bib numbers. He looks instinctively downward to ensure his number is in clear view, and smirks knowing the bib number could not have moved since it is pinned to his white uniform just below the Soviet insignia of a golden hammer and sickle.

"Number 6 2 2 departing," the resonance of the interpreter's accent is clearly understood by all those in attendance. The crowd that lines the trail applauds the Russian's effort as he begins to saunter toward the next section of trail which lies on a ridge called Cavanaugh.

She bends over her husband to steal a kiss in the middle of the commotion. He lifts his head slightly to accept her contact, her companionship. Their lips touch only for a moment. Exchanging a glance and a smile with his wife, J. P. Badillo's attention returns to doffing his damp socks in favor of clean dry ones.

His wife, Susan, tastes the saline on her husband's lips as she has tasted him and his love many times before. Emotional highs and lows have engendered tears of joy and sorrow during their eight years of marriage. Intimacy and depth in which only soul mates can revel have provided a strong loving relationship. "Mmm . . . Nice and salty, just the way I like it," she remarks in a sultry voice, then adds. "You're doing great, top ten I think." She stares into the eyes of her loved-one, half Hispanic, half Native American and ponders, "This man, win or lose, still captivates me."

Badillo replies with his best "B" Hollywood movie impersonation, "Oh, you naughty girl – I love it when you talk dirty to me." Most of his Mexican accent lost to fifteen years of Americanization, he concentrates on tying his shoes properly – snug, but not too tight. "How are things at home? How're the kids?" Juan-Pablo looks-up from his chair to see his wife's blue eyes and her disheveled dirty blond hair draped over her shoulders. Susan's arms are well defined from carrying their two children too often.

Badillo has not spent much time recently with his wife and kids, especially over the past two months. He was happy to take his family to the festivities of the opening ceremony in Los Angeles a week earlier. Since he did not wish to lose valuable acclimation time, he had returned solo to the mountains to complete his final week of preparation. Susan's sister accompanied his wife and kids on the return trip from L. A. two days ago and agreed to baby sit the children while Susan could be part of her husband's Olympic experience.

"Everything's fine, J. P." His wife, who had always supported his efforts to return to the fitness of a world class runner, puts the well-used socks into a plastic bag. "Nice socks!" she exclaims. "What else can I get you, Dearest One?" Her affectionate smile is contagious as J. P. accepts his water bottle. He has little time for small talk and Susan knows that. His wife has "crewed" many times at other endurance events and knows the drill. They exchange another peck.

Badillo grins, "I'm fine, Susan."

"How're legs holding-up, J. P.?" She walks with him a spell.

"Everything's cool. I'll see you at Devil's Thumb, probably around . . ." Badillo notes the time, "a quarter 'til eleven," and mentions, "Nathan's got to be close. Have you seen him come through?" He calls-out his bib number to the attendant, "Number 557 checking-out." He eats a couple of saltines as he proceeds.

"No J. P., I haven't seen him. But, there are so many people and I haven't heard his name called over the P. A. Good-luck!" She shouts above the applause. Once again, as Susan Badillo has witnessed many times during their partnership, the trail consumes her man when he disappears into the forest.

Nathan Washington has been all business during the three mile climb to Robinson Flat. Passing several runners, plus leaving the young Irishman and the Aussie eating trail dust, he has arrived to an ovation of a partisan crowd that only the home country can provide.

"Number 620, Nathan Washington, U S A," the announcer declares proudly. Nathan steps onto the scale eager to complete the medical check. He is nearly six feet tall and tips the scale at 145 pounds. A medical attendant notices his gray uniform is wet, soaked with perspiration, so she proceeds to ask the usual litany of questions.

"You've dropped a few pounds. "How are you feeling? Have you been eating and drinking? Have you been going to the bathroom? Do you have a crew? Can I get you anything?

Washington grins and replies curtly. "Don't worry about the three pounds, it could be the scale. Feeling fine. Yes. Yes . . . And yes." He sees his brother waving from the cordoned area. He returns the wave with vigor. "I think I've answered all your questions. Are we through here?" He looks at the attendant and adds, "Er, no thanks, I have my crew." He moves towards his brother. "Hey Clint, bring the drop bag. I need socks, follow me." Nate and his brother navigate to some portable chairs that are near the medical tent.

"Hey Bro, you're looking great. Top twenty, I think. How're you feeling? He separates the socks that have been folded together and hands one to his brother.

"Doing fine, Clint; where's Gioia?"

"Our cousin dropped me. She's looking for a place to park the car. Christ Nate, this place is a fuckin' nuts. There are more people here than I've ever seen at 'States.' The road is packed. I hope we can get out of here."

"Don't worry, you've got lots of time." He senses his brother's anxiousness and wants to calm him a bit. "I mean, I'm not going to sprint the next twenty-five miles. Take it easy, everything'll be fine." Washington knows from previous experience that his brother and cousin are in for a long day, and he will need them to be alert during the long hours ahead. He takes a small portion of electrolytes from a plastic ziplock and pours some in his water bottle and hands it to his brother. "Fill-it with water, Clint and bring me something to eat too." He finds an energy bar in his bag of tricks and takes a bite of the chewy sweet foodstuff.

"Got it Nate. I'll be quick."

"Thanks." Washington presses his feet delicately with his fingers and sees his first blister on the baby toe of his right foot. He calls for a medic and decides to take the time for a quick repair. "Can I get a band aid from you . . . please?"

"Sure, what's the problem?" The medic grabs a medical kit from the tent.

"Just a blister."

"I could put some second skin on that for you – It will hold better. The medic takes one look at the blister and promptly cuts a piece of appropriate size that adheres to the blister. "Anything else? How's the other foot?" He eyes Nathan's left foot.

"No, it's er, everything's fine, thanks." Washington ties his shoes.

"Here yuh go Bro, coke and water, just the way you like it." He hands his younger brother the cup.

Washington bites down on a few pretzels and chases it with the diluted coke. "Got to go, Clint. Thanks for being here." He acknowledges his brother's presence with a filial hug, takes the water bottle and bids farewell. Washington reflects for a moment, "Thank God he's here." Of course, Clint had always been there, even through the tough times. His brother escorts him to the trailhead.

"Number 620 is checking-out." Clint Washington announces his brother's departure enthusiastically. He sees his brother disappear into the shadows of the forest. People who have lined the trail applaud and offer words of encouragement to America's best hope for a medal in the event. There is one other American in the race, but he's no where to be seen.

Two coaches are simultaneously pleading with their athletes not to drop from the race: one in Mandarin, the other in English. Their runners already have the appearance of beaten man. Faces flushed, rounded shoulders and breathing much too heavily, the two runners are seated in the shade of some large pinion pines drinking what their coaches have given them.

"Eammon, slow your breathing down, man – relax. Here, eat this."

"Christ Coach, just five miles back I was feeling grand . . . running with the American. The last three miles have been hell." He bites into an energy bar, then drains a cup of fluids. "My legs already feel as heavy as bricks. Shit, what am I going to do?"

"The first thing is simple, slow your ass down. Here, take these." His coach gives him two aspirin with another cup of diluted electrolytes. "Eat these too." He hands Horgan some pretzels and recognizes that his pupil is beginning to feel better – regaining his normal complexion. "Eammon, this is a hundred mile endurance run. You'll have your ups and downs. For Gods sake, be patient! How are your feet holding up?"

Horgan contemplates his coach's counsel. "Okay coach, you're the boss, I'll gladly take your advice. One thing's for sure, there's no way I can stay with those guys, unless of course, you want to see me taken away on a stretcher." He snickers at the thought. Horgan notices a blister on his left foot between the big and second toe, and decides to ignore it. He dons a dry pair of socks. "Hand me my other pair of shoes."

"Eammon, you may want to put on the ones you've been wearing."

"They're wet Coach; give me the dry ones."

The coach shakes his head knowing the other pair of shoes will most likely be too tight, since runners' feet tend to swell, especially after sitting. "Okay, if that's what you want."

The Irishman struggles with his left shoe for a moment and then feels a sharp abdominal cramp. He recoils in his chair attempting to alleviate the pain.

"You okay, buddy? What's wrong?"

"Just a cramp." Horgan grimaces, kneading the right side of his abdomen with his left hand.

The contortion of his runner's face almost looks comical. "Let's try the other pair of shoes, shall we?" The coach clears his throat. "Chances are these will fit better."

"Yeah Coach, good idea." Another contorted expression ensues. He takes another moment to massage his gut, then takes the damp shoes and ties them up. "What's the mileage here?"

His coach chuckles knowing the young man is quite aware of the distance covered. "You're a third through and it's time to get moving. Now get out of here!"

The young Irishman turns and sees the Chinese runner departing from the checkpoint. He knows the formidable task ahead and realizes that unless the guys in front literally drop dead, he has very little chance of winning an Olympic medal. "547 checking out," he stubbornly calls out, not ready or willing to give into the worst three letters in distance running: DNF or "did not finish."

The first casualties of the race are reported to race headquarters in the small foothill community of Auburn roughly sixty miles southwest of Robinson Flat. A French runner has severely sprained his ankle and can no longer continue. A Chilean runner has complained of chronic diarrhea since the race's inception and, with the onset of abdominal cramps, has decided to withdraw from the competition. A Romanian runner has fallen and severely bruised his knee cap. He sought treatment of ice and bandages at the Duncan Canyon Aid Station, but the swelling has persisted. Consequently, he contemplates withdrawing upon his arrival at Robinson Flat. Other runners have arrived at Robinson Flat feeling utterly exhausted or suffering from muscle cramping and cannot imagine running another seventy miles. There are five runners unaccounted, most likely lost in the high country after missing one of the myriad of bright yellow ribbons that line the Western States Trail. Two of the runners are South African and have decided to run together on the tenet of abolishing apartheid in their home country. Their demonstration may prove fruitless unless they can relocate the trail and arrive at the Duncan Canyon aid station before the cut-off time of twelve noon.

And the man from Haiti methodically moves on. He is no longer in last position since those who have decided not to continue will be moved to the bottom of the final results. A French interpreter warns of the absolute cut-off time of 1:00 pm for the next checkpoint at Robinson flat. He is a half hour ahead of the cut-off time and feels good after completing a marathon's distance. The Haitian knows he is lucky to be in the race; knows it's too early to think about a finishing line one hundred twenty kilometers away. He contemplates, "*Just get to the next aid station with time to spare . . . just get to the next aid station.*"

Chapter 7 – Deep Canyon One

The pilot pulls back on the throttle to slow his helicopter as a television cameraman zooms-in on the front runner. He and his passenger had departed Sacramento earlier that morning, crossing over the Middle Fork of the American River on a north by northeast heading until their route intersected the Western States Trail. They are five hundred feet above Cavanaugh Ridge when the cameraman spots Yosef Ethiopia. His gait appears efficient, his motion effortless as he proceeds along a dirt trail skirted by gravel and rocks. The second runner, an Egyptian who is five hundred yards behind, lacks fluency and appears to be losing ground.

"Can you take the 'chopper' down for a closer look?" The cameraman speaks loudly into a microphone that is secured to his head. He likes the word that is often used to describe helicopters, especially among military personnel.

The aviator, a veteran of the Vietnam War, immediately chuckles and senses that this cameraman wishes to experience some real combat maneuvers. "No need to shout into the mike; I can hear you just fine. Sure I can take this bird down. Hang on!" He pushes the stick forward and the helicopter descends nose first.

"Whoa! Take it easy there, captain." The cameraman tastes his breakfast for the second time and decides that a little distance is a good thing. "Let's not get too close, okay?" He flips an electronic switch that begins the transmission of the telecast from their flight.

"Roger that . . . are we close enough?"

"Yeah, the distance is fine, just follow the trail. Do you copy?"

The pilot smiles wryly and adjusts the rudder. "Yeah, I copy."

Ethiopia hears the helicopter and knows he has been spotted; knows he is being observed. Currently in first place, he is the hunted quarry – the man the pack wants to catch. Temperatures have steadily risen and with no trees to provide shade, he decides to conserve energy. Yosef eases the throttle back to slow his cadence, shortens his stride length and settles into a more comfortable pace. The Ethiopian has run aggressively for thirty-five miles and knows he has the capacity to win Olympic gold – a status that will surely bring a plethora of accolades and wealth in his impoverished country. He ignores the helicopter, concentrating on his foot strike and the earth moving below his feet.

Imperceptible to the personnel in the helicopter, Ethiopia still appears to hold the same pace. They continue to fly above the trail moving northeast. More runners come into view: a Kenyan . . . then a Russian, a Canadian and an Israeli all appear to be closing in on the second place runner. The cameraman inquires, "How close are these guys to the front runner?"

The pilot contemplates before answering. "They're a mile maybe a mile and a half back." He notes the ruggedness of the terrain and the change in altitude. "At least these guys are running downhill."

"What do you mean by that?" The cameraman doesn't flinch and remains on task.

"Well, they finish in Auburn, right?"

"Yeah, so what?"

"Auburn is at a thousand feet of elevation and they're running above six thousand now. They're basically running downhill, get it?"

For a moment he removes his eye from the lens of the camera and quickly scans the countryside. "I don't know man; sure doesn't look downhill to me."

Stepping over boulders and cobblestones, two runners negotiate a rough downhill stretch just outside of Robinson Flat. Neither look up, instead each remains focused on his foot placement, thereby avoiding the possibility of a fall. They descend to a single track trail with much better footing. "Conrad, what's going on?" The taller Australian inquires keeping his eye on the rugged trail.

"Ah David, good to see you, man. What's going on?" The Jamaican recognizes an acquaintance he had met two years earlier at the Commonwealth Games in Brisbane. He remembers a friendly man who represented his country with a casual manner that was much different from the pompous mind-set of the British expatriates he had known in Jamaica. Both had run the Commonwealth marathon, though not particularly well, finishing well behind the leaders. A friendship had been forged from their meeting and racing in Australia. Here in America, they have become reacquainted.

"Everything's going well. We're in the top twenty. I know that for certain," Conor states confidently.

"So, you're just taking it slow and easy, Mate." The Jamaican emphasizes the last word of the statement, his accent harmonious. Creary recognizes their pace is not so slow, running on a gentle downhill grade. "Do you wish to lead?"

"No worries, Mate, the pace is fine." Conor continues to avoid the occasional rock on the trail. "Do you think the Yank will win?"

"Not if I have something to say about it. There's a lot of running left to do, David. I know I can challenge for the gold medal. Do I sense doubt in you? It's much too early for doubt, don't you think?"

There is a pause from the Aussie. "No doubt, I can challenge too, but the American's one tough bloke, Conrad . . . and very determined to win on his home turf. He left me in a cloud of dust climbing to Robinson Flat. No way could I stay with him."

"You mean he's ahead of us?" Creary wipes a droplet of sweat from his brow.

"I think so."

"Well, so's the Russian, man . . . and he's running for gold too. I ran with 'im this morning for a time and we hardly exchanged a word. He also left me in his dust on the climb to the last checkpoint."

"How far do you think the Russian is in front of us?"

"Not too far ahead. Not too far at all. I know we can catch 'im, maybe the American, too."

The Australian enjoys the optimism of a fellow competitor. "Wouldn't that be something . . . a Jamaican soldier and an Australian doctor challenging for the gold medal."

"Yah man, that would be something. By the way, why do you wear your cap backwards?" Creary asks.

Conor points his thumb toward the center of the solar system. "The sun's behind us – the brim keeps the heat off my neck."

The Jamaican nods and then adjusts his yellow cap accordingly.

Nigel Preverett sees a runner in front of him, his knee heavily bandaged with an ice pack. "Can I pass . . . when there is space?" Despite being in the middle of the pack, he does not wish to lose precious time waiting for a crippled runner to proceed. The Pakistani, as if waiting, perfunctorily steps aside. Dejection etched upon the man's face, Preverett thinks, "The battle lost, he will most certainly withdraw at Robinson Flat."

The Asian runner smiles weakly and utters something, acknowledging that Nigel should move ahead.

Preverett had been in the spotlight throughout the days preceding the race. As the eldest competitor in the race, he had numerous years of experience to draw from and many stories to cite. The interview with the American reporter, Brandon Davis, had gone quite well for the most part. Davis was quite competent, facilitating dialogue with inquiry and humor. A confident man, who had obviously done his homework prior to their meeting, he had begun the interview with one statement and an excellent question:

"Mr. Preverett this is your fourth Olympic games. Ten thousand meters in Mexico City, marathons in Munich and Montreal, and now you come to Los Angeles to compete in a one hundred mile endurance run. What are you trying to prove at the ripe age of forty-five? I mean, most men your age are content to coach or sit comfortably in front of their 'telly' watching the games from a safe distance."

"Mr. Davis, let me preface everything by saying I am not forty-five yet, and I'm no stuffed shirt, so please call me Nigel. No need to be formal." His smile is a bit crooked. "Well, before I retire to my rocking chair with the roaring fireplace and the 'telly,' I have some unfinished business. The one award missing from my collection is an Olympic medal. I plan to pilfer one here, since no one would suspect an old man at the 'ripe' age of forty-four to walk away from the winner's podium with one strung around his neck."

"But, you'll be competing against some men almost half your age."

"Ah yes, one of the oldest debates in athletics – youth versus experience; which will win?" He pauses. "Personally, I think experience is a much more important attribute in a race of this distance. Obviously, I would not be here unless I thought I could win."

Davis wishes to clarify. "You mean the longer the race the more it favors the veterans over the rookies?"

"Yes, I think so, to a point. And of course that 'point' is why there are races in the first place: to determine who's best."

"Tell us about some of your running experiences, Nigel."

Preverett leans back in his chair, revealing teeth that have dire need of dental work. Notwithstanding, his blue eyes peer intently into the lens of the television camera. "Too many experiences to recollect here . . . Suffice to say, that I have run major races on every continent . . . except Antarctica. And if there's ever a race on Antarctica, I'll be there, toe on the starting line, ready to go."

"Yes Mr. Preverett, er . . . Nigel, I believe you will." Brandon Davis recognizes the confidence in this elder statesman's voice. "What races have you competed in . . . globally?"

"I can share a few with you and I think you and the viewers will be surprised to hear that competing in ultramarathons has been popular for years. The Comrades Marathon is a fifty-four mile race that has the largest field of entries of any ultramarathon in the world. I think last year's event had over twenty thousand participating. I am not sure how many finished. Runners from all over the world visit South Africa just to run Comrades." Nigel adds, "I finished tenth there a few years back."

"Out of twenty thousand runners? That's outstanding, Nigel!" Davis sees Preverett accept his praise graciously. "What do you mean by ultramarathon?"

"An ultramarathon is any race in which the distance is longer than a marathon or twenty-six point two miles. Common distances are fifty and one hundred kilometers, plus many fifty mile races are well known. In Great Britain, our most popular ultra is appropriately named London to Brighton - a challenging road race that covers fifty-two miles in the south of England. I finished third there last year. In Italy there is La Passatore, a beautiful run that takes you over the hills surrounding Firenze, er . . . Florence. That particular race is one hundred kilometers. And of course I would be remiss if I did not mention your own nation's JFK fifty mile endurance run held in . . . er, I apologize, I cannot remember the city, somewhere on the Eastern Seaboard, Maryland I think. It's the largest ultra in the North America."

"You have run all those races?"

Preverett nods in agreement, "And then some."

"What is your best finish, Nigel." Davis likes this guy. He is obviously knowledgeable, informative, plus he has an engaging persona.

"I have won numerous races over my career, otherwise, I don't suppose our government would have sent me here to represent Her Majesty. Suffice to say an Olympic medal has eluded me thus far, but just maybe," he reflects a moment, "the Los Angeles games will be different."

After thirty miles he is well over an hour behind the leaders. Not that he is running badly . . . it's just that so many are running much better.

"Number 545, Nigel Preverett, Great Britain." Preverett hears his name announced when he arrives at Robinson Flat. Glancing at his watch, he shakes his head in disbelief - it's already mid-day. The strapping, articulate gentleman from England is not having his best day.

They share a common language and border, yet have only spoken a couple of times since the Iron Curtain separates their countries. Wolfgang Hafner recognizes the regal blue uniform of the German Democratic Republic as he enters the aid station at Deep Canyon I. The red insignia of a hammer and compass is visible just above the bib number. *Mr. Frey, how are you doing?*" He had little opportunity to speak with the East German before the race, since his opponent's team had been sequestered from the remainder of the athletes.

"*Fine, and yourself?*" The East German, Klaus Frey answers automatically without looking up from the table, and then realizes a fellow competitor is speaking in his native tongue.

"*Not bad, ah, not bad at all.*"

"*Ah, Wolfie, it's you,*" shoving a piece of cantaloupe into his mouth. He had heard the moniker describing the West German at the European 100 kilometer championships a year before. "*You must be running very well . . . since you have caught me!*" Both men are standing under a portable canopy with tables of food and drink situated directly in front of them.

Hafner looks up at the attendant and knows the answer to the question, but asks regardless. "*How many runners . . .*" He sees a quizzical look on the attendant's face and realizes the man does not understand German. "I'm sorry, how many runners have passed through, Sir?" His

Bavarian accent evident, Wolfgang hands his water bottle to the attendant and grabs a piece of energy bar. "Electrolytes, please."

"That's okay, sorry I don't speak German," the man offers a genuine apology. "You two are in eleventh and twelfth place, respectively." He promptly turns to fill the bottle.

"Well Wolfie, that makes you twelfth?" Another attendant hands the East German a full bottle. *"See you down the road,"* and then adds with his own Germanic accent, *"Number 5 3 7 checks-out."* He leaves the thirty-six mile checkpoint chewing on a piece of banana.

Klaus's comment about "down the road" is appropriate. The Western States Trail follows a gravel road for the next four miles. For the runners the road is a welcome reprieve from the rocky, root-infested trails that have covered the trail thus far. Many runners will take full advantage of the better footing and increase their pace. Both Germans do just that and Wolfgang wastes little time catching Frey on the gentle downhill. *"Klaus, we have not seen much of you over the past few days. Where have you been hiding?"*

The East German smirks, *"Hiding . . . I have no need to hide from anyone. You know our program Wolfgang . . . we wish to avoid distractions that deter us from achieving our goals. I was staying in a small town north of Squaw Valley named Truckee. It's a quaint little town with some good restaurants. I like it there."*

"Yes, Truckee, I visited the town - nice place. How has life been treating you in the East?"

"Ah, not bad . . . we have our problems, issues. But life is good for me."

"I must ask you something, Klaus. East German athletes have improved in so many different fields, how do you handle all the accusations of drug use, blood doping and such?"

Frey laughs mockingly. *"People in the West have problems understanding our success. They attribute our success to performance enhancing drugs. Bullshit! We simply work harder and longer, that's all."* He squirts some fluid from the bottle into his mouth. Swallows some, then spits the remainder in disgust.

"But we often hear reports of suspected drug use by your athletes. How can all this testimony be false?" Hafner also drinks from his water bottle, but swallows its contents.

"Western propaganda, Wolfie, that's all it is." Klaus is becoming very defensive and increases his pace slightly. *"We are tested just like other athletes. Where is the proof of this drug use?"*

"Okay Klaus, what about you? Have you ever tried anything which helps you run better?"

"Perhaps in my younger days I may have dabbled with a couple of recreational drugs . . . with friends. But I think we all go through phases. But steroids or anything like that, never! Too many side affects, so I have read. I stay clear of that stuff. He pauses and draws another deep breath. *Besides, what advantage would steroids give a long distance runner? I am not a weight lifter or throws athlete."*

Unbeknownst to Frey, anti-anemia medication flows through his blood vessels. His doctor had administered the medication under the guise of a "dietary supplement." Virtually undetectable, Klaus's red blood cell count has been elevated for months. Unfortunately, for this particular East German, so have most of the other athletes' RBC counts been elevated. Since most of the runners have lived and trained at altitude for the past several months, their RBC counts have naturally increased. Altitude training would prove to be an equalizer for all the participants who had acclimated properly for the event.

"And you Wolfie, what about your personal experiences with drugs? I have told you the truth. What has your 'federation' provided?"

Wolfgang recognizes the word that describes his country, plus a hint of cynicism. *"We have no guinea pigs on our national teams, Klaus."* The lie comes easily. Wolfgang is well aware of much steroid use, especially among sprinters and throwers. *"I personally have not experimented with drugs, recreational or otherwise."* Another lie. *"I have been committed to athletics for as long as I can remember."*

The East German scoffs, *"More Western propaganda . . ."*

Both runners see a dry creek bed as they approach a short wooden bridge. The road begins to climb after the bridge and they maintain their pace. Conversation wanes with the increased effort to fight the force of gravity. Both draw from each other's strength and competitiveness as they see a black runner up ahead. No acknowledgement is given to the Kenyan walking up the moderate grade. He looks utterly spent.

Chapter 8 – Deep Canyon II (Dusty Corners)

Three runners enter the Deep Canyon II checkpoint. The Russian, Boroshkov, the Canadian, Jones and the Israeli, Kostinski have moved into the top five and appear poised to challenge the leader. Ian Jones hands his bottle to a young man and queries, "How far is he ahead?" He eats only a few pretzels since he had 'tanked-up' at Robinson Flat, then swallows a cup of diluted coke. Jones recognizes the 100 kilometer world champion, but the Israeli is an unknown quantity. He looks at a rival runner and thinks, "The guy has stayed with us since Duncan Canyon and has not said much."

"You're seven minutes behind; anything else I can get you?"

"No thanks, I'm fine, got to go. Number 525 checking out."

"Good luck you guys. We'll see you in Auburn," an attendant calls-out.

Kostinski acknowledges the assistance of the aid station's personnel, "Thanks, you're all doing a great job."

The Russian remains stoic and reticent as he joins the other two runners on a wide dirt trail.

Since the Israeli's gratitude appears sincere, Jones commences a dialogue. "You're running really well, staying with the world 100 kilometer champion. Not bad, is this your first 100 mile endurance run?"

"Yeah, I must be doing well, since I've also shadowed the North American champ as well." Joshua notes the terrain. They are in the shade of large pine trees, following a jeep trail on a gentle slope running downhill. He takes a quick look at his watch. It's just after noon when Kostinski feels the heat reflecting off the dirt. "It must be 90°," he murmurs. Sweat continues to pour as he settles into comfortable pace, occasionally sipping the cool solution in his bottle.

"You've obviously done your homework. My name's Ian, what's yours?" Jones would not have asked, but thinks, "Looks like the guy will be around for a while - might as well be cordial. And besides, the camaraderie just feels right."

"Josh, and to be honest, my coach did the homework. I only trained following his guidance." The two exchange a brief handshake while running.

"Well, your coach should be commended. After forty miles you're doing extremely well. How do feel?"

"Fine. Legs are a little sore, but that's expected." Kostinski feels the most soreness in his quadriceps. There is also tightness in his upper shoulders and neck. He is approaching the furthest distance he has ever run in his life. A third place finish at the JFK fifty miler in Maryland a year earlier had shown promise. "What about you Ian; how're you holding-up?"

"Doing great, thus far, but it's still early. Much can happen. Believe me, things can unravel in a hurry if you're not careful. Aspirin will reduce the soreness in your legs. Have you taken any?"

"No, not yet. Coach told me to abstain from anti-inflammatories for a long as possible. Maybe at the next checkpoint; Last Chance is the next one, right?" Josh notes the Russian just ahead and Jones on his immediate right. He slows a bit to allow the Russian a five yard advantage, then resumes the cadence to maintain contact. Kostinski looks down and sees puffs of trail dust coming from the Russian with each foot strike. The footing is good as they proceed on a well-groomed jeep trail that is easy to run on. The shade is an added bonus. They're making good progress.

"Your English is excellent, where did you learn to speak so well?" Ian glances at the back of the Russian and wonders when Boroshkov will make his move.

"I went to school in New York and Boston."

"Oh, do you reside in the States?"

"No, I returned to Israel a few years ago and live in Tel Aviv. And yourself, obviously you're fluent in English. Can you speak French?"

"No I can't, but my wife's from Quebec. She's fluent. In fact, if you're with me at Michigan Bluff, I'll introduce you." Not sure why he said that, Jones just feels comfortable around this new acquaintance.

"Well, there's an added bonus." Both men chuckle at the comment. Time and distance pass quickly as their conversation continues . . .

The Russian hears all the gibberish, but understands few words of the runners talking directly behind him. *"Brother, they do like to talk,"* Boroshkov mutters to himself. Regardless, he knows their pace is good along this downhill stretch and predicts silently, *"We will catch the leader, most likely on the next major ascent coming after the river - the climb up Deadwood Canyon to Devil's Thumb."* He likes the sounds of the words as foreign as they are and adds, *"Let's see if these guys will be so inclined to conversation during the next ascent."*

"Remember the Alamo," Washington says to his friend and training partner as he catches him on the downhill stretch after Deep Canyon I. He is running confidently about thirty minutes behind the leaders.

"Badillo counters, "'bout time you caught me. Christ, it's a quarter past twelve. Where've you been?"

"Minglin' with the tourists! How're you feeling, buddy?" Nathan had spoken with a few runners who had attempted to stay with him for short periods of time, the last being a Norwegian who recognized the "favorite" to win. The man had used cross country skiing as part of his training regimen during the long Scandinavian winter. Washington had wanted to learn more, but knew it was a lesson that would have to wait.

"Runnin' well, Nate. Forty miles in and feelin' great!"

"Shit J. P., you're sounding more like a gringo everyday!"

"My wife says, that's 'cause I spend too much time with you!" The shorter Mexican increases his pace slightly to stay with his pal. Badillo knows the man's strengths and weaknesses, and knows with certainty, if he stays with Nathan, great things will happen. "Less than two miles to Deep Canyon II, we're making excellent time."

"You bet, 'Dusty Corners' is straight ahead." Washington uses the nickname given to the next checkpoint – a corner where runners depart the gravel road and return to the dirt of the Western States Trail.

"Ah Klaus, can I ask you one more question regarding politics?"
The two are running towards Last Chance – a name appropriately given to a place where nineteenth century miners tried to make their claim

on the Mother Load or depart before going bankrupt. Last Chance serves as the forty-five mile checkpoint.

"Certainly, Wolfgang, are we not of one heritage?"

"Do you run for your government, the Chief of the Party? To whom do you answer?"

Without hesitating Frey replies, *"The government may support me and give me perks, because of my talents and abilities. But hear this, I, first and foremost, run for myself. Running sets me free. I also run for the benefits provided to my family. The government does not own me. And you Wolfie, why do you run – to represent your government, your Chancellor?"*

"No Klaus, it's the same for me. Running is a selfish sport and I am very selfish about my reasons for running." The West German proclaims his thoughts. *"It is true; running is truly an egocentric sport. But then again, what grand undertaking would not require selfishness and self-absorption."* He sees Frey nod, approving of the comment.

The conversation concludes leaving each man to his own thoughts. Each feels the competitive fire that is internally lit. However, with over fifty-five miles remaining, including three major climbs through the 'canyons,' they continue to pace themselves for a finish line too far away to even glimpse.

Ten miles behind the Germans things are literally heating-up for those runners still on Cavanaugh Ridge. With no canopy, plus temperatures hovering in the low nineties, some of the runners are beginning to experience the ill-effects of hyperthermia. Their legs feel heavier; they do not have the same stride length nor leg turnover to sustain a competitive pace equivalent to the front runners. Some have even relegated themselves to walking flat sections of trail; something unheard of in the previous thirty miles. The back of the pack runners are losing ground rapidly and with little hope of coming back to challenge the leaders, they have decided to run with the intent "just to finish." For these individuals, there is some real soul-searching as to why they have entered this particular race. Some have begun to learn the significance of the Western States motto: 100 Miles – One Day. Others have begun to doubt their ability to complete the run. Many had been selected by their governments to challenge the mountains and themselves. Unfortunately, relatively few will complete the trek successfully.

But such is life: As with any serious endeavor a man can pursue – many are called, few are chosen.

Chapter 9 – Last Chance

Eammon Horgan has regained his composure and confidence. The aspirin taken has reduced muscle soreness, and food has replenished what nature had relentlessly removed. He passed the Chinese runner several miles back on a flat section of trail on Cavanaugh Ridge where Xian Doi had begun to walk. Soon after, when a Japanese runner passed him, the young Irishman made the conscious decision to keep contact. He attempted to speak with Akira Okuda and discovered another runner who did not speak English. "*Another pagan tongue*," he jokingly spoke Gaelic to see if he could rouse a response from the Asian runner. Okuda's facial expression never wavered. The man appeared to be in his own world; calm, focused and resolute.

Horgan had read about athletes arriving to a "flow state" or what Americans call the "zone." The Irish runner observes, "This guy looks to be in the "zone" for sure." The short climb to Deep Canyon II appeared to be a bit of a struggle, but on another flat section, his opponent runs with seemingly little effort.

Okuda increased the pace during the two mile ascent to the previous aid station at Deep Canyon II, trying to lose this "boy" who appears very tenacious. "*A worthy opponent,*" he contemplates. "*The young man has maintained contact for nearly ten kilometers. It is good to have someone pushing me, especially on the descents where runners become complacent.*" And that is where he finds himself; approaching another aid station after running five kilometers on a gentle decline with the Irishman right on his heels. The Japanese runner is exuding confidence at this point as he moves into contention.

"Numbers 552 and 547," an attendant calls out to the other volunteers.

"Akira, Eammon, welcome to Last Chance. What can we get you for you?" The checkpoint personnel quickly peruse each runner. The Japanese runner looks great and even smiles when he hears his name. On the other hand, the young Irishman inhales sharply, and his florid face appears worried. "Are you okay?"

"Aye, fine, thanks. Please fill the bottle with electrolytes." Horgan immediately goes to the table and consumes an orange slice. He hastily chews the pulp, then discards the rind. After taking another slice, his breathing, along with his heart rate, begins to slow and once again, with a brief rest, he regains his composure, plus his complexion. The Japanese runner sits on a chair, swallowing the contents of a cup. His closest competitor shakes his shoe to remove a pebble. "Christ, if I can just stay with this guy . . ."

"Hey Eammon, if you hurry, you can run with us, if not, we'll leave your arse!" David Conor is standing on the far side of the checkpoint next to a Jamaican ready to depart. He motions to Horgan to come along. The Aussie senses a kinship with the younger runner and wants to push him. "We're checking out." He sees the Irishman jogging towards them. The three runners continue down a wide jeep trail running easily after their brief rest.

"Finally, someone who speaks English. How're doing David? He looks at the Jamaican. "My name's Eammon, what's yours?

"Conrad. How's the run going for you, Laddie?"

"I've had some bad stretches, but I'm doing much better now. My coach gave me some aspirin back at Robinson Flat; it helped quite a bit."

Dr. Conor nods in agreement. "Your coach is right to give you aspirin. It's a miracle drug. Just don't take too many; it can really wreak havoc on your gut. Are you eating?"

"A little food at every station and only God knows how much I've drunk already."

"Good idea, Eammon, just be sure to keep pouring the fluids down that ruddy throat of yours." Conrad knows the drill since he had completed a 100 mile endurance run a year earlier.

"And what makes you the consummate expert?" The young Irishman does not appreciate advice from strangers.

His confidence evident, the Jamaican replies, "I'm not an expert, only a man who's experienced going the distance before and knows the importance of putting back what the runnin' takes out." Creary sips from his bottle and recognizes a consistent pace for the threesome.

"Hell, you sound like my coach. You've run this race before?"

"No I haven't, but there's another 100 mile endurance run called the Old Dominion held in northern Virginia. I ran that course last year." Conrad reminisces about a race run in early June through the hills above the Shenandoah River.

"How'd you do? Horgan asks.

"Finished third, but I should've won."

"What happened?"

"I was running well and winning through eighty-eight miles, then missed a trail marker and found myself going the wrong direction." The Jamaican reflects further, "The mistake cost me the race."

"How did you miss a trail marker? I've seen plenty today. In fact, I can't believe anyone could get lost." Once again, Eammon speaks arrogantly, the food and drink having a positive affect.

"It was late, I was tired . . . just missed a turn. In fact, I was lucky that a man on a horse set me straight - straight back on the right path. He," Creary takes two deep breaths before continuing, "convinced me to turn around. Speak of a miracle . . . I could have followed that dirt road for miles before realizing I was going the wrong way."

"What was a guy on horseback doing on the trail in the middle of the night?" Horgan is confused.

"Maybe the man was a relic of the Civil War setting a slave on the right path to freedom . . . a Buffalo Soldier." Creary knows that black soldiers fought for the federal troops and stretches to find a metaphor. But since the man on horseback had been white, he declines to comment further on the subject. "Actually, they were having a horse race at the same time and one of the riders set me straight - straight back on course and back into the race. More deep breaths taken before he concludes his story, "The horseman was a beacon of light to me – a true abolitionist." The Jamaican grins at the allusion.

The Aussie poses a question. "A horse race? That must have been interesting . . . running with horses. What was it like to run with four legged beasts during a race?"

Creary remembers how badly the horses had torn up parts of the trail. "We had thunder showers in the afternoon and the trails got awfully messy. I tried to bypass those sections and the piles of equine dung by staying to the side of the trail . . . and out of harms way. On the other hand, there were some real beautiful animals out there. In fact, some of the horses were in much better condition than the runners."

"What was your time, Conrad?" Conor is truly interested in the run aptly called the Old Dominion.

"I broke eighteen hours and was happy with the finish, though it would have been nice to win."

Eammon contemplates the man's words. "What pace do you think we're running at?"

The Jamaican instinctively looks at his watch - 12:45. "Difficult to say, since I've never run this race. I know we're in the top ten and the next aid station is the halfway point. We'll just have to wait and see . . ." Creary's voice trails-off as they approach the right turn to descend into Deadwood Canyon.

"So Eammon, still think you'll break sixteen hours?" Conor alludes to the brazen statement Horgan had extolled earlier that morning. "Or have you re-evaluated your position and pace?"

Horgan does not answer. He hears the footsteps of an oncoming runner and instinctively turns his head. It's the Japanese runner, Okuda, and he's back, running in the zone. The four runners move into a single file as they enter a trailhead that brings them to the first of many switchbacks they will negotiate to the canyon's basin. What looms ahead is the first of three major climbs over the next twenty miles. The first of which will take them to an aid station above Devil's Thumb.

Across the canyon on the steep ascent to Devil's Thumb, four men are engaged in a war – a war of wills. Rivulets of sweat cover their bodies. Trail dust sticks to their shoes and socks. Their water bottles are nearly empty. Temperatures exceed ninety-five degrees and over a mile of climbing remains to the Devils Thumb checkpoint. A canopy of pine, oak and madrone provides some protection. They breathe deeply trying to cope with the thin air that 4500 feet of elevation sparingly provides. They are all relegated to "power walking" or walking swiftly, but nevertheless, not running.

"Power walking" is the term most often used by individuals to describe walking uphill sections during trail runs. Sometimes the term can be used euphemistically when runners struggle to put one foot in front of another when an uphill grade is simply too steep to run or too steep to expend the necessary energy. This is the case as they approach the halfway point of the race.

Earlier, when the "pack" had caught Yosef Ethiopia, Yuri Boroshkov had attempted to surge and break the race open. But the Canadian, Israeli and Ethiopian are steadfast in their convictions to keep contact. They do not allow the Russian to commandeer the race. All conversation ceases during the two mile, 1500 vertical foot climb from the river to the ridge where an army of race personnel awaits them. The Russian knows that trying to seize the race this early is ambitious. He remains consistent in his pace up the fifteen percent grade and the others respond, not wishing to relinquish their position.

Chapter 10 – Devil's Thumb

"Good afternoon everyone, and welcome to the fifty mile checkpoint at Devil's Thumb. I'm Brandon Davis reporting live at the halfway point of this inaugural 100 mile endurance run in an Olympic games. As we have discovered earlier, a festive atmosphere awaits the participants as they arrive at the aid stations and this one's no different."

The vivacity is tangible as volunteers make their final preparations. There is a bluegrass band providing live entertainment. A small audience has gathered to listen to the band, and two couples are dancing in a nearby meadow.

"These athletes began their quest this morning at six o'clock, nearly seven hours ago and continue their pursuit of Olympic glory. We have some aerial footage taken earlier this morning, showing some of the front runners we will now share." Davis nods to his production engineer to cue the race highlights taken from the helicopter. The transmission begins showing the African runners, plus others in pursuit. "I cannot believe how good these men look. They appear to run effortlessly over dirt trails riddled with obstacles like rocks and roots. It's amazing to watch them, knowing the distance they will challenge themselves to complete.

"The race director of today's event is Norman Sproul, who is a two time finisher of the Western States Trail Run. Mr. Sproul, you have completed this race before. How are these men feeling after running fifty miles?" When the brief video clip ends, the camera finds Sproul.

"Well Brandon, some worse than others." There is an air of collegiality between the two as they have conversed several times over the past week. Brown hair with flecks of gray appears tousled, befitting a man who awoke at 3:30 this morning. The race director appears tired, but alert. There is a great deal of responsibility organizing a 100 mile endurance run, and his face is showing the effects of the stress. "Those who have taken care to drink and eat are probably feeling some muscle soreness and minor discomfort. Those who have not . . . well, let's just say they will not last too much longer. I am certain we'll be adding names to our DNF list at this checkpoint over the next four hours."

"What's a DNF list and why four hours?"

The director looks sympathetically into the camera and states the three worst words of an ultra-marathoner. "DNF stands for 'did not finish,' and since our aid station closes at 4:30, runners arriving after that will be automatically disqualified. Of course, some runners will arrive here exhausted and will not wish to continue. Unfortunately, all who start will not finish."

"That sounds pretty harsh. What if a runner arrives at 4:31 and wishes to continue?"

"The cut-off times must be strictly enforced. We cannot monitor all the runners unless they stay within the parameters established for their safety. It's a matter of logistics when you consider all the variables that go into the management of a race of this length over mountainous terrain. Believe me, the cut-off times are not enforced to disqualify runners. The times are established to ensure safety for all – participants and volunteers."

"You sound like Dr. Logan, the Chief Medical Director, when you say, 'ensure safety.' I guess you want to avoid unnecessary casualties."

"Exactly, and you avoid unnecessary casualties by removing unnecessary risks."

"Understood Norm. Tell us about your experiences on this course, since you've run it twice." Davis uses informal vernacular to set a casual tone.

"Actually, Brandon, I've done Western States three times. Regrettably, I 'DNF'd' once. Two years ago I 'pulled the plug' right here at Devil's Thumb."

"What happened?"

"I just didn't do the things you need to do the day before and the morning of a major race. I really don't want to talk about it and I'm sure your viewers don't want to hear the graphic details." A solemn face peers into the camera, but Sproul forces a crooked smile. "I'll say this, after all the time and energy a person commits to prepare for a race like this one, the last thing you want to do is quit."

Davis points at the silver buckle attached to a leather belt that garners the race director's shorts. "Tell us about how you earned that buckle."

"Many hours of training and many miles logged, that's how I earned this belt buckle. Oh yes, and one more thing, I had a good day as well." Sproul touches the sterling with his left hand. "It's a remarkable feat when you consider what the human body can withstand and what the human mind can compel the body to do." A proud smile follows, "Yeah, quite an accomplishment all right."

"Thank you for your personal testimony, Norm. That surely sheds some light as to why people compete in such extreme events. Well, we've just received an update that the Russian, Boroshkov has overtaken Ethiopia." Davis clears his throat, "Who happens to be from the country of the same name. They will arrive shortly. As race director and obviously a source of information regarding this race, any predictions who you think will win?"

"The Russian is the reigning world champion at 100 kilometers. The North American 100 kilometer champion, Ian Jones, is certainly a contender. The Italian who won the European 100 kilometer championships should not be overlooked and there are a number of lesser known individuals who have the credentials and the ability to win. But in my opinion, I think Washington will win the gold medal today. He has the trail experience and the competitive savvy to win. I'd put my money on him."

"Have you looked at the current standings through Last Chance?" Davis peruses a current catalogue of runners who have checked out of the last aid station.

"No, not since Robinson Flat."

Davis acknowledges the race director's expertise. "Well, Norman all the athletes you mentioned are in the top ten, except the Italian. He was fifteenth at Last Chance. What do you think?"

"Any runner within an hour of this lead pack has the potential to win. So many things can happen - good and bad. Unfortunately, for most, the bad often outweighs the good. The reason I like Nathan's chances is he's local and he knows the course better than anyone else in the race."

"Thank you Mr. Sproul for expressing your thoughts concerning the run." Davis pats the man on the shoulder. "I'm sure we'll have much more to discuss before this day is done.

"Last week I had the opportunity to interview the Russian runner, Yuri Boroshkov. Through an interpreter I learned many things about this man and the country he represents. That interview and much more, when we return."

Yuri Boroshkov looks into the camera. Baldness, plus crow's feet have added years to his appearance. Even for world class athletes, Russian winters can be hard. He has no gray in his blond hair, but nevertheless, looks like a man approaching forty-five years of age, rather than thirty-five. Foreigners have interviewed him before, especially since the 100 kilometer world championships last year. The American commentator appears to be more interested in his profession, rather than his running.

" . . . So you are a professor at the University of Leningrad, a professor of physics. What is your field of expertise, Dr. Boroshkov?"

He awaits the translation of his advisor, remaining reluctant to speak candidly about his work and the country of his birth.

Ten thousand miles away a daughter calls to her mother, "*Mama, Mama, Papa is on the television!*" Yelizaveta Boroshkova enters the small austere living room where she had grown-up near the base of the Caucuses in the Soviet state of Georgia. She puts her hand on the shoulder of her eldest daughter and smiles. This is the first time her child has stayed awake this late. It is nearly midnight when tears begin to well in the woman's ebony eyes – tears of pride and joy. She longs to be with him. The wife knows his strengths, understands his weaknesses, only wishes to aid and assist in his endeavors . . . as she has done for the past ten years.

Her mother and father quickly enter the room to see their daughter's husband who has become a national hero. Yelizaveta's mother cannot believe she is seeing her son-in-law in America, being interviewed on international television. No one predicted such a high level of recognition. It is inconceivable to them.

"*The state university is Leningrad Polytechnic, but yes, as you have stated, I am a physics professor. What more do you want to know?*"

"What branch of physics is your specialty?" Davis looks at the translator and then fixes his eyes upon Boroshkov.

"*Presently, I am working on practical applications of superconductivity. But, what do my studies have to do with these Olympics?*"

Davis listens to a loose translation before replying. "Here in America, we hear very little of Soviet scientific research. Does your government permit you to communicate with the West regarding your work?" Once again, Davis had done his research, learned that Boroshkov is brilliant. He wants more than a mundane interview about the man's running exploits.

Yuri shakes his head, rubs his forehead with his fingers. He sees his advisor look at him wide-eyed, caution expressed. Both men appear nervous. "*Well, certainly there are restrictions, as your country has restrictions.*" Boroshkov muses, "*We're in the middle of a Cold War and this man asks a very sensitive question. What's next: a question about our nuclear arsenal?*"

His advisor does not translate the last remark.

"*I have collaborated with other European scientists regarding my research.*" He wanted to add, albeit, not as often as he would like. "*And collaboration, is it not a two-way street? Sometimes your country has not cooperated with ours.*"

Davis smiles inwardly. The Russian has just opened the door. "Oh really, Doctor and what road-blocks have you experienced when communicating with our government or U. S. based companies? Has our government been unwilling to cooperate with yours?"

"*Obviously, there are certain areas of study that do not present difficulties, such as medicine.*" He knows the Soviet Union has fallen dangerously behind the West concerning medical treatment – his brother one such victim in a socialized medical facility. "*Other sensitive or um, classified subjects concerning national security . . . I do not have the authority to comment.*" The interpreter nods in approval of the response, then translates word for word.

"Granted, I understand the 'sensitive or classified subjects' that cannot be discussed. However, we as Americans know so little of the Soviet Union and its people. What can you share with us?" The American commentator notes a sigh of relief from the two Bolsheviks.

"We live in a vast country in which our government, the Communist Party, works to govern its people fairly. We have some internal issues that have created problems and these will be addressed in the near future, hopefully. But, what nation can boast of having no internal difficulties."

"What we do have is a government that takes care of its people. We have a national form of socialized medicine, our system of public transportation is excellent and everyone in the Soviet Union works. We have virtually no unemployment. Our status as a world superpower goes well beyond our national defense."

Davis nods, "Well stated for a 'comrade' of the Communist Party, Professor, but . . ."

Boroshkov's advisor intervenes promptly, not bothering to translate the last remark. "Like you would state as a 'patriot' of your own country, Mr. Davis. We must conclude this discussion as we have our daily training regimen to consider. The professor and I thank you for your thoughtful questions and hope we have provided greater insight of the Union of Soviet Socialist Republics to your viewers."

Boroshkov appears puzzled as they take their leave from the mezzanine of the Squaw Valley ski lodge where the interview was conducted. *"What did he say?"*

"Nothing Yuri, nothing of merit. The American reporter must be an imbecile if he thinks he can start an international debate with us."

Yelizaveta shakes her head. Georgian eyes do not budge from the set as she quips to her parents, *"I could have translated much better than that clown."* She kisses her daughter on the cheek and reflects, *"Yes Yuri, you are loyal to Mother Russia."*

"How's Yuri running, Liza? How far has he run?" Her father sits in his favorite chair, eyes fixed on the small black and white television.

"He's winning Papa. I think they're almost half-way."

"Almost fifty kilometers?"

"No no, almost eighty kilometers. The race is 100 miles or a little more than 160 kilometers, Papa."

Boroshkov's father-in-law is confused and shakes his head in disbelief. *"I do not even drive my car that much in a month!"*

*   *   *

As the Russian leads three runners into the Devil's Thumb aid station, the American and Mexican close the gap. The two friends have found the energy to jog-walk the steep grade and trail the leaders by less than three-quarters of a mile. They suck air deep into their lungs. Badillo breaks the silence. "We should see the 'thumb' real soon, Nathan," he gasps, flicking a droplet of sweat from his eyebrow.

"Yeah J. P., less than a quarter of a mile and we'll see it."

Both men refer to a volcanic outcrop of rock that was uplifted millions of years ago and aptly named by miners of the nineteenth century. A bystander informs them they are within twelve minutes of the leaders and their confidence soars.

Akira Okuda crosses the footbridge at the base of Deadwood Canyon. The small wooden bridge is suspended above a tributary of the Middle Fork of the American River. He has no idea how many runners he has passed over the last twenty miles, but Okuda knows one thing for certain; he is running well – well enough to lead this pack of *"foreigners"* to the next checkpoint. Directly behind, in pursuit, are the three individuals he entered the canyon with. He will challenge them on this climb – the climb to the halfway point. He smiles the same way he withstands pain – inwardly, and begins to power walk the steep grade.

David Conor responds to the gauntlet laid by the Japanese runner and maintains the pace. There is no conversation as the men contemplate what appears inevitable - the Japanese runner is about to make a move. Creary and Horgan hang on for their dear lives. They lift their knees to negotiate the climb, opposing the gravity and altitude that nature mounts against them. All three respond to the challenge of keeping contact with Okuda.

An ovation welcomes the front runners to Devil's Thumb. "Number 622, Yuri Boroshkov, U. S. S. R." The announcer struggles with the pronunciation, muttering, "At least the next one's easier." Then declares, "Number 525, Ian Jones, Canada. Number 548, Joshua Kostinski, Israel." All three runners wave to the crowd; smiles express

97

their appreciation. Seeing the welcoming committee, adrenaline flows into their bloodstreams, and immediately they forget about the pain and fatigue of their beleaguered muscles. Ethiopia has fallen back.

Jones spots his wife as he steps off the scale. "Genny, bring the bag, '*quickly.*'" He uses one of the few French words he knows. He sees her jogging towards him. They embrace.

The longstanding joke in Genevieve's family is her husband's inability to speak French. Her father would always admonish her. "*What do you expect when you marry a man from Ontario? A nurse no less! Isn't that a woman's job?*"

Jones sits in a portable chair digging into his drop bag. He finds an energy bar and bites down. His wife, who is massaging his shoulders, appears relaxed. "I cannot believe how many people have come here, Ian. From where do they all come? I mean, there are no towns near here." Her Quebecois accent is pleasing to Ian's ear. She reaches into the canvas bag, removes a pair of socks and awaits another request. She has attended to her husband's needs at other races, but has never experienced a race with so much popularity.

"I know Gen; you should have seen the fifty kilometer checkpoint. There were thousands. No thanks, I won't change my socks." Jones removes a small vial of Motrin. Bring me some salty foods and diluted coke, please." She takes his empty bottle and departs to her fulfill her duties. Just before she withdraws into the crowd of attendants and medical personnel, Gen turns and smiles at her beau. He feels goose bumps on his chest and back. Her affect on him is corporal.

Ian had fallen in love with Genevieve the first time he had met her, innocently enough, at a local restaurant in Gloucester near his home in Ottawa. Gen was from the other side of the river; her ancestry French-Canadian. He had discovered they had very little in common. And yet there was the visceral sense he wanted to see her again and spend time with her. Their lovemaking had been the best he had ever experienced. They talked openly about their lives, their desires, their dreams. And once the relationship had developed, commitments were pledged.

One night was simply unforgettable, an occasion when sex is not a perfunctory function. Instead, two people immerse themselves into each other's bliss, connecting beyond anything imagined.

Genevieve had returned to bed after a brief visit to the bathroom and stood over him. It was the middle of the night. No words were spoken. Ian, half asleep, sensed her standing there; her silhouette the only thing visible to his naked eyes. Then he heard her disrobe when her flannel pajamas dropped to the floor. Ian sat up just in time to catch Gen as gravity pulled her to his arms. He truly relished her soft supple skin, kissing and touching and loving in places where two intimate partners know true rapture exists. Ian exercised control, loving unselfishly, letting his woman ravish in the delight of his love . . . bringing her to the pinnacle of pleasure . . . repeatedly. After a time – a long time, she whispered between deep breaths, "*Now it is your turn, my love . . .*" her native tongue adding to the erotica of the early morning hour.

Ian feels fingers rubbing his shoulders and neck as he chews on a salted potato. He touches her hand. "Thanks Gen, got to go. By the way, what time did you arrive here?" He drinks the last bit of coke. He looks up to see Kostinski heading for the exit of the checkpoint. "Hey Josh, wait up."

Genevieve hands him the water bottle filled with the necessary fluids, pecks him on the lips and adds, "I always knew you could go all night, but all day too. *You are incredible my love.*" She smiles as only Genny can and doesn't bother answering the question. The woman had been patiently waiting at the aid station since ten o'clock.

"Was that your wife?" Kostinski asks.

"Yes, that's Genny."

"Okay Ian, get that shit-eating grin off your face. We've got work to do." Josh notes the time: just after 1:00. "Christ, we've been out for over seven hours."

"I know, but we're halfway home." They trail the Russian by fifty meters. Both feel the positive affects of the food, drink and drugs being absorbed into their systems. The single-track trail offers them the respite of running downhill on a gentle grade, enabling the two runners to converse easily. Kostinski runs one step ahead of Jones.

"By the way, how hot is it anyway?" The Israeli concentrates on his foot strike, careful to avoid debris on the trail.

"My wife told me - thirty-seven Celsius."

"No way! That's pushing a hundred. It's not that hot." Kostinski shakes his head in disbelief. The Israeli is acquainted with training in the furnace of the Judean desert. "My guess is low nineties, tops."

"I agree, here, under the trees, it is probably closer to ninety, although it's much hotter than temperatures I am used to in Ottawa. Have you had much opportunity to train in the heat?"

"Oh yeah Ian, much opportunity," Kostinski quips.

"Did you train in Palestine or here in the States?"

"I spent the winter in my homeland and came to the U. S. earlier this summer. Of course, we prefer to call our country Israel. Palestine belonged to the Arabs and we've changed much over the last forty years."

Ian notes a negative connotation. "Sorry Josh, didn't mean anything derogatory."

"Don't worry, Ian. Just a correction we Israelis often make to avoid confusion.

"There is a national park near the Dead Sea called Ein Gedi . . . an oasis in the desert. I spent some time there running in the hills surrounding the park. It's really a remarkable place. And there's Masada . . . ancient ruins of a fortress in southern Israel - a holy place." Kostinski inhales deeply before continuing his description. "Legend has it that a small tribe of Jews held off a legion of Roman soldiers for months before succumbing to the power and politics of Rome. I did numerous hill repeats running up that mountain and actually began to feel sorry for the Roman soldiers who had to fight a group of belligerent Jews."

"Yeah, but not too sorry, I bet. I've heard of Masada - a fortress built on a citadel. But I've never heard of Ein Gedi. My wife and I have discussed the possibility of traveling to Jerusalem, just for a diverse religious experience. Some day I must visit your country." Jones is genuinely interested.

"Where did you spend the summer preparing for the run?" Josh sips from his bottle content to give the Canadian a chance to speak.

"The Canadian Rockies, near Calgary. A friend of mine has a cabin near a ski resort. I spent the summer training above 7000 feet. But

God almighty, it was never this hot! Let me lead for a while, Josh. I'll let you draft for a spell."

"Gladly." Kostinski looks up momentarily to see the Russian well within striking distance and allows Ian to take the lead. He recognizes a kinship with the Canadian, enjoys his company, plus knows they can help one another achieve their goal. He drops back three paces, then resumes the pace that has moved the him into medal contention.

"Fuckin' - A - Nate, you're doing great!" Clint Washington takes the water bottle from his younger brother and departs to fill it, proud of his cute little rhyme.

"Anything I can get for you, Nathan?" Gioia, Washinton's cousin, massages his thighs and calves since Washington has parked himself in a portable chair. She looks up to see her cousin gulping down diluted coke.

"No thanks, Gioia, I'm fine. I'll be here only a minute. Sorry I missed you at Robinson Flat. I heard that parking was a real problem."

"Yeah, here too. We're parked about a mile and a half up the road. But this is too cool, 'Cuz,' I wouldn't miss this for anything. You're in fifth place, about ten minutes behind the leader. An African runner left less than five minutes ago, although he didn't look very good."

She is so proud of her cousin who has overcome much personal adversity. He has not only persevered, but has excelled beyond what his family once thought possible. Running had truly set her cousin free, free from the emotional shackles that result from a tainted love. She sees her eldest cousin approaching with the plastic bottle in one hand and a full cup in the other.

"Nate, here are a couple of aspirin." He watches his brother swallow the aspirin with the cup of water.

"Thanks Bro; got to fly." Gioia and Clint offer words of encouragement. The stiffness in his legs and back quickly dissipating when he walks, Washington departs Devil's Thumb to a thunderous applause. Juan-Pablo joins him. He looks over his shoulder and waves. "See you two at Michigan Bluff." Then Washington calls to an attendant recording numbers, "620 checking-out."

"Number 557," Badillo yells above the cheers. "How does it feel to be the crowd favorite, *friend*?" He emphasizes the last word in Spanish.

"I thought the applause was for you, J. P." They both laugh at that thought – A Mexican in America being favored over a local white boy.

"*Eh man,* too bad we're not in East L. A." Badillo chuckles.

They begin to run. Their next victim: an Ethiopian who's fading fast.

"Hand me the sunscreen, please." David Conor lathers plenty on his shoulders and arms, then smears the remainder on his face avoiding contact near or above his cobalt blue eyes. Conor has learned that sunscreen and sweat are a bad combination, especially when he wears contact lenses. As he quenches his thirst with water, he sees the Japanese runner removing one of his shoes. "Probably picked up a pebble," he thinks. Another orange slice, a few more pretzels and he stands, ready to depart the Devil's Thumb aid station. He grimaces and bears his weight, soreness felt in his thighs and lower back. The Australian murmers, "Superficial pain."

Akira's coach notes the blood. "*Remove your sock, Akira-san. Let me take a look.*" The blood blister between Okuda's big and second toe on his right foot has burst. Okuda winces when his coach applies the antiseptic. He covers the wound with a bandage. "*This is nothing that will deter you from your goal.*" He hands Akira a clean pair of socks.

Akira senses the intensity in his master's voice and witnesses the same intensity in his eyes. Realizing how far he has come over the past forty kilometers he asks the expected question, "*How far is the American ahead?*"

The coach does not bother to answer the question. "*You will catch him. Then you must decide on what to do.*" He hands his protégé a full bottle.

"*And the Russian, will I catch him too?*" Akira has much reverence for the older man and his judgment. Their relationship had been forged at the training center located at the base of Mount Fujiyama years earlier. The coach's training regimen had been demanding to say the least and Okuda's running had improved accordingly.

"*And him, too.*" The coach sounds prophetic. Placing his hand on the shoulder of his charge, he looks intently into Akira's dark brown eyes.

"Only you can make the decision. I am confident you will make the right one. I have instructed you well. You have been a great student of running and have brought honor to me and my training regimen. I believe destiny brought you to this race for reason. Run to your ability and great things will happen." He had waited to give this particular sermon until his athlete was ready to challenge the leaders. Akira is in that position, in seventh place, twenty minutes behind the Russian, only ten minutes behind the American. *"When the time comes, only you will know whether to take command of the race or simply stay with them."* The coach knows this race is much too long to dictate strategy. *"Whatever your decision is - run with certainty, Akira-san; the certainty that you can win."* The coach's confidence is contagious.

Okuda answers with two simple words, *"Yes Master."*

"Number 552, Akira Okuda checking-out," a voice bellows. A thunderous applause ensues. He sips a bit of liquid from his bottle. For the first time the Japanese runner feels an adrenaline rush. He begins to run - with conviction.

What was once a pack of four has been reduced to two. The Jamaican and the young Irishman have fallen behind. The Japanese runner wastes little time in catching the Australian. And as the succession of runners continues, so does the succession of vegetation. At an elevation of 4000 feet above sea level, deciduous trees of oak, manzanita and madrone are slowly replacing coniferous stands. The arid smell of dried grass and herbs is ubiquitous. There is much more scrub under the canopy. Poison oak is everywhere. Runners have been warned about this pesky perennial, especially if they are relegated to the use of foliage when toilet paper is unavailable.

Runners are spread across nearly fifteen miles of trail. The two South African runners who were lost for nearly two hours have relocated the Western States Trail and are ahead of the twenty-four cut-off time. They're bickering about whose fault it was to have missed the yellow ribbons marking the course. Somewhere between Red Star Ridge and Duncan Canyon, they had missed a turn and followed an unmarked trail. The two men had made the monumental mistake of not retracing their steps when they had not seen trail ribbons, instead, opting to continue their merry way down the wrong path. Good fortune had led them to a small group of hikers who were encamped near a small alpine lake. The backpackers had redirected the two nomads to the trail located on a ridge a fair distance away. To say the two South Africans are pissed-off is an understatement. Of course, the burden of blame falls squarely on both their shoulders. Returning to the gravel road they pass an Indian runner and the Haitian who appear content to set their own pace. No longer "dead fuckin' last," they begin the gravel road ascent to the checkpoint known as Deep Canyon II or Dusty Corners. It's 1:30 in the afternoon and the temperatures have eclipsed the century mark.

"Ciao Lamo, how does it go?" Girolamo's fiancée smiles, showing pretty white teeth in contrast to the tan-olive skin of her face.

"Ciao Sabrina, how do you stay? I'm a little tired, but doing much better now that I see you!" The Italian has moved up and at present sits in twelfth place. Pavin has entered the aid station with two German runners. He is thrilled that his girl has arrived to help. *"Can you bring me some crackers and something to drink, please?"*

His coach interrupts. *"I will bring it. Sabrina, just stay with him. Here Girolamo, drink this."* The coach recognizes the importance of having this woman in his runner's life. He sees Sabrina begin to rub her lover's legs and witnesses the connection that exists between the two of them.

"What is in the drink," Sabrina inquires.

"Yogurt, banana, juice and electrolytes . . . I've been drinking this stuff for the past year. It agrees with me." He shakes a few pebbles from one of his shoes and then looks at his watch. It's 1:30.

"Why is this aid station called the Thumb of the Devil, Lamo? I see no devil, nor thumb."

Pavin laughs. *"I am not exactly sure, but supposedly there is a large rock near here that sticks-out from the earth and it looks like a thumb . . . coming up from hell. I have not seen this rock, perhaps you can find it before you leave."* He sees his coach approaching and stand above his fiancée who continues to massage his legs.

"Good luck, my love." She stands, hugs him warmly and hands her fiancé the water bottle.

He drinks the contents of a cup and then grabs the pretzels putting a few in his mouth. "*I will see you at the next aid station. A thousand thanks.*" His smile vanishes as he directs himself to the next section of trail and another canyon to conquer. The soreness in his legs and neck is manageable.

The Italian hears his name. "Number 549, Girolamo Pavin, Italy," followed again by a generous applause." He cannot recollect a race where thousands of people have lined the trails - in the middle of nowhere. Adrenaline surges. Pavin savors the moment as he departs Devil's Thumb, halfway to the finish line.

Chapter 11 - Michigan Bluff

Volcanic magma cooled millions of years ago and uplift slowly raised the piece of igneous rock through crust. An angular portion of the rock breached the surface when erosion removed soil surrounding it. Like an iceberg, the majority of its girth and weight lay well below ground. The four inches of exposed granite are covered by a layer of foliage and remain invisible to those runners who have passed this section of trail west of the Devil's Thumb checkpoint. The East German never sees it coming.

Klaus Frey, Wolfgang Hafner and Girolamo Pavin are three Europeans who have competed against one another before. Hafner had attempted to stay with the Italian a year earlier at the European 100 Kilometer Championships and ultimately had to let Pavin go. On some obscure roads in Holland, near the capitol of Den Haague on a cool autumn morning, Pavin had buried the remainder of the field when he consistently ran three minute, fifty second pace nearly the entire distance. His time of six hours twenty-four minutes was last year's best – even better than the Russian who currently leads the race. And now, Pavin, who had caught the Germans just before the last checkpoint, is pushing the pace . . . yet again. Both Frey and Hafner lengthen their strides to match the Italian's, who is five meters ahead on a narrow stretch of trail just west of Devil's Thumb.

"We must stay with him." Frey breathes heavily into the left ear of Hafner. *"If you move up on his shoulder we can draft on him a bit."* Frey is drafting on the left shoulder of the West German.

"I know. We can't let him go." Hafner increases his tempo and quickly cuts the distance to less than two meters. *"You know this will be difficult . . . to stay with him. He is running well. Maybe we should let him go. There are eighty kilometers remaining."* Hafner's confidence wavers.

Frey smirks. *"Who said this was going to be easy? If you cannot keep contact, then step aside and let me by."*

Hafner slows for only one step and moves to the right side of the trail.

Frey begins to pass on the left. *"Thanks Wolfie, best of . . ."* His left ankle rolls outward parallel to the ground. Searing pain shoots up his left leg as the audible sound of ligaments and tendons rip. He shrieks and instinctively reaches for Hafner's shoulder as he falls forward. *"Shit!"*

"What's wrong?" Hafner turns for a moment to see Frey falling to the ground, grabbing his lower leg obviously in extreme pain.

"I turned my fucking ankle. Damn it!"

"Christ Klaus, that was your ankle? I heard the crack. Are you okay? What did you step on?"

"Dumb shit no! I am not okay." He looks upward knowing his race may well be over. The East German knows when the ankle balloons outward, the swelling and pain will not permit him to run adroitly. He sees the Italian return shaking his head. A face with intense dark eyes looks down, reminding Frey of his older brother who often intimidated by size and strength. Pavin forces a smile and his intensity wanes, revealing a youthful face and a kind soul. A small crucifix dangles outside of the Italian's singlet. *"What do you smile about, Pavin? What's so fucking amusing?"* He shifts his weight toward the Italian.

Pavin speaks no German. He reaches into his short's liner and pulls out a small plastic bag. "Motrin." He hands Frey two pills. *"Good luck,"* he says and takes his leave.

"What did he say?"

"Something about good fortune, I think."

"Wolfgang, you better go too . . . stay with him. You can do it. I'll be along soon."

Hafner watches Frey swallow the two pills with one gulp of fluids from his bottle, well aware that the battle is lost for this opponent. No way will he return . . . not in this race. He glances at Frey sympathetically, then turns, chasing the Italian down the gentle decline that will take them to another series of switchbacks. The trail drops to the base of El Dorado Canyon.

Frey slowly stands and bears his weight. The throbbing in his ankle continues. He walks two steps backwards and kicks some leaves from the trail with his right foot. Ten centimeters of rock are visible above the surface. The East German shakes his head in total frustration, in total disgust. *"Damn it,* he repeats and then looks eastward and considers returning to the Devil's Thumb aid station. Looking at his wristband, Frey reads the numbers that indicate weight, pulse, blood pressure, and for the first time, contemplates quitting. He ponders for a moment, then looks in the opposite direction and begins to jog westward. *"Only eighty kilometers to go, I am halfway finished – halfway home!"*

Frey awkwardly favors his right leg.

"How're you feeling, J. P.?" The American has not heard any comments from the Mexican since leaving the last checkpoint. Both perspire heavily despite their descent. Washington squirts some water into his mouth.

They are about halfway down the canyon on an eastern slope, facing directly below the scorching sun. Incendiary photons strike the rocky trail. Adjacent boulders absorb the sun's mid-afternoon heat as well, reflecting the searing energy toward the runners. Since there are fewer trees to provide shade, the effect of the bare rock surrounding the trail is like that of an oven, with the runners served as the main entrée.

"It's got to be 110 degrees, Nate."

"Yep, pretty close. How you holding up there, buddy?"

Washington is a step behind Badillo. They have been exchanging places every ten minutes on the narrow trail sections, each allowing the other a brief reprieve of breaking the trail. "You want me to take the lead for a while?"

"Nah, I'm good for now."

"Hey J. P., what were the temps like last year in that race you won?" Washington refers to a 100 mile endurance run that follows trails over the San Gabriel Mountains northeast of Los Angeles.

"Not this hot. Maybe mid-nineties - tops."

Badillo is proud of the fact that after withdrawing from Western States in late June, he had returned to his American hometown of L. A. to win the Angeles Crest 100 Mile Endurance Run in late September. The win had landed him a position on the Mexican National Team. He carries two bottles, one of which is filled with water. Juan-Pablo squirts a large dose on his forehead and under his cap. He winces since the bottle's contents are not much cooler than the ambient temperature.

"So 'Bad Ass,' you still think that Angeles Crest is tougher than Western States?"

"Sorry Nate, no question – much tougher. You should try it. In fact, the race is next month. I'll get you an application." Badillo grins.

"Well, what makes that course so much more difficult?"

"I told you before, remember? The course is really similar to this one through seventy miles. After that it becomes difficult, very difficult . . . almost impossible. In fact, I was the only runner to break twenty hours."

"Oh, that's right; you're referring to the two consecutive climbs: three thousand feet to the top of Mt. Wilson and then another major ascent just after that. Doesn't sound all that tough, buddy." Washington smirks.

"You're right. It wouldn't be so bad if the climbs came earlier in the race, but at seventy-five miles plus . . . it'll bust your balls. Like I said, I'll get you an entry form. The race director would love to see you run his course."

The two arrive at the bottom of the canyon. Temperatures are slightly cooler when the two runners cross the wooden footbridge over El Dorado Creek. The trail leads directly to the next major climb – the climb to the checkpoint at Michigan Bluff.

Dr. Chad Logan fixes his eyes on his next patient. "What seems to be the problem?" He sees fear in the eyes of a runner.

An interpreter who speaks both Spanish and Portuguese intervenes. She hands the Brazilian runner a cup of water. "His skin is dry and he appears faint and out of breath, Doctor."

Despite liking the pleasant Hispanic voice of the attendant, Logan replies, "I can see that. Tell me something I don't know."

"Um . . . like what, Doctor?"

The checkpoint leader re-examines his list of runners who have passed through Devil's Thumb. "Number 521, Carlos Ontiveros, Brazil. He's lost five pounds, Chad."

He looks at the interpreter. "Ask when he last went to the bathroom."

The interpreter translates word for word, then naively replies. "There are no bathrooms near here, Doctor."

Logan rolls his eyes upward. He hears the attendant laugh. "Ask him when was the last time he urinated."

The woman nods her head. "Oh, I am sorry, I misunderstood." She rewords the question and awaits the reply. "He does not remember."

"What color was his urine?" Logan persists to identify the problem.

When Ontiveros answers the doctor needs no translation. "He's out of the race. Cut off his wristband. Blood in the urine, dehydration, plus he's not even sweating. There's no way we can let him continue. Please explain to him that he has been disqualified for medical reasons and bring him more water. He stays put until I discharge him from this checkpoint."

The man from Rio sits in a portable chair fifty miles from the starting line and fifty miles from the finish. His day is done, the race a loss. He holds two paper cups full of water and sips from them until both are empty. Placing one inside the other he lays them gently on the ground and looks at his watch: 2:15. Feeling alone and abandoned an emptiness envelopes his mind and body. Runners are being attended to, others are checking out. One runner has his left hand on the trunk of a large pine and continues to vomit. Another calls for assistance in obvious pain. The runner has blistered feet.

Ontiveros shakes his head, unfamiliar with the state in which he is relegated. Since his training had often exceeded two hundred kilometers per week, months of preparation appear to be wasted. He contemplates the sacrifices he has made, then puts his head down and thinks, *"Why has God forsaken me? I know I am better than this."*

The translator arrives with two more cups of water. She notices a man whose spirit is broken, and attempts to console him. *"Here, drink this, my friend. You will be back. There will be other races, no?"*

The Brazilian has no reply, except for the despair etched upon his face. Silent tears drip from his nose, and still no perspiration is visible.

*   *   *

The Russian is analytical in all facets of his life and subsequently, has done his homework. Boroshkov studied several opponents before leaving the Soviet Union. His "sources" had compiled dossiers on certain individuals who would most likely compete for medals in his event. The research had revealed much detail about their personal lives as well as their running accomplishments. Three individuals provoked the most thought concerning preparation in knowing the opposition. They were the Canadian, the Italian and the American, and without question, all three would fiercely contend for Olympic gold.

The Canadian had been raised in a small town near his nation's capitol of Ottawa. He works part time at a local hospital for a cardiologist, plus volunteers at a clinic where patients seek rehabilitation from heart ailments. Ian Jones runs full time. He had been married for less than a year when he won the North American 100 Kilometer Championships with a venerable time of six hours twenty-two minutes – the best time ever recorded on his continent. Jones has been running competitively for a number of years and no doubt, will draw from his experience to contend for a medal. His life appears full and his future promising.

The Italian is younger. Girolamo Pavin is enrolled at the University of Turin working toward a doctorate in pharmacology. He decided to take a sabbatical when the Italian Olympic Committee selected Pavin to compete in the Olympics after winning the European 100 Kilometer Championships. He too, seems content, planning a marriage with his fiancée later on this year. His progress to world class status has been swift and is nearly complete. However, he lacks experience. His file revealed few ultramarathon races and only one marathon near his hometown, the Turin Marathon, which he won in two hours twenty minutes two years ago. Pavin's weakness may be exploited during the later stages of the race . . . if he can run that far.

The American is a bit of an enigma. The transition from collegiate to national class runner was well underway when his personal life took a sharp turn for the worse. Presently, his work schedule as a fireman allows much flexibility in training. Boroshkov considers Washington to be the most committed of all competitors. This is the champion's homeland, his territory, and most likely, the American will do just about anything to defend it. Yet on the other hand, personal turmoil may have left "the favorite" lost and confused for a time, perhaps even vulnerable. Records show very little data about the American after his divorce five years earlier. He just seemed to vanish for a couple of years, then reappeared running ultramarathons. The champion of the Western States Trail Run appears poised to win an Olympic medal.

Boroshkov dares not turn to see the two runners pursuing him up the slope to the next aid station. He has done more running on this climb than he had an hour before. The incline is gentler, permitting a better pace. People line the trail under sparse vegetation and applaud when he runs by. He glances at his watch: 2:20. *"The aid station must not be too far away,"* he infers. The Russian is thankful since his water bottle is empty and temperatures have soared over the past hour. *"An inferno,"* he mutters, *"It must be forty-five Celsius or worse."*

A switchback provides the opportunity to peek downward at the trail below to see if the two are still in pursuit. Through the brush Boroshkov is surprised to see only one has responded to the increase of pace and heat. *"It is the Jew, and the man appears focused and resolute,"* he thinks. His concentration returns quickly to the trail. He knows nothing of Joshua Kostinski, but acknowledges that at ninety kilometers, the Israeli must know what he is doing . . . because he is doing very well.

"Hey Ian, how're you doing?" Nathan Washington sees the flushed face of a competitor who is overheating fast. He passes Jones quickly with Badillo right on his shoulder.

"Oh, I've been better." They are all walking . . . albeit, the Canadian is walking slowly. Jones feels pounding between his ears as he does his best to negotiate the ten percent grade.

"Not too much further to Michigan. Hang in there, buddy."

Jones nods. "Thanks for the encouragement, Nathan. Boroshkov is not too far ahead."

. . . And the Japanese runner is not too far behind. "Christ, this guy is not going to back down," David Conor mutters and continues to mull over the possibility of dropping back. "If I can only stay with this guy – just within stone's reach, I got a chance." He glances backward to see no one, and realizes if he loses Okuda, he loses an opportunity to catch the leaders. Sweat drips from a dimpled chin, soaking his torso. The Aussie notes his bottle is nearly half empty when he squirts fluid in his mouth and immediately corrects himself thinking, "The bottle is half full. God damnit, think positive!" Both men are running well up a gentle grade toward the next aid station at Michigan Bluff. The heat is tolerable for the physician from Melbourne. Training in the heat and humidity of the Australian tropics has acclimated his body well.

"You can hear Don Henley's, 'Boys of Summer' playing on someone's stereo system nearby. Everyone's anticipating the arrival of the first runners to the fifty-six mile checkpoint." Davis speaks loudly since the music is being amplified to the point of distortion. The camera pivots to reveal race personnel making preparations, and a thousand people lining the streets. The place is packed.

"Good afternoon everyone, I'm Brandon Davis reporting live from the gold mining boom town of Michigan Bluff about seventy miles northeast of Sacramento. This is the place where Leland Stanford earned his fortune during the Gold Rush of the nineteenth century. Today, this quiet foothill community has been transformed into a medical checkpoint and an aid station for the runners who will complete their fourth major climb of the day. Certainly it's the worst, since temperatures have soared above 110° in the canyons. It's an oven here and I'm only standing . . ." Davis looks upward and the camera follows his cue. ". . . under the shade of this magnificent oak tree. I am but a mere mortal, and these athletes are attempting to achieve immortality. It's difficult to conceive what these men are attempting to accomplish, but just to give you an idea . . ."

Davis points his index finger east to the horizon where the camera zooms-in on thunderhead clouds above mountainous terrain. "The first ridge you see is where the previous checkpoint is stationed at Devil's Thumb. The second ridge beyond the first is Last Chance. But way off in the distance, where the clouds tower above that bluff; that's Robinson Flat. The runners have covered twenty-five miles since leaving that bluff and that's only one quarter of the distance they will run today. This is an amazing perspective."

He pauses and then continues his commentary. "When we Americans think of the 'Boys of Summer,' well, we have always thought of baseball players. Today, I've re-evaluated. These men are the boys of this particular summer. What these men are doing goes far beyond what I thought humanly possible. And yet, they push-on. The leaders are about to arrive here and at the other end of the spectrum; there are runners who have not even reached Last Chance – the forty-five mile checkpoint. Those runners have earned my respect as well. They will not compete for Olympic glory; their aim is solely to finish and be part of the Olympic movement. Truly remarkable! Yes, these men are truly the 'Boys of Summer.'" At that instant, the song is broadcast in full stereophonic fidelity. Recorded video tape shows numerous runners negotiating one of the many climbs, followed by a clip showing runners entering the Devil's Thumb checkpoint.

The effect is dramatic.

Climbing to Devil's Thumb is Nigel Preverett. "My God," he mutters, "it's bloody hot." A natural spring has delivered water adjacent to the trail. He removes his Union Jack bandana from his neck, squats on the trail, dunks the cloth into the clear water and squeezes the contents. The cool water is refreshing as it pours from his head to his shoulders and trickles down his back. A Swedish runner stops and does the same. "Is it hot enough for you?" Preverett sips some water from his bottle.

"When they said that temperatures would exceed forty Celsius, they were not exaggerating. Do you think the water is potable?"

"Maybe, but I would not take the risk. The aid station is not too far off." The English gentleman notes the soiled uniform of a competitor who has given his best, but remains miles behind the leaders. He is taller and younger with Scandinavian character.

The Swede asks, "You are referring to the possibility of microbes, yes?"

"Girardia is common in this region and not very pleasant if ingested." The two commence to walk up a steep grade. "What's your name?" Preverett extends his hand.

"Per, Per Olafsson and yours?" Olafsson uses his left hand since his right is occupied with a bottle.

"Nice to meet you, Per; my name is Nigel."

Continuing their ascent, both runners soon begin to breathe deeply.

"Do you think we are ahead of the cut-off time?"

"Well ahead of the twenty-four cut-off, but unfortunately, so far behind the lead pack." Preverett senses that all his time and commitment to training will be for naught. Once again, no Olympic medal, no Olympic glory, only the satisfaction of knowing he will not surrender until he reaches the finish line. He sees Olafsson pulling ahead, power walking faster than his body can presently muster. "Godspeed, Per."

"Thank you, Nigel. Best of luck to you too."

"We know so little about Joshua Kostinski, except for the information provided in his profile. Oh yes, we know he can run, don't we." Brandon Davis forces a smile as he prepares to describe a runner whom no one knows anything about. "He was born and raised near the Sea of Galilee in the town of Safed and served in the Israeli military before coming to the United States. Kostinski ran cross country and track at Albany State University and at present resides in Tel Aviv. He holds his nation's marathon record at two hours eighteen minutes, which he set in Boston last year. This is his first 100 mile endurance run. "At this point he is the only competitor pressing the Russian for the lead. What can you add, Norm, about the man running in second place?"

"No question, he's a dark horse in the race." The camera focuses on the race director. "No one has even heard of this guy. Many naysayers were dispelling the notion that this guy could stay with Jones and Boroshkov just six miles ago. And yet, we're well past the halfway point of the race and he is dispelling the notion that he can't stay with the Russian. That's the beauty of international competition – You never know who will step up, and who will fall flat on their face."

"Do you think his training in the desert has given Kostinski an advantage, considering the heat?"

"You don't have to be a rocket scientist to answer that question, Brandon."

The commentary is disrupted by the obstreperous crowd welcoming the front runners.

"Who is the Jew?" Boroshkov feels a cold wet towel draped over his shoulders; feels his heart rate and breathing begin to slow. He swallows a cup of electrolytes.

"Slow down, Yuri. It is not vodka." The advisor does not wish to see his athlete become ill from drinking too much cold liquid too hastily. *"I am not sure who he is, but I did read his profile. I think this is his first ultramarathon. He has run two hours eighteen minutes in the marathon, more or less."*

"Bullshit. This may be his first 'official' ultra, but he has run these distances before or he simply would not be here."

"Do not worry comrade, your talent and experience supersedes his youth and inexperience."

Boroshkov does not respond to the rhetorical comment and peers across the aid station to take a close look at the challenger. The Israeli is seated, and an older man is squatting in front him talking. There is no question the man doing the talking is the coach. He sees Kostinski pour a cup of water over his head and for the first time through the cascade of water their eyes meet.

"Josh, you can take this guy. You're having a great day. Here drink this." The coach realizes that his athlete is performing well beyond what he had hoped. He had conversed with Kostinski weekly about training strategies and preparation, but never dreamed he'd be in a position to win. Thinking the impossible, "the kid actually has a chance," the coach asks, "How're holding up?" He sees his pupil swallow the contents of the cup, simultaneously chewing on a piece of banana.

"I know I can stay with him . . . for now. But he's really moving well, especially on the up-hills."

"Just . . ."

"I know Coach, 'keep contact at all costs.'" Kostinski sets his eyes on the older Soviet runner. "How old is the Russian? He looks as old as you!"

"Very funny, Josh. He's not much older than you. Besides, don't think about that Commie bastard. Concentrate on your pace, the trail, what you need to take in. Christ Josh, you're having the race of a lifetime – savor it."

116

Josh smiles. "Commie Bastard, Coach? I thought you never mixed politics with sport."

"Normally I don't. But I'm just pumped-up, that's all."

"You told me you have never coached an Olympian before, right?"

"Yeah, so what?"

"Well, that means you've never coached a gold medalist before either."

"Now you're talking, Josh. Run with confidence."

Joshua Kostinski pulls his eyes away from Boroshkov and takes his water bottle from his coach. He stands, feeling the ache in his legs, lower back and shoulders caused from running nearly sixty miles. He soon limbers as his walk becomes a jog. "Number 547 checking-out." A thunderous applause results when he runs through the gauntlet of spectators. Kostinski cannot believe it. He's taken command of the race.

"My friend, you become the hunted now." The Russian no longer thinks like an analytical physicist. He has become the hunter. *"Let us see how well you are able to maintain the pace."* Boroshkov is ten meters behind as the two leaders follow a dirt road leaving Michigan Bluff. His blue eyes keenly focus on the back of his prey – an Israeli runner who appears clearly vulnerable.

"Yah man, I would like to stop too, but there's no time to waste. We must press-on." The babbling brook looks inviting to Conrad Creary as he and the Irishman cross the small wooden footbridge over El Dorado Creek. Creary envisions his favorite waterfalls nestled in the hills near Port Antonio. With its sparkling water and lush vegetation, it resembles the biblical setting of Eden.

"I'm just bullshitting, Conrad. Christ, we're still in the top ten. We still got a shot at a medal." Eammon Horgan reasons, "Although not as good a chance as Conor and the Japanese runner who left Devil's Thumb just when we were arriving. We're running well. No runner has passed us since the last checkpoint. How're you holding up in the pleasant California sunshine?" Eammon smiles at his wit, since conditions are not so pleasant.

"Not too bad. I think it's worse in Jamaica."

"How can you say that? Your country is an island for god's sake. Does it really get this hot?"

"No man, but the humidity is much worse. The sweat sticks to you like flypaper, and you can overheat if you're not careful. In fact, the worst condition I've ever been in my life was after a four and a half mile foot race," the Jamaican reminisces.

"Four and a half miles, that's a short one. What happened?"

"The race was at five o'clock in the afternoon – ninety degrees and ninety percent humidity. I ran too hard for too long and passed out at the end. I remember the last two words I said to my coach when I crossed the finish line: 'Help me.' Then everything went black."

"Jesus, I've never become unconscious in my life." Of course the Irishman recollects a time or two when he drank too much and 'almost passed out.' "It must have been pretty scary. When did you come out of it?" Horgan sips electrolytes from his bottle.

"I was out for only about five minutes. They used smelling salts to wake me up. The irony is I almost passed out again. After the smelling salts revived me, I started to hyperventilate. One of the runners on our team shoved a paper bag in my face until my breathing slowed."

"It actually sounds pretty funny, Conrad. Did you win?" Eammon begins to breathe deeply as they begin a moderate ascent up the canyon wall towards Michigan Bluff.

"No man, that's the funny part. I was the best runner on the Jamaican Defense Force team and finished tenth. Now every time I return home my friends badger me about it." Creary feels his dry throat and quenches his thirst. His water bottle still has plenty of liquid.

"Yes, friends can be annoying. But how many of your teammates are running here in the Olympics?" Their conversation slows. They hear footsteps approaching from the rear. The two instinctively increase their cadence to avoid being passed. Eammon recognizes the accent. It's the German.

"Let us pass when possible," Hafner requests. Creary and Horgan step aside as Pavin passes first, with Hafner right on his heels. "How are you two doing? The heat is miserable, yes. But at least here there is shade."

Creary acknowledges, "Yah man, miserable."

118

The four men make good progress on switchbacks leading to the Michigan Bluff checkpoint. It's a quarter of three and near the ridge of the canyon, it's 100 degrees - in the shade.

Badillo steps off one of the scales as Washington simultaneously steps off another. "J. P., I'll see you on the other side of the checkpoint." The Mexican waves as he approaches his wife. "Hey Clint, Gioia, how're we doing?"

"Shit, Nate, you're closing in on the Russian." Clint is clearly psyched for his younger brother. He is confident that his sibling can catch anyone on this trail. "There's another runner too - the Israeli's hanging tough. Give me your bottle. The usual? What happened to the Canadian?"

"Ciao Nathan, have you seen Ian?"

Washington looks up from the chair in which he is seated. They are situated under one of the many oaks located in Michigan Bluff. He recognizes an attractive woman with dark brown hair that is highlighted with copper tone. Concerned ebony eyes look down. "Oh, hi Genny." He feebly attempts to chew and talk at the same time. "Ian's struggling in the heat. He should be here soon." Gioia massages his shoulders.

"Will he arrive soon, do you think?"

"He's fine. Just having a rough spell. He'll come out of it."

"Thank you Nathan."

"Who was that, Nate?" Gioia watches the woman disappear into the crowd of spectators. She places a cool damp towel on the shoulders of her cousin.

Nathan sees Susan attending to J. P. and touches his cousin's hand. "That's the Canadian's wife. I met her earlier in the week. They make a fine couple . . ." as his voice tapers off he mentions, "and so do J. P. and Susan."

*   *   *

He misses her . . . still misses her badly, and tries not to think about her. Though at times, he can't help himself. How Nathan Washington's life had changed one dreadful day five years ago.

Married for two years, Nathan's personal life appeared in order. He

119

had finished forestry and fire science classes at Humboldt and later decided to fight fires professionally. The work hours permitted ample training time to pursue his real passion. He had landed his first job outside of Sacramento in Folsom and subsequently, he and his wife had moved from Arcata to their new home. The two had lived in their new home for over a year seemingly in marital bliss, when in one fell swoop, his entire world came crashing down.

After a shift he had been scheduled to work was reassigned to another fire fighter, he had returned home one Sunday morning to hear voices coming from the bathroom. One he recognized . . .

"My husband never touches me like that . . . never makes me feel the way you do . . ."

The other voice he didn't. "I guess that's why you've invited . . ."

In rage, Nathan threw the shower curtain back and in an instant saw a man he simply was not - blond, barrel-chested and virtually no body hair. The stranger had his hands cupped around his wife's breasts as both her hands clasped the shower nozzle. The punch missed the intended target as the man ducked and parried the blow. Instead, the fist caught his wife squarely on the nose, knocking her against the shower's tiled wall. The man recovered quickly, smiting Washington's face. Practically knocked unconscious, Nathan fell to the floor. When he propped himself against the opposite wall he gasped, "How could you do this to me? How could you do this to us?" Thoughts of alibis, lies and deception quickly filled his head, and the thoughts turned his stomach.

Washington refuses to recall much of that fateful day, except the man's pleading for him to remain on the floor, and that he did not wish to hurt him anymore. Did not wish to hurt him! The man (and his wife) had done far more damage than the one punch that sent Nathan reeling. Tears mixed with blood from his lip and nose. The saline, sanguine taste combined with bile sickened him - that he would never forget.

After a time, his wife had attempted to contact Nathan - to patch things up. She was contrite and wanted to discuss things rationally; attend counseling sessions and possibly work things out. Dismissing his wife and any rational thought, he expressed himself explicitly. "You broke our vows; you broke my heart and most importantly, you broke our home. I can never trust you again."

Nathan Washington has not trusted anyone since, deciding instead to immerse himself in the one activity where he finds solace and confidence. His running excelled. His social life waned. Nathan felt content to live alone, and the only person with whom he truly confided was Clint. Clint had been there for him, always offering brotherly advice and giving support when necessary. Clint's wife had tried to arrange dates for her brother-in-law occasionally. Nathan had politely declined the offers stating, "I am already happily dating two women – Betty Palm and Five Finger Mary."

Clint's comment was always the same. "You sure make a great manage a trois!" Clint's attempt at French always sounded guttural at best.

Unfortunately, the woman remains in his head. Especially at night, when he lies alone . . . too many fond recollections to recount, and only one indelible memory he can't forget.

"Hey Bro, J. P.'s leaving." Clint hands the water bottle to his brother. "What's wrong?"

"Nothing Bro. See you at Foresthill."

"Why's he upset?"

Gioia shakes her head. "I don't know; he just got real quiet all of a sudden."

Chapter 12 – Foresthill

She stands tall beside the trail and watches the runners pass, poised to run. Taut muscles from years of conditioning workouts are the products of the long distance regimen. Running the trail has given her valuable lessons of knowing what lies ahead. She too, is a Western States Trail finisher - completing the 100 mile trek successfully on four different occasions. Another runner passes, muscles tense, she's ready to move.

"Whoa girl. Be patient. The last runner will pass soon, then we'll go." Andrea Gibbons gently pulls the reins and pats her Arab on the neck. She and Diamondhead have been through much together. She knows the horse very well, knows her temperament, plus her limitations. The equine in turn trusts the master, trusts her judgment and commands. Mutual respect exists between the two of them. "We're not racing today girl, only helping out a bit."

The master garners a different silver belt buckle on her blue jeans that bears the "100 Miles, One Day" inscription. Instead of Western States Endurance Run, the words "Western States Endurance Ride" are beautifully engraved on this fine piece of sterling. Andrea and Diamondhead have completed the arduous Tevis Cup ride four times over the past six years. Both are in excellent condition as they have prepared for a ride and tie event in late August. They wait patiently near the trail a mile west of Last Chance.

Diamondhead's ears perk as she turns her head to see another oncoming runner. Andrea looks too, simultaneously standing on her stirrups to see the man approach. "There he is, Girl, number 545. Now we can go." Gibbons does not recognize the uniform of the Haitian runner, but offers an encouraging smile. He returns the favor and waves. Andrea's official title today is Trail Sweep. She will trail the last runner down into the American River Canyon and follow any straggler up to Devil's Thumb, making sure all runners remain accounted for. She carries extra water, some food, plus a medical kit in case an emergency arises.

The Haitian continues to plod along, twenty minutes ahead of the twenty-four cut-off time. He begins to attack the switchbacks with an aggressive pace, knowing he needs to make up time on the descents. Once again, he finds himself as the last runner on the course. The Indian had not stopped at Last Chance, but decided to press on in an attempt to catch the South Africans. He feels gravity's positive effect, and his confidence returns as he free falls to the canyon's basement.

"I'm standing here at the Michigan Bluff checkpoint with Joshua Kostinski's collegiate cross country coach, Jeff Thornburg, who is 'crewing' for the Israeli runner today." Brandon Davis had located the coach after Kostinski departed to discover some pertinent information about the current leader in the race. The interview is being recorded for later transmission. "So what do you think of your athlete today? Is everything going as planned?"

"I think much better than either of us expected." The coach, a man in his early fifties with gray and girth to show for his years, speaks with a thick Bronx accent. "He seems to be running well right now, but with forty plus miles of trail remaining, much can happen. The Russian is pressing the pace, and there are others who are within striking distance. This race is far from over."

"You sound somewhat apprehensive, Mr. Thornburg. Is there a potential problem you can foresee?"

"Please call me Jeff, and problems, certainly yes. Just to name a few: there's hyperthermia, hypoglycemia, muscle necrosis, not to mention total exhaustion. Get the picture?"

"Not really, Jeff, your vocabulary is a bit challenging. You obviously have a history in this sport. Can you explain in simpler terms?"

"Actually, the longest race I've ever run is the New York City Marathon, but that was years ago. Just to simplify the terminology, there're a lot of bad things that can happen when the body overheats. I mean just look at the Canuck who just arrived; he's already spent. Josh had been running with him for thirty miles - since Duncan Canyon. Now look at him." Thornburg shakes his head, laughs and gestures in the direction of the Canadian. "That could happen to anyone . . . even if they're vigilant about drinking and eating. Things can go from bad to worse in a hurry – in a big hurry."

The camera pivots, finding Ian Jones seated with his hands covering his face and head down - the forlorn posture of a beaten man. A woman is speaking to him. "Agreed. So what gives your athlete an advantage at this point in the race? Why is he winning?"

"Certainly, living in Israel the past three years has acclimated his body to running in the heat. Beyond that, I'm really not sure, except I will say, he is one of the most talented and tenacious runners I have ever coached. In fact, I'm learning just how tough this kid can be."

"Did you travel to Israel to train Kostinski?"

"Unfortunately no; I couldn't arrange to leave my post at Albany State, even though I was tempted to go for a visit last Christmas. But with the wife, my kids, and there's even grandchildren now . . . just too many family commitments."

"Then how did you coach him?"

"By phone. We conversed weekly about his workouts and how his training progressed over the past year. Josh came to New York earlier this spring and trained with some of my collegiate runners. He moved to Mammoth, er . . . wherever that is, earlier this summer, then moved into Squaw Valley's Olympic Village about three weeks ago. He knows the course pretty well."

"You must have a good rapport with him since he asked you to be here."

"Honestly, I'm surprised that Josh invited me. I mean, he's been out of school for over four years and I have little experience at this distance. I am honored to be part of this."

"Your humility is refreshing to hear, Jeff." Davis nods approvingly at the man from New York. He had often interviewed athletes and coaches who were thoroughly arrogant with their conceited comments. This man is different. "Of course, who has experience coaching athletes who run 100 mile endurance runs?"

"Good point, Brandon. Good point."

She looks into eyes that were once lucid and cobalt blue. Now they appear drawn, gray and incapacitated. "Ian, are you okay?" Genevieve is worried. Her husband, who apparently has had enough, looks beaten.

He inhales deeply and mutters, "That last climb kicked my ass."

"Ian, what are you saying?"

Another long breath taken. "Nothing Gen, I'm all right. Just get me a wet towel would you – please?"

Her man looks exhausted, plus sounds disturbed. *"God,"* she thinks, *"he looked so good just ten kilometers ago."* Genevieve sees Ian shaking his head, rubbing his hands through his auburn hair. She drapes a cold damp towel over his shoulders and hands him a cup of water.

"Thanks Gen, get me a salted potato, would you?"

She crouches in front of him, putting her hands on his thighs and stares directly into his eyes. "What happened, Ian?"

"It's the fuckin' heat." He quaffs the cup of water in one swallow. "The last climb was pure misery. I even had to stop once for a breather; something I never do in a race."

Genevieve rarely heard her husband cuss. *"Shit* Ian, it has to be over forty degrees. What did you expect?"

"'Shit Ian' . . . such harsh language for a lady, even if it is in French." He smiles at the mockery. "Maybe you've been in this country too long, Dearest One."

"It is good to see you smile. I'll fetch you that potato."

"And a cup of coke, too."

Genevieve rolls the potato in salt and then carefully pours water into a half cup of coke diluting the beverage. "Here you go my dear, enjoy." She sees some color returning to those eyes - the eyes that initially attracted her to him three years ago this summer. "Feeling better?"

After another deep breath between chews, he responds, "Oh yeah, much better. How long ago did Nathan and er . . .?" Jones had met the Mexican runner earlier, but cannot recall his name.

"He left with another runner about . . ." She glances at her Swiss watch, "fifteen minutes ago."

They both hear the announcer declare the arrival of two runners. "Number 552, Akira Okuda, Japan. Number 511, David Conor, Australia." More applause follows.

She sees fear in his eyes once again. "Ian, you're in fifth place for goodness sake. You can catch the American, the Russian too. But you must believe."

Ian looks into her brown eyes which express faith and confidence. He stands, feeling stiffness and soreness fifty-six miles of trail running cause. Low blood pressure makes him feel light-headed as well. He feels her lips press against his and draws strength from them. Ice water pours over his head and he withdraws a step. His wife is standing there, empty cup in hand with a guilty smile – a lover's smile. "Thanks Gen, I needed that. I'll see you at the next checkpoint." He waves at the checkpoint personnel in charge of checking-out runners.

"Number 525, Ian Jones, you're looking good, 'Oh Canada.' Good luck!" The attendant records the departure time in her log - 2:50, and returns a friendly wave. Another thunderous applause follows when the North American 100 kilometer champion exits Michigan Bluff.

Jones glances at his chronometer. "Looking good my ass, I feel like shit," he mutters.

"Ian Jones, the current 100 kilometer North American record holder has faltered a bit. He departs the Michigan Bluff checkpoint in fifth place. We had the opportunity to interview Ian earlier in the week and he disclosed some interesting strategies about training for a 100 mile endurance run." Brandon Davis nods at the engineer to roll the video clip which is broadcast live.

"Hmm . . . How does one prepare for a 100 mile endurance run?" Jones shakes his head, rubs his right eyebrow and then laughs. He has a thin face with a prominent nose. Thick wavy auburn hair is combed behind his ears. His deep blue eyes reveal a man who is relaxed and easily approached. "Actually, I feel more confident talking about the preparation for a 100 kilometer world championship than a 100 mile endurance run." He pauses for a moment to collect a thought or two. "Please do not misinterpret what I'm saying. I know I've prepared extremely well for this event – akin to preparing for a 100 kilometer race."

"'Extreme,' now that's a word I have associated with this event. Tell us what you do on a given day, Ian." Davis holds the microphone under the narrow chin of the Canadian runner.

"It's probably better to discuss what I do during a given week of training since the day to day stuff can vary. I've been averaging between 180 and 200 kilometers per week for the past five months. I often run twice a day or ten to twelve workouts a week depending on my work schedule. Believe me Brandon, there's a huge commitment of time and energy toward preparing for any long distance event. Whether it's a ten k run, a marathon or an ultra, you will invest the appropriate time or you will not succeed. I know I'm going off on a tangent, but whether you're an elite runner or novice, the decision an individual makes to commence a serious training regimen is the crucial first step towards becoming a successful runner. Without the initial decision to train seriously, a person will be wasting his or her time."

Davis smiles into the camera. "Obviously, you're no novice, Mr. Jones. Tell us what you do during a typical week."

Jones clears his throat, knowing he could give a litany of information on his training strategies. Instead, he keeps it brief. "Generally speaking, I run twice on Mondays. Monday morning is an easy run of eight to ten kilometers. The evening run is longer and tougher. I usually run a fartlek workout in the afternoon."

"Pardon me, Ian. Fartlek, what is that? I mean it sounds like you're expelling gas when you run." Davis chuckles at the thought.

Jones ignores the comment since he's heard the same joke numerous times, especially from American athletes. Canadians never laugh at the same stupid joke twice. "Actually, it's a Swedish term used to describe running swiftly, followed by recovery runs at a slow pace. Then you alternate with varying distances or times depending upon what you wish to accomplish."

"Oh," the commentator clears his throat, not wanting to appear ignorant. "And what exactly are you trying to accomplish with this kind of workout?"

"Well Brandon, in a nutshell, I am building cardiovascular strength, plus, exercising fast-twitch muscle fibers."

"Okay, not too technical." Davis does not want to burden the audience with a crash course on human physiology. "So what's on the menu for Tuesday?"

"After a morning workout of another easy run, the afternoon workout is pure speed and always moderate to difficult in intensity."

"Pure speed?"

"I go to the local 400 meter track and run intervals. It's never a pleasant workout. Instead, I push myself well beyond race pace." There is a serious tone in Jones' voice. The face of a man, who has eclipsed the threshold of pain too many times to count, peers into the lens of the camera. "Wednesdays and Thursdays are easier, mostly mileage. Fridays are another tough day. After a morning run, I gear up for another afternoon session of intervals or hill repeats and . . ."

"Hold on for one second, Ian. You said that Tuesdays are not pleasant and Fridays don't sound like much fun either. Do you find this pleasurable? I mean, when does running become fun, or doesn't it?"

The Canadian ponders for a moment. "It's difficult to explain. I mean there's a philosophy that describes why people participate in distance running. Why they, er . . . we take our bodies to the ultimate limits of endurance. For me personally, the incredible feeling of accomplishment after a workout or a race is magnificent; it's simply sublime. I'm not sure if you can comprehend what I'm trying to say, but in an eccentric sense, yeah, it's fun."

"If you say so, Ian. One more question regarding your training strategies. With all this mileage you run in a given week, what is the longest run you do?"

"Which brings us to Sunday, Brandon." Ian Jones scratches his beak, and answers, "Fifty kilometers. There is a trail system near my home in Ottawa. Believe me, I know it well. Cross country skiing in the winter, running the trails the remainder of the year. It's a great place to escape and immerse myself in running and just being."

The man's sentiment is palpable. There is calm to his countenance. Brandon looks away from the camera and into the sincere blue eyes of an athlete who has obviously sacrificed much to be here, and asks one final question. "With all that you've described, is your preparation adequate to win?"

"A coach once told me, 'always plan ahead, prepare sufficiently, and always enter a competition with quiet confidence and fierce determination.'" The North American 100 Kilometer record holder concludes the interview saying, "Oh yeah, I can win this race. Of course, there are 150 other guys thinking the exact same thing."

"Akira-san, sixth place, you have improved your place in the race, plus you have closed the gap on the leader; only twenty minutes behind. How are you feeling? Are the blisters okay?" The coach puts his hand on Okuda's shoulder and attempts to assess the damage caused by running ninety plus kilometers. *"Do you wish to change socks?"*

"No Master, my feet are good. Who is the runner who came in with me? He is a worthy opponent . . . for a Christian." He had seen the Australian cross himself when leaving the Devil's Thumb checkpoint and thought, *"There is the man's weakness."*

The idea of Christianity not only perplexes the Buddhist from Hokkaido, but as far as running long distance is concerned, he thinks Christianity is a detriment. In a sport that requires one to internalize pain, to run through the threshold of agony, praying to an outside deity for help makes absolutely no sense. Instead, Okuda believes the athlete should look deep into his own soul and find the strength to surpass what others find humanly impossible. Another concept that eludes Okuda is the whole procession of faith dealing with a son who is the incarnate of his father and born of a virgin woman! When has that ever existed in natural history? What a crock of bullshit the West has fed its people for centuries.

Once again, he touches the talisman around his neck and looks at his adversary. The man's face is flushed, his sandy blond hair matted from sweat and grime. His eyes are open, but clearly lack focus. *"Please fill my bottle with electrolytes, Master; I will not be here long."*

"Akira-san you should eat something. Here, eat this." The coach hands his athlete a plastic bowl filled with rice covered with soy, plus a pair of chopsticks. *"The salt will do you good."*

"Dave, you okay?" An American friend, whom the Australian had recruited to crew, hands him a cup of electrolyte fluid and half a sandwich.

"Bonzer, fuckin' bonzer. I don't know if I can stay with Mr. Nippon over there." Conor looks over to see Okuda who is drinking and eating. His closest rival appears totally relaxed, within his own element. "The guy is tearing me up on the ascents. I mean, I can stay with him on the downs, but the last climb was hell."

"Dave, speaking of hell, welcome to hell's hole! It's got to be well over a hundred in the canyons. Eat and drink, relax a minute. The food and fluids will do you good. Anything else I can bring you?"

Conor bites into a vegemite sandwich and tastes the salty spread. "Thanks Mate. Yeah, bring me some . . . libation - coke and dilute it with some H-2-O, pretzels too." The physician from Melbourne is no longer thinking like a doctor. He begins to regain his composure and glances at the Japanese runner to assess the man's fitness. "Fuck, he looks great."

"Yeah, but his uniform is dirtier than yours. Hey buddy, you're in sixth place! You're doing great. Well over halfway. Hang in there." He hands his runner the diluted coke.

"Thanks for the encouragement, but actually I'm in seventh place, he's in sixth." David Conor points his thumb towards Okuda while finishing his sandwich.

"Bullshit, butthead. Better to think of the bottle being half full, not half empty."

"Yeah I know. I tried that once already. It worked on the last climb. By the way, have you ever thought of becoming a midwife? You're pretty good at this coaching stuff – good support therapy and such."

"Very funny, Conor. Right now it's difficult enough 'crewing' for you!"

"Shit, he's getting ready to go. Hand me my bottle, Mate." The Australian looks over to see the shorter runner receiving a final instruction from his coach. "I wonder what the h - e - double l those two are speaking about, like it'll make a difference at this point." He snickers, then states, "You're right, sixth place."

"That's the spirit Dave – stick with him."

"*Keep pressing Akira-san and you will catch the American by the next checkpoint, maybe even the Russian.*"

Okuda finishes the contents of the bowl and nods in agreement, completely identifying with his coach's prediction.

"*Many things can happen over the next seventy kilometers – many good things!*"

"Number 511, David Conor, Australia; number 552, Akira Okuda, Japan." A roar erupts as a thousand spectators witness a clash between two competitors that is about to unfold. The attendant records their times and notices only twenty minutes separate the first seven runners. "Hey Jack, check this out – We've got ourselves a race."

Inaudible to the cheering crowd that has gathered at Michigan Bluff, and unbeknownst to Conor and Okuda, a runner arrives determined to catch the leaders before his day is done. "Number 549, Giro . . . lamo Pavin, Italy." His name badly mispronounced, the attendant escorts the Italian to the scale and looks at his wristband. "Your weight looks good. Anything I can get you?"

Pavin smiles and answers in Italian. "*Everything is fine.*" He breathes deeply, trying to recover from the difficult ascent to the checkpoint. Girolamo sees his fiancée and coach approach. "*Ciao, Sabrina, Salve maestro. What's everyone cheering about?*"

The coach replies as Sabrina hugs him. Both are happy to see Pavin, but for different reasons. "*You just missed the Japanese runner. I think the other man is from Australia. Give me your plastic bottle.*"

"*You are soaked Lamo. Did you stop for a swim?*" Sabrina grins.

Pavin steals a look at his woman. "*You have always liked it when I sweat, my dear.*" His dark eyes have always had the habit of piercing the girl's heart and finding her soul. Now is no different. He smiles at the allusion and sees her blush. "*Bring me orange slices and water, please.*"

"*Certainly, naughty one. I'll be right back; do not go away.*"

"*How do you feel, Lamo?*" The coach places a wet towel over his head and assesses his athlete. He looks great. "*The Germans, where are they?*"

"*The East German turned his ankle badly. The West German will be here shortly, along with two others. I do not want to stay here long.*" Sabrina hands him two orange slices. The smile has vanished from his salt encrusted face. He swallows a cup of water.

His coach easily recognizes what happened during the last climb. Not only had Pavin proven his prowess while running road races, he had shown a real talent for trail running. There had been a trail championship series near Davos, Switzerland the summer before and the Italian had won the 100 kilometer event easily. Repeating similar tactics, Pavin simply pulled away on the previous ascent, allowing contenders to eat his trail dust. His athlete is having a good day.

Pavin stands to depart. His coach dispenses two Motrin. "*This will help alleviate the inflammation.*"

"*I know it, Coach.*" There is soreness in his lower back and quadriceps.

Sabrina tucks the crucifix under his singlet and pats her fiancé twice on the chest. With her eyes fixed on Pavin's, she says, "*In the den of the wolf, Lamo . . .*" She gives him a peck on the lips.

The coach repeats, "*Yes Girolamo, in the den of the wolf!*"

The Italian's nostrils flare. Knowing the aphorism's significance he whispers inaudibly, ". . . *and death to the wolf.*" Pavin departs, his muscles already beginning to limber.

Despite being dusty, the jeep road west of Michigan Bluff has the benefit of having large evergreens and oak to protect the runners from the afternoon sun. The lead runners are hugging the side of the dirt road that is under the shade of secondary growth. It is a flat section of trail, so the Russian and the Israeli alternate positions occasionally. Drafting is not only permitted in distance running, runners are encouraged to "draft" whenever possible.

The Russian wishes he can speak English to ascertain if living in Israel is as nice and beautiful as a Jewish colleague at Leningrad Polytechnic proclaims Palestine to be. Yuri had often listened to his colleague whine every time he had applied for an exit visa for his family. The government had always rejected the application for the obvious reason of not wanting to lose the Soviet Union's most precious resource – its people. Discussions had always escalated into debates, sometimes very heated ones.

The Jew would always return to his office, which he shared with Yuri, aggravated that the Soviet government would not permit him to emigrate to Israel. He seemed always eager to vent his frustration to anyone who would lend an ear and comfort him about his unfortunate situation.

"*I cannot believe how close-minded and pig-headed those bureaucrats at the visa office are. They do not understand how important my religion and faith are to my family and me. They cannot begin to understand how difficult it is to be Jewish in this Soviet state. All I wish to do is contribute to the one place where I can find religious asylum and avoid all the anti-Semitism that I am obliged to experience here.*"

It was the last comment that aggravated Yuri the most. "*Anti-Semitism does not exist in Israel! Are you insane? That's where you would be hated and despised the most. Do you think the Palestinians are going to welcome you with open arms? What about the Lebanese, the Syrians or the Egyptians?*" He shook his head in disgust. "*I listen to you complain about our Soviet state's unfairness to the Jewish community. But, you are permitted to practice your faith. You are given as much latitude as the Orthodox Christians regarding assembling for prayer and their blessed sacraments. Why do you continue to whine about living in the most powerful country in the world?*"

"*That's just the point. I am second-class citizen of a country I no longer wish to be part of. I would make a much greater contribution to the state of Israel than I presently contribute to the Communist Party. You are Communist, Doctor Boroshkov. You have been indoctrinated to think like a Communist and learned to live like one. My freedom to choose where I want to live, and where I wish to practice my faith has never been granted. My dream is a simple one: To live on a kibbutz and contribute to the welfare of a Jewish State. I would like my children to experience that as well – to know what religious freedom is all about. That, they will never find here.*"

"*Perhaps Comrade. But you speak fluently, as an educated man; one who is literate and well versed in language, plus the sciences. Well my friend, who educated you, provided you with a job, continues to provide medical treatment to your family? Our government has a vested interest in your well-being and does not want to squander one of our most prominent physicists. Perhaps you should try to be more loyal to the state that has given much and that you most obviously detest.*"

"*And perhaps 'Comrade,' our government should allow people to choose where they wish to live and ultimately, what they want to do.*"

"*Certainly, I can agree to that . . . after such people have paid their debt to the people of the Soviet Union.*"

"*At what cost, Doctor Boroshkov? A life sentence!*"

"*A life sentence at our university is certainly much more agreeable and productive than, hmmm . . . let's say a research station in the province of Siberia. In fact, I bet you can find religious freedom there!*"

"*Is that what you wish to see, Yuri – that I am transferred to Siberia? Will you inform the KGB of our discussion?*"

"*Only if you don't stop the whining, Comrade Rubinchik.*" He then patted his colleague on the shoulder and chuckled as he walked out of their spartan office.

*　　　*　　　*

The Russian squirts some water into his mouth and swallows the cool liquid, feeling its soothing effect as it passes to his gullet. He sees an attendant ahead with a red flag pointing at the single-track trail that leads to the next decent – Volcano Canyon, the last of the three canyons. Yuri has run nearly 100 kilometers and feels strong. As expected, there is soreness in his quadriceps, calves and shoulders. He knows there are a few blisters on his feet, especially between the toes. No matter, Boroshkov is confident he can win, since the Israeli, who is right on his heels, is beginning to labor. The pace too, is swift. The Russian recognizes the four minute per kilometer gait he is holding on the flat sections. The next ascent he will dispatch this opponent who has been relentless thus far. Yuri thinks, "*I will bury him on the next climb.*"

"*Hey Nathan, what's happening, friend?*" J. P. Badillo speaks Spanish, then immediately changes to English. "You haven't said much since Michigan Bluff. Are you okay?"

"You seem to get along pretty well with Susan, don't you?" Nathan exhales and then swigs some electrolytes into his mouth. The liquid is still cool and refreshing to drink. The large trees adjacent to the dirt road provide shade, permitting the two runners to make good time along this stretch.

"Uh . . . yeah, I guess so. What the hell are you thinking about, man?"

"I don't know. Sometimes I think about my ex-wife. Wonder what it would be like if she was here – crewing for me."

"Christ Nate, this is no time to be thinking about past relationships." He blurts a couple of Mexican expletives. "Stay focused! We've got a chance to make history here today. We're reeling in the front runners like fish on a line. Come-on, snap out of it. What do you think our pace is?" Badillo knows the pace is better than six-thirty per mile, but he wants to distract his training partner from his "what if" attitude.

"I know you're right. But I saw the concern on Ian's wife's face, and just thought to have someone close, er . . . intimate . . . for support; that might be nice."

"Oh that hurts, Nathan. I thought we were much closer than that! By the way, who's Ian? Are you trying to make me jealous, big boy?" The Mexican's lisp sounds comical.

The American chuckles at the response. Washington is glad to have companionship at this stage of the race – at this stage of his life. J. P. is a good friend and a good listener. "Thanks buddy. By the way, I figure around six-thirty pace, give or take. We should be seeing the turn to drop into Volcano Canyon soon."

"Very soon," Badillo replies. He squirts some fluid into his mouth, contemplating Washington's initial question. "Yeah, me and my old lady - we're pretty tight."

The heat is omnipotent. It's just before three and even in the shade west of Michigan Bluff, the Canadian feels like he's being cooked alive. He is relegated to walking just to catch his breath. Ian Jones feels exhausted and helpless. Then the inevitable happens. He hears footsteps and turns to see an Australian and Japanese runner - the first of many whom will pass him over the stretch of trail that connects Michigan Bluff to the Foresthill checkpoint.

Volcano Canyon is an appropriate name since it comes complete with its own magma chamber. The afternoon sun has baked the surface of the trail and the adjacent rocks. Reflecting heat, plus the sun's direct rays have caused the ambient temperatures in the canyon to rise above 110°

Fahrenheit. There are no trees, no protection. Heat waves can readily be seen rising from the surface of the trail. The Russian and the Israeli approach the canyon's trough just as the Mexican and the American reach its trailhead. One mile of trail separates them. It's three o'clock and little perspiration can be seen on their skin – it evaporates as soon as it is secreted.

The West German, Wolfgang Hafner spots the Jamaican who is preparing to leave Michigan Bluff. The sheen reflecting off his black skin is not sweat, but cold water the Jamaican has poured over himself. He thinks about the heat that the man's black skin absorbs compared to his own pale complexion and concludes, *"Being white must have distinct advantages when running on hot sunny days."* He walks over to meet Conrad Creary, his German accent prevalent when he speaks. "Are you ready to run, my friend?"

"Post-haste," Creary replies. "What happened to Horgan? I haven't seen 'im."

"Who?"

"The Irish runner I was with. We came in together."

"Sorry, I have not seen him."

"Hope he's okay. Seems like a nice young man. Although, I believe he is learning a lesson in humility."

Hafner acknowledges, "We will all learn a similar lesson today."

The two men report to the attendant who is recording bib numbers and then they depart Michigan Bluff between the applauding masses.

"Well my good son, you have two choices: slow-up or blow-up."

Eammon Horgan's face is flushed with blood. He has not been able to slow his breathing and his heart rate remains above 180. He gasps, "Jesus Christ, that last climb was a bitch. I haven't felt this bad . . ." Rubbing both his hands through his reddish hair, he looks at his soiled shoes, "ever! And God help me, I'm barely half finished."

His coach who is standing in front of him instructs, "Look Eammon, you just need to slow down. Conserve a bit. And for God's sake, try to slow your breathing. Concentrate! Drink this."

The young Irishman feels his pulse dropping. Horgan realizes what his coach's wisdom can provide. He is very deliberate when he swallows the beverage. "Oh great, more electrolytes. Thanks coach, this tastes like piss."

"Well, I'm not exactly sure what piss tastes like, Eammon, but it probably contains similar salts. Here, eat this too." The patient coach hands him a salted potato. "You're in tenth place . . ." They both hear the announcement of a Norwegian runner followed closely by a Korean. "All right, twelfth place. But the point is you can finish this race. You just need to think a little. Regain your composure. What I'm asking is do you want to finish?" He looks seriously into the light azure eyes of the youth seated directly in front of him.

"I've come too far to quit, Coach."

"That's the spirit, Laddie. So don't be an imbecile. Slow down and use the brain God's given you."

Horgan's breathing slows. He chews a few pretzel sticks. "Get me some coke, Coach. This stuff makes me sick!"

The coach returns quickly with two cups of diluted coke. "Drink it slowly."

The brash Irishman immediately chugs the first and smiles. "Okay, Coach, just joking. I'll slow down." He puts the second cup near his right foot and finishes the potato.

The coach recognizes the face of a competitor who is recovering quickly. "Do you need anything else, son?"

"Yeah, maybe an orange slice or two . . . and a cookie for desert."

The mentor contemplates, "His stomach's fine – that's a good sign."

Dr. Chad Logan wipes the top part of the Swiss runner's hand with an alcohol swab and then smiles at his patient. "You'll be fine. We'll get some fluids into you stat." The man had passed out for a moment after vomiting. He still appears delirious, but at least has regained consciousness. Logan carefully inserts the needle into the vein and waits to see blood enter the syringe. He attaches the intravenous unit to the syringe, removes the surgical tubing from the man's arm and begins the slow drip. "Lay back and relax; you're going to be here for a while."

Lastly, he cuts the wristband officially disqualifying the participant and says, "Welcome to the trail of broken dreams, number 6 1 2." His patient hardly notices.

The man who is under an IV drip understands little English. But listening to the sympathetic voice of the doctor has a soothing effect. He cradles his head in his hands, closes his eyes and falls asleep. Another victim has fallen to the day's heat, an onerous distance and the consequence of having a bad day - an Olympic torch extinguished, another ambition unfulfilled.

Dr. Logan has not left the Devil's Thumb checkpoint. He hands the wristband to the attendant. "How many DNF's is that?"

"I think were up to twenty-two here. I have no idea what the total is, Doctor."

"Doesn't really matter," he adds, "they'll be others." Logan looks at his watch – it's just after three.

The aid station will remain open for another hour and a half.

Andrea Gibbons looks down from the embankment near the bridge that crosses the North Fork of the Middle Fork of the American River. Diamond Head has found a plume of grass and chews the vegetation. She sees a runner who has doffed his shoes, laying prone in the water, eyes closed and appearing totally relaxed. His long black hair spreads-out as the weak current purls around him, slowly pulling the man downstream. "Hey, you there! You okay?"

The Indian runner immediately stands in the shallow pool. He answers politely, "Yes Miss, I am fine; just taking a breather from this terrible heat. And you? Is it hot enough for you today?"

Gibbons looks across the bridge to see the Haitian runner disappear on the trail that climbs to Devil's Thumb. "Are you dropping out of the race?"

"No Miss, I need only a brief rest and then I'll be on my way. Are you a race official?"

"Yes I am. Where are you from?"

"I was born in a small village north of Delhi. You would not recognize the name."

"Oh really, try me." She observes a good-looking man with attractive dark eyes, thirty-ish, thin chin and shoulder length, wavy black hair. He seems to be in fine spirits, well educated too.

"I was born in a small town called Chamoli in the Uttaranchal region of northern India." He likes the girl who appears confident on horseback, her light brown hair neatly combed into a single pony tail. Her hazel eyes are also pleasing.

"You're right, never heard of it. But, aren't you worried about being disqualified?"

"Disqualified? For what, Miss? By the way what is your name?"

"My name's Andrea and you could be disqualified for not making the next cut-off time, er . . . number 546. And what's your name?"

"My name is Indraneil Kamath, but all my friends call me Neil." He bows respectfully to the woman, his chin touching the surface of the stream. "A pleasure to meet you, Andrea."

"Thank you, Neil. But we haven't got all day."

"Oh no Andrea, that's just the point, we do have all day . . . and all night too. And there is no person who I'd rather have accompany me to the finish line than a fine lady like you." Kamath walks to the water's edge and stands on a large boulder to dry his feet before donning his running shoes. He removes an embroidered white scarf from his neck and rings the excess water. Kamath never removes his probing eyes from the woman. He sees a broad smile and grins in return.

"Would you like a dry piece of gauze? How're your feet holding up?" Gibbons sounds genuinely concerned. She reaches into her bag and pulls out a large bandage. "This will help."

Kamath takes the cotton gauze and dries his feet, wiping any excess water from the toes. "A few blisters here and there, but nothing too serious," he mentions.

As he crosses his left leg and lifts his foot, Andrea notes a large blister on the ball between the first and second toe. "That's a nice one. You better have someone take a look at that when you get up to Devil's Thumb."

"I will take your advice, Andrea." He finishes tying his shoes. "By the way, I must be the last runner. I wonder where the leaders are."

Gibbons glances at her watch. "Well Neil, quite a few miles ahead of you. Do you think you can cover fifty more miles?"

"Oh yes. I have relations who are Sherpa. We may not be known for our speed, Andrea, but our stamina is renowned worldwide." Kamath smiles at the sexual allusion.

Gibbons ignores the final comment. Her mind has returned to the race. She looks at her watch, 3:15 . . . "The lead runners must be approaching Foresthill by now."

". . . Commie bastard." Kostinski grins, thinking of his coach's remark. He has followed the Russian into Volcano Canyon, and the two runners cross a dry creek bed and begin to climb. He recognizes the trail having trained on this section of the course two weeks earlier. The canopy of oak and pine is a welcome sight, once again providing shade. He feels some chafing under his armpits and on his nipples. "I'll grease-up at the next aid station," he contemplates. "The road should not be too far." His breathing increases to compensate for the incline.

Joshua Kostinski is well aware that no Israeli national has won an Olympic medal - ever. He has been schooled on the turbulence that Jews and more recently, Israel has endured during the twentieth century.

*   *   *

The XIth Olympiad, or the Nazi Olympics held in Berlin in 1936, had been the first time racial and religious discrimination had been used as an argument to boycott an Olympic games. German Jews as well as Gypsies had been removed from the German National Team prior to the games and a number of countries were appalled at the disparity between how athletes of Aryan descent were treated compared to non-Aryans. Many Jews attempted to form their own Jewish Athletic Associations, but ultimately were barred from competing on a national or international level. Despite the efforts of many Americans to lead a global boycott, forty-nine countries participated in the games hosted by the Nazi Party in Berlin – the largest number of nations to participate in an Olympics up to that time.

Within the American Jewish community there was mixed sentiment. Many individuals boycotted the games, others participated.

Without collective action, many American Jews decided to compete. This appeared to be the case in most industrialized nations, where men and women of Jewish faith and descent made the decision to compete or boycott depending on their own ideals and beliefs.

The Munich Olympics of 1972 are entrenched in the minds and hearts of the Israeli people. In fact, most Israelis can tell you exactly where they were and what they were doing when a group of Islamic Fundamentalists seized control of the dormitory where the Israeli national team was housed. Two Israelis were initially murdered and nine hostages were held captive until they too, were executed. Another lesson on anti-Zionism for the world to witness, their nation grieved. Unlike other terrorist acts, this horrific incident occurred during a time when goodwill is promoted, along with international harmony – the spirit of the Modern Olympic Games. The Muslim fanatics violated these sacred ethics.

Certainly, there would be retaliation, as the Israeli government would hunt down those parties responsible. The Bible quotes the Babylonian ruler Hammurabi in the book of Exodus, "An eye for an eye and a tooth for a tooth." The Israeli military and their intelligence operations, the Mossad, would seek swift and complete retribution. But unfortunately, the lives lost could never be replaced, and the scars left on the Twentieth Olympic Games would never completely vanish. Life goes on and so does the hatred between Jews and Muslims, between Israelis and Palestinians.

Kostinski and his classmates were on lunch break when their teacher requested everyone return to class. She announced that something terrible was happening in Munich, Germany - at the Olympics. All the students and faculty assembled in their small auditorium to watch the only television in the school, witnessing the drama unfold. Later that evening the carnage was revealed. An American announcer had initially declared that the hostages had been set free and then later corrected himself: A grenade had exploded inside a helicopter killing all the hostages. Snipers shot several of the terrorists killing a few and three of the assailants were taken prisoner. A botched rescue attempt had been the pitiful explanation.

Kostinski never forgot. His classmates had been competing in a school wide Olympics. He was scheduled to run the 1500 meters the following day on the school's 300 meter dirt track. The race was cancelled along with the remainder of the events.

He had always been taught to tolerate the local Palestinians, but never to trust any of them. He had little interaction with them. But for the first time, after the tragedy of the Munich Olympics, Joshua Kostinski heard a racial slur he would always remember. Not from some uneducated troglodyte he would expect, but instead, from a highly revered faculty member. After the incident, when hostility was rampant over the massacre, he overheard a conversation between the school's director and his science teacher. They were discussing security and how to prevent a similar calamity at their kibbutz. Two words concluded their short discussion: "Fucking Arabs!" For Joshua, personally, he knew well of the conflict. In fact, he had fought Palestinians in a few skirmishes during his three year stint in the military. Yet, he had never repeated those odious words. On the contrary, Kostinski learned to respect the enemy and ultimately, respect all of his opponents.

$$*\qquad\qquad*\qquad\qquad*$$

The asphalt of Bath Road is another welcome reprieve from the rugged trail. Kostinski continues to follow Boroshkov, who has not walked since the last ascent to Michigan Bluff. He finishes the last bit of the tepid liquid in his plastic bottle. Spectators have lined the road and applaud the frontrunners as they pass. Their applause sounds distant to the Israeli. His breathing labored, he struggles to maintain contact. Joshua attempts to lift his arms and knees, compensating for the pace and incline. The reigning 100 kilometer world champion appears in command and in total control of his capacities. Joshua attempts to relax taking deeper breaths and shaking his hands. He imagines reaching out to God, his hands searching for the Almighty . . . and God touches his hand, mind and soul. He closes his eyes for a moment drawing strength from the vision. But the vision is fleeting, and so his strength follows. Running nearly sixty-five miles has taken its toll. Kostinski slows to a jog and begins to walk.

"Good afternoon everybody and welcome to Foresthill – the sixty five mile checkpoint in today's race. We are here with race director Norman Sproul. Thanks for joining us again, Norm. I guess your local rock group is playing appropriate music. 'Born to Run' by Bruce Springsteen, Jackson Browne's, 'Running on Empty.' Did you help select the songs?" Brandon Davis appears cool, calm and collect, having changed into a clean white polo shirt with the network's emblem embroidered above the pocket. His light brown hair is neatly combed. He places the microphone under the chin of a man who is holding up well amidst all the trials and tribulations of directing an Olympic 100 mile endurance run.

"No, Brandon. I have little to do with the entertainment provided. I am happy to delegate all responsibilities to the captain of the aid station. He brought in the rock and roll. But I agree, the music certainly adds to the festive atmosphere." Sproul adjusts his sunglasses and then sneezes loudly. "Sorry about that. Excuse me for a second." The race director removes a red handkerchief from his back pocket and quickly blows his nose."

"Allergies Norm?"

He grimaces. "Yes, that and fatigue."

"How are the runners doing? I mean, from what I've seen everyone seems to be doing fine?"

"Well some better than others. We've had our share of casualties. Of the 162 runners who started this morning, thirty-seven have officially withdrawn. That was the last count. We are posting the DNF list on the other side of the cordoned area." He points to the opposite side of the aid station. "They'll be others."

"DNF - did not finish?"

"Correct, Brandon."

"Anyone notable you can mention?"

"Not really. All the heavy hitters are still in the running. Boroshkov and Kostinki remain one, two. Washington and Badillo are knotted in the third spot. They'll work together to catch the lead runners."

"Work together? What do mean by that?"

"Runners often 'draft' or exchange places occasionally on flat sections or gentle down-hills."

"What does that accomplish?"

"A runner who 'drafts' conserves ten to fifteen percent of his energy when he's behind a lead runner; very effective when running long distances."

"And that's legal?"

"In running, yes. In some cycling events, no."

"So what you're saying is that strategy is being implemented out there between aid stations, Norm."

"Absolutely, much strategy. What to eat and drink, and how much. Whether to run the up-hills or walk them. Whether to run aggressively or pace yourself and remain patient. There is much to think about during the run. What's really interesting is the decisions an athlete makes can cost him the race. And I'm not talking about winning, I'm talking about just finishing! Just ask the thirty-seven who are no longer running."

"Most likely we'll talk to a few of those who DNF'd later today. Anyone else in contention?"

"The Aussie, Conor and the Japanese runner are battling, plus the Italian is coming on. This is shaping up to be a great finish."

"We interviewed the Canadian, Ian Jones, the North American 100 kilometer champion earlier in the week. Do you still think he's got a chance?"

Sproul shakes his head. "I saw Ian at Michigan Bluff, and he looked like he was in a world of hurt. I doubt he'll recover."

Their interview is interrupted when the cheering crowd announces the arrival of Boroshkov. The dusty trail coming into Foresthill is a gentle downhill slope and the Russian makes the most of it. He steps on the scale and looks benignly at the attendant waiting for the approval sign to step down. When the attendant nods, Yuri moves to a chair and hands his assistant the water bottle. *Bring me orange slices and a salted potato too.*

"Immediately, Comrade. Here are water and pretzels to start."

Boroshkov sees a young woman approach with a large wet sponge, water dripping from its porous exterior. He smiles and gestures for her to give it to him. "Thank you," he replies, his heavy accent easily recognized. He shuts his eyes, squeezing the sponge above his head. The cold water re-energizes his spirit. Boroshkov bites into a potato and swallows some coke. "*I wanted electrolytes, Comrade.*"

"*That is in the bottle, Yuri. The sugar and caffeine will help you. Just trust me, alright. Do you wish to change socks?*"

"*No, I will wait until I cross the river. Remember to bring the extra pair of shoes as well. Meet me on the far side.*" They both hear applause. "*It must be the Israeli. I do not want him to see me.*" Boroshkov finishes an orange slice and gulps the last bit of coke. He sees his assistant pick up the plastic bottle.

"*I'll walk you to the exit of the aid station. Here is your bottle, Yuri. Are you ready to leave?*"

"*Yes, let's go.*" As they walk to exit the Foresthill aid station, he looks at the KGB delegate and says, "*You know that I am about to enter no man's land, Doctor.*"

"*No man's land? What do you mean, Comrade?*"

"*I have never run more than 100 kilometers in my life.*"

His advisor nods. "*Yes Yuri, I know that . . . but you have run 100,000 kilometers in your life time.*" He hopes his confidence is contagious.

"*Perhaps not quite 100,000, but close,*" Boroshkov pensively adds. Both Russians smile at the thought.

"Number 622, Yuri Bor . . ."

The advisor's voice is interrupted by the din of the crowd growing louder and louder. Hundreds of spectators are jogging to the opposite side of the Foresthill aid station. All begin to join in, adding to the raucous.

". . . USA, USA, USA, **USA, USA, USA . . .**"

"*It is the American.*" The assistant turns to find Boroshkov's eyes, but instead, sees only the back of his runner moving well over the pavement. He looks at the attendant. "Number 6 2 2 . . ." He's interrupted again, this time by a race official.

"I know, Yuri Boroshkov checked out. No worries, we got him."

Chapter 13 – Todd Valley

Clint Washington stares at his brother's nemesis, wanting her to vanish. "What the fuck are you doing here?" He eyes Nathan's ex-wife whose alluring hazel eyes, short strawberry-blond hair and taut little tits infuriate him. Clint intrinsically despises her for what she did to his younger brother. "You have no business here, woman!"

"Well isn't that just like a big brother, always protecting little brother? So, shove it up your ass, Clint. I can be anywhere I choose." She ripostes a glare of equal disdain. "We've been divorced for five years. I am sure Nathan has moved on – put our relationship behind. I said I was sorry once. I am not going to repeat an apology, especially to you!"

Washington shakes is head, points his finger and goes nose to nose. "You fucked him over once; I won't let you do that again. Not today, no way today." He sees his cousin walking over to join the argument. Spittle appears on the corner of Clint's mouth. He's as angry as a rabid dog.

"USA, USA, USA . . ." The chant is so loud; they continue to yell at one another.

"Look, Nathan is going to be here any second. He doesn't need this. Get the picture?" Washington takes a deep breath and attempts to calm himself.

"Oh yeah, I get the picture. Once again, big Clint imposing his will, always . . ."

"Don't patronize me. This is neither the time nor place." He puts his hand on Gioia's shoulder and never removes his eyes from Nathan's ex. "Deal with her would you, I've gotta grab Nate's bag."

"Hi Carol." Gioia smiles to lighten the mood. "Clint's right about one thing - this is not the time or place. Nathan's in the battle of his life. There's a lot at stake here. Can you at least give us some space . . . at least till the end of the race?" She wishes to avoid a public confrontation and looks benignly at the other woman.

They have little in common. Gioia is taller, with light brown eyes, long brown hair and is well endowed. "We just don't want any distractions . . ." She waves her hand above her head and acknowledges the boisterous crowd that has gathered. She chuckles, "Like there aren't enough distractions already."

The young woman acquiesces. "You're right Gioia, my timing could be better. I just wanted to see for myself."

Gioia thinks, "No shit, Sherlock! Your timing could be a hell of a lot better." Nathan's cousin restrains herself, not wanting to continue the discussion. "Maybe we'll see you in Auburn. Okay, Carol?"

Nathan's ex-wife does not answer. She smiles sheepishly and disappears into the flock of spectators that have gathered to see the front runners enter Foresthill.

"Christ Nate, I've run in some big races before. But, I don't ever remember seeing this many people at an aid station. What a rush! And talk about home field advantage – they love you, man." J. P. Badillo absorbs the crowd's energy, and for a moment feels no soreness, no pain.

"Hey J. P., they're cheering for you too. And you're right; this is one hell of a welcoming committee! I wonder how far we're behind."

"We got to be close. I heard one guy say five minutes and another say three. We made good time on Bath Road."

"Agreed." Washington instinctively squeezes his bottle to empty its contents into his mouth, but nothing remains.

After their steady climb up Bath Road, the two runners are on a wide trail that leads into the Foresthill aid station. Another gauntlet of humanity greets them as they proceed. Both had run the entire ascent from the bottom of Volcano Canyon to the Foresthill Divide – a road that parallels the Middle Fork of the American River. They're enjoying a gentle descent with ample shade. When Nathan Washington and Juan Pablo Badillo check in, the cheers ease to a few people yelling encouraging remarks.

"J. P., my man, you're doing so well!" Susan is all smiles when she hugs her husband. "Do you want anything?"

"*Yes, my love.*" He speaks Spanish initially, then returns to English. "Bring me a half 'p, b 'n j' sandwich, diluted coke   and two aspirin." He hands his water bottle to one volunteer, "Electrolytes please," he requests. Then the Mexican motions to another to bring a soaked sponge. "*Thanks.*" Badillo squeezes the cold water on his head and the back of his neck. "Christ, this feels great! Thanks Susan, more coke and dilute it with plenty of water." He bites into the peanut butter and jelly sandwich, and delights on some solid food.

"Yes, your highness, immediately." A wry smile follows.

The volunteer returns with his bottle. "Here you go, number 5-57. Anything else I can do for you?"

The Mexican tosses the aspirin into his mouth and takes a swig from his bottle, then grimaces. "This is way too concentrated." He pours out half the fluid. "Fill the rest with water, would you?"

The volunteer takes the bottle complying with the request.

Susan returns with two cups of diluted coke. "*How do you feel, my husband?*" She begins to massage his thighs. "How're those big strong quads holding up?"

Badillo feels the power of love when he looks at his wife, her expressive eyes still captivating. His quads are sore, but that is not his concern at this point. "What would I do without you?"

Eight years earlier she had gone to Montreal to watch her husband run, but solely as a spectator. Now she is his crew and an integral part of the race. Susan answers sarcastically, "Probably not be as much of a 'Bad Ass,' Badillo!"

J. P. nods approvingly. "So tell me pretty woman, how far is the Israeli and the Russian ahead of us?"

"Oh, I thought you'd never ask." She bats her eyelashes repeatedly and then answers seriously. "The Israeli left just as you arrived and the Russian runner – maybe four and half to five minutes before that. You and Nate have definitely made up ground." She looks over and sees Washington on his feet and delivering some last minute instructions to his crew. "Nathan looks like he's getting ready to go. Are you sure you don't want me to meet you at White Oak Flat?"

"No, let's stick to the game plan. Meet me on the other side of the river and remember, bring socks. Gotta' fly." Badillo grabs his water bottle, gives his wife a peck on the lips and walks to the west side of the aid station. He sees his friend jogging towards the check point's exit. "Hey Nate, ready to run?" He checks his watch; it's 3:20.

They depart on an asphalt street heading southwest. The gentle decline is a welcome grade. When the chant resumes, "**USA, USA, USA . . .**" their adrenaline surges and their spirits soar.

Susan tidies up before departing the aid station. She collects a few pieces of garbage and sees Nathan's crew doing the same. They meet at the same garbage can. "I guess the work never ends during one of these runs."

"Not until the finish line." Clint Washington looks at a woman with sandy blonde hair, a soiled white halter-top and tan shorts. "I think were all going to be tired when this day is done. You're J. P.'s wife, aren't you?"

"Hi, I guess I should have introduced myself earlier, but I wasn't sure if, er . . . that was okay. Any ways, my name's Susan."

"Hi, I'm Clint, this is Gioia. Nice to meet you." They exchange genial handshakes. "And yes, it's okay. Nathan has talked about your husband. I'm glad to see they're working together . . . we'll just have to see how the race plays out."

"By the way, I don't want to be forward, but I saw you arguing with a woman earlier. Is she a race official? Is there a problem?"

"She's no race official. That's for sure." Clint's voice elevates.

Gioia smiles and pulls a few strands of hair behind her ear. "That's Nathan's ex-wife. She showed up unexpectedly. We thought . . ."

"That bitch just wants to jump on the bandwagon, that's all."

"Clint, shut-up, would you? She's gone for now . . ."

"Hopefully for good!"

"Like I told you earlier, she shouldn't be a problem." Gioia sighs and then looks over to see Susan's blue eyes wide open.

"I'm sorry I didn't mean to pry into family matters . . ."

"That's just the point – she's no longer a member of our . . ."

"Clint, that's enough. I'll meet you at the car." Gioia watches her intractable, older cousin grab Nathan's bag and stomp off.

"Please forgive him, Susan, but he and Nathan are very close. I guess he harbors more anger and resentment than Nathan."

"I gathered as much."

Their discussion is interrupted by an announcement. "Two runners incoming!"

Susan looks to the east side of the checkpoint to identify her husband's closest competitors. "I wonder who it is."

"Whoever it is has certainly made up some ground since Michigan Bluff." Gioia's curiosity takes her to a vantage point where she can see the runners arrive. "Shit, it's the Japanese runner." She observes a man of smaller frame who is entering the checkpoint looking more like a man out for a Sunday jog, rather than a man who has run sixty-five miles.

"Is that the Australian behind him?" Susan remembers a navy blue uniform with stars imprinted on the singlet. The uniform is a different shade of blue. "Did he change his shirt?"

Gioia's response is immediate when she recognizes the flag on the sky blue uniform. "No, it's the Italian! Nathan told me about him. He won a European championship last year."

"I wonder what happened to the Australian."

Gioia does not bother to answer the obvious.

The Australian decided to make a pit-stop before reaching Bath Road. He had left the trail just after crossing a dry creek bed and found a tree in which to brace himself. Squatting was not the problem – standing afterwards was. The pain shot through his thighs as though someone had stabbed knives into flesh. Lower back spasms followed. He sat on his heels to stretch tightened muscles. A panic wave rushed through his body as well. David Conor has never felt this type of pain before.

How he handles the adversity will ultimately decide his fate in the event. The pain in his quadriceps does not pass. It is not a typical dull soreness; instead, it is sharp – piercing sharp and very deep. He tries to stretch his quadriceps, but more back spasms result. His body is revolting against the distance and the harsh conditions that he has endured. Conor prays, "God, just get me to the next aid station. Please, just get me to the aid station."

"What part of Germany are you from?" Conrad Creary is enjoying the company on this flat section of jeep trail leading to the drop into Volcano Canyon. He is aware that his pace has slowed considerably, yet, progress is steady.

"I am from Landshut, a small city east of Munich." Wolfgang Hafner is tired. He has run nearly 100 kilometers and feels fatigue setting in fast. Hoping to displace some of the pain and weariness with conversation, he asks, "What part of Jamaica are you from? I have never visited your country. It is a relatively small island, is it not?"

"Yes, very small - less than half the size of Cuba. I live on the north side of Kingston near a section called Barbican Heights. It is where I grew up." Creary thinks back to a small tenement with a corrugated zinc roof and outdoor plumbing. Living at poverty level by Western standards, his mother worked six days a week to put food on the table and clothes on his back. He would only see his father on weekends, since the bauxite mines are located in the country's interior. His lifestyle has significantly improved since graduating from UTEP and enlisting in the JDF as an officer. "What line of work are you in? I mean, besides running." The Jamaican squirts some cool fluid into his mouth.

"I work at a local brewery where we inspect our product before we bottle."

The Jamaican recalls the speech in the Olympic Village a week before the race. "Yah man, I remember your dissertation about the high standards of brewing beer in Germany – The Purity Laws, right?"

"Yes, the laws have been enforced for centuries and our brewery surpasses those standards, producing wheat beer of the finest quality."

"Wheat beer? Never heard of it. What's it like?"

"It is different, with particles of the hops, barley and wheat still in the beer. It is not filtered and tastes, er . . . grainy." The German wishes he could sit back on his favorite chair, kick his feet up on an ottoman and drink a cold one right now.

"Well Wolfgang, we have breweries in Jamaica, too. There's Red Stripe, our nation's lager and two stouts are produced as well: Guinness and Mackeson. We have a cliché. Drink Guinness! It's good for you."

"Yes, I have heard the slogan." Hafner does not wish to pursue this discussion any further; does not wish to have another disagreement over who brews the better beer. *"Besides,"* he thinks, *"how could any speck on a map, especially west of the prime meridian, produce any beer worth tasting?"* The West German squirts solution from his bottle into his mouth, and then changes the subject. "What is your occupation?"

151

"I am a soldier – an officer in the Jamaican Defense Force."

"A soldier? Why does a small island need a military?"

"For the same reasons a big country needs a military," Creary thinks. "What a stupid thing to ask." Then he answers, "To protect national interests."

"My father was a soldier too - a colonel of an armored column. Though, that was a long time ago."

"He was a high ranking officer – you should be proud." Creary does not associate the German's father with the Nazi Party. "I am lucky to have superiors whom have given me much latitude to train. I had hoped to return to my home seeing family and friends with an Olympic medal around my neck. To walk among them knowing I have accomplished what no Jamaican distance runner has ever accomplished before. The way I'm running right now, I'll be lucky to make it to the finish line."

"Nonsense!" Hafner recognizes that they have slowed, but not to a standstill. "We are still running. No one has passed us since the last checkpoint. I may not win a medal, but I know I can finish this race. Regardless, being an Olympian is reward enough." Wolfgang Hafner had changed his attitude on the last major climb when Pavin surged and he could not respond. He contemplates where the Italian may be.

"I like your attitude, Herr Wolfgang. Maybe, we'll go the distance together." Conrad feels the faith and makes a conscious decision to stay with the German runner.

"You mean Herr Hafner, Conrad. Herr is like mister."

"We always address friends informally in J A. Take it as a compliment. Cool runnings, my friend." Creary smiles and sees a fellow competitor nod in approval. He looks ahead and spots someone holding a red flag. "Volcano canyon, irie - the last major canyon."

The German goes first and immediately feels the heat when the canopy disappears. He swallows a large gulp of electrolytes and notes the liquid is still cool. "You are correct, this is the last canyon, but we are far from the last climb." They both look at their watch simultaneously: it's 3:30 and the temperature in the canyon is still 110 degrees.

*   *   *

Albino Pavin hopes to hear about his son's quest before the network signs-off from its Olympic coverage. The time is 12:45 AM and he is intent on remaining awake, despite the medication. *RAI Uno*, the Italian network televising the Olympic Games, is about to conclude their evening broadcast. Since his son had not been running with the leaders, the network had been broadcasting other events, only providing occasional updates on the race. He is having difficulty keeping his eyes open.

Liliana hears her husband snore. *"Albino, come to bed. You are so tired you cannot even keep your eyes open."* Pavin's wife, a woman in her mid-fifties, is concerned that her husband will over-stress his body. The chemotherapy had been taxing enough earlier in the week. Now her husband appears gaunt and totally fatigued. She reflects, *"If the cancer does not completely ravage his body, the drugs certainly will."*

"I know Mamma, the program is almost over. Last I heard, Lamo was in eighth place. He is moving up. I just want to hear the latest news of the race." The elder Pavin rubs his forehead. He is sitting on his favorite reclining chair, legs prone. *"God has blessed me in one way and condemned me in another."* He shakes his head trying to find solace in the fact that at least he is still alive. *"You know six months ago when the doctors diagnosed my cancer, I prayed that I would be alive this day . . . and God has at least granted me that. But nevertheless, I should be there. Life can be so unfair."*

"I know Albino, but that is life. I am thankful that you are alive . . . not to watch Lamo run, but to witness the development of all your children. You must rest now." She too, prays the cancer does not consume her husband – that he lives to a ripe old age. *"Please come to bed now."*

"In a moment, the telecast is almost finished."

In a moment, the elder Pavin begins to snore again. His wife takes a light blanket to cover him. She shakes her head and kisses her husband on the forehead. *"Please God, do not take this one yet. He is impossible to live with, but he would be impossible to live without."* She hears the announcer refer to the 100 mile race.

"We have an update on the race across the mountains. Girolamo Pavin has arrived at the 105 kilometer checkpoint in sixth place, running

153

with a Japanese competitor. They still have over fifty-five kilometers remaining." A video clip of Okuda and Pavin entering the Foresthill aid station is broadcast. "*The Russian, Boroshkov, appears to have taken the lead . . .*"

Liliana Pavin looks at her husband and decides not to wake him. She walks closer to the television set and begins to pray. "*And please, Mother of God, watch over that one too. "Hail Mary, full of grace, the Lord is with thee . . .*"

The two runners exemplify fluency in motion. The Italian is five centimeters taller than the Japanese runner. There are subtle differences in their style and cadence. Regardless, they are moving well over a groomed trail west of Foresthill. Both are veterans of distance running and recognize their pace of four minutes per kilometer. Every five minutes, one slows and allows the other to pass. They are working together, drafting which improves efficiency and their overall time. Perspiration soaks their bodies' head to toe as the two breathe heavily to compensate for their solid pace.

The Italian does not veer from the trail to urinate. Since the trail offers privacy, there is no need to leave the trail to find vegetation. Girolamo Pavin slows, then withdraws his genitals from the inner lining of his shorts and while continuing, relieves himself. He notes his urine is pale in color and concludes that he is drinking enough fluids. Many runners utilize this same strategy to save valuable time. He looks at his watch. It is almost four o'clock when Pavin contemplates, "*The temperature must still be over forty Celsius.*" He drinks from his bottle, swallowing a healthy portion and then accelerates in front of the man from Japan, taking his turn to break the wind for the other runner. When he passes Okuda he glances at the Asian runner and observes only stoicism. Pavin predicts, "*We will have an opportunity to test one another later . . . when we challenge each other for the lead.*"

"Well Norm, it looks like we have ourselves a close race. Less than thirty-five miles to go and six runners are within fifteen minutes of each other. Any predictions?" Brandon Davis savors the moment. A competitive race, plus the network's broadcasts have generated much national interest. Ratings are rocketing.

"Anyone of those top men can win. Since they're all experienced distance runners, the race may come down to who has the best day or more precisely, who has the best finish." Sproul removes his sunglasses. "Once again, I will reiterate, Washington knows this course better than anyone. Home field advantage could definitely have an impact on today's competition. As we witnessed earlier, the crowd's behind him all the way."

Davis nods in agreement. "Is there anyone who can come from behind and catch the leaders? Possibly one of the Africans?"

"That's always a possibility. But with the way the frontrunners are moving, it will take a monumental effort to overtake them. As for Ethiopia," Sproul clears his throat, "the runner, not the country; he ran valiantly for forty plus miles, but has dropped back considerably." The race director looks at the entrance to the Foresthill aid station, then at his watch. Live music is still playing; however, there is a lull in the action. "Apparently, we have a bit of a gap."

"Where does the course go after Foresthill? I know they are running southwest to Auburn, but can you briefly explain what lies ahead for our intrepid Olympians?"

Norman Sproul contemplates the question literally . . . then, allegorically. "The next aid station's near an open space called Todd Valley. That's about five miles from here. Five miles after that is the checkpoint at White Oak Flat; then comes the river crossing at about eighty miles. No bridge there, they'll have to ford the river on their own." He anticipates the announcement of another runner arriving, but only sees people dancing to rock music. "Actually, the course gets much easier once the runners leave this checkpoint. It's generally all downhill until the river crossing at Ruck-a-Chucky."

"Ruck-a-Chucky?" Davis smirks. "What kind of name is that?"

"Just a name given to a location near the river with lots of big rocks surrounding the site where they'll cross. I'm not sure of its origin. But more importantly, you asked, what lies ahead for those runners who have braved some of the harshest conditions nature can throw at them . . ."

"I'm sorry, Norm, but what do you mean by 'it's all downhill from here to the river?'" Davis wants the race director to elaborate on the course before the philosophy lesson commences.

"There are no major climbs for the next fifteen miles. The trail has a good surface – not as rocky . . ."

"What about Ruck-a-Chucky?" Davis laughs. "I'm sorry Norm, but the name is amusing."

"Right Brandon, very amusing. As I mentioned before, the course does get easier, but their task will become more painstakingly difficult. Any person who runs sixty-five miles feels the adverse effects. The altitude, the heat, the distance . . . will test their resolve and stamina beyond comprehension, especially with those who have never run 100 miles before."

"Do you know any other competitors who have completed a race of this distance besides Washington?"

"Several. The Mexican, Badillo, won the Angeles Crest 100 Mile Endurance Run last year. He's running with Nathan as we speak." The race director pauses for a moment. "That should be an interesting battle down the stretch . . . a battle among friends. Oh yeah, the other American in the race won the Old Dominion 100 Mile Endurance Run last year as well."

"In Virginia, right? What's his current standing?"

"He's a non-factor at this point. The Old Dominion is an East Coast version of our race. The course circumnavigates a portion of the Shenandoah Valley . . ."

"No one else, Norm?"

"I think the Jamaican, Creary, ran Old Dominion too, but I'm not sure where he finished."

Brandon Davis hears the music abruptly change. "I recognize this song. Men at Work's, 'Down Under.'"

"Men at Work?" Sproul is confused, never having heard the song before.

"I have heard some Australians say the song is so popular, it just may become their next national anthem." Davis chuckles at his own prediction.

The camera focuses on an incoming runner who is hobbling into the aid station. David Conor smiles and waves, appreciative of the welcome. The music sends goose bumps down his spine. The applause echoes through the small foothill community as he proceeds to a scale to be weighed and checked-in. An attendant with pretty green eyes assists him off the scale. Annette Edwards recognizes a man she had met while working the Duncan Canyon aid station earlier that morning. She looks at his wristband. "Your weight's good. Anything I can get you, number 511." She offers the runner a seat near a table with food and drink.

"Yes, you can get me a new pair of legs – these are thrashed." Conor rubs his thighs and shakes his head. "I'm bloody well spent!"

"You're doing great, Mr. Conor! Here, drink this. Can I get you something to eat?" Annie sees a man approaching with a drop bag.

"Hey buddy, how're you doing?" David's American friend is genuinely concerned. "You didn't look so good coming in. What happened?"

Conor looks at the waist of the woman who's assisting. "That's a nice belt buckle you're sporting there, Sheila. You win it?"

Edwards smiles proudly. "Oh yeah, I won this one last year." She ignores the name thinking the Aussie is too fatigued to know whom he is addressing.

"This one? You mean, you have others?"

"Only one other. I have finished this race three times. I did not break twenty-four hours on my first attempt."

"Well then . . . er, what did you say your name is?" Conor sees an opportunity to draw from experience.

"I didn't. My name is Annette Edwards, not Sheila."

"Okay, Annette. Sorry about the name, no insult intended. What do you recommend as a remedy for these aching legs?"

"You need salt and lots of fluids. Let me get you a salted potato with some electrolytes. Have you taken any aspirin today? It's worked miracles for me!"

Conor motions to his friend. "You heard the lady, be a good bloke and fetch me some provender and grog."

157

"Yes, Herr Doctor." His friend snaps his heels together, then salutes. "Listen shit head, get some food in your gut before taking the aspirin."

"No worries Mate, I will."

Edwards laughs at the exchange. "Are you really a doctor?"

"Yes, a cardio-pulmonary physiologist."

"Then, why do you ask me what you obviously already know?"

"In case you haven't noticed, I'm in trouble. I have thirty-five miles remaining and if I can glean some information from you that is helpful, then I will take the fullest advantage. Since you've run these distances before, 'obviously' you've been in dire straits before. Is there another suggestion you can give me?" Conor bites into the potato and simultaneously chugs a cup of electrolytes.

"Yeah, in fact, there is, but you don't want to hear it." Edwards looks empathetically into the blue eyes of the Australian.

"Oh yeah, try me, Annette."

"Slow down, Doctor Conor, simply slow down."

David Conor smiles and looks at his watch. "Shit," he mutters, "it's after four." He bites into the other half of the vegemite sandwich, then swallows some diluted coke. The Aussie looks up and makes eye contact with the young woman. "I'm afraid, that's not an option." He looks at his crew and requests three aspirin. "I will not be here much longer."

Near the base of Volcano Canyon, in a dry creek bed, Ian Jones sits on a large rock wondering if he can continue. Dizziness has persisted since Michigan Bluff. Last week during one of his many training runs, the climb up Bath Road presented no difficulty. Today, the molehill looks more like a mountain with its pinnacle far from view. His water bottle has little fluid when he considers the necessity to move on.

"For God's sake," the Canadian contemplates, "I can't stay in this hell hole forever."

Only the trees and rocks hear his doubt. A searing breeze sways the treetops.

"I can make it to the next check point. I am not a cripple for Christ's sake," he insists. The Canadian has not prayed in quite some time, but contemplates that prayer certainly would not hurt. He thinks of a quote from the Bible to give him strength. "Though I walk through the valley of death, I fear no evil for you are by my side with your rod and staff, give me courage . . ." Jones cannot recall the entire passage, so he thinks about a parody of the scripture instead. "Though I walk through the valley of death I fear no evil, 'cause I'm the baddest mother fucker in the valley." On that note, he stands and begins to walk up the gentle grade. He removes the cap form his water bottle and finishes its contents, tilting his head back to get every drop. He ponders, "The power of prayer . . ." Then after a hundred meters his head begins to spin again, and another runner passes.

Juan Pablo Chacarito Badillo sets his coffee eyes on the man dead ahead. "Hey Nate, we're about to catch another runner – it must be the Israeli." Dry weeds slap against his legs. Star thistle spines puncture his skin near his ankles and shins, but he hardly notices. His sights are set upon the back of a competitor who is fast approaching. He breathes deeply, working harder to catch the front runners.

Nathan Washington does not bother to look up, concentrating on the trail and his next foot strike. "How far is he ahead?"

"Less than 100 yards." He sees the man in a white uniform disappear into a stand of evergreens. *How are you feeling, friend?*"

Once again J. P.'s Spanish breaks up the monotony of the trail. Nathan smiles inwardly. "Doing fine considering, we've been running for over ten hours."

"Doesn't time pass quick when you're having fun."

"That's right, Badillo, capital F U N!" Washington chuckles.

The Mexican tries not to think about the Russian who remains out of sight. He squirts some electrolytes into his mouth ignoring the sharp pain in his left knee. "Did you take some drugs back at Foresthill?"

"*Yes Mister*, only the finest recreational pharmaceuticals from your side of the border." The American laughs at the sound of his own accent.

"Very funny, Nate. '*Yes Mister*,' you sound like one of those stupid gringos who come into my restaurant trying to order their meals in Spanish. I cannot tell you how foolish they sound." The Mexican reflects upon a joke he heard a while back. "Hey Nate, what do you call a person who speaks three languages fluently?"

"Oh no . . . here we go again, another 'Bad Ass' joke."

"Just humor me Nathan."

"Okay, J. P., you tell me. What do you call a person who speaks three languages?"

"Trilingual. What do you call a person who speaks two languages?"

"Er . . . bilingual, I guess."

"Very good. And a person who speaks only one language?"

"Hmmm . . . monolingual?"

"No, nice try – an American!" The Mexican snickers, knowing he has caught his friend off guard.

"Which reminds me . . ." Nathan pauses for a moment. "Is your wife fluent?"

"No, not fluent, but she speaks very well. In fact, it was her Spanish that brought us together at the community college I went to in Southern California many years ago. She was a tutor in the ESL program."

*   *   *

Growing up in a small village in Northern Mexico taught Juan-Pablo Chacarito Badillo about the importance of family and community. He remembers working with his father on their modest ranch and farm, plus helping his mother around the house on occasion. Chacarito Badillo knows his roots and is proud of his heritage. His family's village is situated amidst the mountainous terrain of the Sierra Madre in the state of Chihuahua, where his ancestors, the Tarahumaru, have lived for centuries. Running has been part of the Tarahumara culture and lore since time recorded. They run to travel, run to communicate, run for enjoyment and run to compete. Stories of men chasing deer or horses to exhaustion are common among the tribes. Like the east Africans, running is in their blood. The Tarahumara prefer a more traditional name, calling the men of their people the Raramuri – the ones who run.

An American who was visiting the region studying the language and local customs of his tribe discovered Badillo and his innate talent. The

160

man convinced Juan-Pablo to move to Los Angeles and enroll at a local college. Since he had an uncle living in East Los Angeles, the decision to move there and enroll at Pasadena City College was made easier. Three years later he completed a liberal arts course of study, simultaneously learning the English language. His English, like his running, excelled.

During that time a young woman was completing her own course of study in Castilian Spanish. Susan met J. P., innocently enough, while gaining practical experience – teaching English as a Second Language at the college. She was fond of this man from the onset, whom appeared more Native American than Mexican.

The transition to a world class runner came after college. Juan-Pablo joined an enclave designed to help Spanish speaking Americans continue their training after college. In fact, Badillo liked the title of his club – Aztlan. He won several road races culminating in a third place finish in the Los Angeles City Marathon. A year later, he finished the Olympic Marathon in Montreal. It was somewhat of a disappointment, finishing seven minutes and more than a mile and a half behind the leaders.

After the Montreal games, Badillo retired in anonymity. Except for the photographs hanging in the restaurant, or a few of the more precious awards he has not tucked away in a closet, no one would ever suspect this mild mannered Native Mexican to be a fierce competitor. Later, when he heard about the Western States Trail Run, J. P. thought, "One more race, one more chance."

The Mexican enters the Todd Valley aid station first. The American is right on his heels. There is no crowd, no crew, no television cameras. The Israeli is seated on a chair, a cup of liquid in his left hand and breathing heavily. His face is without expression.

"What can I get you guys?" A young woman smiles at Badillo first, then at Washington.

Washington already has an orange slice in his mouth. He swallows the pulp and juice, spitting out the rind. "Fill it with electrolytes, please." He hands the attendant a bottle, then shoves a few pretzels in his mouth.

"Do you have any aspirin?" J. P. feels an ache in his left knee, and prays the aspirin will quell the soreness, reduce the swelling.

"You okay, J. P.? Didn't you take aspirin at Foresthill?"

Badillo lies, not wanting to bring attention to the injury. "No, with all the commotion, I forgot." When the attendant hands him a full water bottle he asks, "When did the Russian leave?"

"I'm not sure. It wasn't too . . ."

Another woman who is recording bib numbers interrupts, "Five minutes ago. Are you guys ready?" She records their bib numbers, plus the time of departure of the second and third place runners: 4:15.

Nathan snaps back, "You bet! We're out o' here." He grabs his water bottle and takes a last look at the Israeli. "Thanks much, see you in Auburn."

"Christ Nate! Did you see the look on that guy's face? I don't think we have to worry about him."

Nathan Washington shakes his head. "I just pray we don't end up like him. By the way J. P., what's an ESL program?"

"Come on Nate, get with the 'program.' ESL – English as a Second Language."

Chapter 14 – White Oak Flat

The section of trail passing through Todd Valley is flat, mostly open, but with the occasional stand of secondary growth. Temperatures have finally dipped below the century mark and under the canopy, the column of mercury does not reach ninety-five. Runners have an opportunity to make good time through this section . . . that is if they have the legs to take advantage of the easier conditions.

The Israeli continues to sip on fluids, seated under a large Ponderosa Pine. Joshua Kostinski bites into a peanut butter, jelly sandwich and then washes it down with coke. He chews slowly, methodically, appearing to savor each bite. "I kept the demons at bay for as long as I could," he thinks.

An attendant interrupts his thoughts. "How's that taste, number 5 4 8? Anything else I can get? Just let me know." The young woman smiles.

"Please, call me Josh. No thanks, I'm good for now." He reaches for his water bottle and swallows some of its contents. "I will not be here too much longer." He takes another deep breath. "I just needed to take a break. How far have we run?"

"Seventy miles, I think. You've been running for over ten hours. I can't imagine running that far . . . you guys are amazing!"

Kostinski offers gratitude for the comment, then adds, "My coach once told me if you can imagine, then you can accomplish. All you have to do is believe."

"And Josh, do you believe you can still win this race?" The attendant, a woman in her mid-twenties, looks directly into the lethargic eyes of a man who appears utterly exhausted. A man with an oblong chin, dark matted hair, sable eyes and a three-day beard stares back.

"Maybe not win, but certainly finish." Kostinski stands to gather himself before proceeding. "Top the bottle with electrolytes, please." The brownies look appealing, so he grabs one and before biting into the chewy morsel, he smiles at the young woman. "Number 5 4 8 checking out," and repeats the words he has often heard today, "See you in Auburn."

Thirty miles ago at Duncan Canyon, he was pleading with his athlete to stay with the front runners – even challenge them. Now at Michigan Bluff, he is pleading with his runner to stay in the race. Xian Doi of the People's Republic of China has overheated. He feels nauseous and dizzy. No food or drink appeals to him. He is shaking his head, wanting to withdraw from the competition. Simply put, he's had enough.

"*I know you will regret quitting if you stop, Xian. You must continue.*" Doi's coach sees fatigue in the eyes of his pupil, but he does not see exhaustion. "*You have worked much too hard to end your journey here . . . at a place where you do not belong. You belong at the finish line with those who cross it. You deserve much more than this. Try to drink and eat something. You will feel better if you do.*"

"*I am not hungry, Coach. I feel like throwing-up.*" Doi puts his face down ashamed of what he has become. His pace has been reduced to a crawl. That, coupled with the number of runners who have passed him, has completely shaken his confidence. Sweat drips from his nose. He looks at his coach searching for an answer. "*I do not think I can continue.*"

The coach looks at his watch. "*You have run over ninety kilometers in a time of ten and one-half hours. Seventy kilometers remain, and you have over thirteen hours to complete the run. Xian, you need only to run five and one-half kilometers an hour – the pace of a snail! Take some time to collect yourself. Here, drink this. It will settle your stomach.*" He hands his charge a cup of herbal tea, then opens a container of rice spiced with soy and ginger.

His stomach accepts the offering of the tea; its soothing effect readily felt. Doi watches his coach pour another cup from a full thermos. "*Thank you, Coach. This is much better than the vile liquids I have had today.*" He sips the tepid brew. "*My legs actually feel fine considering the distance and terrain. Maybe some food would be good.*"

"*This is a simple dish. You will feel better. Try some.*" The coach hands Xian the bowl with a pair of chopsticks.

Doi puts his face into the bowl and scoops a portion of the rice into his mouth. The salty taste agrees with his palate. "*Perhaps you are right, Coach; the finish line is where I belong.*"

The coach thinks of an old Chinese proverb. Rephrasing the words into current application he adds, "*Xian, you have sown the seed, placed the first brick and taken the first step. You only need to complete the journey to fulfill your destiny.*"

Xian Doi stops chewing momentarily and nods in agreement.

The tissue is swollen and inflamed. Engorged with blood and lymph, the anklebones cannot be seen under the distended skin. Klaus Frey grimaces as his coach pokes and prods the joint. "*I can give you something for the pain. Do you wish to continue?*"

"*What do you think? I have been running, albeit much slower than before.*" He looks into his coach's eyes searching for a solution to the problem. Frey trusts the judgment of his mentor.

A young man returns his water bottle filled with electrolytes. Both acknowledge the effort. There is much commotion surrounding Michigan Bluff as runners continue to enter and exit the aid station.

"*You are limping noticeably. If you had ten kilometers to reach the finish line, I would say that you are foolish not to finish. However, with seventy kilometers remaining, you are foolish to continue. Why risk further injury? There will be other races.*"

"*There is something special about this race, Coach. Perhaps it is the camaraderie or accomplishing what few people thought possible. Perhaps, it is just plain pig-headed stubbornness. I want to continue.*"

"*You said the Italian gave you Motrin, correct?*"

"*Yes, that is what he told me.*"

"*Are you sure the pills were Motrin?*"

"*He had no reason to lie to me. Stop being so cynical.*"

The coach removes a vial from his bag. "*You will need to eat something before you take this.*" He places a large white pill in Frey's hand.

"*This is much larger than the other two I took. What is it?*"

"*Motrin, eight hundred milligrams. This should reduce some of the soreness. Let me get you something to eat.*"

Before the coach turns his back to go to the food table, Klaus asks. "*Are you sure this is Motrin?*"

The East German coach sardonically smiles. "*Now who is being cynical?*"

He hands Klaus a plate of food and examines his athlete's left ankle again. *"You know there could be a fracture. You know that you will encounter much tribulation attempting to finish this race."*

"I know Coach. But isn't that what life is all about – enduring the struggle? In fact, isn't that what you have taught me about running and how it pertains to life. I cannot let this opportunity pass." He drops his eyes to the pill in his hand and hopes for the best.

"Do not take it yet. I will be back shortly. They have boiled some potatoes. I will bring you a small portion."

As Klaus Frey chews on a salted potato, his coach tightly wraps an elastic ace bandage around the injury. *"This should keep the swelling under control . . . for a time. Do not remove it."* The coach loosens the shoelace, replaces his shoe and then tightens the lace accordingly to the larger fit. *"There is no disgrace not finishing, especially given your present condition."*

Frey pushes on the armrests and stands carefully. *"How long until the medication takes effect?"*

"Fifteen to twenty minutes. Be sure to keep drinking, since the dosage can cause dehydration."

The East German smirks, *"You mean like today's heat can cause dehydration?"* He sees his coach laugh. *"I know there is no disgrace in not finishing, but I have come too far to quit here."* He begins to walk toward the exit of the aid station and sips from his water bottle. By-standers applaud. An attendant records his bib number and for the moment, Klaus Frey forgets the pain and begins to jog.

The American is pushing the pace. Nathan Washington continues to run aggressively, trying to catch the Russian and challenge for the lead. Badillo had stopped to go to the bathroom; said he would catch up before the next aid station. When Washington arrives at the wide dirt road that leads to White Oak Flat, he sees the lead runner for the first time. The other competitor is about three hundred yards ahead, kicking-up wisps of fine powder with each step.

Spectators who have lined the road applaud and shout, "Looking great, Nate . . . You've got him . . . He's fading fast . . ."

Washington no longer listens to the encouraging remarks. Instead, his focus circles like a bulls-eye on the back of the Soviet runner who continues to run this section. Regardless, he's gaining ground.

There are no cars permitted on the dirt road leading to White Oak Flat. The race committee did not want vehicular traffic impeding the progress of the runners, nor did the idea of runners breathing excess dust generated by cars sound particularly appetizing. The sun is beginning its decline towards the western horizon, but the ambient temperature still remains ninety-five degrees. There are no trees. Both runners carry bottles empty of fluids. Their shoes and socks are covered with rusty trail dust – their uniforms filthy from dirt, grime and sweat. Neither cares about self-image, despite the fact that they have become the focal points of the race. Their hearts and souls continue to pour forth as they proceed along the Western States Trail. There is still over twenty-five miles to run.

"Incoming runner," the attendant calls-out. "Number 622, Yuri Boroshkov. Welcome to White Oak Flat. What can I get you?"

The Russian hands his bottle to a svelte, elderly man wearing a visor and sunglasses. "Electrolytes, please." Boroshkov looks at his shoes and sees moisture seeping through. His feet are very sore and he hopes the moisture is sweat, not blood. Regardless, a few blisters or sore muscles will not deter him, no matter how invasive they become. The man from Leningrad has experienced this type of pain – numerous times. He bites into an orange slice, swallows the pulp and juice, then tosses a couple of pretzels into his mouth. Yuri grabs two cups of water pouring one into a cup of coke to dilute and with the other he dowses his head. He sees a sign that is posted and asks the man, his heavy accent prevalent. "Three marathons down, one to go? What does this mean?"

The old man points at the sign and translates slowly and loudly. "This means, you have run three marathons and you have only one marathon left to run. Do you understand?" The attendant attempts to assist to the best of his ability.

Boroshkov responds, "Yes, thank you. I have run 120 kilometers and I have forty-two remaining." He adds in Russian, *"I may not understand your popular language, but I am certainly not deaf!*" He glances at his watch – it is a quarter before five.

"Yes, er . . . that is correct. I am sorry. I do not speak Russian."

"That is okay. I do not speak English very well." Yuri senses a runner approaching and reaches for one last morsel before departing – a homemade chocolate chip cookie. He takes his leave with a full bottle in hand.

Another attendant announces the arrival of the second place runner. The Soviet runner hears the name and turns to see a man on a mission. A stern look combined with the runner's fu man chu embody an intensity Boroshkov has not observed today. At such a close distance the red letters U S A are clearly legible on the soiled gray uniform. Boroshkov reflects as he begins to run, "*Well Nathan Washington . . . it is about time - I have been waiting for you.*"

Chapter 15 - The River Crossing

Ian Jones steps out of the SAG wagon into the blistering sun. He adjusts his cap to shield his eyes. A white van that was used to transport supplies to an aid station is now used to ferry runners who can no longer continue. Jones has officially withdrawn from the race. A television camera captures the dejected face of a beaten athlete. A microphone immediately confronts the Canadian who spots his wife, and only wishing to be consoled, motions for her to come over.

"Ian can we get a brief statement from you?" Davis bears witness to a man who appears utterly depleted, with eyes recessed deep in their sockets, stooped posture and a grimace, indicating an aching body.

Jones sees his drop bag in Genevieve's hand and concludes she has not heard the disappointing news. "Brandon, give me a moment please." He looks at his wife, smiles meekly and then adds, "Hi Gen, we will no longer need the drop bag."

She observes his wristband has been removed and a uniform with bib number soiled with a rusty powder – the same color as the dirt surrounding Foresthill. "What happened, Ian?"

Brandon Davis glances at his watch and interrupts politely. "Ian, we must depart for the Ruck-a-Chucky checkpoint promptly." He avoids laughing at the comical sound of the name. "Can you give us a brief summary as to why you've dropped-out?"

Spectators have surrounded the camera and crew.

"Sure Brandon," he replies discontentedly. He watches his wife drop the canvas bag she had carefully prepared. A large red maple leaf is visible on it. Jones feels her embrace and then looks into ebony eyes that fill with tears. He has never DNF'd in a major competition before, and the emotional wounds are as apparent as the physical exhaustion. "I'm okay, Gen. Just wasn't my day." Ian kisses Gen's cheek.

Davis glances over to the man behind the camera and points at the couple. The despair on the man's face is visceral, and not wishing to miss an opportunity, he begins the brief exchange. "We're here with Ian Jones at the Foresthill checkpoint. The North American 100 kilometer champion, one of the favorites in today's competition, has withdrawn from the race. Can you tell us what went wrong since Michigan Bluff?"

His left arm rests comfortably on Genevieve's shoulder. He feels her support – both physical and emotional. "In one word Brandon, heat." He looks upward at a cloudless blue sky. An attendant hands him a cold bottle of flavored seltzer water. He takes a long drink and wipes the excess from his lips. "Thanks. You guys have been great today." He returns his attention to Davis. "The heat was overwhelming."

"What exactly, were you experiencing, Ian?"

"Dizziness mostly. It seemed like every time I got going, my head would spin. I stopped a number of times trying to collect myself, but after a few minutes of running, the dizziness would return. In fact, when I reached the bottom of Volcano Canyon and attempted to walk the climb to this checkpoint, even an ambulatory pace created problems for me. I realized I could not continue."

"Well, you're not alone. The DNF number is almost fifty. Ian, one more question; do you think you'll return here and try this race again?"

The Canadian removes his white cap into which his nation's emblem is embroidered. Scratching his head he chuckles cynically. "This is not the best time to ask that particular question, Brandon. I think I've had enough of the Western States Trail for a time."

Genevieve returns a kiss and simultaneously wipes a tear from her own cheek. "Oh, we'll be back here again. I know my husband well, and I am certain he will wish to correct what went wrong today." Embracing the man she loves, Gen repeats, "He'll be back – I know that for sure."

"Howdy Chad, how're we doing?" Norman Sproul appears content and confident that his race is going as planned. Many runners have since passed the checkpoint, the American appears poised to battle the Russian, and the race has not encountered any major catastrophes. Everything looks as if the race is going as planned. "Are you all right?" He recognizes the face of a concerned physician. The two men are standing under a portable canopy located in the middle of the Foresthill checkpoint.

"I'm fine, Norm . . . but it's the one hundred 'n ten runners left in the race I'm worried about. It's only five o'clock and we've already lost a third of the field. Christ, this could result in the worst finishing percentage in the history of Western States."

"Listen Doc, this is not June. Temperatures are the worst that runners have ever encountered in the history of the race. Everyone is accounted for and most runners are making steady progress. Temperatures are on the decline - the worst is over so to speak. We anticipated a high DNF rate, Chad. Given the conditions, it's expected. No one has been hospitalized . . ."

Dr. Logan smirks, "No Norm, not yet, but the evening's still young."

For many runners, their situation has deteriorated. Most are relegated to walking the ascents, have slowed their pace considerably on the flats and descents, and stopping at the aid stations for extended periods has become the norm. Many ask the same questions:

"How far until the next aid station?"

"How far have I run?"

"Should I continue?"

"What am I doing here?"

Many have lost confidence.

On the other hand, when the participants arrive at the aid stations, volunteers greet them offering emotional support. The assistance helps the runners immensely, enabling them to continue after a brief rest. These same volunteers have worked the Western States Trail Run before and have seen the worst a race of this distance can cause. All are genuinely concerned for the runners' welfare and give of themselves selflessly. One underlying theme at Western States is: Without volunteers, there is no Olympic 100 Mile Endurance Run.

Klaus Frey is in the rear seat of another SAG wagon, left leg elevated. Elastic wraps hold two plastic ice bags firmly in place around his ankle. Teeth clenched, he is in obvious pain. The medic who accompanies him has never seen an ankle as swollen as Frey's. His lower appendage looks more like a case of Elephantiasis than a severely sprained ankle. Unfortunately, the East German speaks virtually no English and consequently, there is no communication between the two individuals.

"Hey Doc, you better take a look at this." The nurse, a man in his early thirties, is another veteran of Western States. He looks worried.

Chad Logan walks over to the van and sticks his head in. The swelling is so bad the toes look more like little knobs than digits. "What the hell did you do to that foot of yours?" Logan decides not to remove the ice bags. "Do you speak English, number 5 3 7?"

"I am sorry." Frey shakes his head and speaks German. "*Where is my coach? I need to speak to him immediately.*"

"Find me a German translator, stat!"

"Okay Chad, right away." The medic departs to a location where a number of volunteers await instructions. "We need someone who speaks German . . . in a hurry. It's an emergency."

A young woman speaks up promptly. "Yes, I speak German. What can I do?"

The medic points to the white van. "Please go over and assist the Doctor. A runner is injured and we have no idea what he's saying."

She jogs over to the van. "Hi, my name is Katherine. What can I do?"

Logan skips the formalities, but notices a younger woman with sandy blonde hair, high cheek bones and a figure just as appealing under a white blouse. Her snug black shorts accentuate her slender figure. "Ask him what he did to that foot."

"*Good afternoon.*" The translator begins with the appropriate salutation. "*What is your name?*"

The beauty of the young woman initially surprises Frey. "*Ah . . . Frey, I mean, Klaus. Are you German or American?*"

"*I am German, born in Stuttgart. But the good Doctor has not requested that I come here for us to become acquainted.*"

"*I would love to visit Bavaria – Stuttgart in particular, perhaps to purchase a Mercedes or Porsche.*" Frey forces a weak smile and looks over at the doctor. The physician appears quite concerned.

Logan recognizes the words, then interrupts. "What are you two talking about?"

She smiles at the doctor revealing a small gap between her two front teeth that adds a unique flavor to her visage. "Give me a chance, Doctor."

Logan pleads, "Er . . . Katherine, please ask about the foot at once."

"*The doctor is very concerned with your left foot. What happened?*"

Wishing to impress the young lady Frey answers, "*Tell the Doctor that it looks worse than it is. It is only a sprain. I will be fine, I am certain. Please have someone find my coach and bring him here.*"

Katherine points at his foot. "*Mister Frey, that looks much worse than a sprain.* Um, Doctor . . ."

"My name's Logan."

"Well Dr. Logan, he says it's only a sprain and he wishes to speak to his coach."

The medic speaks up. "I'll see if I can find him."

"Put an announcement over the P. A. system," Logan suggests, then returns his attention to the translator. "Ask if he has taken any medication today."

The translator follows his instructions. "He says he has only taken Motrin for the swelling . . . to reduce inflammation and soreness."

Logan scratches his chin and shakes his head in disbelief. "Ask again and impress upon him the need to tell the truth."

After a short discussion Katherine replies, "He insists he is telling the truth. Why would he lie, Doctor? What do you think is wrong?"

The Chief Medical Director does not respond. He knows there is a blood clot somewhere near his ankle and surgery will be necessary to restore the circulation that has obviously become impaired. Logan has also read about the side affects of anti-anemia medication and knowing which type of medication will be instrumental in the treatment of the clot.

Frey's coach arrives and inquires without emotion, without concern, "*Good afternoon; where is my athlete?*"

"Do you speak English?" Logan leers at the coach wanting some direct answers.

"No, I am sorry. I speak very little English. Is there a problem?"

The translator intervenes. "*The doctor is concerned that Klaus has taken something that has caused his ankle to look like that.*" She points at the left foot of Frey.

173

"*Nonsense. It is only a bad sprain . . . I will give him a healthy dosage of Motrin. I can take care of my athlete now. We have our own physician. Klaus, can you walk with me to our vehicle?*" The coach remains stoic.

"Katherine, what did he say? Ask the coach if he has given his athlete any medication today . . . or over the past month." Logan persists knowing that anti-anemia medication must be taken for long periods of time, if it is to have the satisfactory result of incrementing red blood cell counts.

"Chad, I already asked. The coach assured me that the ankle is only a bad sprain and that he only gave Klaus Motrin at the last checkpoint. He's definitely upholding party-policy. He wants to take him to their team's physician."

"Bullshit! This guy needs surgery and he needs it now. We're taking 'Klaus' to a hospital. Explain to the coach, he is welcome to accompany his athlete. The closest hospital is a thirty minute drive from here."

Logan looks at the young woman. "Katherine, you got all that?"

"Yes, um . . . I will translate . . ."

As she translates, the Doctor looks at the driver of the SAG wagon. "Take him to emergency. I will call ahead and notify them that you're coming."

He looks at the coach who disagrees with the decision, shaking his head. "Katherine, tell that fool this is not open for discussion. Tell 'coach' to get in the van. You better go too, just in case your services are required at the hospital."

"Certainly, Dr. Logan . . . What do you think the problem is?"

"Do you know the translation for blood clot or thrombus?" He looks at the East German coach again, then towards the front of the van. "Drive safe," he exclaims, then closes the door behind the passengers.

*   *   *

And a river runs through it . . . Natural springs combine with snowmelt to cascade water from the peaks of the Sierras to the lowlands of the Sacramento and San Joaquin Valleys. The American River and its tributaries have carved the canyons in this region on the western slope of the Sierra Nevada for millions of years. Dams have impeded the river's progress, but its waters remain ever present, ever flowing. Whether Native American, gold miner or recreational fisherman, the river has provided valuable resources for centuries. The Western States Trail follows its serpentine path, crosses its banks and continues westward to the Sierra's foothills. If Cougar Rock represents the flagship mark of the Western States Trail, then without doubt, the American River wholly defines the trail itself, and ultimately the race run upon it. Runners, like the flowing water, continue to move steadily southwest, albeit, some faster than others.

Twenty-five miles separate the two lead runners from the last two. Each pair approaches a river crossing. The Russian and the American descend on switchbacks toward the major checkpoint at Ruck-a-Chucky, and the Haitian and the Indian are about to arrive at the bridge that crosses El Dorado Creek midway between Devil's Thumb and Michigan Bluff. Their paces are indicative of their positions. The front runners are running at 6:30 per mile pace on their decent. The runners in the rear plod along three minutes per mile slower. Regardless, all make steady progress. Each tempts fate by pressing their respective paces to attain their ultimate goal – to reach the finish line. The time is 5:15 post-meridian and 100 runners separate the aforementioned four individuals.

"I have been following the progress of this race since its start at six AM this morning. A shotgun blast sent 162 Olympians on a journey of a lifetime – a race of 100 miles across the Sierra Nevada. Good evening everybody, my name is Brandon Davis and if you have not been following this ground breaking event, I will update their situation . . ."

Davis speaks enthusiastically knowing the transmission is reaching East Coast viewers during a prime time slot. A day that began with an above average audience has soared to an Olympic following. People from all over the country are calling to inquire and comment about the race:

"Is this really possible?"

"This must be a bike race, right?"

"How can human beings run 100 miles?"

"The race must be a multi-day event with different stages like the Tour de France, right?"

"I have trouble driving my car 100 miles."

"No way! This must be some kind of hoax."

"Who are you guys trying to bull $#@*, any ways?"

Regardless of the color commentary elicited by the audience, there is a heightened interest - a fascination clearly evident by the viewers who have tuned-in to Olympic coverage.

Davis continues his report, "Presently, we have a battle of the Cold War raging on. Nathan Washington, a native Northern Californian finally caught the Russian runner, Yuri Boroshkov, just after the seventy-five mile checkpoint. Boroshkov is well known in the circle of ultramarathoning, having won the 100 kilometer world championship last year. Washington, a two-time winner of the 100 mile race held on this same course, is currently challenging the leader. Capitalist versus Communist. The big red machine against the red, white and blue of Uncle Sam. This could develop into quite a confrontation by race's end.

"Behind them is a Mexican runner, Juan-Pablo Chacarito Badillo, a resident of Reno, Nevada who knows the trail well too. In close pursuit is an Israeli runner, Joshua Kostinski who actually led the race at one time. And there are two athletes who have gained quite a bit of ground over the last fifteen miles; an Italian who is the European 100 kilometer champion, Girolamo Pavin, and from the island of Hokkaido, Japan, Akira Okuda. Our latest communication from the previous checkpoint at White Oak Flat reveals that less than fifteen minutes separate the top six places. Stay tuned, as we'll bring you more coverage of the race, plus, a candid interview with the top American in the race."

The American River surges behind Brandon Davis as he reports live from Ruck-a-Chucky. Runners refer to the checkpoint by its more appropriate sobriquet – the River Crossing. Since there is no bridge, the runners must ford the current with only the aid of a guide rope tethered to two vehicles on opposite sides of the river. The Plimsouls' rock song, "A Million Miles Away," blares from portable speakers. Fifty volunteers, plus hundreds of spectators await the arrival of the front runners. Large granite boulders are readily visible on the banks of the river . . . and the sun has dipped behind the canyon's walls. Temperatures will finally begin to cool.

"Nathan Washington is a runner in the purest sense. Some people run to live – that is to improve their fitness and health. Nathan Washington is not one of those. He lives to run. Running is in his nature, part of who he is and what he is all about. I had the opportunity to speak candidly with one of America's finest distance runners, and his insight into endurance running is not only engaging it's downright illuminating." Brandon Davis nods at his production engineer to role the clip.

"Nathan, how many people have told you that you're crazy, even insane to run 100 mile endurance runs?" Davis shakes his head in disbelief at such a preposterous notion – running 100 miles.

The two men are seated under a large lodge pole pine at the Squaw Valley ski resort. The reporter looks at a man with thick reddish-brown hair who is clean shaven, except for the mustache. The man has a pug nose, though not flattened like a boxer, an angular chin with a slight dimple and innocent blue eyes. His face reveals a boyish charm, especially when he chuckles.

"Fewer now, than before. Initially, everyone thought I was nuts. Even my college coach, who I still remain in contact with, tried to convince me not to run distances longer than a marathon. But what I've discovered is that over the past three or four years, more people are becoming acquainted with the sport of ultrarunning and no longer consider having me committed to an asylum." A nervous chuckle follows. "What I'm saying is . . . it's doable, given certain parameters, the most important being preparation." Nathan feels somewhat anxious since he has never received national press coverage before, and the man conducting the interview is somewhat of a celebrity, having covered sporting events worldwide.

"We spoke to the Canadian, Ian Jones earlier in the week about his preparation. Do you think your preparation is much different than his?"

"No, my training is not unlike Jones'. We probably share many of the same techniques and strategies. Certainly, there are subtle differences."

"Name one."

The American clears his throat. "I swim and sometimes, even fly."

"Fly?"

"My senior year at Humboldt, I was diagnosed with a 'possible' stress fracture in my right tibia, er . . . I mean shin. So my coach had me cut my weekly mileage way back. Instead of running, I would swim - and I mean I swam a lot." Washington pauses, biting his lip.

Davis suddenly senses sadness in the persona of the man he is interviewing. "Please continue, Nathan."

"My ex-wife was a member of the swim team – one of the better swimmers in the conference. That's how we first met." Washington slouches a bit and rubs his index finger and thumb through his mustache.

"Sore subject?"

"Not really, it's been several years since . . . Well, she taught me many things and unfortunately, not all good, but she did teach me the butterfly stroke and to this day, I still do swim workouts as part of my cross training."

"So that's what you mean by 'fly,' right?" He sees Washington nodding, but his eyes clearly lack focus. "Nathan, why do you run?"

The runner smiles. "For the longest time I ran because I was good at it. Maybe not great, but certainly competitive. Lately, it seems, running has become therapeutic. It's really helped me overcome personal adversity."

"Your divorce?"

"Yeah, that and my Dad's death a few years ago."

Davis is surprised by the man's candor. He's an open book ready for publication. "You and your father were close?"

"My father was a good man – a real gentleman. Oh, he had is problems just like anyone else, but a good man nonetheless. I guess we were as close as anyone might expect. I miss him."

"Did your father run?"

Washington chortles. "No way. In fact I remember the first time I told Dad I was going to run Western States, he laughed and said, 'Whatever makes you happy, son.'"

"So what possesses you now, in this particular event? What drives you, Nathan?"

"Running makes me feel good, Brandon. I don't think my day would be complete without it. I like fighting fires, and I do get personal satisfaction from my work. But running sets me free, takes me to a better place – a runner's high so to speak."

"Yes, I've heard of that. Some people equate the affects of long distance running with prolong drug use; that running can become habit forming or even addictive."

"Yeah, I've read an article or two that suggest endorphins produced in the base of the brain can induce feelings of euphoria. Whether that's a type of addiction is debatable. But I will say that when I'm running, the sky appears a bit bluer, trees are greener and my whole outlook on life is much improved. And that's better than any recreational drug can provide."

"What do you hope to accomplish running 100 miles in these Olympic Games?"

"Certainly, I want to win. When Shorter won the '72 Olympic marathon in Munich, he changed the face of running in this country forever. Bill Rogers, with his wins at Boston and New York, has added zest to a nation caught up in the running boom. A gold medal here, on this course, in these Olympics, would have a similar affect on the sport of ultra-marathoning. Ultimately, I think we all want to make a difference in the world we live in. I guess this would be my contribution."

"And if you don't win?"

"I think the publicity of this Olympic race will help greatly, regardless of my place or time. Nevertheless, I remain optimistic."

"And what do you think your chances are?"

Washington rubs his fingers through his mustache again. "Winning or just finishing?"

"I know you understand the gist of my question, Nathan." Davis smiles.

"My chances are good - very good. I did a workout a couple of weeks ago that indicates I'm in the best shape of my life. All I need is God to grant me a good day . . ." The American ponders further before disclosing, "and if He condemns me . . . well, I'll just have to deal with the pain." He follows the thought with more laughter.

"What's so funny, Nathan?"

"Nothing really, just thinking about all the things that can happen running 100 miles on dirt."

"Okay, so what's the workout you referred to?"

"I ran eight repeat miles all under 4:50 with five minutes rest between each interval, and I did the workout here in Tahoe at altitude. 72's on the track, like clockwork."

"I'm sorry, Nathan, but what do you mean by '72's?'"

I ran each lap at seventy-two seconds or better for each of the repeat miles. Trust me. It's a tough workout."

"No doubt." He reaches over to shake Washington's hand. "You're a remarkable man. Thanks for taking the time . . ."

The American grabs the rope with his right hand to level himself before entering the river. Washington is totally oblivious to the hooting and hollering of all the spectators who have hiked down to the River Crossing to see the progress of the front runners. The Russian is five meters in front, in waist deep water – his white uniform soiled from kicking-up eighty miles of trail dust. He had attempted to surge past Boroshkov on three different occasions. But the Russian returned the salvos with surges of his own. The American remains in second place.

He sees Boroshkov dip his white cap into the river and pour its contents on his bald head, then replace it. Washington dips his head into the current and then throws his head back releasing a plume of water. The cold liquid provides a welcome reprieve from the heat of a long day. The water tastes salty - his perspiration mixing with the river's clear fluid. He stumbles on the rocky bottom, then recovers quickly, the rope giving ample support. The river is swift, but manageable. He crosses without incident.

Washington exhales deeply as he walks up the embankment. "Hey Clint, what's happening?"

"Glad to see you finally caught the Commie bastard. How're you holding up? What can I get you?" He pats his younger brother's back.

Washington sits in one of the portable chairs and quickly removes a shoe, then the sock. "Two cups coke, two cups electrolytes and dilute everything. Shit, nice blisters."

"You want me to get someone to look at that?"

"Nah, fuck it. Twenty miles to go, I'll just deal with it."

"Is it bleeding?" Clint is concerned. He sees skin that has obviously been chafed to the point of disfigurement.

Washington laughs. "No, not yet." He replaces the soaked sock with a clean dry one.

"I'll be back in a minute, Nate."

Gioia is all smiles. She drapes a cold wet towel over his shoulders. "You sure have gotten your share of sun today."

"That's an understatement. Am I sunburned?"

"Not too bad." She removes the towel and rubs aloe moisturizing lotion onto her cousin's shoulders.

"Christ that feels good, Gioia. I think I'm in for a real dogfight with that guy over there." He motions in the direction of the Russian, who appears to be changing shoes, then takes a healthy bite into an energy bar.

"Do you think you can beat him, Nathan?"

"I don't know." As he bends to tie his shoes, stomach muscles tighten. Washington quickly sits upright and messages an abdominal cramp. "At times I feel like he's just toying with me – that he'll drop me at any time."

"Bullshit Nate. You can take him." Clint hands his brother a cup of diluted coke. "This is your course – your race." Then he adds with his best French accent, "Twenty miles to go and voila, zee gold medal iz yours."

"Clint, you gotta promise me one thing; either stop talking like that, or take some lessons!" He swallows another cup of fluids and looks at the Russian. Boroshkov's blue eyes appear galvanized as he prepares for the assault of another climb.

The Russian looks to his left and sees the jeep trail leading upward from the river. The next climb is two hundred fifty meters vertical over a distance of three kilometers. *"He has pressed the pace since he caught me. No question, he is a worthy opponent."* Boroshkov looks over to see the Americans chuckling. *"They all have a good disposition. Who is with him?"*

"What do you care, Yuri?" His advisor wishes to disregard the question.

"*I am curious, that is all. He appears to have surrounded himself with good people.*" Boroshkov bites into a banana.

"*I think that is his brother. I am not sure who the woman is.*"

"*That would be nice, Doctor; to have my brother here. He would be of immense help, immense importance. I wish he was here, that is if he were alive . . .*"

*　　　*　　　*

Yuri Boroshkov had lost his brother three years earlier – a victim of an outdated medical system. One night his brother had been admitted to the hospital with excruciating abdominal pains – torsion of the small bowel had been the official diagnosis. Surgery was required to correct the problem. The surgery corrected the problem, but unfortunately created another life threatening complication. Sepsis was what the attending physician called it and initially, the doctor sounded optimistic. "*We will need to cycle your brother on antibiotics. The medication should control the spread of the infection.*"

"*What infection?*" Boroshkov demanded to know.

The attending physician, an infectious disease specialist, explained. "*Sometimes bacteria can infect the area where surgery has taken place, especially at the site of the intestine. The intestine harbors numerous strains of gut flora and some can infect a wound. However, the antibiotics should remedy the problem.*"

The medication had no such effect. Since the bacteria were resistant to the antibiotics being administered, a high fever persisted. Another surgery followed to find an abscess located somewhere in his brother's abdominal cavity, but the procedure was to no avail. The infection continued to spread, first to adjacent tissues, then to vital organs. In two weeks his brother was dead from "complications" brought on by his twisted gut. He had lost someone very close to him – someone whom he often confided his most profound secrets. Boroshkov and his family grieved. His brother was twenty-six, and like Yuri, he was a runner.

"Thirty kilometers remaining, Comrade. The longer he stays with you, the more confidence he will gain. I do not think you want this race to finish with a sprint, do you?"

Boroshkov bites into a salted potato and then swallows the remaining contents in his cup. *"I am sorry Doctor, what did you say?"*

"Yuri, where the hell is your mind? Concentrate! Your brother is gone, but I know he would want you to win this race. The American is weak – nothing more than a spineless capitalist. Thirty kilometers to run and you will join an elite group of Soviet athletes who have won Olympic gold medals. Do not disappoint the Party or your country."

Boroshkov does not reply. He swallows some fluids from his bottle to wash down the potato. Standing to begin the ascent of another canyon he mutters inaudibly, *"The American may be a capitalist, but he certainly has a spine . . . or he would not be here with me."*

"Twenty miles to go Nate. You can beat this guy. This is your turf, your course, your race. Don't deny yourself this opportunity. This is your destiny Bro; I can feel it!" Clint has become animated in his methods to motivate his younger brother.

"I know Clint, but I don't think I have ever run against a man of his caliber . . ."

"And he's never run against a man of your caliber, Nathan." Gioia intervenes, handing her cousin a full bottle of fluids. She offers a confident smile. "You can win this race, Cuz."

"Thanks guys. I'll see you at Highway Forty-Nine." Washington sees Boroshkov take three steps, then he immediately begins to jog the ascent. Once again, he follows the leader, matching the Russian stride for stride. Nathan winces, feeling the skin of his blistered feet shift. His quadriceps and lower back have tightened as well. Spectators applaud. The sound of the river begins to fade. The American thinks, "Contact at all cost."

Across the river two runners are arriving simultaneously as the two leaders depart. Juan-Pablo Chacarito Badillo limps noticeably. The Israeli steps off the scale first. His weight is fine. After a long descent to the

River Crossing, their pulse and breathing have slowed accordingly. "Juan-Pablo, I'll see you on the other side, okay?"

"Thanks Joshua, I hope so."

Badillo mutters a loose translation, *"A bad fuckin' wheel."*

The Mexican had heard Americans use the phrase to describe a variety of running injuries pertaining to a limb. He sits on one of the portable chairs under a nylon canopy. The ambient temperature is much cooler here.

A nurse examines his left knee. "You have some swelling on your lateral excruciate. How painful is it?"

Badillo is in his own world contemplating the inevitable. The aspirin has had little affect on the soreness or the swelling. The descents had been particularly difficult with much acute pain - like a large needle that punctures deep into flesh.

"You do speak English, don't you?" The woman had overheard the brief exchange of the two runners at the scales. When the nurse applies moderate pressure to the outside of his knee, the Mexican immediately reacts.

"Christ yes, I can speak English! Take it easy on the knee." Badillo shakes his head. He looks at the portly, middle-aged woman and asks, "Is there anything you can give me? I really want to continue."

"We're only allowed to give aspirin or ibuprofen. What have you been taking today?" She straightens Badillo's left leg and gently messages the swollen area. The injury is common among distance runners.

"Just aspirin. What do you think my chances are?"

"That depends on the extent of the injury and how much pain you can deal with. Can you walk on it?"

"The pain isn't too bad when I'm walking, but the down-hills are a killer."

"Well number 557, with twenty miles to go, I think that answers your question. Do you want me to bring you some ice or aspirin?"

"Nah, that's okay, my wife's on the other side." Badillo stands and takes one long breath. Muscles have stiffened considerably and in particular, rigor mortis has set-in between his shoulder blades. He glances at his watch before gripping the rope with his right hand. It's 6:00. "Eighty miles in twelve hours - not bad."

184

An attendant speaks loudly above the rushing water of the Middle Fork of the American River. "I'm sorry, did you say something?"

"Incoming runners!" The public address system blares. Both men turn simultaneously and see two men run the last switchback before arriving to the checkpoint.

He sees Susan waiting patiently on the other side. She looks concerned. The Israeli is standing ready to depart, his coach offering words of encouragement, no doubt. The Mexican yells, "I said eighty miles in twelve hours is a good time." He steps into the river and steadies himself, the cool water inviting after a long day in the sun. He doffs his cap into the swift water and pours its contents over his jet black hair. Juan-Pablo inhales deeply, closes his eyes momentarily and prays for salvation.

The attendant nods approvingly. "An excellent time! Good luck number 557."

"*Thank you, my friend.*" He offers a left-handed salute.

The two men seated in portable chairs change their socks. They eat and drink to replenish what nature has taken. Like their countries on a globe, they sit opposite one another. They have little in common, except for the passion that drives them and this race that enthralls them. They request basically the same things, ask the same questions. One speaks Japanese, the other Italian. While many runners have melted under the day's scorching sun, Akira Okuda and Girolamo Pavin have shined through. They are on the brink of moving into medal contention.

Their coaches attempt to deliver exhortations that will inspire their athletes beyond anything they have personally experienced. Initially, both comment, "*Relax, stay within yourself. Stay focused.*" However, since neither coach has ever run this far in one day, they are at a loss for words. Each one stares at his protégé, proud of what his runner has accomplished thus far, and astounded at what he has endured. And each coach ponders, "*Thirty kilometers remain to fulfill a destiny – coaching an Olympic champion.*"

The two competitors echo their replies and comments to their respective coaches. "*Do not preoccupy yourself, Maestro. I am focused.*" Pavin smiles and looks at Sabrina who is placing a wet towel on his shoulders. He pauses briefly to kiss his fiancée's hand.

"*Master, I am relaxed and running well within myself.*" Okuda quaffs a cup of electrolytes and then bites into a piece of melon, delighting in its juicy sweetness. "*The Italian is a good running companion. We have worked together and continue to make good progress. How far are the front runners ahead of me?*"

"*Less than ten minutes. Excellent!*" The Italian feels confident. "*We have cut their lead in half. I saw the Mexican leave. He was walking.*"

"*What about the Israeli? Was he walking too?*" The Japanese runner ties his shoes; the dry socks feel good against chafed skin. "*The American and the Russian were both running the incline? Then I will do the same.*"

The two depart the river within seconds of one another and within seconds both are breathing heavily. Pavin allows Okuda to take the initial lead, then promptly closes the gap. The two mile climb is another formidable obstacle the two men negotiate. The higher they climb, the warmer the temperature becomes. Within five minutes the sun's oblique rays shine upon them and they pass the Mexican, who appears to be hobbling. There is no exchange of words or gestures.

When they reach the Green Gate, an ovation welcomes them to another trailhead, which leads to the Auburn Lakes checkpoint, less than four miles distant. Then, after a few minutes on a flat, single track trail, the Israeli steps aside allowing the challengers to pass. The two are running well, averaging four minutes, twenty seconds per kilometer on this section. Both are positive they will soon catch the leaders. "*It's only a matter of time and distance,*" each man thinks.

Eammon Horgan struggles to keep contact with another runner. Every time a runner passes, he attempts to match an opponent's pace. But within a minute or two, the runner pulls ahead and leaves Horgan walking, gasping for air. He is approaching exhaustion and with over thirty miles of trail remaining his confidence, once again, is shaken. He is jog-walking with a Yugoslavian athlete who speaks little English. Their dialogue is limited as they walk together for a brief encounter.

"Dusan Majic, my name is." The man from Croatia is taller with a muscular frame. He has light brown hair and dark eyes. "Pleasant to meet you, Eammon. Where do you live?"

"Nice to meet you, too. I'm from Ireland." Horgan replies not knowing the extent of Majic's vocabulary.

Majic smiles and points at the shamrock on the Irishman's uniform. "I know your country. Where in Ireland?"

"Oh, I'm sorry. I'm from Cork, in the south."

"Everything is green, yes?"

Horgan grins. "Yes, everything is green. And where is your home, Dusan?"

Majic begins to jog. "My home is near Dubrovnik on the Dalmatian Coast. You must come visit. The sea is beautiful. I like to bathe and swim there."

Horgan thinks, "You look more like a swimmer than a runner." He holds his comment, concentrating on the increased pace. He sucks air deep into his belly. "I got to stay with this guy . . . at least till the next checkpoint."

But the Todd Valley checkpoint is nowhere in sight and consequently, Eammon Horgan begins to fade – again. The Slavic runner leaves him walking in the dust, his legs slapping against star thistle that line the trail.

Chapter 16 – Auburn Lake Trails

Far away on a plateau in East Africa, above the Red Sea, a young man carefully adjusts the frequency of his shortwave band radio. It's a Grundig receiver of the best quality. The national television station broadcast in their regional capitol of Asmara had concluded its broadcast hours earlier, and after a short nap, Zechariah Ethiopia is trying to ascertain the whereabouts of his brother. He glances at the simple clock, the only adornment of an entire wall, and notices the time is nearly five AM. Zechariah Ethiopia had learned from earlier reports that his brother, who had been winning the race through fifty kilometers, had begun to fade after eighty. He commented to his parents before they went to bed, "*I am worried about Yosef. We have not heard anything in a long time. I hope all is well with him.*"

Even from ten thousand miles, Zechariah can feel the presence of his brother's spirit, and what he feels is not good. He attempts to locate the broadcast band of the BBC radio network. "*God almighty, he has run for twelve and a half hours. I pray that he is fine and running well.*" Ethiopia sighs, "*160 kilometers, what was my brother thinking?*"

His Coptic beliefs assert that he prays to God directly. The Ethiopian's belief in their Orthodox faith is absolute, the Son of God being mere incarnation of the one true God. He prays in the regional language of Tigrinya.

"*Please God watch over him and guide him, give him strength beyond measure and grant peace unto his body and soul where ever . . . There it is; I have found it.*" The glass face of the radio reflects a near perfect, mirror image of his brother's face. Yosef and Zechariah Ethiopia are identical twins. They have grown up together, knowing each other's thoughts without speaking a word. To say the least, they are close, as only identical twins can be. His English is limited, but he understands names and numbers without problem. Listening attentively to the BBC, Zechariah notices his reflection on the glass of the tuner. He sees his brother's face . . . something is not right.

Sweat drips from his nose, breathing labored. Salts have crystallized on his orange national uniform, and dirt has stained it. Yosef Ethiopia forces a bite of banana down his throat, then almost wretches it back up. He has reached deep into his reservoir of talent and ability and now finds only nausea and pain. Exhaustion is imminent. The East African from Eritrea had run the five plus miles from Todd Valley to White Oak Flat, without walking a step. He has second thoughts about continuing.

An older gentleman with thinning, gray hair hands him a full water bottle. "Just as you requested, mostly electrolytes with some water. Anything else I can do for you, number 542?" The man's demeanor is upbeat.

His face drawn and gaunt, Ethiopia rubs his forehead with thin fingers, searching for a solution. "I do not feel well. What can I do to feel better, Sir?"

Seeing the ashen face of a runner in trouble the attendant contemplates, "The first of many . . ." Then he asks, "What do you expect number 5-42? You've run seventy-five miles. Do you really think anyone feels good after running three marathons? What is your name?"

He takes a long drink from the refilled bottle. "Yosef Ethiopia." The beverage stays down.

"Yeah Ethiopia, I remember now. You're the guy who showed up at Robinson Flat, er, bare footed. You were winning for a while, right?"

"I am no longer in that envious position." Ethiopia thinks about how good he felt early on, and how much his race has changed over the past four hours.

"No, but you can finish this race, if you want to. Yosef, when was the last time you ate some solid food? I mean besides a slice of banana."

"This morning I ate two pancakes before the race started."

"Shit, you haven't ate nothing solid all day?"

"No, I did eat a couple of pancakes before . . ."

The race attendant sees a look of confusion. "I mean during the race, Yosef! What have you eaten during the race?"

"My coach thought it best that I drink only liquids during the race and avoid solid foods that would upset my stomach."

"Let me bring you something. Don't go away."

The man from Ethiopia mutters aloud in his native dialect of Tigrinya, *"Where can I go? I am utterly exhausted and I have no clue where I am."*

"Here, eat this. It'll do you some good. And wash it down with this. This'll get you jump started – for sure." The attendant hands Ethiopia half a peanut butter and jelly sandwich, and a cup of diluted coke.

"What do you mean . . . uh, 'jump started,' Sir?"

"It'll give you some energy. Believe me, you'll feel better." The attendant avoids adding, "That is, as long as you don't throw it back-up."

Ethiopia, nonetheless, remains discouraged. Runners continue to pass through the White Oak Flat checkpoint barely slowing a step. "When did the first runner pass through?"

The attendant looks at his watch. "Over an hour ago, Yosef." The man pauses, then adds, "I doubt you'll be on the medal stand tomorrow. But you can finish this run. Are you feeling a little better?" He sees the younger man has regained some of his ebony complexion.

"Yes Sir, I am. Thank you. Is there anything else you can recommend?"

"Yeah, in fact there is. Take these." The attendant takes two white pills from a medicine dispenser and hands Yosef the medication with a chocolate chip cookie. "And one more thing, slow down. Conserve some energy. I know you can make it to the finish line."

"What are these, Sir?" Yosef decides to stand. He reads assurance in the eyes of the elder attendant.

"Aspirin and a homemade chocolate chip cookie my wife made yesterday. Believe me, that little morsel will give you some get up and go!"

"Get up and go," Ethiopia ponders. *"These Americans are full of aphorisms, not to mention horse manure as well."* He laughs at the thought.

"That's the spirit Yosef, glad to see you're feeling better. Number 542 checking out," he yells to another attendant recording bib numbers. "See you in Auburn."

Ethiopia recognizes the name of the city tantamount to the finish line and responds, *"Yes my friend, see you in Auburn."*

190

The Aussie looks over toward the Ethiopian and sees him grab a water bottle to continue his quest. For David Conor the race has come to inexplicable halt. He pours water over his head and feels the cool liquid drip between his shoulder blades, then shakes the excess from his dirty blond hair – even dirtier from the trail dust that coats the individual strands.

"Well number 511, what else can I get for you? You've been here a while." An attendant hands Conor a full bottle of fluids.

Conor shrugs his shoulders and laughs. "A new pair of legs would certainly help, and since we have become intimately familiar with one another, please call me Dave."

"Okay Dave, what's wrong? What can I do?" The attendant, a woman in her mid-thirties, appears genuinely concerned. "Your weight's fine. You look like you have all your faculties together. Er, I mean at least you're coherent."

"My quads are spent. The pain is excruciating even when I'm walking. And the thought of another descent into a river's canyon sounds about as appealing as shoving a couple of stilettos into my thighs." Conor continues to shake his head in disbelief and mumbles, "I cannot believe this has happened."

"Dave the heat has been relentless. Almost half the field has already DNF'd. You're not alone." She rubs his left quadriceps gently.

The Australian cracks a half-smile. "Thanks for the discouragement."

"Have you tried massaging your legs?"

"At Foresthill."

"Aspirin?"

"Six in the last four hours."

The attendant shifts to his right leg. "Have you drunk enough fluids?" She knows if he hasn't, then it's too late to begin now.

"Gallons." Conor rubs his temples with both hands. He looks despondent. "There's nothing else for me to do."

"Hey, David W. Conor, how're you doing mate?"

David looks up and sees his compatriot looking fresh and jolly-good. "Well Lindsey T. Eagle, I was wondering when you were going to catch me. I was getting bored waiting for you. You having a good day?"

"Could be better. And since when do you deserve the royal treatment, Doctor?" Eagle eyes the woman rubbing Conor's thigh while handing his water bottle to another attendant.

"Comes with the price of admission, I gather."

Both men chuckle. Conor groans and almost leaps from the chair when the attendant strikes a nerve with her thumb. "Sorry Dave, I'll try to be more careful." The attendant reduces pressure on the muscle.

"No worries, Sheil, um . . . I'm sorry, you didn't tell me your name."

"Margaret, but all my friends call me Peg."

Conor looks earnestly at the attendant. "Well Peg, regardless of what happens to me, the support personnel in this race have been unbelievable - unparalleled to any race I've ever run." He sees the woman smile.

"So get off your arse Conor, time to roll. Let's get on with it and stop all this lollygagging about." Eagle shoves a cookie in his mouth and guzzles a last cup of fluids before his departure.

"Linds, I'm afraid I'm going to be here awhile. You'll have to carry the torch for the both of us."

"Hell, carry a torch I will not! Too bloody hot for that, mate; I'll carry the Southern Cross instead." Eagle pulls on his soiled, navy blue singlet. He looks into the eyes of a fellow countryman and thinks, "I've seen that forlorn face before – his day is done." The Aussie casually salutes his team mate and declares, "Number 512 checking-out." He turns to begin his decent into the American River Canyon.

David Conor looks down at the woman kneading his muscles methodically, attempting to relieve what only time can. He touches her hand gently. "Margaret, I've had enough."

"But I'm not finished. Let me . . ."

Conor interrupts, a furrow forming above his brow. "But I am. My race is finished." He holds up his left hand with the medical wristlet. Dr. David Conor takes in a big gulp of air. "Please remove it."

"Are you sure David? There's a lot of time remaining. You can . . ."

Eyes moisten. The Australian feels a warm soughing breeze come up the canyon wall. He tucks a lock of dirty blond hair behind his right ear. Pinching his dimpled chin with his thumb and fore finger, Conor contemplates, "Six months training lost, an Olympic opportunity blown." The Aussie sucks in another deep breath and looks into the eyes of the woman directly in front of him. Relinquishing his participation he sighs, "Just cut the damn thing off."

His tone is decisive, just like his words.

"Good evening everyone and welcome to the Ruck-a-Chucky River Crossing. I'm Brandon Davis." Once again the reporter is right on cue to begin another live remote broadcast after what has been a long, extraordinary day. A spotlight shines, illuminating his face against the twilight's shadows as dusk approaches. His ebullience and energy manifest a personality that appears right for the task. "It's just after seven o'clock and the race leaders are approaching the eighty-five mile check point at Auburn Lake Trails. The American and the Russian still lead, however, according to our latest report, the Italian, Girolamo Pavin and the Japanese runner, Akira Okuda are gaining ground. As you can see behind me, there is still a great deal of activity as runners continue to cross the river."

The camera pans a view of the scene. Two runners are visible holding the anchored rope as they ford the river. An athlete is sitting on the far side changing shoes and socks. Another individual is beginning the climb toward the Green Gate. And when the camera returns to the smiling face of Davis, he announces, "Pavin and Okuda have cut the lead to less than five minutes." He pauses for a moment. The track "King of Pain," recorded by The Police, can be heard above the sound of rushing water. Davis clears his throat and then continues. "The Japanese and the Italian are the antithesis of one another. We have edited some footage that we feel demonstrate the cultural and personal diversity that exists between two world class athletes that happen to be running together at the same time and in the same place." Davis nods at the program engineer to roll another video clip.

The man's slanted eyes appear calm and resolute. There is an unmistakable tranquility in his demeanor. Through an interpreter he responds to Davis' question. *"Running has brought depth and meaning to my life.*" The Japanese runner collects his thoughts. "*My life is like a book - each word a second, each sentence a minute or an hour; each chapter, a time in my life - perhaps an accomplishment, perhaps a failure.*"

The interpreter pauses to reflect on Akira Okuda's personal commentary. "I have learned much through success and failure – never celebrating too long in victory, nor dwelling on defeat. Running encapsulates my life, with crests and troughs; the pages of my book are written, and my life unveils new discovery. These Olympic Games represent a chapter in my life. An Olympics that will no doubt enrich my life – an experience I will take with me forever, win or lose."

Okuda pauses for a moment and glances at his coach. "*I am honored to be a participant, honored to represent my coach and honored to represent my country.*" The Japanese runner lowers his eyes and bows in deference to his mentor.

The other man's brown eyes are oval, confident and affable. He holds his fiancée's hand and answers the same question much differently. "*The reason why I run? That is an easy question. I am good at it.*" Girolamo Pavin smiles at his fiancée, then pecks her on the lips. "*God has given me a special ability – the ability to run longer and harder than anyone in the world. And naturally, yes, I believe I can win.*"

The interpreter grins and then continues the translation. "What is the cliché I have heard before? Yes, second place, is that not the first loser?" All chuckle at the comment. "Regardless of whether I win or lose, there will be other things in my life. I plan to marry . . ."

He kisses Sabrina again.

"My profession? I plan to open a pharmacy near my home in Torino. No doubt, I will continue to run. Whether or not I continue to compete at an elite level, only God knows that." The Italian contemplates the next question. "My coach? He makes me atone for my sins."

The winsome brunette offers a swift prod to his ribs. "*What sins do you refer to my dear?*"

Pavin laughs. "*He has been a good influence to me. I listen to him, but ultimately, I do what works best for me. Sometimes he becomes frustrated when I decide not to follow his instructions about training or diet. I understand his frustration, but I am a grown man and not a child anymore.*"

Davis asks, "Please Girolamo, could you be more specific about diet, since we have heard much about training already?"

Pavin waits for the translation and then answers, "*According to my coach I should eat so many grams of protein, so many grams of complex carbohydrates, so many grams of simple sugars, so many grams of fat, etc., etc., every day.*" He snickers adding, "*According to my mother, I should just eat, stop.*"

Davis inquires, "Stop? What do you mean by that?"

The translator replies, "I am sorry, I mean period. According to my mother I should just eat, period."

Davis chuckles at the interpreter's translation, and after examining the svelte runner he responds, "Tell Girolamo I agree with his mother."

The Japanese runner offers a different testimony.

"*I trust my coach completely and follow his orders explicitly, without question. I am the apprentice in the sport of running, he is the master.*"

The interpreter continues the translation. "I have much to learn. He has been very patient with my steady progress. You ask me about diet. I have followed a strict diet monitoring my protein and carbohydrate intake. I eat very little fat. I know there is fat in the fish I eat and we cook our vegetables in oil. Sweets are a rare treat. Does that answer your questions, Mr. Davis?" The translator bows his head forward in another gesture of respect.

"Yes, thoroughly. Akira, you have spoken much about running and diet. What about other aspects of your life - professional, personal?"

Okuda articulates, "*There will be time for those other, um . . . distractions later in my life. I have immersed myself in my master's training regimen and I have learned to live in the present. The past is a fleeting memory, Mr. Davis and the future unknown. It is best to live in the here and now. Yes, the Latin phrase sums-up my thoughts best - Carpe diem.*"

"Seize the moment." Brandon Davis nods in approval.

Davis looks at the Italian and scratches his forehead. "I mean why a hundred miles, why not the marathon or ten k?"

The interpreter parrots the question.

Pavin's fiancée giggles. "*He's crazy; we all know that.*" She brushes his hand with her soft lips and gazes at her man with much affection.

Pavin appears serious for the first time in the interview. "*In French I have heard a phrase, 'Ne plus ultra' or nothing better or the best. I believe this race will bring out the best in me . . . hopefully, not the worst.*" He listens to the translation.

"It is difficult for me to explain, except that I believe I am here for a reason: to attempt something beyond what I thought incomprehensible or even possible, and as I said before, I have arrived to win."

"Well I certainly understand the incomprehensible part, Mr. Pavin." Brandon Davis sees that the Italian exudes confidence. There is passion in his countenance. "And one more question, Girolamo. What has been your most difficult workout in preparing for this race?"

The Italian listens to the interpreter and responds without hesitation. "*The metric pyramid workouts are the most demanding.*"

Davis looks quizzically at Pavin. "What's a metric pyramid?"

The Italian's handsome face smiles into the camera. "*Let me explain. There are two parts to a pyramid: one, going up the pyramid and two, going down the pyramid. After a warm-up, I go up the pyramid. I run 500 meters, then rest briefly. I run 1000 meters, then rest. Then I run 1500 meters, then rest. And I reach the top of the pyramid running 2000 meters, and then after that I rest for five minutes.*" Pavin pauses.

Davis appears confused. "That's it?"

The translator remarks without consulting Pavin, "Oh no Mr. Davis, Girolamo has not finished . . . Then I go down the pyramid - another 1500 meters, then 1000 meters and then another 500 meter run, resting again for five minutes."

Davis remembers tougher workouts described by the Russian, the Canadian and the American. In comparison, it doesn't sound all that difficult. "How fast are you running during the pyramid workout, Girolamo?"

The Italian flattens his eyes. *"As fast as I can. And one more thing, Mr. Davis, just to be sure I have prepared more than enough, I run the pyramid again, for good measure."* Another confident smile ensues.

"His toughest workout, Mr. Davis?" The interpreter translates and sees Okuda scratch his neck before replying.

"Without question, the hill repeats I run at altitude. In Sapporo, near my parents' home, there is a ski resort that has many trails going to the top of the mountain."

"The distance is about six kilometers from the bottom to the top and the elevation gain is over one thousand meters. I attack them with intensity running up the mountain, then without rest, I run down the mountain with equal . . . ah . . . what is the word?" The interpreter is at loss for the correct translation. "Gusto."

"Gusto?" Davis snickers when he thinks of a beer commercial.

"Is there a better word?" the interpreter asks in an earnest tone.

"No no, I understand completely."

Okuda concludes his oration. *"Mr. Davis, for the past six months I have been diligently writing a script that will bring success. This race will bring closure to another season of training, and another chapter in my life will end. I hope the conclusion of this chapter will bring an exclamation point, not just a period."* For the first time during the passive interview, the man from Japan offers a genuine smile, bowing deferentially to the commentator.

"I'll say this much. They may be from opposite parts of the globe, but they share, along with many runners I have spoken with, something unlike anything I've observed before - a true passion for their sport and an undeniable potential waiting to be unleashed." Davis signs off. "We have to take a station break, then we'll return to our studios in Los Angeles."

The Haitian runner asks the aid station attendant, *"What time is it?"* He chews on half a peanut butter jelly sandwich and points at the wrist of the attendant.

The young man glances at his digital watch and shows the runner, whose brown face is streaked with crusted salt, the face of his watch. "I have 7:30, number 545. Is there anything I can bring you?" He observes that the man appears alarmed about something.

"*At what time must I depart this aid station to avoid disqualification?*" He drinks a cup of fluids.

The only word the volunteer understands is *disqualification.* "Disqualification? I am sorry I don't understand what you're asking . . ."

Another attendant, a French teacher from a local high school understands completely and intervenes. "*I am not sure what the time of disqualification is, but I can find someone who knows. I will return quickly.*"

The Haitian smiles broadly, feeling confident he can finish this race of resistance . . . this test of endurance. "*Thank you, Madam.*"

*　　　　*　　　　*

The Haitian had been interviewed prior to departing for the Los Angeles Olympics. In fact, the brief interview had been conducted at the Port-au-Prince Airport just prior to the team's departure. The dialogue was broadcast on the national television station that evening, bringing recognition not only to the athlete but his family as well. The Haitian runner had been transformed into "movie star" status in a heartbeat.

"*In which event will you compete, young man?*" The news reporter, one of the anchors at the local television station, had indiscriminately selected athletes as they waited for their flight. The man she speaks with is slight like many other Haitians, but differs having well-defined thigh and calf muscles. He wears the national uniform - a white polo shirt with the country's national insignia on the breast. His navy blue shorts are clean and pressed.

"*I am a runner. I will compete in an ultramarathon.*" The athlete's face is calm and unpretentious.

"*What is the distance of your race?*" The reporter has never heard the term ultramarathon.

"*The race is 100 miles in length.*" The man's eyes remain fixed on the reporter's eyes, never wavering.

"*100 miles? I have never . . .*"

"This is the first time they will include such a race in the Olympics and . . ."

"But 100 miles! That is a distance of . . ."

"160 kilometers." The runner grins at the thought of his quest, plus the lasting impression he will leave with the lady conducting the interview.

"How do you prepare for such a distance?" The young woman is perplexed.

"Many kilometers of running and many climbs to the Citadel."

"Are you from Cap Haitian?" She had climbed to see the fortress on the north side of the island.

"My family is from there."

"What do you hope to accomplish by running 100 miles?"

"I hope to compete and finish the race. The run will be my greatest athletic accomplishment." He refrains from adding, *"An accomplishment no one can ever take from me, not even our corrupt government."*

"Do you think you will win?"

The Haitian runner laughs, knowing there are too many great distance runners in the world . . . knows he's lucky just to be part of the Olympic team going to Los Angeles. *"No, I seriously doubt I will win. But I carry enough pride and passion to finish. Ne plus ultra."* The runner smiles, showing his white teeth behind full lips, then turns his head towards the coach of the team when the announcement to depart is heard. *"Well, I must catch my plane."*

The reporter wishes she had interviewed the young man earlier. *"What a great feature story it would have been,"* she thinks and then calls-out. *"Mm, Mister, if you please . . . what is your name?"*

The Haitian runner turns as he's walking away, *"My name? Xavier-Francois Simeon. Thank you, Miss Louyot."* He recognizes the woman from seeing her on previous newscasts.

The young woman watches the man disappear behind the glass doors leading to the aircraft and whispers, *"Good luck Mr. Simeon."*

There is little commotion at the Foresthill checkpoint since the vast majority of runners have either passed through or dropped-out. The attendant speaks slowly. *"Xavier, you must depart within one-half hour.*

The time of disqualification is 8:00 and that time is absolute. Do you comprehend?"

"Absolutely. You speak French very well." He smiles at the woman who has assisted.

Simeon remembers the translation of the race director the day before. *"The absolute cut-off times at the aid stations will be strictly enforced tomorrow,"* the French interpreter had stated. And thus far, he has remained ahead of those times. In fact, he is building a little cushion. *"Thank you for your assistance, Madam."* The Haitian stands to exit the aid station, water bottle in hand.

"Xavier, you forgot your, er . . ." The sedulous attendant cannot think of the words for fanny-pack so she improvises, *". . . your purse."*

"My purse?" He sees the fanny-pack in her hand. *"Ah yes, my pack. Thank you much, Madam. You are too kind."*

The woman blushes, *"Yes, your pack."*

Inside the pack are a change of socks, an energy bar, plus one item all the men in the race will require – a flashlight to illumine their path through the night. And the night for Mr. Simeon will be a long one – the longest of his life. Of course, he will not be alone.

The man from the poorest country in the Western Hemisphere walks to the exit of the Foresthill aid station. Temperatures have cooled. He sees the sun's reddish-orange glow, plus a ferrous tint on the western horizon, and thinks, *"100 kilometers completed, sixty to the end of the race. I can finish this race . . . and no one can ever take this race, this experience from me, ever."* Simeon states proudly, *"Number 5-4-5 leaving."* He tugs at his bib number. Xavier-Francois begins to jog between the few onlookers who have remained to see the back-of-the-pack runners.

Their applause is a thoughtful gesture.

Chapter 17 – Pointed Rocks at Highway 49

More than a marathon's distance separates Simeon from the front runners at the onset of dusk. The two leaders traverse a ridge above the American River. The trail is single track with scattered oak, pine and manzanita adjacent to it; poison oak is visible among the scrub. The arid smells of late summer with dried grasses and herbs permeate the air surrounding them. Music is detected, echoing from the ravine below.

The American hears his opponent's foot strike, plus the Russian breathing down his neck. "Not unlike my own," Washington contemplates his own toils and then grins at the thought of the college professor who taught him the double negative. He glances at his watch, but can't see the digital read out in the twilight. "Shit, Brown's Bar and I can't shake this guy." He had caught Boroshkov on the descent to the river crossing and had even taken the lead on occasion. But the Russian remains steadfast - his conviction to keep contact at all costs. Every time Washington opened a lead on a downhill section of trail, Boroshkov closed the distance on the next uphill.

The twice champion of the Western States Trail Run has not been in this position before – namely, being contested this late in the race. In his two wins at Western States, by ninety miles, he had opened a considerable margin on the remainder of the field. This race, however, is much different since Boroshkov refuses to yield to the indefatigable pace. The American has launched several offensives to take command of the race and the Russian, who has his own reservoir of talent and experience to draw from, will not concede the lead.

Numerous times during Boroshkov's illustrious career as an elite, world class runner, he has battled against the best and come out on top. Despite fatigue and the inexperience of running 100 miles, he continues to attack the ascents and maintains contact with Washington.

Familiarity with the Western States trail has certainly given Nathan Washington a clear advantage on the descents. Conversely, Yuri Boroshkov's tenacity on the ascents has proven to be the equalizer in the gold medal confrontation. They have been running together for nearly fifteen miles and both feel the adverse effects of running ninety miles.

Virtually every part of their bodies ache. Soreness has encroached on joints, ligaments, tendons and muscles, but their minds remain lucid and fixed on running to win. More than a battle of wills or a test of athleticism, each man aspires to be an Olympic champion - neither man ready to surrender.

This battle is not one of nationalism. The media can hype about capitalist versus communist, Christian versus atheist, physicist versus fire fighter. Instead, this is a race between two men whose running is at the core of their existence. Each aspires to a greater good which is much more than a medal dangling from his neck as he stands on a podium hearing his country's national anthem. The challenge is to win and be considered the best in the domain of ultra-distance running and ultimately, separating himself from all others – that's what each man strives for at this juncture of the race, at this juncture of his life.

The American side steps a rock descending into the ravine and the Russian follows suit. Each runner concentrates on his foot strike and cadence. Both men exhausted, pushing themselves beyond limits, look forward to a brief rest at Brown's Bar. The American recognizes the music of the "Beach Boys" playing on an eight track stereo. Alternately, the Russian recognizes the sound of a portable electric generator. The aid station is nearby, right around the next corner. Their breathing has slowed somewhat during the descent to the aid station.

Boroshkov hears the loud rock and roll and contemplates, *"Mindless music, that's all I've heard all day - another dissolute cacophony. Have these local Americans not heard of classical music or smooth jazz for that matter?"* He sniggers at the thought and for a moment the empirical harmony of "St. John's Night on Bare Mountain" composed by Modest Petrovich Mossorgsky stirs Yuri's memory, assuaging the miles compiled against body and mind.

"Welcome to Brown's Bar gentlemen; what can I get for you?" A portly man with a well-used, grimy-green John Deere cap welcomes the front runners.

Washington responds first. "Just fill the bottle with coke and dilute it with some water please. I won't be here long."

The Russian reaches for a piece of energy bar on one of the portable tables and relishes the sweet chocolate taste. "Coca cola please," his accented words even more difficult to understand while he masticates. He grabs a cup of fluids and washes down the morsel.

The attendant points at his bottle. "What can I fill it with, er . . . Sir?"

Washington recognizes the attendant from a previous trail race. "His name is Yuri." The American looks over at the Russian, and for the first time takes a moment to size up the man challenging him for Olympic gold. He's shorter, bald and appears much older. "Yet despite the appearance of an inadequacy or two," Washington thinks, "the guy can run." He raises a cup of coke in the air to salute the Russian's presence this late in the race.

Boroshkov hears his name and replies, "Yes, electrolytes in bottle." The American is smiling, so he returns a toothy grin and raises his cup, acknowledging a fellow competitor. "Thank you, Nathan." Yuri Boroshkov takes a moment to look into the eyes of an opponent. "*A fierce competitor,*" he contemplates, "*but I will break the American by the end of the race.*" The Russian takes his bottle from the attendant and hears another attendant call-out his bib number . . . then the American's.

"Runners 622 and 620 checking-out. May the best man win."

Washington waves, then immediately overtakes Boroshkov on a rocky, downhill section of trail that returns to the American River - his agility evident on another descent. Once again, he hears Boroshkov in pursuit and knows the race is far from over. "The Russian ain't gonna quit," he senses. Washington illuminates the dial of his watch – it's after eight. "Fourteen plus hours of runnin'," he quickly calculates. Refocusing on his next foot strike he predicts, "This is going to be a fuckin' dogfight 'til the end."

"*I cannot believe I have run this far and I am running well - still.*" Boroshkov glances quickly at the shoulder of the American, then returns his focus to the rocky earth moving under his feet. The Russian, who approaches 145 kilometers, refuses to relinquish his position. He knows that aerobically, he is the superior athlete. *"There are two major climbs remaining,"* he predicts, *"on the next one, he will eat my dust."*

The front runners are less than ten miles from the finish.

"You can do it! Less than twenty miles to go. You're looking great, 5-50." Few spectators recognize the cross of St. Andrew, the national emblem that covers the runner's singlet: a yellow diagonal cross with opposite green and black coloration. The Pan-African colors represent the sun, the land and the hardship endured by Jamaicans of African descent. "Cool runnings, Creary. Irie!"

Conrad Creary absorbs the encouragement of the crowd that has lined the jeep trail. He offers a weak wave and a weaker smile to his audience. Ten miles behind the leaders, Creary is walking the incline to the Green Gate. Several runners have passed him and he, like many of the participants, are content just to finish. The thought of dropping-out is repulsive. His face is long and drawn as he breathes deeply during the 900 foot climb. He anticipates the next flat section of trail . . . "I'll start running then. Run the flats and downs, walk the ups . . ." He had heard the survival strategy before when discussing late race tactics in ultramarathons.

*   *   *

The runner from the Caribbean island nation, who had returned last summer after completing the Old Dominion 100 Mile Endurance Run, was somewhat of a local hero. People in his locality of Kingston would stop him to speak about the race. People were astonished, learning of his accomplishment. Despite not winning the race, he had performed admirably and the ultra runner received considerable national attention. One of the interviews that ensued upon his return demonstrated that public interest and media coverage went far beyond athletics.

"Nice belt buckle, Mr. Creary," the reporter commenced the interview referring to the sterling award merited by a runner who completes a revolution of the George Washington National Forest, west of the United States' national capitol. The embossed words "TOP TEN" in the upper left portion of the buckle indicated Conrad's overall performance. "Third place is commendable. Were you satisfied with your performance?"

"Thank you. Yes, quite satisfied considering what happened late in the race."

"I heard. You were lost for a time, correct?"

"Yah man, lost for a time." Creary remembered the horse rider who offered directions to a wayward runner.

"Conrad, you were winning at the time. How exactly did you become lost?" The reporter initiated his cynical probe of a young man who may have been treated unfairly.

"There was a bridge, a left turn and I missed it. That's all. Truly unfortunate."

"Do you believe someone tampered or removed trail markers? Perhaps they didn't want you, a foreigner, to win."

"What do you mean by 'they?'" Creary appeared puzzled.

"Isn't it ironic that you were the only one to become lost near the end of the race?"

At that point Creary easily determined the nature of the interview and began to laugh. "You're thinking conspiracy, man?"

"Maybe conspiracy is too severe of a word, but duplicity may account for you not winning."

With a smile a mile wide and a crinkle in his broad nose, the Jamaican shakes his head. "For one thing, I was not the only runner to get lost. I spoke with a runner from California who not only took that wrong turn, but also took another early on. I'll never forget what he said, 'The furthest I've ever run in my life – 105 miles.'" Creary chuckled. "In fact, it was the assistance of a horse rider who kindly turned me around and set me straight."

The reporter, a known advocate of the Socialist Party, knows of the United States' intervention in the Caribbean and has read numerous articles about his country. One in particular, "Jamaica: A Show Case for U. S. Foreign Economic and Political Policy," stirred his national sentiment. He feels that the capitalist party had usurped control from the socialist party without a fair election. And the current members of the Jamaican parliament, the Prime Minister included, are merely puppets of the American executive branch. He continues to probe for an exclusive story. "Come on Conrad, how can you be so naïve to think that a Jamaican can be treated fairly in the United States?"

The man who earned an undergraduate degree at the University of Texas, El Paso, and who ultimately decided to return to his home, wasted no time in responding. "Not only was I treated fairly, but as one of the few foreigners competing, I was catered to. People went out of their way to demonstrate civility and good sportsmanship. What I have no idea about is what you are searching for, Sir. Obviously, you have your own agenda or maybe you've been misguided about my experiences at a race in the U. S. In fact, I know I will return to the state of Virginia to run Old Dominion again, and God willing, this time I will win."

The interview was never broadcast.

Creary listens to the applause trying to assimilate the captive energy into his own personal quest. Winning is no longer the objective. Even finishing in the top twenty is remote. "But ah man," he thinks, "just to finish this race, an Olympian, will be truly satisfying." He sees the right turn at the Green Gate and after adjusting his fanny-pack, he squirts fluids from his water bottle into his mouth. When Conrad steps onto the single track trail, the Jamaican begins to jog.

Two miles ahead, somewhere between the Green Gate and the Auburn Lake Trails checkpoint, Wolfgang Hafner is running well. Hafner hears footsteps approaching from the rear, and instinctively increases his tempo. The two men – a Greek and a Czechoslovakian are running better and need little time to overtake the West German. He recognizes the Czech runner who commented on his favorite beer, "Prazdroj" or as Hafner had tried to correct him, "Pilsner Urquell." Wolfgang smirked at the time preferring the Germanic name. Now he strains to keep contact.

*   *   *

Without question, the two individuals who are running together represent countries that have had men, who in their day, set standards from which all other performances would be measured and compared. They were individuals whose accomplishments far exceeded what were once thought as humanly possible.

Phidippides, the Athenian courier who ran twenty-two and a half miles from Marathon to Athens to announce his army's victory over the Persians, collapsed. Dying from exhaustion or more likely, complications from dehydration, he proclaimed their army's success. The modern day marathon is named for his extraordinary feat of endurance and remains a tribute to the legacy of long distance running.

As for the current distance of 26.2 miles, the marathon was later designated at the fourth modern-day Olympics held in London in 1908. The distance from Windsor Castle to the Olympic Stadium at Shepherds Bush was used as the marathon in that particular Olympics and became the benchmark for all marathons worldwide.

Emil Zapotek, a Czech runner, achieved the greatest performance of any long distance Olympian in the modern era or perhaps, even dating to ancient times. Zapotek remarkably won all three distance running events at the 1952 Olympics in Helsinki, Finland. He claimed three gold medals: one in the 5000 meters, another at 10,000 meters and a third in the marathon. No athlete has ever duplicated that particular performance, albeit, Lasse Viren of Finland came close in 1976. Viren won the five k and the ten k, but finished a distant fifth in the marathon.

Hafner slows no longer willing to expend the necessary energy. Stepping to the side of the trail to urinate, he immediately senses his breath slowing. A luminescent glow stick dangles from a branch of a nearby shrub. Ambient temperatures have cooled, nevertheless, sweat flows. He gazes to the western horizon. An indigo inversion layer above the Sacramento Valley gives his panoramic view an aesthetic backdrop. The distance lights of Auburn are visible, twinkling like starlight. Venus, the evening star, is in full phase – brilliant, like an aircraft with its landing lights directed toward the earth's surface. The last vestiges of daylight are quickly fading. His vision impaired, the onset of night is imminent. The West German sips water from his bottle, then looks at his watch and presses the illumination button – 20:30. Hafner carefully removes his flashlight from his fanny-pack, not wishing to spill its other contents. He switches it on and points its beam at the single track trail beneath his feet.

Despite the fatigue of running over 130 kilometers in fourteen and one half hours, he continues a respectable pace toward a finish line fast approaching.

The American has opened a seventy meter lead on the challenger when he reaches the climb to the Pointed Rocks checkpoint. Better known to runners as Forty-Nine Crossing, it is the last major checkpoint before the race's end. Highway Forty-Nine is a winding, north-south route through the gold country of Northern California – henceforth its name. The Western States Trail crosses the highway in the ninety-third mile of the race. An entourage of personnel awaits them, including race staff, friends and comrades.

The Russian pumps his arms, lifts his knees and continues to run the fifteen percent grade. The American is power-walking, less than fifty meters ahead. Boroshkov closes on his quarry. Like a pendulum he feels momentum swing in his favor; knows the time to make the decisive move is ripe. Yuri surges upward on the single track trail and two simple words are exhaled between deep breaths, "Pass please." The trail is difficult to see in the darkness of twilight. Heavy brush and oak prevent the little light available to filter through, but the 300 meter vertical has worked in his favor and the American steps aside.

Washington, aware that Boroshkov is making a move, finds the gear necessary to keep contact. His head throbs like two kettle drums pounding between his ears when he feels the added burden of an increased pace. "To keep contact . . . at all costs," his collegiate coach had emphatically stated on more than one occasion. "There's another long downhill not too far ahead – the drop to No Hands Bridge." Nathan nods imperceptibly at the thought. "God willing, I'll drop the Russian there." Vehicles driving on the highway are audible – the checkpoint must be close.

A boy who is standing on the outcrop of boulders waves a flashlight. "Incoming runners," he proclaims. A portable generator produces the power necessary to light the staging area of the Pointed Rocks checkpoint. A hundred spectators have assembled to bear witness to the Olympic runners arriving and departing the final major checkpoint. An enthusiastic applause welcomes the front runners.

"*Comrade, you had me worried.*" He smiles proudly at his athlete. The assistant peers into the eyes of a fatigued runner. He sees his charge begin to slow his breathing. "*You can beat this American – beat him on his own soil.*"

"*Doctor, I need a flashlight.*" Boroshkov is all business. "*Get me some fluids and be quick, I will not stay here long.*" The Russian finishes the tepid contents of his bottle and hands his assistant the empty bottle. A cramp pulls on his right calf with an unexpected spasm. He quickly moves to a table to stretch before proceeding.

His assistant follows. "*Yuri, are you all right?*"

"*Yes, fine. Please get me the electrolytes.*"

"*Immediately.*"

Boroshkov glances over to see the American attended by his crew; knows the American will not quit until he crosses the finish line. "*You are a redoubtable opponent, Nathan Washington.*" He flicks on the flashlight to be sure it is operative and then drinks the contents of a cup, followed by more liquid from his bottle - its contents cooled by the addition of ice. "*Thank you Doctor, you have been of immense help today.*"

"*Ten kilometers Yuri . . .*" The Doctor too, looks over to see what the Americans are doing, "*and you become an Olympic champion.*"

"God damn it, Nathan, you can beat this guy!" Clint Washington has his right hand on his brother's shoulder. He looks directly into the eyes of a runner trying to gauge the level of exhaustion and observes listless eyes staring outward. "You know the trail, you know what it takes. The Russian knows jack-shit. Come-on Bro, don't deny yourself victory. This is destiny, Nate. I can feel it. Olympic champion - it's got a nice ring to it, doesn't it?"

The American's vacuous face nods, agreeing with his brother's words of encouragement. Washington doffs his stained cap, tucks a lock of ruddy-brown hair behind his left ear and scratches his head. Delusion appears imminent. "I'll need my flashlight, Clint." He takes a cup of coke from his cousin. Nathan senses a sibling's warmth when Gioia rubs his shoulders, but at this point Washington simply feels numb all over - the climbs' detrimental affects easing when he rests briefly.

209

"Nathan, are you okay? Six and half miles, Cuz, then it's over. You can finish this race." Gioia conceals her concern, not wanting to alarm her cousin.

"Finish this race? Bullshit, you can win!" Clint had seen this drained, empty look before. More importantly, he'd seen his brother recover from the brink of collapse to win a fifty mile endurance run. He hands his brother a full water bottle, plus a piece of energy bar. "Gut-check time, Bro; the Russian's getting ready to go. Stay with him. You can beat him."

A highway patrolman escorts his brother to the road crossing. He sees Boroshkov jogging to join Nathan – limping apparently. Traffic on Highway 49 is being controlled by the local California Highway Patrol.

An attendant calls-out, "Numbers 6-20 and 6-22 checking out."

Clint Washington repeats under his breath, "You can beat him, Nate."

Gioia overhears and replies, "I'm not so sure, Clint." She touches the shoulder of her elder cousin. "He looks totally exhausted."

The boy on the outcrop of rocks waves his flashlight and yells at the top of his voice, "Runner incoming, runner incoming." For a moment everyone is quiet, surprised that someone has caught the leaders. Spectators and staff turn to see who is arriving to challenge for the gold medal. "There's another light," the boy exclaims. "Two runners are coming in!"

Boroshkov and Washington hear the applause behind them and instinctively increase their cadence as they jog up a short grade above Highway 49. Someone has closed the gap considerably.

Clint sees the first runner approaching, then looks over at his younger cousin and shakes his head. "Fuck, it's the Italian . . . and the bastard's smiling."

Chapter 18 – Robie Point

A serpent slithers under a canopy of darkness, through the scree and scrub of the Western Sierra foothills, in search of prey; its senses heightened by hunger. With infrared imagery and a keen sense of smell, the pit viper focuses on stimuli coming from the brush ahead. It slows and begins to coil ready to strike. A small mammal continues to forage for seeds and dry grass near its burrow unaware that its existence is in grave peril. Without malice or hatred, the snake strikes with uncanny celerity and accuracy. The rodent attempts to leap from its attacker's fangs, but feels the deep laceration above its left shoulder, venom injected. In panic and in flight, the vole flees from the snake's jaws and prances into a thicket – away from its burrow. The snake stealthily follows, instinct controlling its purpose. Within seconds red blood cells lyse, the venom spreads causing further internal complications. Muscles shudder; the critter convulses and falls onto an open area not far from the strike. The vole, now in shock, shakes uncontrollably. The Pacific Diamondback approaches and with rhythmic alimentary contractions, swallows its prey whole. Satiated, it lays outstretched next to a rock to rest a spell, directly on the Western States Trail, a mile west of the Auburn Lakes Checkpoint.

Three runners abruptly stop, bumping into one another reminiscent of a Three Stooges re-run. The first's flashlight prompts the rattlesnake to live up to its reputation. With its slit eyes and imposing four foot frame the rattling sound in the warm night is intimidating to say the least. Adrenaline courses through the runners' veins, their fatigue quickly forgotten. No one wishes to contest the snake's territory. Conrad Creary, Xian Doi and Yosef Ethiopia are all inherently terrified of snakes. Yosef speaks first. "Maybe we should kill him." They have crept backwards another ten feet giving the snake ample space.

"With what?" Creary replies, "Our water bottles?"

"I do not know, perhaps with a stick or rock." The two turn around and see Doi searching the ground and muttering in Chinese.

"*Stupid gutless foreigners! I will remove the snake from the path myself.*"

211

"Well I'm not going into the brush to search for a switch. I would probably be unlucky enough to find its mate." Conrad shivers at the thought.

"Then what do we do?"

Xian returns smiling having found a large branch and begins to prod the snake. The snake strikes with vengeance determined to hold its ground. As the three men recoil, Doi trips and practically falls into Creary's arms.

Ethiopia points his flashlight at the coiled serpent, its tongue flicking occasionally. "Oh my God, he refuses to move." Ethiopia does not know the gender of the snake, but uses the masculine pronoun knowing all snakes must be the direct descendents of Satan.

"What's happening boys?" An American approaches, a slight drawl evident in his speech.

The voice is familiar to Creary and he is relieved seeing a familiar face. "Byron, Byron Hall. 'Tis you? Is it really you?"

The two exchange a handshake and a brief hug. "Hey Conrad! I wondered if I was going to catch you." Byron Hall, the second American in the race and winner of the Old Dominion 100 Mile Endurance Run a year earlier, is not having his best day. The two competitors had become acquainted a year earlier when Creary had finished third in the same race.

"I'd thought you'd be up with the leaders, Byron."

"Yeah, me too. Unfortunately, I've taken a wrong turn . . . or two today. So here I am," the American laughs, "back with you guys." Hall is from the state of Virginia and has been running endurance runs for a number of years. His light brown hair and boyish face belie his thirty-one years.

Doi speaks in Mandarin. "*I hate to break-up the reunion, but we have a big problem on our hands.*" He points his flashlight at the coiled rattlesnake, which immediately begins its staccato.

"A rattlesnake is what stopped you guys?" Hall's eyes sharpen on the predator. "What's the big deal?" He looks into the whites of the two black runners' eyes and sees fear. "It's just a rattlesnake for Christ sake. Any of you guys got water left in your bottles?" The two men promptly hand their bottles to Hall. The Chinese runner observes and follows suit. The American shakes his head and smirks, "I only need one." Grabbing the Jamaican's bottle, he motions towards the snake. "Okay, you guys point your flashlights at the snake."

Once again, Doi follows the cue and smiles, understanding the strategy.

Hall side steps the three men, then squirts the snake directly in the face. The viper freezes, then slowly retreats, slithering into the bushes adjacent to the trail. "Rattlesnakes hate water," he says matter-of-factly. Hall promptly begins to jog. "Okay boys, let's get on with it." The Virginian illumines the dial on his watch with the press of a button, "Shit, it's already after nine."

The four men in queue begin to run a flat section of trail on a ridge above the Middle Fork of the American River. The footing is good along the single track, so their pace improves accordingly. Ethiopia speaks, "At least you were right about using the water bottle, Conrad."

At an altitude of 580 feet above sea level, a concrete slab stands – a testament to early twentieth century engineering, and the lowest point on the Western States Trail. The arched overpass, an abandoned railroad trestle, passes over the Middle Fork of the American River just above its confluence with the North Fork. Water cascades well below the span. A group of spectators and race officials have assembled to observe the front runners as they approach the Mountain Quarry Cement Bridge - better known as "No Hands Bridge." The bridge has concrete abutments with no side rails, but its sizeable girth provides plenty room for safe passage. Two race officials converse checking their log to be sure everything is in order to record the runners correctly. No Hands Bridge is just three miles from the finish.

"Flashlight!" One of the spectators yells, pointing directly above herself at an embankment that overlooks the trail on which they are standing.

"There're four lights," another person observes.

One official calls to those assembled, "Please make room for the runners."

Four runners descend on a series of short, rocky switchbacks that lead to the foot of No Hands Bridge. Each man is intent to hold his position over the narrow trail, which widens considerably as it crosses the gravel surface on the bridge.

"Number 620 . . ." one official declares.

The American's six foot frame is carried by long, gangly legs. He's over striding when he reaches the level ground adjacent to the aid station. Deeply concerned about his body hitting rock bottom as well, Washington whispers, "Only wimps walk across No Hands." The reigning Western States Champion hears the cheers from the spectators, but recognizes his pace has deteriorated considerably. He's breathing heavily on the down hills too, and knows ultimately, he'll be lucky to hang on.

". . . Number 622 . . ."

The Russian is hobbling noticeably; his perspiration on his bald crown reflects light from a nearby light post. On the descent he feels tightness in his calf; on the ascents the pain is stifling. *"Five kilometers remaining . . . must keep contact,"* he murmurs inaudibly. Moving toward the last major climb, the World 100 kilometer Champion's confidence wavers. Doubt has crept into Borshkov's mind.

". . . Number 549 . . ."

The Italian has gained much self-assurance over the last fifteen miles. The intensity in the eyes of the European Champion is clearly evident. Pavin has finally caught the leaders and with their decline, knows victory is at hand. His pace is fluent and his running appears effortless. Poised to take the lead, and with the widening of the trail over No Hands Bridge, Pavin asserts, *"Pass on your left, please."* He tucks a lock of dirty brunet hair behind his left ear, then squirts his face with water. Girolamo Pavin passes the Russian first and then the American.

". . . Number 552 . . ."

The Japanese runner, whose short black hair is plastered with sweat and trail dust, sees the Italian making a move. Okuda concentrates, his dark eyes focused on the back of the soiled blue singlet in front of him. He inhales sharply and using short efficient strides, increases his canter - matching the Italian's. He too, runs confidently. *"This is a good place to be – good karma,"* he asserts to himself. *"I can take him by the end of the race."*

A race official removes his walkie-talkie from its holster. "Norm, Curtis here. Do you copy?" He pauses. "Norm, it's Curt. Are you there?"

"Yeah, Curt. What've you got?"

The official looks at his watch. "Four runners through at 9:15, over."

The race director looks confused. "All together?"

"That's a ten-four, buddy. Numbers 620, 622, 549 and 552 have just crossed No Hands. Get ready for 'em. Should be a hell of a finish. I'll be in touch, out."

Sproul quickly records the four bib numbers, immediately recognizing all of them. "Roger that. Thanks Curt. We'll be ready. "

Upon exiting the bridge, Pavin and Okuda waste no time running a hill charge up the moderate grade to the outskirts of Auburn and the last checkpoint at Robie Point. The runners negotiate 600 vertical feet over a mile and a half of trail. The finish line is another mile and a half of road, downhill to the finish from there. Early in the race this grade would have presented no problems to any of these four individuals. However, for the American and the Russian, the molehill has become Everest. As in any number of races that Washington and Boroshkov have run, they've learned to find a new gear at this juncture of a race, especially on an acclivity of this slope, is difficult at best, impossible at worst.

"Lift your knees, pump your arms, you're almost home, Nate!" Washington flashes on his coach's strident voice, blaring evocations of encouragement. Yet when he attempts these simple tasks, there is simply no response. After nearly ninety-eight miles of trail, heat and running forward, his body is ready to shut down. The American looks up and points his flashlight directly ahead. A drop of sweat finds Washington's left eye and he blinks hard to remove the sting. Opening his eyes Okuda's sullied white uniform swiftly fades to black. Washington shakes his head, disappointed and continues to walk the moderate grade to Robie Point.

Boroshkov immediately realizes what is happening, and knows he has to go – now. "Pass please, Nathan." The Russian sees the American step aside and when Yuri increases his step, the calf muscle strains due to the additional stress. He winces as he goes by Washington. His jog is only slightly faster than the American's power walk, if in fact, he is "power walking." Yuri opens up a fifty meter lead on the man directly behind him. He still jogs, glancing ahead to the trail's abyss, hoping to see Okuda or

Pavin. Only the tapering of an empty trail can be glimpsed in the darkness. He returns his attention to the trail's dirt. Another cramp in his right calf quickly spreads to his hamstring, and then lower back spasms follow. He grimaces knowing he has to slow down. Yuri Boroshkov steps to the side of the trail to urinate. He does not bother to look at the color. It is of no relevance at this point. The Russian hears the labored breathing of the American. He sees Washington squirt fluid in his mouth; sees him swallow hard. The fifty meter lead has quickly vanished when he steps on the trail to resume his quest - for a bronze medal.

Chapter 19 – Placer High School,
Auburn, California

"Good evening and welcome to Placer High School in Auburn, California – the finish of the inaugural Olympic 100 mile endurance run." Directly behind Brandon Davis, the camera focuses on the yellow Western States banner, which hangs above a cinder track. The large blue text "Western States Trail Run, 100 miles – One Day" is printed in script and clearly visible. Stadium lights illuminate the surroundings. The place is packed. "Thousands of people have come to this quaint little town to witness the finish of a truly remarkable event. This morning 162 athletes representing one hundred five countries embarked on a journey across the Sierra Nevada. Ninety-five runners remain in the race, but only four contend for Olympic gold.

"I'm Brandon Davis and we're here with today's race director Norm Sproul, who's been on the go since four o'clock this morning. I see where you get the nickname 'Stormin' Norman.'"

"Well Brandon, it requires a great expenditure of energy to run a race of 100 miles, but in my humble opinion, it takes even greater energy to direct one!" He chuckles at the thought. Sproul continues to exude enthusiasm despite the onset of fatigue.

"No argument here Norm. I have heard the term 'extreme sport' often today. What exactly constitutes an extreme sport?"

"I think any athletic contest that takes the participants to the extreme limit of their physical, mental and even emotional capabilities. This race certainly falls into that category."

"I have heard similar comments about the Iron Man Triathlon in Hawaii."

Sproul shakes his head and reflects a moment, "There's no comparison. They're completely different events and I have complete respect for anyone who can swim two and a half miles, ride a bike 110 miles, then run a marathon all in the same day. But there are advantages in that race you will not find here."

"Advantages? Norm, you've just described nearly 140 miles of distance, if my math is correct."

"Oh, don't get me wrong, Brandon. It's a tough race, no question, but there are numerous advantages. For example, you have the luxury of using different muscle groups within each discipline of the swim, bike, run format. A person is buoyant in water, has the mechanical advantage of gears and weight distribution on a bicycle and the run . . . well, I think that's toughest part. Plus, I want to add that the Hawaiian course is fairly flat. Running 100 miles over mountainous terrain . . . like I said, no comparison. It's just you and gravity out there."

Davis shakes his head looking at Sproul's silver belt buckle and recognizes the man's gift for the power of persuasion. "Sounds like you have given this some thought, Norm."

"Yeah, I guess I have. A number of people have approached me comparing the two races. In my mind, it's like comparing apples and oranges. However, I would like to draw one comparison regarding the two races."

"You just said there's no comparison, Norm." Davis grins, thinking he has just shackled the logical reasoning of the race director.

"Just one, Brandon. Please indulge me." Norman Sproul smiles confidently. "If you want to test your endurance, then complete the Ironman Triathlon. If you want to test your soul, run Western States."

The stadium's loudspeakers crackle to life and the announcer declares, "We have our first runner who has arrived at Robie Point. Number 549, er . . . Girolamo Pavin, from Italy." The man behind the microphone struggles with the pronunciation of the name and inadvertently mispronounces the country. He looks over the list of entrants' names with their corresponding bib numbers and contemplates, "This could be a long night."

"Well Norm, as always, you have shed light on this event helping me and our viewers better understand this sport of extreme endurance. I am sure you have many things to do."

"Actually, only one task remains this evening, Brandon."

"Only one?"

"I will congratulate each and every runner who crosses the finish line."

After running many miles of desolate trail alone or accompanied by few runners, Girolamo Pavin is greeted by a throng of spectators who have come from parts of Northern California, Nevada and even Oregon to welcome the finishers to Robie Point. He hears shouts and applause but understands few words. Most important though, he blocks out the extraneous noise, concentrating on the road beneath his shuffling feet. Pavin is transfixed, eager to bring this race to closure. *"Don't turn around, never turn around – this shows weakness,"* Girolamo recalls one of his coaches stating emphatically when he was younger. The Italian looks to his right, between the masses, and recognizes the last ascent before the finish. Victory fuels his fire. With his last bit of reserve and the utmost resolve, he races the last climb. No longer hearing the Japanese runner, he thinks, *"No one is with me – the race is mine."*

One-half mile below Robie Point, on a steep incline, Pavin had surged and Okuda could not respond. The decisive move had little to do with differences in nationality or religion or culture. European verses Asian. Catholic versus Buddhist. West versus East. The celebrated diversity in the Olympic Games would have no bearing on the outcome of this race. Instead, the race came down to one simple concept. The Italian runner would have a slightly better day than the Japanese runner.

Both men had prepared exceptionally well. Both men had devoted a myriad of hours, running a myriad of miles. Perhaps coaching strategy played a role in the outcome. Perhaps a few molecules of glycogen remained in the Italian's liver or necrosis of muscle fiber was worse in the Japanese's. Maybe it was the constipation that Okuda experienced at the onset of the race or the Italian's strategy to conserve early and come from behind. Regardless, the Italian is about to begin the celebration of a lifetime, and he will not be celebrating alone.

Akira Okuda arrives at Robie Point less than minute behind the leader. Dizziness accompanies him along with a vigorous ovation. He sees a table with cups of water, electrolytes and coke distributed evenly and neatly on the table. Light-headed, Okuda grabs two cups; one of which he pours on his head, the other he immediately quaffs. He is proud that despite being disoriented, he did not pour the coke and drink the water.

Okuda looks to his right and in the distance, moving up the incline, sees the back of Pavin's singlet disappear as the Italian crests the final hill. Shaking his head he returns his concentration to the liquids on the table and sees his flashlight still glowing. *"I will no longer need this."* Akira flicks it off. The Japanese runner looks down at his shoes and wiggles his toes. He barely feels them. Everything below his waist is numb.

An attendant at the table looks at Akira, "I'm sorry I didn't understand. Can I help you, number 5 5 2?" She asks loudly to be heard above the raucous.

Okuda replies, "I do not speak English. I am sorry," his words equally as loud, but heavily accented. He removes his headband, looking at the red circle imprinted on it and begins to walk the final ascent. The headband is no longer clean and white. *"I stayed with him as long as I could,"* he ponders. *"There is no shame in that."* The man from the Land of the Rising Sun takes a last look behind. No flashlights. He too, is all alone - in second place.

The Italian arrives at the stadium entrance waving a small Italian flag that he has picked-up from a bystander. The place erupts. The entire route from Robie Point to the finish has spectators lined three deep. When the crowd simmers Girolamo Pavin is on the far side of the track 150 meters from the finish.

The stadium's announcer requests, "Let's give Girolamo Pavin a real Olympic champion's welcome." Another eruption follows.

Within the crowd, Pavin's coach and fiancée are making their way to the finish line. Both are practically in tears. The coach asks, *"Can you believe it, Sabrina?"*

"I am sorry, what did you say?" She's screaming to be heard.

"Nothing. It is nothing."

Pavin feels his emotions rising, so he takes a deep breath to quell the flood. He reaches into his soiled singlet and removes the eighteen carat gold crucifix. Impassioned by the moment, the Italian kisses the precious metal and crosses himself, paying homage to his God and the Son who was sacrificed. Arms raised above his head, he runs the last 100 meters into Olympic history.

Girolamo Pavin is the first man to finish a 100 mile endurance run in any Olympic games - modern or ancient.

Norman Sproul is holding a large ceramic medallion. There is a cougar embossed on the front with the Olympic rings below. Inscribed are the words 100 MILES – ONE DAY, FINISHER and the year 1984. Sproul holds back his disbelief. He cannot believe that this "rookie" from Italy has beaten the local veteran. "Congratulations Girolamo. Great race." He sees tears mingling with sweat on the face of a champion when he places the medallion around Pavin's neck. Sproul offers a warm handshake and an embrace.

Pavin looks at the medal and recognizes the race's logo. "*Thank you. Thank you for everything.*" He hears his fiancée's voice calling from the bleachers.

"*You won, Lamo! You won!*" Sabrina cries out, her hands clasped high above her beaming face.

The runner grins at the race director and shrugs his shoulders. "*I must go.*"

Sproul speaks no Italian. He places his left hand on Pavin's shoulder and motions at a digital clock adjacent to the track. "Fifteen hours forty-one minutes. Well done!"

Pavin looks, but the time is meaningless to him. He returns another smile of gratitude and then jogs over to Sabrina and his coach.

"*I cannot believe you won, Lamo. You are fantastic.*" She bends her supple body over the railing to kiss her fiancé. A teardrop falls onto the face of the champion.

Pavin feels it just before their lips touch. Simultaneously, he holds his hand up and shakes the hand of his coach. After the kiss Girolamo hands the small Italian flag to Sabrina. "*For you, my dearest one.*"

"*I had no doubts, Girolamo,*" the coach declares with an earnest smile. "*Here, take this for your victory lap.*" He removes a large Italian flag from his leather satchel. "*As I said, without doubt.*"

When Pavin reaches for the flag, an announcement and an ensuing roar welcome the silver medalist. "*I will wait for Okuda to finish.*" Sabrina and Coach are looking across the arena unaware that Girolamo is speaking

"*I am sorry. What did you say?*" Both respond in chorus.

Pavin shakes his head. *"Nothing of importance."* With the Italian flag draped around his shoulders, Pavin returns to the finish line to welcome a fellow competitor.

The standing ovation continues until the Japanese runner crosses it. At which time Akira Okuda squats, leans to the cinder track and kisses the track, paying homage to the earth that has helped carry him to this place at this point in time. Okuda lowers his head to the race director and accepts the medallion graciously. He sees Pavin waiting in the background.

Once again the race director offers his best sentiment on a job well done - another handshake, another hug. He motions to the clock: 15:45:03. "Outstanding, Akira, truly outstanding."

Okuda bows in deference.

For the first time, under the stadium's lights their dark eyes meet. Both smile at one another knowing the sacrifices each made to get here. The Italian, taller with a slightly bigger frame, has a two day growth of whiskers on his face, and in contrast, the diminutive Japanese runner lacks facial hair. Both are covered with a day's worth of sweat intermixed with trail dust. There is mutual respect between the two runners. Pavin is the first to bow and offer his sincere congratulations. *"You are a worthy opponent, but an even better ally. You helped me win this race . . . you pushed me."*

Okuda speaks not one word of Italian, but understands the tone of honor and respect. *"You have been of great importance to my performance today. Thank you, Pavin-san."* He bows again.

The only word that the Italian recognizes is his surname. Pavin motions with his finger circling in the air. *"Please take a victory lap with me."*

Okuda holds up one finger. *"One moment, please."* He sees his coach, his mentor at the rail adjacent to the track and walks over. *"I did the best I could today, Master."*

Okuda's coach reaches below the railing and places his hand on the head of his protégé. He feels grime, one product of a day's journey. *"That is all anyone can ask, Akira-san. I am very proud of what you accomplished today. You have brought great honor to your country, your family and to me. You have completed something truly extraordinary."*

"You are not disappointed?"

222

He reaches into his canvas bag and unfurls a large Japanese flag, then drapes it over the shoulders of his runner. *"We will talk later. Right now, I want you to live in the present and enjoy this moment – you deserve this."*

"Thank you, Master."

Okuda's coach watches the two runners begin their victory lap, and then looks over at the Italian coach to acknowledge their victory. He sees the other coach wave, affirming their athletes' performance. The Japanese coach bows deferentially toward the Italian; then recedes into the crowd of spectators inconspicuously.

The ovation is deafening.

Twenty miles behind the leaders on the south side of the River Crossing, Nigel Preverett sits on a lawn chair, barefoot. His feet, chafed and blistered, are wrapped in a clean towel. The song blaring on the audio system is familiar. He knows the words and lip-sings, "I was born in a crossfire hurricane, and I howled at my ma in the drivin' rain . . . I was schooled with a strap right across my back . . ." There is commotion and conversation around the aid station. An attendant, a middle age man, brings a plate of food and two cups of fluids, which stirs him from his song. "Ummm . . . lovely victuals. Thank you, Sir. What's all the natter about?"

The Rolling Stones' tune continues, ". . . I was washed-up and left for dead . . . but it's all right now, in fact, it's a gas, I'm Jumpin' Jack Flash . . ."

"Matter?" The attendant appears puzzled. "Nothing's the matter."

Preverett chuckles. "What's all the chatter about my good man?"

"Oh, we just received news from Auburn. The Italian, er . . . Pavin just crossed the finish line."

"Ah, Girolamo Pavin, I am not surprised. Excellent runner." Preverett pronounces the name correctly.

"We are! Surprised that is. We really thought Washington would prevail given his record here. Do you know him?"

"Washington or Pavin?" Preverett smiles knowing what the attendant meant. He bites into a peanut and jelly sandwich and swallows it with a cup of diluted coke. "Yummy." The British runner sounds somewhat sarcastic.

The attendant likes the man's sense of humor. "Do you know Nathan Washington?"

"No, not really. But Pavin, I know well enough. He won the European 100 kilometer championship last year – a tenacious sort, if you know what I mean."

The attendant recognizes Great Britain's flag on the front of the runner's singlet. "Were you there?"

"Yes I was . . . finished tenth in the same race," Preverett remembering the race well.

"Really, that's awesome! How would you compare running 100 kilometers to this race?" The attendant is genuinely interested to hear the comparison.

"Running 100 kilometers is undoubtedly a race of endurance. This race . . ." Nigel takes a deep breath and shakes his head, "it's a battle of survival."

"So I've heard."

Preverett reaches into his drop bag and removes a clean pair of white socks. "By the way, did Washington finish second? I heard he was in contention."

"No, he didn't. A Japanese runner did. Hmmm . . . can't recall his name though. Anything else I can get you, number 544?" The attendant sees another runner wading across the river. "Got to go."

"Thanks much for your assistance," he replies biting into an orange slice. The veteran of numerous marathons and ultras is left to his revel in his reverie. He sees a waxing gibbous rising just above the treetops. The river has cooled the environs considerably. Twenty miles from the finish line and God knows how many hours behind the winner, Nigel Preverett knows he will finish this race - well within the allotted time.

The British runner had visited Oxford in May for the thirtieth anniversary celebration of Roger Bannister's breaking the four minute mile barrier. Preverett had met the man more than once. Their ages are not that far apart. He knows that Bannister averaged better than fifteen miles per hour during his world record performance. Preverett looks at his watch

– it's almost 10:00, nearly sixteen hours of running. He inhales deeply and then titters at the calculation of his own speed in this race - better than five miles per hour. "Different race I suspect," chuckling again, he finishes tying his damp shoes.

Nigel recollects an old photograph of his father in uniform. As a young boy, maybe five years old, he is hoisted on the shoulder of the patriarch of his family. Often, as an adult, Nigel has thought of his father, wondering what he would think of his son running outlandishly long distances. "This race, even more ridiculous – 100 miles on foot for God's sake." He sees a runner walking up from the river's edge. "I've kept it warm for you," he says, happily offering his seat to a Hispanic runner. The son of a World War II fighter pilot descends from solid roots - has inherited the right stuff; if not to win, then certainly to succeed. The man from the U. K. looks up the trail and sees the next ascent and mutters, "Better get on with it."

A mile and a half from the finish the American is overwhelmed. Nathan Washington has never seen so many people at Robie Point at one time. He waves off an attendant who offers a cup of fluids. Boroshkov is right beside him.

"You can beat him Nate . . ."

Another voice registers, "Take him, Nate."

"Less than a mile, you can . . ."

"Hang-on, you can beat him . . ."

Among the cheers, he recognizes only one - his ex-wife's. Washington attempts to jog, but exhaustion prevents that. His breathing labored, he walks the final incline. "With a downhill just ahead, I will run that," he hopes.

Boroshkov observes the American's failed attempt to run the last ascent. He too, attempts to jog, but must immediately slow the pace, his right calf tightening precipitously close to tearing flesh. He joins Washington with a novel thought which he decides to share. In heavy accented English three words come from his mouth, "Nathan, finish together."

Washington can barely discern the voice behind the words. The crowd is simply too loud. "I'm sorry, Yuri. What did you say?" He continues to walk

"Finish together, Nathan." This time the Russian offers a hand.

Washington almost stops. "Finish together?" he yells, and then mutters, "Are you nuts?" Something peculiar happens subsequently in his mind, however. He looks into a man's eyes that are genuinely declaring a truce. Next, he looks at the hand offered and then instinctively turns to see if anyone approaches from the rear. "No one's there," he thinks, "and after twenty-five miles of racing against each other - hell, why not." He takes the Russian's right hand firmly and looks directly into recessed pale eyes, "Finish together."

"Come on Washington, take him . . ." The American ignores his audience's pleas. Stadium lights come into view as the two competitors jog the final descent and enter the backside of the track.

The roar can be heard a mile away.

The stadium announcer declares, "Numbers 620 and 622, Nathan Washington and Yuri Boroshkov . . ." There is no desperate finishing kick, no flailing arms nor finishing collapse. Just two men from opposite sides of the planet, hold hands, one's right hand grasping the other's left high above their heads as they cross the finish line. Both share the satisfaction of the moment, but for these two highly competitive individuals, the moment is fleeting.

Washington sees the clock that has tentatively stopped: 15:52:20. "A P. R.," he immediately thinks, then shaking his head in disbelief, "not good enough."

Norman Sproul senses the man's disappointment. "You ran a great race, Nathan. A personal best too, no less. Nothing to beat yourself up about." He places the finisher's medallion over Washington's head and turning to the Russian he repeats the same task. "Congratulations, Yuri. Your performance will always be remembered. A sub sixteen hour effort on this course is exceptional, especially since this is your first time here." Sproul hangs the medallion and shakes both men's hands.

The Russian understands little of the comments bestowed upon him by the race director, but denotes the manner in which the comments are delivered. "Thank you, Norman. This was . . ." Boroshkov searches for a correct translation, "an incredible, er . . . race for me, even because I do not win." Then he turns to Washington, the man whom he had researched in detail, and after running forty kilometers with him, has become much better acquainted. "You are an incredible man, Mr. Washington." Yuri Boroshkov kisses the American on both cheeks, then looking over his shoulder at the infield of the track, he says in Russian, "*I think I will sit down now.*"

"What did he say?" Nathan is surprised with the public display of affection. Not sure how to react, he watches Boroshkov find a chair and begin to untie his shoelaces.

Sproul chuckles. "I think he likes you, Nate. I mean, I didn't get any kisses."

"Very funny, Norm."

Clinton Washington navigates his way through the bystanders and sees his brother sitting near a medical tent. "Hey Bro, what's happening?" Initially upbeat, he does not want to annoy his brother after seeing him finish in a draw for third place.

"I tried Clint. Just didn't quite have it today." Nathan unties his shoes. "I think I'm going to need a medic . . ." Blood and sweat are intermixed with soil on his filthy socks.

"Get the fuck out o' here. Didn't quite have it today! Shit! You ran the fastest time of your life on a scorcher of a day on this God forsaken trail. You should have no regrets."

Washington, repressing his disappointment, acknowledges, "Yeah, I guess you've got a point."

"Damn straight. Now what can I get you?" The older brother still aware of his role; knows his brother needs to continue to drink fluids and eat.

Gioia approaches. "Great race, Cuz. We really thought you were going to win." She rubs Nathan's shoulders.

"Me too." Nathan points over to the Italian, who is being interviewed, his tan face illuminated by a portable light affixed to a television camera. "He had other plans." Washington bends to examine his feet. "How far was I behind?"

"About ten minutes, Nate." Clint looks askance at his younger brother. "No regrets, remember."

"Yeah, you're right. A bottle of water Clint, and do me favor . . ." He looks over at the Russian who is talking to his coach. "Get a bottle for Yuri too."

"You want me to get that . . ."

"That's right Clint; get the 'Commie bastard' a drink. It's just a nice gesture that's all." He sees his brother walk toward a long formica table with a variety of beverages and foods. Washington looks toward the other side of the medical tent and sees the Japanese runner being assisted by medical personnel. "A lot of good people affiliated with this race, Gioia." The American takes in the warm night air and looks up at the stadium seating. "I've never seen so many people here."

Another familiar voice answers. "That we do agree on, Nathan."

Washington turns to see the silhouette of his ex-wife standing in direct line with the light fixtures of the stadium.

"Hi Gioia, I hope I'm not intruding."

"No, not at all, Carol. Thanks for your patience and understanding today. We just didn't want any distractions."

"What brings you here?" Nathan inquires cynically.

"I just came to meet the latest Olympian celebrity. You've been on T. V., radio, in the newspapers. You've become a household name." The woman pauses, feeling a little uncomfortable. "Honestly, I just want to say congrats, Nathan. That's all."

Clint arrives and hands his brother an icy-cold bottle. "And now that you've offered your 'congrats,' you can turn around and get the f . . ."

His brother's hostility evident, Nathan intervenes, "That's all right, Clint. Be cool." But he's thinking, "Funny she should use the word 'honestly.'" The American and Russian raise their bottles toward one another, their lime-flavored drinks savored.

Carol ignores the older sibling and flicks her short strawberry blonde hair back from her eyes. "I saw you were winning at the River Crossing. When did you lose the lead?" Washington's ex-wife is familiar with the Western States Trail.

"No Hands Bridge. Those two guys surged," he motions to the men who finished in front of him, "and I had nothing left in the bank to withdraw." Washington belches, then laughs, "Excuse me."

"Nathan, how about a cup of soup? You should try to eat something." Gioia sounds concerned. She continues to rub his shoulders.

"My stomach isn't quite ready." Washington sips gingerly from his bottle. "That feels great, Cuz. Thanks much."

Carol agrees. "Gioia's right, Nathan. The sooner you put something solid inside yourself, the better you're going to feel."

Nathan shakes his head, his anger brewing. "What are you doing here, Carol? Do you really think this is the time and place to become all chummy? I could give a flying f . . ." Nathan stops in mid-sentence when he sees Brandon Davis walking towards him with a cameraman on his heel.

Clint's grinning. "That concludes this conversation."

Carol is visibly flustered. "I just thought . . ."

"No, that's just the problem. You weren't thinking." Gioia very protective of her cousin adds, "You have no business here."

Nathan refuses to even look at his "ex." Instead, he attempts to calm himself prior to the post-race interview, which he knows is inevitable.

"I'll say this much . . . she sure has a nice ass." Clint watches the woman return to the stands.

Gioia rolls her eyes. "No shit, Sherlock. There lies the crux of the problem."

*　　　　*　　　　*

The doorbell rings, awakening Albino Pavin from a deep slumber. Pavin is still in his recliner. The elder man feels stiffness in his lower back and shoulders. The dry chalky taste of medication still lingers. He stretches a bit to orient himself before answering the intercom. "*Yes, who is there?*"

"*Albino, he won! Lamo won the race!*"

Pavin is rubbing his eyes and yawning when the declaration finally sinks in. "*Oh my God, the race! I forgot . . . the time difference.*" He looks

229

at the clock, then immediately turns on the television, flipping through the channels looking for an Olympic update. The doorbell chimes again. Returning to the intercom, "*Sorry Augusto*," he depresses the gate switch.

His long time friend enters through the kitchen door extremely excited. "*RAI Uno, Albino, try channel one.*"

And there on Italian national television with sweat still visible on his forehead, under stadium lights, the drawn, gaunt face of a champion smiles into the camera. "*Mamma, come quickly! Lamo is on the TV.*"

"*What has happened?*" The woman enters wearing a white, light cotton robe. "*Hi Augusto, how are you?*" She yawns noticeably. "*I wondered who rang the doorbell at this early hour.*" She gives the man a snide look.

"*Liliana, you must see this,*" Augusto explains. "*Your son has won.*" The man points to the television set.

"*. . . an unbelievable race. I never thought I could hold the pace for so long. But at 150 kilometers, I was still running well with enough strength and stamina to run to the finish.*" The younger Pavin is holding a cup of soup and sipping it carefully between the commentary. Another man is translating to English.

Augusto guffaws, "*150 kilometers! That is crazy! A race of 100 miles - leave it to the Americans to introduce that distance.*"

"*I knew I was going to win when I passed the American with less than five kilometers remaining. Everyone thought that this was his race, which he would win. When I surged passed him, I never looked back.*" The Italian takes another swallow of broth and follows it with a bite of chicken and noodles. "*He is a fine competitor with much experience here. However, I knew if was close, I would make this an exciting finish.*"

Brandon Davis looks at the translator. "Please tell Girolamo he certainly made this race an exciting one and thank him for the interview." Davis sees Pavin nodding.

"*One more thing, Mr. Davis, if you please.*" Pavin pauses for a moment and then resumes speaking in an earnest tone. "*I wish to dedicate this race to my father who taught me how to run and how to compete. He is sick presently and I know this will make him feel much better. Papa, this is for you!*" Pavin raises the cup of chicken noodle soup with one hand and the medallion with the other. Lastly, he adds in Latin, "*I came, I saw, I conquered.*" The Italian grins ear to ear.

Liliana and Augusto look over to see Albino's reaction to the dedication. The man is speechless and withdrawn. Pavin recollects a time when he looked down at his younger son with tattered shoes, who had a gleam in his eye and an undeniable potential – a potential that has now come to full fruition. Tears are evident. He blows his nose with an embroidered handkerchief.

"*Congratulations, Papa.*" She hugs Albino affectionately. "*Our son looks too tired and too thin. He needs to come home to his Mamma for a while.*" The woman smiles at the thought of fattening her boy and spending time together. "*Okay Augusto, would you like a coffee?*"

"*Yes, thanks.*"

Liliana Pavin walks into her kitchen and looks out the window above the sink. She turns on the water which feels cool to the touch. The morning is already warm and humid. The cherry trees are in full green foliage. "*Father, Son and Holy Spirit*, Liliana Pavin whispers, "*Thank you for this.*"

*   *   *

"*Mamma, Mamma! Papa finished third.*" The young girl is ecstatic hearing the news of her father on the television. She sees her mother walking toward the small living room from one of the two bedrooms in her grandparent's modest apartment.

Yelizaveta Boroshkova sits next to her eldest daughter. An old clock with roman numerals denotes the time. It is just after ten in the morning. Mrs. Boroshkova knows her husband too well - knows that a third place finish is not good enough; not good enough for Yuri and certainly not good enough for a Soviet Olympic athlete. Not to curb her daughter's enthusiasm or innocence she agrees, "*Yes Elena, third place is very good.*" Watching the newscast she learns that Yuri finished with an American named Washington – that they finished together. "*That is odd*," she thinks, "*Yuri finishing in a tie. My husband is much too competitive . . .*"

"*See Mamma, there is Papa.*"

And there on the black and white screen she sees something contrary to what she has come to know of her husband. The anchorman informs, *"Yuri Boroshkov, in an act of sportsmanship and diplomacy, has joined hands with the American, Nathan Washington to finish even for the bronze medal. Comrade Boroshkov completed the race of 162 kilometers or 100 miles, run on trails across the Sierra Nevada Mountains in the state of California, in fifteen hours fifty-two minutes. He was passed by the eventual winner, an Italian, Girolamo Pavin and the second place finisher, a Japanese runner, Akira Okuda, both of whom finished approximately ten minutes ahead of Boroshkov and Washington."*

"Mamma, what's wrong?"

Boroshkov's wife knew of his intentions to step-up to the longer distance, to best a field of international runners and return to Moscow, not only the reigning world champion, but also an Olympic champion. Now that she has learned of his third place finish, though respectable, it is not what her husband had in mind. She has difficulty suppressing her own true emotions. *"I regret we cannot be there to celebrate with your father."* Yelizaveta smiles weakly, then asks herself, *"Why a draw?"*

"Why a draw, Comrade Boroshkov? Why not beat the American on his home ground – beat him soundly in the last kilometer or two?" The KGB advisor observes Washington and Boroshkov exchange their salute. *"I am perplexed."* The advisor shakes his head in disbelief.

"You have no clue what you are talking about, Comrade." Yuri is grateful to have finished with a respectable time and place. Sitting on a lawn chair in an arena brimming with spectators, he takes in the surroundings – the stars above, a moon rising in the east, the warm night air, people assisting after a long day. He adds, *"This has been a great race – a great experience."* The Soviet runner continues to massage and knead the muscles in his right calf. *"Nothing I could have done could have better prepared me for this, except of course, running the race before . . ."* Looking at his advisor he adds sardonically, *"and I was not permitted to do so, was I?"*

Boroshkov reflects on the topographical maps, the personnel profiles of the competitors in the race, plus the actual physical and mental preparation. The Russian physicist smiles upon a simple calculation. *"162 kilometers in less than sixteen hours: I averaged better than ten kilometers per hour over mountainous terrain. Not many men can say they have done that.*"

"*But you lost, Yuri.*" The advisor attempts to define his reality of the race.

"*Doctor, that depends on your definition of losing. Be useful now and fetch me a bowl of soup; I am hungry.*" Boroshkov hears the man grumble indignantly that he should have been "hungrier" during the race. When he bends over to untie his shoes, a sharp abdominal spasm forces him to promptly sit upright.

"Can I help you with that?" An attendant sees the Russian struggle and squats to remove his shoes.

Before Boroshkov can protest, she has already untied one of his shoes and is quickly doing the same to the other. When the woman sees the filthy, blood stained socks she offers, "Let me get a podiatrist for you."

Boroshkov begins to speak, but she has left to find assistance. He shakes his head. "*Americans can be so impetuous.*" He carefully removes one of the socks revealing disfigured toes with blackened nails. Blood blisters have popped as well and chafing has removed some skin covering the Achilles tendon. "*The human foot is a work of art and a masterpiece of engineering,*" he quotes Leonardo Da Vinci, laughing at the sight of his hideous feet.

"I am sorry I don't speak Russian, but let me have a look at those feet." The Podiatrist begins an examination.

". . . What made you decide to share third place, Nathan? Is this a signal to end the Cold War?" Brandon Davis places the microphone under the chin of a man he has come to admire and respect.

The American sips the flavored seltzer water and then answers, "It was actually his idea." Washington points his thumb toward Boroshkov.

"His idea?"

"Yeah, we'd been running together for twenty-five miles, pushing one another I guess, and then, going up the last climb, he mentions finishing together."

"But I thought Boroshkov doesn't speak English."

"And I don't speak Russian. But he made himself understood." Washington pauses for a moment and rubs his index finger and thumb through his mustache. "Just seemed like the right thing to do."

The reporter nods approvingly. "You were leading the race for a time. When did Pavin and Okuda pass you?"

"Less than three miles from here. There's a climb coming up to Auburn just after No Hands Bridge. Those two guys passed me like I was standing still. I was surprised Boroshkov didn't go with 'em. I think he hurt his leg though. I mean the guy was limping the last six miles – a lot."

Davis thinks, "That's got to hurt too - leading ninety-seven miles into a hundred mile race and not win." Then he asks, "Are you satisfied with your performance today?"

Collecting his thoughts along with another smile, Washington answers, "It would've been nice to win." He pulls a tress behind his ear and recalls, "My college coach once told me, 'On any given day anyone can win . . . Put yourself in that position and anything is possible.' I did that today and just came up a little short."

"You sure did, Nathan. Er, I mean you put yourself in a position to win. Many people I've spoken with considered you the favorite."

"Well Brandon, that's why we have races: to see who's the best and who's not."

"Regardless of the outcome, I'm sure your collegiate coach is very proud of what you accomplished today."

"And Dad would be too." Placing his hand on his brother's shoulder, Clint Washington interjects a personal thought into the post-race commentary.

"So what do you think of your brother's performance?" Davis moves the microphone to the two individuals standing adjacent to the bronze medalist.

Gioia speaks first. "He's still a champion to us."

Clint laughs and then adds, "He should have beaten the Russian."

"Which brings us back to the original question, Nathan; Do you think your decision to finish with Boroshkov will enable people to understand, that maybe, after working together for a time, we're not that different after all?" Davis makes his own decision to solicit a response that encompasses a broader subject than just distance running.

Washington looks over at Boroshkov and sees a medic tending the Russian's feet. "Maybe the symbol of an American and a Russian crossing the finishing line together will have a positive effect. No one can say for sure. But I do know one thing; that's what the Olympics are all about – bringing people together from all parts of the world to engage and compete with one another. Only good can come from that."

A low din of cheers is heard outside the confines of the arena – escalating to a stentorian crescendo. "We have another finisher . . . er, three finishers." The stadium's amplifiers resonate the announcer's voice once again, when three runners arrive – sprinting.

There will be no draw for fifth place. The Korean runner who had opened up a lead on the ascent to Robie Point had lost it on the descent to the finish line. His shorter legs unable to maintain the frantic pace, he is no longer in contention. The West German is on the right shoulder of the Czechoslovakian when the two reach the far corner of the track. Both men have track experience. Both men can generate a sprinter's foot speed. Both men are at the pinnacle of fitness and both men definitely have their national pride at stake. When the two reach the final straight, there are seventy-five meters remaining and they are dead even. Flailing arms, knees lifting, legs driving into the ground; both men collapse when they reach the finish line – the German a half step better than the Czech runner.

There is a thunderous groan from the audience.

Norman Sproul yells, "Can I get some help here?" He immediately goes to the German runner who appears worse. He crouches and sees the man gasping for air, eyes rolled back in his head. "Try to slow your breathing. Got to get up, Wolfgang. Walk it off." The race director knows the best way to prevent blood from rushing to the head.

After passing a Greek runner at No Hands Bridge, Wolfgang Hafner had caught these two on the last climb above Robie Point, then raced the final 1500 meters with vengeance. Wolfie, now aware of the race director, asks between the heaving, *"Did I beat him?"*

"What did you say? Are you all right?" Sproul observes the German's breathing begin to slow. He sees the pupil's of the competitor's eyes are not dilated, and then takes a deep breath himself. "You okay?"

The Korean runner who retains his composure crosses the finish line soon afterwards. The Czechoslovakian runner stands, but remains incapacitated, inhaling deeply to collect his breath, hands on his knees, head down. The Korean offers a hand which the Czech runner accepts weakly and then walks over to Sproul and Hafner extending his right hand.

The race director stands and shakes firmly. Sproul holds up his left hand. "Please wait a moment." Jogging to a nearby table, he grabs three medallions and returns quickly. "Got a little something for you guys." Beginning with the West German, who is still lying, he congratulates each man. "Wolfgang . . . Vaclav . . . Baik . . ."

The stadium announcer speaks into his microphone attempting to pronounce each name correctly. "We have the unofficial results. "Finishing in fifth place from the Republic of Germany . . ."

More applause follows, intensifying. The Greek runner arrives, and the crowd, looking for any excuse to revel in their Olympic experience, cheers fervently.

"This is gonna' be a long night," Sproul laughs.

"What did you say?" Hafner yells, accepting assistance to stand.

The race director points to the infield of the track. "Get something to drink. We have soup and goodies of sorts."

The Czech and Korean runners do not understand the words, but understand the general directions. Hafner offers his hand to the Czech runner. "*Congratulations, good race.*" The three men walk off the track, arms on each other's shoulders.

Once the applause subsides, the speakers crackle. The announcer clears his throat. "Finishing in fifth place with a time of sixteen hours, twenty-two minutes twelve seconds, from the Republic of West Germany, Wolfgang Hafner. Finishing with the same time from Czechoslovakia, our sixth place finisher, Vaclav P . . . s . . . er, enic . . . ka. In seventh with a time of sixteen twenty-two thirty-five is Baik-il Han from the Republic of Korea, and the latest finisher in eighth, from Greece, Yannis Taptelis. His unofficial time, sixteen hours twenty-four minutes."

The man behind the stadium's microphone had announced other Western States' finishes. He had pronounced difficult names in the past. Looking down the international registry of entrants with their abridged profiles he discloses publicly, "This is gonna' be a long night." The man hears his voice echo around the arena and then sheepishly switches the mike off.

Sproul chuckles, "Hey, I was just thinking the same thing."

Susan Chacarito Badillo looks at her despondent husband seated at the Highway 49 Crossing aid station, his head hung. "You're not thinking about quitting, are yuh?" She had seen J. P. in tough situations before, but the knee, obviously a concern, has him re-evaluating. "Can you walk on it?"

The Mexican scratches the black stubble on his chin, then looks into the eyes of a woman who knows him too well. "*I have doubts*," the man's Hispanic tongue forthcoming as exhaustion has set in.

Susan repeats the same questions in Spanish.

An aid station attendant hands him a small plastic bag of ice. "Can I get you some aspirin or Motrin?" Her hair is light and her eyes appear gray in the artificial light of a kerosene lantern. She speaks with a slight British inflection.

Juan-Pablo asks, "Is there a difference? I mean is one better than the other." Badillo searches for a quick remedy, so he can run the last six miles.

The attendant, a nurse who appears thirtiesh replies, "Not really. They'll both reduce inflammation. It just depends on what you've taken today. You shouldn't mix one anti-inflammatory with another, though."

"Thanks for the info Doc, but I'm looking for a quick fix; something to take the edge off." J. P. removes the ice bag from his left knee.

"Oh, I'm not a doctor. Just a nurse I'm afraid. I believe there is a physician on staff. Should I call him over?"

Susan intervenes, "No thanks, we're fine." Then she muses, "The last thing we need is a second opinion." The wife of a veteran endurance runner knows her man's capabilities . . . knows he'll be a pain in the ass to live with if he doesn't finish this race.

The nurse performs a speedy exam of the knee. "Oh my, your left lateral excruciate has certainly bared the brunt of your efforts today." She pushes tenderly . . .

237

Which immediately elicits a grimace and groan from Badillo. "That's okay nurse, er . . . What's your name?" He reapplies the ice to his knee.

"Penelope, and if I may add, number 557, there's nothing wrong with withdrawing. No need to punish yourself, if you know what I mean. There will be other races."

Susan Badillo reasons, "No need to punish yourself! That's the nature of the sport, Penelope." She hates the sound of the name, especially the tone and manner in which it was delivered. "Please excuse us for a minute, 'Penelope,'" more stress placed on the woman's name.

The nurse shrugs, "Just offering my two pence, Mam."

"Look Chacarito-Badillo." Susan pauses becoming more patient. "Dearest, you remember last year when you DNF'd? How disappointed you were – for months. Now, think about how you'll feel if you don't cross that finish line. I know it's not what you wanted, but remember what we have always told each other. You can't always get what you want . . ."

"Yeah I know; you get what you need." The statement is a summary of their lives. "But really Susan, I've finished an Olympic marathon before. There's no need to kill myself . . ." Shaking his head, he finishes a cup of fluids. "Just to finish . . . I can run this race again next year."

"Next year! You sound like that stupid nurse, Penelope." She pronounces the other woman's name with scorn - as an insulting twelve year old would. "I asked you this before; can you walk on it?"

"Yeah, I can hobble to the finish," he answers equivocally.

Admonishing her husband Susan takes the ice bag from her husband. "Then that's what you're going to do. Now be a good boy and let Mommy wrap that leg for you."

The Mexican smiles wryly. "And they call me 'Bad-Ass' Badillo."

Joshua Kostinski walks the last incline to Robie Point – disillusioned and exhausted. The Israeli has run numerous races in his life and yet, has never felt this utterly depleted. He squirts water onto his face, then into his mouth. "Only one thing left to do," he ponders, "finish the fuckin' race." Joshua had heard the remark from his collegiate running buddies, when they had not performed as they had hoped. Thinking of his collegiate coach waiting at the finish line, he feels somewhat apprehensive. "God, I felt so good for so long," he reflects, "then the demons jumped on my back . . . Hell, there're still clawing at my throat!" Kostinski chuckles at the thought.

"Lookin' good there, number 548. Less than a quarter mile to Robie Point. The spectator, a young man, recognizes the Star of David on the runner's jersey. "Go Israel! Almost there."

Wanting to sound grateful, but not believing the estimation of distance, Joshua waves and says, "Thanks." He had received much input from well-wishers on the trail during the day and found for the most part, most had no clue of what they were talking about. Totally fatigued he thinks, "'Lookin' good' – I know I look like shit, because I feel like shit . . . and a quarter mile to the next checkpoint - I bet that's a crock of bullshit too. It's at least a half mile, if not more." Laughing at his own cynicism he mutters, "Must be another demon."

A raucous crowd greets the Israeli, along with his coach who is standing in front of the station's beverage table. The elder man places a cold damp towel on the shoulders of his athlete. "Just thought you might need a little encouragement before your last push to the finish line." The coach points to the crowd and continues, "So I brought a few friends."

"Thanks coach. I appreciate the thought." Kostinski declines a drink from one of the attendants. "Not quite what we had hoped for, Coach. I mean when the wheels started to come off, they came undone."

"Don't sound so, er, deflated, Josh. You've run a great race."

"Good metaphor, Coach . . . Wheels – deflated, good one." The two men walk toward the final ascent. "What place am I in?"

"Twelfth, I think." The man recognizes his runner's sense of humor; recognizes that he is cognizant of what's around him. "You've done good kid. I'm damn proud of you."

Kostinski points his flashlight at his chronometer. "23:02:30 and counting . . . 'Takes a lickin' and keeps on tickin'.'" The man born in a small middle-eastern country surrounded by four hostile borders chortles, "Just like me."

The coach removes the damp shawl from his runner's shoulders. "See you at the finish, Josh."

Runners are strewn over thirty miles of trail. From Todd Valley to the Placer High School track in Auburn, flashlights bounce and wobble - some solo, some in queue. Illuminating their path to the finish line, bright yellow ribbons quiver in a light evening breeze, intermittent phosphorescent glow sticks provide an additional means to stay the course, and a large gibbous moon is overhead. Like fireflies fluttering toward a lantern, these runners are drawn to a finish line; a finish line that will endorse an accomplishment few people will appreciate and fewer will understand. For these spirited souls, the lantern is the moon above and the finish line, just as visible in their minds, is eidetic. Their quest will only be fully complete when they cross it.

Vomiting his guts up for the umpteenth time, Eammon Horgan sits dejected at the Auburn Lakes checkpoint. Every time he swallows anything, he throws it right back up. The man whose goal was to finish the race in sixteen hours is relegated to a position he has experienced few times in his life. "Fuck, the last time I felt like this I was in a drinking contest with one of my buddies."

One of the attendants laughs, "What were you drinking?"

After a dry heave Horgan answers, "Paddy's."

"Whiskey? Well that's pretty stupid. Didn't anyone tell you distance runners can't drink, especially the hard stuff." The attendant walks over and places a couple of antacid tablets in the runner's hand. "Think about the amount of body fat inside yourself. Any booze you take in goes straight to your liver and brain. How much did you drink?"

"We split a bottle."

"A bottle? How big of a bottle?"

"In this country, you'd call it a fifth."

"A fifth! God almighty, that could have killed you." The attendant eyes a man who should be committed, not commended.

"Ah, when it comes to the drink the Irish possess no fear, and for that matter," Horgan adds with a wry smile, "no brains either."

"What have to been eating and drinking today?"

"No Paddy today, that's for sure." The young Irishman belches and refrains from up-chucking any last remnants in his stomach. "Jesus, Mary and Joseph; when's it going to stop?" He looks at the tablets. "Do you think these'll help?"

"Sure, if you can keep 'em down." The attendant turns to welcome another runner entering Auburn Lakes.

Eammon feels saliva gathering in his mouth, so he spits to remove the excess. There are two cups of fluids next to his chair; one filled with carbonated cola, the other with water. Neither looks inviting.

"Well Eammon Christopher Horgan! How the hell are you?" Nigel Preverett had met the younger runner last year in Brighton after the two dueled for a top ten finish. Both had succeeded, but the young Irishman had proven to be the better runner on that day, finishing second. Preverett sees a speckled face without much complexion, and eyes recessed deep in their sockets. "What the bloody hell has happened to you?"

Initially Horgan does not recognize the man who's speaking, although the accent is too familiar. The intense brightness of a kerosene lamp prevents the identification of the man in front of him. "Eighty-five miles of running has happened to me." He leans over for a better look at the man addressing him. "Oh Nigel, it's you. What a pleasant surprise," he says sarcastically.

"Now now, Eammon, be a good sport. Neither one of us is having the day we expected." The British runner has spoken to several runners during the course of the day and wishes only to express propriety toward a fellow competitor.

"You've caught me at a bad time, Nigel, er . . . whatever, Preverett," Horgan answers bluntly. The Irishman has met few English he likes - most for whom he feels total contempt.

Growing up in Cork two hundred miles from Belfast and Derry, Eammon Christopher Horgan and his family have been far removed from the turmoil and violence that has besieged Northern Ireland. Eammon has read numerous political and economic, partisan leaflets requesting support for the cause of removing English rule from Ireland. Despite not being actively involved, much to the relief of his parents, he completely empathizes with Irish nationalism.

Looking up at the elder British runner, he sees a pompous, conceited man who is obviously running better than he is - perhaps, even flaunting his own performance. "I'm not in a cordial mood at the moment." Another loud burp follows. "You best be on your way and leave me to my misery."

Preverett senses the underlying hostility. Knowing the history between the Irish and the English, he has come to the realization that the hatred between the two European island nations must come to an end some time, and the sooner the better. Too many innocent victims have been consumed over a territory long ago sanctioned to Great Britain. He squats down in front of the young Irishman, and with the stalwart voice of a veteran asks, "You're not thinking about quitting, are you?"

Horgan is pinching the band clasped to his wrist, looking at the vital data written on it - Wt 142, BP 108/65, HR 52. He raises his head. The man looking at him is old enough to be his father. Thick gray hair, thin lips, a nose that appears to cover half the Brit's face, and lines on his forehead and face that match the man's age. "How did you know my middle name?" the Irishman inquires suspiciously.

"At London to Brighton last year; when they called your name at the awards ceremony." Preverett nods, "You ran an excellent race. Wasn't that your first ultra?"

"You have an excellent memory, Mr. Preverett. Do you always commit names to memory?"

"Only when I know I'll be racing against them in the future." The British runner laughs and adds, "Senility hasn't quite crept in yet."

"You've got a lot of experience in running, don't you?" Horgan lowers his guard.

"More than I care to remember, and I will say this much; I've vomited in races and came back to finish." He grabs the cups next to Horgan and drinks them in two gulps. Wiping liquid for his chin he says, "Thanks for the drink, Laddie." Preverett stands feeling stiffness in his legs, lower back and shoulders. Holding his forearm under the lamp, he reads, "Just past eleven, Eammon. Fifteen miles in seven hours, do the maths lad; you can crawl to the finish with time to spare."

Horgan realizes that the older man is not the typical pompous ass that he has come to equate with being British. That the center of civilization may in fact, lie some where beyond England's shores. His boyish charm returns. "Yes, 'tis some where inside a shamrock, Nigel."

He touches the three-leaf clover stitched onto his singlet, knowing its kinship to the Father, the Son and the Holy Ghost.

"What's inside a shamrock?" The British runner queries nonplussed.

Staring into the bluish-gray eyes of an opponent he replies, "Maybe the solution to my problems." He chews the two tablets provided, tasting the chalky residue. "I'll see you at the finish Nigel, er . . . What's your middle name? James? Graham? Chadwick?" The Irishman smirks at his own inquiry.

"That's the competitive chap I remember from last year. Good to see you're feeling our oats again." Turning to an attendant recording bib numbers he acknowledges, "Number 544 checking out. Thanks for everything. You guys have been great."

"Hey Preverett, your middle name?" Horgan follows the query with another loud belch, content that nothing has come up.

Preverett replies smugly, "I'll let you know later, if not at the finish line, then certainly at the awards ceremony. Now get off your arse and continue your quest, Cristoforo." Nigel enjoys pronouncing Latin forms of names, and with a final remark, "Cheerio," the man from Manchester flicks on his flashlight and departs into the darkness of a warm summer night somewhere in the Sierra foothills of Northern California, leaving the young Irishman to his thoughts.

Eammon's angular face, which was like a blade's edge a few minutes before, has softened into a dull sheen. He thinks of his mother who had always provided strength and conviction – the matriarch of the Horgan family. The toast she offered prior to his departure was fittingly Celtic and inspirational. Now he repeats the words to gather himself before a final push to the finish line. "May the road rise to meet you. May the wind always be at your back. May the sunshine warm your face and the rain fall softly upon your fields, and until we meet again, may God hold you in the hollow of His hand." The woman has foresight.

Standing naked in the shower, both hands on the nozzle, he looks down at the swirling water flow into the drain. The warm water rinsing his back and legs is mixed with sweat, soil and blood - remnants of a day's work being washed away. Girolamo Pavin feels a wash cloth softly scrubbing his back. "*Please use your hands, Sabrina. I prefer your touch over cloth.*"

"*As you wish my dear. Anything for my Olympian.*" She embraces him feeling the soapy film against her breasts. Slowly and methodically, she works her caress lower and lower, massaging as she cleans - the soap removing dirt, her touch removing soreness. Sabrina feels herself begin to stir. She has done this a hundred a times and knows the nuances of the cleansing ritual with her fiancé. Alone with her man, with only the sound of rushing water she asks, "*Are you happy that I am here with you, Lamo?*" She scrubs layers of dirt and speckles of blood from his calves and then winces when she sees his feet.

"*Without doubt, Sabrina.*" Pavin is in his own world – contemplating an astonishing accomplishment that will open a world of opportunities. He too, winces from the sting of soap washing chafed skin and blisters on his feet and toes.

"*And do you love me, my husband to be?*" Sabrina has positioned herself in front of her man scrubbing his shins, knees and thighs; each scrub followed with a soft kiss.

"*Yes, without doubt, my love.*" Girolamo feels her lips press against him more passionately; her soapy hands cleansing the most sensitive parts of his body. The woman has his undivided attention. He sees only the top of her head and shoulders, water cascading over olive-tan skin. Sabrina's hands are moving rhythmically over his legs, chest and buttocks. Her attention to detail is incredible. "*You are not repulsed by what you see, my Dearest One?*" The woman's eyes express desire and pleasure.

Sabrina fondles his genitals, kissing his sinewy abdomen and strong thighs. Rubbing, tugging, sucking, wishing only to please – his touch is irreplaceable. Lamo's hands are no longer on the spigot. Instead, he pulls her gently upward and she kisses him every centimeter of the way. Their lips meet, tongues lash-out; they're enraptured in the moment. Sabrina delicately moves the crucifix and places it on the nape of his neck. She feels the cool tile against her back as her man anchors himself and she braces for the most passionate love-making. Their bodies entwined as one, she adds between profound breaths, "*Lamo, you are the luckiest man in all the world. Is it not true?*"

Pavin gasps, *"My God, without doubt my love, it is true. Without doubt."*

The stadium's loudspeakers crackle to life. "Finishing on the track in fifteenth place, making the final turn for the homestretch, from Tanzania, Ibrahim Cheyo." A modest applause ensues since the large crowds have dwindled to a few loyal supporters. "His unofficial time is seventeen hours, fifty-five minutes.

"And just entering el stadio, one of our local favorites, representing Mexico, Juan-Pablo Chacarito Badillo." The announcer's accent sounds comically American. "J. P. currently resides in Reno and is finishing the Western States Trail Run for the second time."

The cooling effect of rushing water is cleansing. Half way across the Middle Fork of the American River, Indraneil Kamath immerses his head into the sacred water. To Indraneil, the earth, the wind and all waters are sacred. Kamath is a devout Hindu. He throws his head back, and water sprays from his long black hair. Moonlight reflects off the river and he looks to the sky and thinks, "Light to guide me on my path to enlightenment . . . and the finish line." The river exhilarating, Indraniel feels revived.

In his youth he had participated in a Ceremony on the River near the headwaters of the Ganges – a holy place called Haridwar. The pilgrimage to the five sacred bathing pools represented a reincarnation of his life on earth and a rebirth of his soul. The purging effect of the water is most memorable, and thus every time he showers, bathes or swims, his mind and body feel cleansed.

"Number 546, you better get the lead out of your pants! You're barely ahead of the cut-off." An attendant, a strong burly man reaches his hand out, offering assistance to a diminutive runner arriving on the bank.

Kamath keeps his right hand secured on the line and clutches the man's thick forearm with his left. Stepping onto the embankment, he encounters a man twice his size with a full beard. "You are too kind, Sir. But I can assure you, I have no lead in my pants." The Indian puts his palms together, half bows and then laughs.

"I just wanted you to be aware of the time and you're . . ."

"My predicament?" Indraneil is well aware of his situation and totally in command of his faculties. "I assure you that I am fine. Thank you for your assistance."

The attendant hands Kamath his drop bag. Many runners, who looked more dead than alive when they arrived at Rucky Chucky, had decided to cash it in, forfeiting their wristbands. "You seem to be in good spirits, number 546."

"Please, my name is Neil." Looking into his drop bag, he finds a dry pair of socks and sneakers. Kamath acknowledges, "I am having a good day, Sir; perhaps not a great day, but a good day nonetheless."

"Can I get you anything?"

"Yes, you may. Thank you. A cup of tea would be nice." The Indian feels a chill as cold water drips onto his back.

"Anything else?"

Indraneil has not eaten much since Foresthill and decides it's time to consume some solid food. "Crackers, banana, orange . . . anything you have is fine." With a soiled towel he dries his feet, before donning dry socks and sneakers. He peers across the river to see other flashlights approaching. Kamath had passed several runners since the last checkpoint, most of whom resembled casualties of war more than runners attempting to finish a race. He shakes his head and says, "The walking wounded." Someone had mentioned the phrase at the trail-briefing yesterday and now he witnesses the race's full effect. The phrase clearly applies.

The bearded man observes the Indian chomp into a cracker that has been lathered with peanut butter. "Very perceptive, Neil. So you better get the lead out, before you become one of those 'walking wounded.'" He sees the dark eyes of a competitor come into clear focus. The slight man exudes calmness that belies intensity.

"I'll be on my way soon enough my good man. Thank you for your prompt and dutiful attention." Indraneil finishes another cup of tea, and then stands to continue.

"Finishing twenty-fourth in a time of eighteen hours, forty-five minutes from the state of Virginia, Byron Hall." The applause is sparse, since it's after midnight and most of spectators - the sane ones – have long since departed. Large incandescent bulbs burn brightly on the tops of four towers, illuminating the arena. People are milling about the infield catering to the runners who have completed their quest. Other race officials communicate with inbound checkpoints, monitoring the progress of runners whom remain in the race.

"And entering the stadium," the announcer pauses seeing a runner moving swiftly on the far side of the track, "number 5-42, Yosef Ethiopia appears to have some gas left in his tank." He remembers the East African is the only runner in the race whose surname is tantamount with his national origin. "Yosef hails from the province of Eritrea in Ethiopia."

The race director welcomes another finisher – the twenty-fifth. "Congratulations Yosef, you have run an admirable race. You should be very proud."

Ethiopia, who had run the final downhill mile attempting to catch Hall, accepts the medallion graciously. He exhales responding, "Thank you, Sir. You and your people have been wonderful to me all day. I am truly grateful." The man's tone is genuine, and his East African accent is refreshingly melodic.

Sproul looks into the depleted dark eyes of a competitor who has obviously sacrificed much to get here. Not only in today's race, but also the sacrifice when one considers the man's remote past. "For your first time on this course, you ran a tremendous race – even leading for a time."

Hall intervenes, "You sure did, buddy. You should be damn proud." He shakes the Ethiopian's hand. "And how about that rattlesnake too?" The American laughs, recollecting the look on the Ethiopian's face.

"What rattlesnake?" Sproul has not heard of any snake encounters during the course of the day – one of his worst fears being an athlete bitten on a remote section of trail.

"Oh, we had a squabble with a four-footer near Auburn Lake's."

"That certainly was . . . unsettling," Yosef's fear resurfacing.

Sproul chuckles, "Part of the total Western States experience."

Hall places his hand on the shoulder of a fellow finisher and wishing to be a good host he asks, "What do you say we go grab some grub?"

"Grab some grub?" Ethiopia looks perplexed. "What is grub?"

"Come on, I'll introduce you to some of the finest grub this side of the Pecos."

Sproul interjects, "Another part of the total Western States experience."

"*And another stupid American idiomatic phrase*," Ethiopia adds, chuckling in his own native dialect of Tigrinya.

He squats behind a large woody shrub adjacent to the trail near the Auburn Lake Trails checkpoint. His gut has been reeling since leaving Todd Valley and every bite of food or sip of fluid brings another flush. Rectum raw, frustration setting-in, Xavier-Francois Simeon pushes to relieve the pressure that has been mounting since his last stop. Diarrhea accompanied by minor cramps has slowed his progress immeasurably. When Simeon stands to carefully wipe himself, he spots another flashlight approaching. Then as quickly as the runner passes, the Haitian sees another runner come into view. Another pang in his abdomen, he massages the area gingerly. He shakes his head in disgust, bows his head and prays, "*My Lord, I have not asked much in my life, but I implore you now; Give me the strength to continue and finish this race.*" Simeon gazes into the starry heavens searching for an answer. Many more stars are visible in the arid sky of California compared to the humid tropical environs of Haiti.

*   *   *

A few weeks before leaving the western region of Hispaniola for the Olympics, he had gone for one of his early morning runs where his parents live near Cap Haitien. Simeon always observed impoverished people wherever he went, and this run was no different. Skeletal faces would always peer from huts or from under perpetually worn hats. Smaller children with inflated bellies would always follow, grinning at him and wishing to join the crazy runner who would appear from time to time. The run was fairly flat as he followed a dirt trail north to the coast. Upon arriving to a rocky shoreline over-looking the Caribbean Sea, he stared north. The ocean mirrored the sky – indigo-blue. A crescent moon was still visible on the western horizon. "*Thank you Lord, for this moment, this opportunity. I am truly blessed.*" Xavier-Francois speaks French fluently, but he always prays in his native Haitian Creole. His preparation complete, he knew he was ready to run.

A large gibbous moon illuminates the trail. He has his flashlight turned on, but soon realizes there is substantially more light coming from our neighboring satellite than his toy-sized, C-battery flashlight. Xavier-Francois Simeon is surprised to feel how well his body is holding up, despite the diarrhea. He sips some fluid from his bottle, electing to spit it out, rather than swallow. He crosses himself before stepping onto the trail and whispers, *"Please Lord, do not desert me."*

Simeon hopes he can run some distance before his next bathroom break. If he cannot, his goal of finishing may be as fleeting as the contents of his gut.

"Two runners have just arrived and they look in high spirits." The announcer continues, "Let's give them a warm welcome, "Xian Doi of China and from Jamaica, Conrad Creary." Few people on the infield pay attention to the declaration, since their activity revolves around those who have finished and need medical assistance, or those remaining on the trail that still need to be monitored. Doi's coach is there, so is an assistant from the Jamaican national team. When the two runners cross the finish line together handshakes are exchanged, and hugs too.

"Congratulations you guys. You've done really well!" Norm Sproul greets both with finisher's medallions. He points to the clock. "Nineteen hours, twenty-seven minutes. Great job!"

Creary and Doi solicit their respective coaches as to their final position at trail's end. Their coaches reply in unison, twenty-ninth; albeit one answers in English, the other in Mandarin.

An attendant walks over and points at their wrist bands. "We'd like to get your final weight and blood pressure. Please come with me."

Creary responds first. "Do you need our wristbands?" He attempts to remove it.

"Oh no," the attendant replies. "In fact, you may want to keep it as a memento. Most runners do."

Doi observes the dialogue between the attendant and Creary, then asks his coach. *"What does she say?"*

Doi's coach offers a warm smile. *"Just follow the woman, Xian."*

Creary looks at his watch and mutters an obscenity in patois, then says, "it's one thirty – in the morning! I just want to sit a spell."

The attendant, a woman in her forties, grins. "You will. Once I get your weight, you can sit while I take your blood pressure."

Creary chuckles. "Mam, you have a kind heart."

Doi inquires again. *"What do they say, Coach? All I wish to do is . . ."*

"I know Xian - you wish only to sit down." He observes a puzzled look on his runner's face.

Vangelis', "Chariots of Fire," is playing on an eight-track stereo – at full volume. The progressive music is so loud that it can be heard by incoming runners a kilometer away as an echo resonates up the ridge to the Western States Trail. Four kerosene lamps burn brightly, illuminating the amphitheater known as Brown's Bar. The checkpoint has enticed weary runners to stop for a short break before continuing their assault to the finish line, sixteen kilometers away. A Norwegian runner approaches Brown's Bar, walking the single track trail, exhausted and ready to call it quits. Another runner, the Swede, Per Olafsson sits near a lantern, sipping on some chicken noodle soup and contemplates the same fate. Mats Larsen eyes a fellow Scandinavian when he enters the aid station and pulls a chair adjacent to Olafsson. His breathing labored, Larsen mutters in Norwegian, *"I can no longer continue. It is done."* He rubs his hand against his forehead and feels the crust of sweat intermixed with trail residue.

Olafsson pulls a lock of his blonde hair from his eyes and finishes a morsel of chicken noodle. *"For me too . . . maybe."* Olafsson's stoicism belies his true feelings. The portion of trail from the River Crossing to this checkpoint has been extremely slow-going. More walking than running and frequent rest stops have left the Swede feeling frustrated and despondent. *"I too, am not sure if I can continue."* Per wiggles his toes, feeling the dirt, sweat and blood which have accumulated over the past ten miles of trail. When he had changed his socks at the River Crossing and examined his feet, he had witnessed the carnage of eighty miles of trail running. Olafsson knows his feet are a mess. *"I feel I have nothing left to give my body."*

"Hey guys! You're looking swell. What can I get for you, number 560?" The aid station attendant, a portly man in his mid-forties, looks directly at the Norwegian, scrutinizing the runner's condition. "I have something for you. It'll make you feel better." The attendant brings a cup of soup and crackers.

Larsen looks up at the attendant and replies, *"Your energy. You can give me your energy . . . But you can certainly keep those legs."* Both runners laugh at the thought.

"And what is wrong with my legs?" The attendant replies in fluent Swedish.

Olafsson clears his throat and apologizes immediately in English. "I am sorry. I think we are all fatigued beyond sanity." The runners exchange a sheepish glance.

"Well then, I would question any man's sanity who attempts to run 100 miles. But more importantly, I would commend the same man for completing such great athletic feat."

Both runners recognize the man's intellect, plus his articulateness. Larsen requests, "You can inquire for a ride to the finish line, um . . ."

The attendant offers his name in Swedish. *"My name is Karl . . . Munz."*

All three men grin, recognizing the heritage of the attendant. "Karl, I think I've had enough. I'm done." Larsen accepts the cup of soup.

The heavy fellow sits in a portable chair that appears to strain under his weight and girth. "Obviously, I'm no expert in running 100 mile endurance runs, but during my youth I did run a marathon or two." Holding his watch under the lantern, he reads the time. "And I'm no dummy either. You guys have been running for twenty hours, and you have your wits as well. With ten miles left and apparently four hours of time remaining, you would be foolish not to finish." As he stands the arm rests of the portable chair bend to support him.

The two runners are stunned. An overweight American has just lectured them on the importance of completing the race. Both men shake their heads in disbelief. Larsen glances at his watch first. *"You know he's right. I have run faster than four minutes per kilometer during my long runs. We surely can run four kilometers an hour to end this run, can we not?"*

Olafsson nods and replies in his best west-coast slang. "You bet your ass we can!"

"Incoming runner!" Another attendant calls out, "Number 544."

Nigel Preverett does not bother to sit, nor does he acknowledge anyone in the immediate surroundings. He has been adamant about keeping a consistent pace and momentum since leaving Auburn Lake Trails. Preverett, who is immersed in the race, avoids lingering or exchanging civilities. He grabs a couple crackers and washes them down with a tepid cup of broth, followed by two shots of diluted coke. "Number 544 checking-out. Thanks men." Nigel departs with a chocolate chip cookie in his mouth, a full water bottle in his left hand and a flashlight in his right."

Olafsson remembers the Englishman's name. "Nigel, we'll come with you. Number 602 departing."

Nigel turns and sees two men leaving the checkpoint directly behind him. "Oh, Per, I'm surprised to see you. Thought you would have strutted to the finish by now."

"Strutted? I have struggled . . . much over the last fifteen miles."

"He's not the only one who has struggled," Larsen adds.

"Ditto that my good man. My name's Nigel, what's yours?" He hears Larsen's reply, and then the man from the U. K. leads a threesome to a steep rocky descent. With three flashlights and a large moon reflecting sunlight above them, the trail is well lit and subsequently, the three men make good time picking their way over the fist-sized stones. The sound of cascading water quickly replaces a fading refrain of Vangelis' "Chariots of Fire." The American River flows adjacent to a relatively flat section of trail leading them to their next ascent to Highway 49 Crossing.

The earth approaches the end of another complete rotation on its axis. Another fraction of its revolution around the sun will soon come to closure as well, and when the day is done, time will have run out for those obstinate souls who have refused to give in to their compulsion to quit. For most, their mode of transportation has become relegated to the "Western States Shuffle" – a jog, then walk survival approach of just getting to the next tree or glow stick or aid station. Runners are moving southwest and see the large moon with a hint of orange dropping towards the inversion layer on the western horizon. And like the moon which appears just out of reach, so goes the finish line as well. The interval of time between aid stations has become progressively longer and longer as their pace has become slower and slower. The lights of Auburn have been visible for hours – so it seems. Their progress is abhorrently slow to the point of ad nauseam. Many check their chronometers repeatedly, praying the next aid lies just around the next bend. For the runners who remain steadfast in their conviction to finish, the Western States Shuffle has taken on a different meaning. Perhaps "death march" has become more appropriate. And unfortunately for those remaining on the course, none of whom have ever completed a race of this length, the death march continues.

"Entering the stadium, the forty-third finisher, from Australia, number 512, Lindsey Eagle." There is a distinct holler and a yelp heard from the shadows in the bleachers. Eagle looks up to see a fellow Aussie hobbling down the stairs.

David Conor is all smiles when he reaches the finish line to offer a congratulatory hug to one of his own. "Great job, Linds. You've done your country proud."

"Thanks Dave. Wish you could have accompanied me to the finish."

"Here Mr. Eagle, let me give you this token of our appreciation. Congratulations." Sproul puts the finisher's medallion around the man's neck and shakes his hand heartily.

Only a glimpse of disappointment can be gleaned on the face of the other competitor who could not muster the will to continue. Tapping his quadriceps, Conor replies, "Just wasn't my day, Mate, but there'll be other races."

An attendant requests that Eagle accompany her to the final stop before the finisher is dismissed. "We'll need to get your weight. How are you feeling, number 512."

Eagle smirks, "Oh, I've been better."

"Bloody hell, Linds! You've just run the longest race of your venerable life. You're entitled to feel a bit dour." Conor nods, approving of the other man's completion of task. "Besides, now you've become part of an elite corps of runners. Not many can say they've run 100 miles in a day. You can!"

"Thanks Dave. Hearing that from you means a lot." Lindsey Eagle looks up from the scale he's standing on and sees the young woman recording his weight. "What was my time, give or take?"

The attendant interjects, "Looks like you lost a few pounds, er . . ."

"Lindsey." He smiles at the young woman when their eyes meet. "What's yours?"

The favor's returned, "Christine, and 'give or take,' twenty-two hours, six minutes, seven seconds."

Conor adds smiling, "and one hundred five milliseconds – 'give or take,' Linds."

The announcer interrupts their conversation with another declaration. "We have another runner who has just arrived at Robie Point. Er . . . number 544, Nigel Preverett of Great Britain."

"Looks like the old Pommie's going to finish – God bless him. David Conor glances at his watch and concludes, "I should be home in bed. It's after four AM."

Indraneil Kamath continues the grind up the steep grade. Not running a step since leaving the river a half mile back, he forces himself to inhale deeply as he negotiates another ascent. An occasional car passes on the highway above the trail. Kamath can hear the cars, but the only things visible in the dense vegetation are the trail illuminated at his feet and the intermittent glow stick hanging on a leafy branch. The Indian is convinced he has run a smart race with a sound strategy. He has told himself repeatedly, "Just keep moving. I can do this." Finally a voice of optimism cries out in the warm morning's air and it's of the sweetest sound.

"Incoming runner!" Then after what seems the grandest hiatus, a man asks, "What's your number?"

Indraneil sees the orange hue of the moon on the western horizon and realizes time is running out. "Number five forty-six." He hands his water bottle to an attendant and then flicks his flashlight off. Walking over to a table filled with a variety of snacks and beverages, Kamath asks, "What do you recommend?"

A man stands to assist. "Whatever your stomach has handled all day and night, er . . . number 546. I certainly wouldn't change anything at this point."

Kamath chews on a piece of energy bar and simultaneously swallows two cups of coke. "Thank you for your suggestion, Sir. I will take it to heart."

"Where are you from?" The man observes the other's dark complexion and long black hair pulled back in tightly bound pony tail.

Kamath smiles and points to his singlet. "You do not recognize the flag here."

The attendant looks perplexed and shakes his head. "No, I am sorry . . ."

Kamath, too, is perplexed. How can Americans be so ignorant? The second most populated country on the globe with the greatest English speaking population . . . "I am Indian . . ."

"You don't look indian . . ."

"Not Native American," Kamath withholds a laugh and thinks, "You blithering fool."

"Oh! Indian." The man clutches his head, aware of his own ignorance. "Please forgive me, but it's after four in the morning and I'm . . ."

"Hah Rama! It's after four . . ." Indraneil looks around and sees runners lying on cots or sitting in chairs totally incapacitated. "Casualties of the battle," he ponders.

The attendant is resolute. "You have almost two hours to run seven miles. You're in great shape. You will finish number 546." The man has put on a pair of glasses.

Kamath nods, "Yes I will. Thank you for your vote of confidence."

"You speak English really well."

Without hauteur or conceit, he informally salutes the man behind the table. Then murmurs, "Yes I do, and probably better than you."

As he approaches Highway Forty-Nine a police officer greets him. "You ready to go?"

The Indian calls to the attendant recording bib numbers, "Number 546 checking out." Indraneil switches his flashlight on and jogs across the pavement, only to be greeted by another ascent. He grimaces and then whispers, "Hah Rama, when is it going to end?"

One and half miles ahead of the Indian, the Haitian is working his way along a flat rocky section of trail above another road – the Auburn-Foresthill Divide. A canopy of trees and brush prevent moonlight from seeping in. No Hands Bridge is in his immediate future. Xavier-Francois Simeon has not eaten nor drunk since the Auburn Lakes Checkpoint. On the upside he has not defecated for some time and the cessation of minor abdominal cramps has improved his disposition, somewhat. On the downside, hypoglycemia is taking its full effect. Sore muscles he once felt are completely numb. His focus has waned considerably as he has difficulty picking his way over the many large rocks that sabotage the narrow dirt trail. *"Just keep running,"* he repeats between deep breaths. *"I can finish this . . ."*

A rocky specimen seems to levitate from the ground when his big toe crashes into an immoveable object. The face plant knocks the wind out of him, and for a moment he is stunned. His flashlight has disappeared. He grovels around in the darkness as a blind man would for a lost cane. Winces of uncertainty rapidly swell into shear panic. Simeon stops for a moment, attempting to erase the doubt that has crept into his mind. *"Relax, you will find it. Just relax."* He facilitates the relaxation technique by slowing his breathing. A dull pain is discernable on his right knee and he touches warm fluid oozing from the wound. The incident angers the Haitian. *"Jesus Christ,"* he yells skyward, *"What do you want from me?"* Simeon continues his search, having no clue where the flashlight went. He observes an embankment to his immediate right and realizes if the flashlight fell there, he will have to run blindly on this dangerous section of dirt, rock and brush. Standing to properly assess the damage to his body the Haitian whispers, *"Thank the Lord, nothing serious."* His eyes soon adjust to the darkness and the void becomes a tapering trail, beseeching him to move forward – one step at a time.

Indraneil Kamath is running. The trail is a gentle decline with good footing and he makes the most of it. Despite sheer fatigue, the Indian knows he is close to achieving what many thought impossible. Many of his friends and family in northern India, near the Himalaya, had trekked 100 miles. The distance was not the question. The element of time was the question: completing the 100 mile trek in one day – that was the question.

Thinking back on the day's events: the people he had met, the scenery he had witnessed and the plethora of sensations, from despair to elation . . . the man is awestruck at the magnitude of his accomplishment. Kamath points his flashlight at his watch, then quickly back at the trail. It's four twenty. Another flashlight soon appears less than fifty meters ahead and his confidence waxes; just like the phase of the moon vivid on the western horizon. Indraneil squirts a solution of electrolytes into his mouth and contemplates, "Another person to pass."

Simeon is unskilled running in darkness, plus is frustrated that he cannot move faster. The Haitian can barely detect the rocks on the trail and stumbles occasionally. Xavier-Francois has lost track of time as well. He jog-walks off the trail and into the brush. "*Shit, I cannot see anything.*" The Haitian quickly back tracks to the trail and resumes an ambulatory pace. He mutters, "*World class athlete my ass . . . I am nothing more than a helpless invalid. First the diarrhea, now I am blind as a bat.*"

Soon however, a light appears below the embankment. He hears voices and calls out. "*Hello, can you hear me? Can you help me?*"

An attendant jogs up the embankment and finds the runner with no flashlight, no water bottle. He sees the man's leg and sock are stained in blood. "Holy Toledo, you look like you've been put through the ringer there, buddy."

"*I am sorry I do not speak English, but I have need of assistance.*"

"I don't understand a word you said, partner. But let's get you to the aid station and have a look at you." The man declares, "Number 5-45 coming in."

His friends had been cynical when they heard of the Olympic event in which Indraneil had qualified. "You must be mad. How can you run 100 miles across mountainous terrain in less than one day?" Kamath had listened on more than one occasion.

Even his mother had doubted his abilities. "You have spent much time in the mountains with your father and uncles, but my son, you are being irrational. One marathon in one day is foolish in my mind; running four in the same day, that is insanity."

Kamath had reassured his mother. "It is a simple calculation, Mother. I need only to average better than four miles per hour and I will succeed. And like the calculation, my goal is simple too: I wish only to finish the race and not necessarily compete to win." The pundit of pure athletics had paused for a moment and then added, "Competing to win . . . that would be irrational."

Indraneil has adhered to his strategy all day: slow and consistent will finish the race. "Like the tortoise," he had contemplated during the day. That was the cliché several Western States finishers posed. "Run like a tortoise, eat like a pig and drink like a fish." The trail has become rocky – again. He adjusts his pace to account for the obstacles. Kamath feels the punishment of another moderate descent, his quadriceps aching painfully from the pounding. No difference, the finish line is so close; he can taste the sweet sensation of success.

"Hey Curt, you got an extra flashlight for this guy." The attendant appears concerned as he treats the deep gash directly upon the right knee cap of the Haitian runner. "Here, hold this."

Simeon shakes his head, *"I am sorry . . ."*

The attendant places cotton gauze onto the runner's hand and has him apply pressure to the wound, attempting to stanch the blood flow. "Curt, what do you say about that flashlight?"

"I know I've got one in my bag; just hold on a second."

"You'll probably need stitches to close the wound, er . . . number five forty-five."

"His name is Simon Francis, I think." Curtis hands the runner a flashlight and sees the attendant apply a fresh dressing to the wound. "Whoa, that's a lot of blood. Can he continue?"

"I don't know Curt. You want to try and stop him." The attendant knows that a man who has run ninety-seven miles will not quit with three miles remaining. He tapes the gauze firmly to the man's leg. "It's patch work, but it's the best I can do given the circumstances."

Simeon senses the finality of the treatment and stands to continue. *"Thank you for your attention. I am truly grateful. Thank you very much."*

The brief rest has the done the runner good. Regardless of stiffness and soreness, he feels better. Before leaving the aid station he walks over to the table with food and beverages, and decides to drink fluids, plus eat a salty item or two before departing. There is a bulletin board with bold letters and numbers printed. He comprehends the information with ease. *"Only five kilometers remain,"* he translates. Simeon nods when he glances at his watch. *"Ten less than five o'clock."* The Haitian hears the attendant call out that other runners are arriving to the checkpoint. It's of no relevance. He flicks the flashlight on. No Hands Bridge awaits his crossing . . . and so does the finish line.

He has not thrown up for nearly three hours – not since leaving Auburn Lake Trails. His stomach settled; the antacid tablets had been the remedy. The young Irishman crests the top of the last climb above Robie Point. No one is around – no one in front, no one behind. Not one spectator to welcome the conquering hero; Eammon Horgan is all alone. He breathes in the warm morning air, taking in the solitude of his surroundings. Touching the Celtic cross suspended on a leather choker, he ponders the day's events: such a promising start, such an awful collapse. Street lights glow, illuminating a residential zone.

Horgan recalls what a philosophy professor once said when coping with depression or despondency. "It's always darkest the hour before dawn." Removing the soiled cap from his head, a lock of hair falls in his face. Eammon looks at his own shadow cast on the ground and remembers a psalm he had heard at a wake earlier in the year when a friend of the family had suddenly and tragically died. The priest concluded the eulogy, "Weeping may remain for the night my friends, but remember always, rejoicing comes in the morning." He smiles at thought, then pulls his thick reddish hair back and replaces the cap. Morning has arrived.

A sparrow chirps in a nearby sycamore. A squirrel chatters in another. A neighborhood dog barks. The silence broken, Horgan awakens from his reverie. His watch indicates that it's just after five AM and looking eastward he sees a faint glow above the mountains from which he has come. Instinctively, the young man nods and reflects the time, "Time to bring this race to a close." He points to the sky and shouts in his own native Gaelic tongue. "ERIN GO BRAY!"

The descent on asphalt is another welcome reprieve. Gravity with no trail obstacles has distinct advantages. Horgan easily increases his pace, inspired by the sight of the stadium's lights. He enters the cinder track and hears the announcer's welcome. "Number 547, Eammon Horgan of Ireland, is finishing his first 100 mile endurance run. Congratulations Eammon, great job." A modicum of applause follows.

"Well Mr. Horgan, about time you made it." Norman Sproul grins, brimming with the knowledge of a Western States finisher who has finished in the twenty-third hour. "Incredible experience, isn't it?"

"I'm not sure if 'incredible' is the word I would use right now, Norman." The Irishman removes his cap to accept the finisher's medallion. "Not that it really matters, but was my place?"

"I'm not certain of place, fifty-something I think, but your time is 23:07 and change. Not bad considering this is your first trip down the Western States Trail." He offers his hand. "Congratulations."

Horgan forces a laugh when he shakes the race director's hand. "And probably my last trip too."

"Don't be so hasty with your judgment. Many runners reconsider, once they've given their bodies . . . and minds ample time to recover."

Horgan shakes his head. "Well, if you mean a decade or two as ample time for recovery, then maybe . . ."

"You're young. Something tells me you'll return . . . before the end of this decade."

Horgan laughs, "You're quite the seer, Mr. Sproul. But right now, all I want to do is find a comfortable chair to sit my arse." Stepping toward the infield, the Irishman thinks of a passage from Saint Paul. "I have fought the good fight, I've finished the race." Then the man from Cork turns to the race director and adds, "Maybe the word isn't 'incredible,' Norman. The word is indelible."

"Thanks for the compliment, Eammon. We'll see you at the Award's Ceremony." The race director nods at the reply and thinks, "The young Irishman has grown, considerably."

Chapter 20 – Award's Ceremony

"Good morning every body and welcome to Placer High School in Auburn, California. We're here to share in the celebration of the longest running event in the history of the Olympic Games." The camera expands its view to include Sproul, who sports a stained visor with sunglasses perched on the brim of the cap. "Along with me is the man in command, race director Norman Sproul." Brandon Davis appears refreshed in front of the camera after a good night's sleep, shower and shave. In sharp contrast is the disheveled appearance of the race director who has not rested, nor showered, shaved or even changed his clothes. "If you were not with us yesterday, let me bring you up to date on this extraordinary race. Yesterday morning, 162 courageous runners, starting at the base of Squaw Valley, attempted to run 100 miles to the finish line located directly behind me. At five fifty-five this morning the last runner crossed under the banner." The camera pans toward the finishing area and focuses on the yellow banner with navy blue script, "Western States Trail Run, 100 Miles – One Day."

At nine thirty, the morning is already warm – eighty-five degrees warm. Wisps of clouds disperse, remnants of an alpine thunder shower from the day before. Otherwise, the sky's enamel blue canopy is perfect.

"Actually, we had a few 'unofficial' finishers complete the run after the allotted time." The camera finds Sproul rubbing his eyes with his knuckles.

"Unofficial finishers, Norm? What do you mean?"

"There were a few stragglers who completed the run after the six o'clock deadline." Sproul scratches his facial scruff absent-mindedly. "Despite not qualifying for the finisher's award, I will find a way to recognize their achievement."

"Who were the unofficial finishers?"

"I was afraid you would ask me the particulars. Unfortunately, the roster is with a couple of my assistants who are checking the different aid stations' data entries. We have to be sure that all the runners who crossed the finish line are indeed official finishers."

"Can you tell me how many 'official' finishers completed the run?"

"That I can tell you, Brandon. We had seventy-three runners cross the finish line before six AM this morning. And I'm proud to say we only had a couple of incidents that required hospitalization."

Davis inquires in a serious tone, "Nothing serious I hope?"

"I'll have to consult our Medical Director, Chad Logan, before I comment on particulars. But I haven't heard of any fatalities."

"Fatalities?"

"What I mean is that all runners are accounted for and I am not aware of any life threatening incidents or accidents."

"I understand, Norm. One hundred sixty-two men started this race, only seventy-three finished. That's less than half the field. Was that expected?"

Sproul crosses his arms, purses his lips and gestures a "such is life" expression. "Yeah, we expected it. Temperatures reached 112° in the canyons and didn't dip below eighty. Conditions were brutal out there yesterday. And that's the challenge: overcoming what nature throws at you and going beyond what you thought possible. For the seventy-three runners who crossed that finish line," Sproul pauses a moment before continuing his reflections, "and even those who didn't finish; experienced something indescribable. Something they will take with them forever." Despite fatigue, the man's thoughts are lucid. "I can attest from first-hand experience, this race, this course, this trail; it captivates you beyond reason."

Davis senses the emotion. It's visceral - to the point of touching the man's core. "Yes Norman, I can see that. We have to take a short break. We'll return with the medal presentation after these messages. Please stay tuned."

When the camera swings on its turret, a view of the bleachers and the entire stadium reveals thousands of spectators have returned to witness the award's ceremony. Hundreds more are streaming in. Once again, the place is packed.

A recording of the Italian national anthem, *Brothers of Italy,* is playing on the stadium's sound system. The television camera focuses on the four men collectively, and then zooms-in on each individual, fading from one to the other. Three of the men have medals suspended on their chests. Only the Italian is touching his. He has shaved the dark stubble from his face and is all smiles, no tears. Pavin holds a bouquet of flowers which he will deliver to his fiancée at the conclusion of the ceremony. The Japanese and Soviet runners stand stoically, but honorably, respecting the formality of the medal presentation. No question, there is a look of disappointment on the American's face. The anthem concludes. The ovation commences.

"Well, there you have it, a befitting finale for a remarkable event." Brandon Davis begins a final soliloquy. "I have had the opportunity to cover sporting events worldwide, but in all my experience, I have never witnessed such effort, cooperation and proficiency of all whom were involved in this race of endurance. From the race director to every volunteer, and to the runners themselves, each person contributed to the overall success of the race . . ."

Girolamo Pavin's coach has handed his runner a magnum of champagne, and a photojournalist prepares to capture the moment.

Pavin laughs, shaking the bottle vigorously. He uncorks the bottle quickly, allowing the cork to shoot into the audience which has overflowed to the infield of the track. A photographer snaps the picture just before being sprayed by the effervescent fluid. Other bystanders feel the cool moisture stick to their flesh. The Italian takes a long swallow and then hands the half-filled bottle to Okuda. *"Drink! Drink!"*

Before the Japanese runner can respectfully decline, he is clutching the bottle and looking for any excuse to return it to Pavin. Akira shakes his head, not wishing to insult his rival. *"Thank you, no Giro-san, I prefer not . . ."*

Pavin is obstinate. *"Take some, drink it. It is life."*

When the crowd observes what's happening, the throng chants, "Chug, chug, chug . . ."

Okuda does not understand the words, but sees the Italian gesturing to drink and remembers a saying he had learned long ago in school: *"When in Rome . . ."* He gulps a portion of the contents into his gullet and then wipes the excess from his lips. *"Thank you Giro-san."* Akira returns the bottle to its owner and waves to the audience.

An obstreperous cheer ensues.

The Italian passes the bottle to the Russian, who in turn drinks a healthy portion. His stoicism vanishes, replaced with a genuine smile. "You drink, Nathan Washington." Briefly, he peruses the man he had studied extensively, the man who was supposed to win – the overwhelming favorite. Watching the American drink, Yuri thinks, "*You are truly a great runner, but you are even a better man.*"

Washington had refused to take part in a coin toss to decide who would receive the only bronze medal available. He had tersely insisted to give the medal to Boroshkov, who in turn insisted on giving it to Washington. The American won-out when he explained through an interpreter, "Tell Yuri I would be insulted if he did not accept something from me when offered in 'my house.' Please, take it. I can get another medal later." The Russian had reluctantly accepted.

Boroshkov feels fluid spill on his head and drip down his face. Washington has doused him with champagne. He sees the American laugh at the boorish prank. "*And you are a bastard's son as well, Nathan Washington.*"

Washington acknowledges, "Got'cha!"

"I know that every man who arrived at this race had a story to tell - a story of preparation, dedication and sacrifice. For those seventy-three men who successfully completed the run, they have a story of triumph as well." Davis continues, "We have attempted to show you a glimpse into the world of endurance running – ordinary people attempting the extraordinary. We have witnessed uncompromising despair and absolute elation. It appears we didn't have just one winner today, we had seventy-three. I saw exultation on the faces of those who crossed the finish line - an unforgettable look of accomplishment and achievement. No question, all the runners will take this experience with them forever – to share with their family and friends where ever these intrepid athletes call home.

"We return now to our studios in Los Angeles and the preliminaries of the track and field competition at the Coliseum. I'm Brandon Davis. Farewell from Auburn, California."

The camera man flicks a switch. "And that's a wrap."

"Yes it is." Brandon Davis takes a deep breath. His equivocal thoughts about this assignment at the XXIII Olympiad have become unequivocally clear. An inaugural event of a bunch of unknown, misguided, foolish men, traipsing 100 miles across the mountains has transformed him. "These men . . . and women, every single one of them, have earned my respect - from the Olympic champion to the last volunteer." He too, will never forget.

The camera man nods. "Ditto that for me too, Brandon." It's been a pleasure working with you."

In the middle of the stadium, on the make-shift wooden platform, Norman Sproul stands behind a podium and speaks methodically into a microphone. "Can I have your attention? Can I have your attention, please? We would like to begin the awards ceremony at this time." After a long pause, the race director exclaims, "Well, we did it!" There is a roar, followed by thirty seconds of cheering and applause. Sproul holds his hands high to quiet the crowd. "Before we begin with the awards, there are several people I gotta' thank." He sees Davis loading a van on the far side of the infield. Pointing his index finger towards the journalist he acknowledges, "Brandon Davis and ABC, thanks so much for the outstanding coverage of our race." He claps his hands a few times and the spectators are happy to oblige the recognition of a job well done.

Davis waves before stepping into the van and his eventual departure.

When the multitudes simmer, he points at one of the medical tents. "Chad Logan, M. D., are you in there?"

Logan appears near the entrance of one of the tents and waves.

"Sproul inquires, "No casualties, right Doc?"

The doctor yells, "Plenty of casualties, but nothing of permanent consequence, Norm."

The crowd demonstrates their approval.

"Gatorade, Exceed, Coca Cola, Motrim, Safeway, Levi Straus have all donated items and invested into the success of this Olympic edition of the Western States Trail Run. I speak for the foundation when I say, we are truly grateful."

Sproul waits a minute for the crowd to quiet. "And lastly, I would be totally remiss not to thank, from the bottom of my heart, the thousand volunteers who have graciously given of themselves throughout the entire event. Without you, there is no Western States."

After a long pause, waiting for the few hoots and hollers to subside, Norman Sproul begins the presentation of awards. On the platform there is a table stacked with small white boxes, plaques and two large trophies – the Cougar Trophy presented to the winner of the race, plus the Robie Cup with the names engraved of past champions. "As is custom we will begin with those individuals who . . ." Clearing his throat he smiles, "Those tortoises who completed the run and then move onto the more . . ." Another brief pause follows, "the swifter."

"Last, but certainly not least, from Krakow, Poland; Tomaz Weglowski.

Stepping from the crowd, a man with thinning blonde hair ambles gingerly up three stairs, obviously in much discomfort. He grins, hearing the mispronunciation of his surname.

"Tomaz is our first 'unofficial' finisher. Despite not meeting the mandatory twenty-four hour time limit, we still would like to give him an award befitting a true stalwart." Sproul hands the man a handsome Western States plaque. "Tomaz completed the course in twenty-four hours forty-six minutes." Applause follows.

Tomaz neither speaks nor reads English, but is cognizant of the tone of the race director and the beauty of the award. He accepts the award amiably, shaking the race director's hand. *"Thank you, I am honored to be recognized."*

Sproul speaks no Polish. Holding his hand up, he motions to the Polish runner to stay on the platform. "Next from Ica, Peru; Marcos Honor. Marcos finished in twenty-four hours forty minutes."

The spectators acknowledge each recipient with a suitable round of applause.

Nathan Washington feels the pats on his back and shoulders, and hears the numerous salutes.

"Congrats Nate . . ."

"Great run, Nate . . ."

"Third place isn't bad - great job."

Washington offers cordial salutations and thanks in return while weaving through the people who have congregated on the infield. He spots Badillo with his wife and kids and moves in their direction. "Hey J. P., missed you down the stretch, buddy. What happened?"

Susan places her arm around her husband, her other hand holding onto one of the children trying to escape. Susan scolds the child, insisting on better behavior.

Juan-Pablo appears subdued. "Knee problems, Nathan. Just wasn't meant to be, not this time anyways." His younger son is holding onto his right leg – the leg without the wrap. "I was fine until we reached Foresthill. Then the downhill stretch really started to take its toll." He shakes his head, placing his hand instinctively on his son's shoulder – offering support and receiving some too.

"Sorry to hear that, man. How bad is it?"

"There's swelling, but I don't think there's permanent damage." Badillo removes a cap with an Angeles Crest logo embroidered into it and scratches his forehead. "I mean I didn't feel any crack or snap or anything like that – just a whole lot of hurt." The man avoids cursing in front of his children. "Frustrating Nate, very . . . frustrating."

"What's the plan now?"

Susan intervenes. "We're going to collect our buckle, then head for home. Right, Darlin'?" She pecks her husband on the cheek.

"I saw your time, J. P.; sub eighteen hours and a top twenty finish. Not bad considering your knee." Washington nods approvingly.

"Not what I wanted, Nathan." The Mexican feels an emptiness inside that a consolation award will not satisfy. "I really thought we, er . . . I had a shot."

"And our last two unofficial finishers, who missed the twenty-four cut-off by mere minutes, from South Africa, Ernest Van der Zandt and Retief Greyling." When the men arrive on the platform, Sproul hands each man a distinctive walnut plaque with the words engraved: "Sub 30 Hour Finisher."

Both men accept their award and sincerely thank the race director, exchanging handshakes and smiles.

The race director announces. "Ernest and Retief would have arrived sooner, but instead, they decided to take a more scenic route." He pats both men on their shoulders and invites the dozen other unofficial finishers to come forward. "I cannot translate what I'm about to say to these fine men, but if you can," pointing to the audience, "please pass the following message onto them." Sproul collects a few well intended thoughts. "I, er . . . Excuse me. We . . . we challenge you to return here and run our race again. I personally would like to see you all come back and become 'official' finishers of the Western States Trail Run."

Van der Zandt requests the use of the microphone from Sproul. He looks at the audience for a moment and petitions, "Only if you come to South Africa, Norman and run our Comrades Marathon." The man from Pietermaritzburg grins, returning the microphone.

There is much cheering and shouting when Sproul declares, "That can be arranged, Ernie." He waits for the athletes to exit the stage. "We now begin the recognition of those finishers who completed the run in under twenty-four hours. Each will receive our coveted award - a sterling silver belt buckle with the words engraved, '100 MILES, ONE DAY.'"

Taking one of the white boxes from the table, he requests, "From Finland, finishing with five minutes to spare; I won't even try to pronounce the name of his home town. Anders Hamalainen, please come on up. Anders finished seventy-third in a time of twenty-three hours fifty-four minutes." He looks into the crowd to find the recipient noticeably limping.

Hamalainen elects not to use the stairs and accepts his buckle from the race director in front of the platform. "Thank you, Norman. You and your staff have done fine work." The Finnish runner accepts the white box, but does not open it.

"You're welcome Anders, great run." Sproul hands the Finnish runner the microphone. "You must pronounce the name of your home town. Please?"

The man grins and replies eloquently. "Certainly, I am Anders Hamalainen from Uusikaupunki, a city on the North Sea."

Sproul grasps the microphone and says, "Now you guys can understand the importance of bib numbers!"

"Where's the hardware, Bro?" Clint Washington had not heard the news about the single bronze medal awarded to the Russian. "You tied the guy, right?"

"There was only one bronze medal here, so they gave it to Boroshkov." Nathan appears unconcerned.

"They gave it to the Russian! What the hell for?" Clint responds cynically.

"No worries Clint; I'll get another one later. It's no big deal."

Both men are sitting in the bleachers of the stadium with their feet propped on the bench in front of them, sipping on bottles of water; Nathan's thirst not completely quenched.

". . . Finishing sixty-fifth in twenty-three hours thirty nine minutes, from Cap Haitian, Haiti; Xavier-Francois Simeon."

Simeon limps to the platform, his injured knee stitched and bandaged. He fixes his eyes on the race director and says, *Thank you for your great race. You have given me something that I will cherish for the rest of my life. I will never forget what happened here. Ne plus ultra!*" He takes the white box and shakes Sproul's hand firmly.

Norman Sproul appears confused. "I'm sorry I don't speak French, Mr. Simeon."

An Algerian finisher overhears the statement and translates, then adds, "I believe the Haitian speaks for us all. Peace, harmony and blessings be upon you." The North African runner half bows touching his chest, lips and forehead, a sign of Islamic reverence.

Sproul steps back to the podium, truly touched by the statements of both men. "Your welcome; but believe me, you all have given much in return."

"That's Nathan, always the gracious host. Can't you just be an asshole once in a while and raise some shit?"

"You know Clint, that's what I love about you – always the diplomat. By the way, where's Gioia?"

"From Delhi, India our sixtieth finisher; Indraneil Kamath completed the run in twenty-three hours twenty-nine minutes."

". . . of course I can ride a horse." The Indian finds his conversation interrupted by the announcement to come forward and receive an award. Kamath touches the woman's hand with whom he is talking. "Please wait. I'll be just a moment, Andrea." He looks into the hazel eyes of the rider he had met the day before and sees a sincere smile reply to his request.

"She's mingling with the tourists." Clint watches the proceedings with little interest. He has attended several awards' ceremonies and finds little difference with this one. "You know I hope this ends soon, 'cause I'm bored shitless."

"Won't be too much longer, Bro. There were only seventy finishers."

"Swell."

". . . finishing fifty-fifth, from Oslo, Norway, Matts Larsen. Matts time was twenty-three hours seventeen minutes."

". . . from Malmo, Sweden, finishing fiftieth in a time of 23:02, Per Olafsson."

"Hey Nate, you're not going to give one of your long-winded sermons about what a great event this has been or what this race means to you or anything like that, are you?" Clint Washington tugs on his sunglasses, peering over the rims at his younger brother.

Nathan does not bother to look at his older brother. "Not this time, Clint. Speeches are for the winners." He sees the queue of twenty-three hour finishers disperse into the crowd.

Norman Sproul grabs the one remaining plaque on the table and then quiets the crowd. "Usually, there are age group awards we give to runners at our annual Western States event. Since this is an Olympic event, we excluded the age division awards. However, we've made one special exception." The race director pauses, sipping on bottled water. "To the first master's finisher, the first finisher forty years or older, I am happy to present this Master's Division award to an individual who is forty-four years young – our most veteran participant. And I should add that since we only had one finisher over forty, awarding this plaque is a cinch.

"He has a breadth of running experience – worldwide. A veteran of three Olympic games . . . he has demonstrated true mettle and resolve in a number of venues." Sproul pauses to commit to memory time and place. "I am pleased to present the Master's Champion plaque to the eldest runner in our race who completed the run in twenty-two hours twenty minutes; the forty-fifth finisher overall, from Manchester, England; Nigel William Preverett."

The roar is deafening.

Preverett ambles to the stage, enjoying the moment. He has never received this type of reception – ever. He shakes Sproul's hand and accepts the plaque and belt buckle yelling, "Any excuse to revel in the moment, eh Norman."

Sproul passes the microphone. "They're all yours, Nigel."

Preverett faces his captors, doffing his cap equipped with havelock, and placing it under his arm. "I am honored to stand here today, a finisher of the Western States Trail Run." He pauses momentarily and then continues, "I had not conceived that this race would attract so many quality people, and I'm not just talking about the competitors." He points the microphone at the audience.

Another loud roar amplified by the sound system resonates throughout the stadium.

"You have all done a superb job preparing and presenting a race that is unparalleled to anything I have experienced before. I wish to commend all those who assisted in yesterday's event. Indubitably, the success of such an event depends on race personnel and the race personnel assembled here are the finest."

More applause and cheering interrupt Preverett's speech.

The British runner removes the sterling buckle from its box and holds it on his waistline. Grinning, he declares, "I only have need of a fine steed to make this picture of the American West complete. Thank you all."

Clint Washington claps. "Hear that Nathan. The acceptance speech took less than a minute. Remember 'KISS' when you get up there, okay?"

"Keep it simple stupid?" Nathan looks at his brother quizzically. "Keep it simple, stupid? What do you think I intend to do? Speak in parables or paradigms, innuendos or just pure rhetoric. You know me, Clint. If I can't impress 'em with my intellect, then . . ."

"I know Bro; you'll baffle 'em with your bullshit." Clint shakes his head, annoyed. "KISS stands for keep it short, stupid!" He sees his cousin approaching. "Hi Gioia, what's happening? Meet any cute guys?"

Their cousin smiles. "In fact I did - a cute Spanish guy . . . I think he's Spanish."

Nathan replies. "Good to hear, Gioia. What's his name?"

"Eduardo, er . . . something or other. He said he's from Pamplona."

Clint laughs. "Did you ask him if he's been chased by any 'cute' bulls lately?"

". . . Finishing thirty-ninth in a time of twenty-one hours twelve minutes, from Yugoslavia; Dusan Majic.

"Our thirty-third finisher is from Cameroon. Paul Sonkin completed the run in twenty hours four minutes."

"In sixteenth place from Copper Canyon, Chihuahua, Mexico; Reno's own Juan-Pablo Chacarito Badillo. J. P. finished in seventeen hours fifty-seven minutes."

Susan kisses her husband softly. "Keep your chin up, Hubby and go pick up your second Western States belt buckle." Susan reaches for their younger son who is being held by her husband.

Badillo shakes his head. "You come with me."

"Come with you? What the hell for?" she asks puzzled.

"Just come with me," J. P. reasserts. "Just come with me."

"Okay, if that's what Daddy wants, that's what Daddy gets."

When the family of four arrives on stage, Sproul smiles since he has witnessed this scene before. "Congratulations, J. P. – great race."

Instead of taking the white box, Badillo asks for the microphone. Facing the audience he begins his personal dedication. "I'm sure I speak for all the family men who rely on the support of their loved ones to help

272

through the daily grind of work, training and life. I dedicate this race and this belt buckle to my wife, Susan. I wouldn't be here without her."

Susan is awestruck. She sees her husband take the white box and remove its contents. J. P. holds the belt buckle for all to see; its sterling face shimmering in the midmorning sunlight. She feels her husband's lips press against hers.

"This is for you, Susan – forever."

The cheers can be heard throughout Auburn.

"The twelfth finisher is from Tel Aviv, Israel; Joshua Kostinski." Sproul sees the Israeli runner making his way to the stage. "His official time is seventeen hours thirteen minutes. Joshua was leading for a time yesterday. Let's give him a fine round of applause."

When Kostinski arrives, he hops easily onto the stage and shakes the race director's hand. "Great race, Norm. May I say a few words?"

"Certainly." Sproul hands the microphone to him and steps backward three paces.

The Israeli inhales deeply before speaking. "During my life many people have asked me, with all the turmoil and violence in the world, why I still believe in God and specifically, why Judaism remains my faith."

A hush descends on his audience.

"I have often answered this query with an adage; for those who believe, no explanation is necessary, and for those who do not believe, no explanation is possible.

"Before coming here, people asked me similar questions about running 100 miles. Why run 100 miles? What are you trying to prove? And I answered similarly; for those who understand, no explanation is necessary and for those who do not understand, no explanation is possible." Joshua smiles at all those assembled and then shouts, "You understand! Thank you so much, I will not forget you!"

The man born in Israel, raised on a kibbutz and educated in the United States is an inspiration to all who listen.

The applause is frightfully loud.

"I would like the bronze medalists to come up here: Yuri Boroshkov of the USSR and Nathan Washington of the USA."

The chant resumes. "usa, USA, **USA, USA** . . ."

273

Norman Sproul holds his hands up, attempting to quiet the crowd. "Please, please . . . I'm sure each man has something to say." He hands the hometown favorite the mike first, hoping Nathan can quell the flood of noise coming from the masses. "There all yours, Nate."

"Thanks a lot, Norm." Washington covers the mike and smiles at Boroshkov. Would you like to say something?" Before the Russian can protest, he hands him the microphone and then raises both hands.

The spectators soon quiet themselves, wishing to listen to what the foreigner has to say.

Boroshkov steps forward to commence his address. "Thank you very much . . . for your hospitality. I wish I can speak English better, but I am not good at speaking your tongue." Yuri collects a few thoughts and then translates the best he can. "You all have a great race with great people helping. You must be very . . . er . . . *proud*. I am sorry I cannot think of the word."

A few people in the audience who speak Russian recognize the word and translate for those around them. Everyone nods, approving of the Russian's efforts.

"I may not return here, but I know with certainly, I will not forget this race and as important, I will not forget you."

The two Americans on stage look stupefied. Sproul acknowledges, "I guess he can speak English."

"Good enough in my book," says Washington. The American hands the Russian an open box showing the Russian his latest acquisition. "Congratulations Yuri. You ran a great race."

"Thank you, Nathan. You are a great runner and a great man." Boroshkov hands the American the microphone and steps behind the race director.

"Ultra running has taken a huge step forward today." Washington pauses to allow the spectators to settle before continuing. "My older brother told me to keep this short, so I will heed to his wisdom." The American looks at the audience and recognizes one man in particular. "Ten years ago a man came here to ride one hundred miles on his horse, and when his horse came-up lame, rather than withdraw, he made the 'lame' decision to tackle the distance on foot." Washington chuckles and then adds, "We all owe him a dept of gratitude for demonstrating that anything is possible when one considers the potential that exists within us all. Gordy, raise your hand." Washington sees the man with light hair and a tawny beard raise his right hand, appearing astonished for the recognition. "He certainly merits all our praise considering his contribution to our sport, or all the blame depending on how you want to look at it."

Speaking passionately, the bronze medalist proceeds. "Last month two hundred fifty runners completed the Western States Trail Run, and one hundred sixty eclipsed the twenty-four hour barrier – the largest number of finishers ever. Our sport is growing leaps and bounds, and all of you who have participated, whether finisher or DNF'er, are a testament to what the human spirit can conquer." Washington pauses, waiting for the energy to wane.

"Surely, I want to thank all the volunteers who worked through the day and night, yesterday. I know it's been said often, but without your dedication, without your hard work, there is no race. And lastly, I want us all to recognize the one man whose diligent work of coordinating the enormous task of putting this race together – an Olympian in his own rite, Stormin' Norman Sproul!"

Washington yells above the cacophony of sound rising from the stadium. "Congratulations Norm, once again, you've put on a great show."

The race director waits a full minute, hoping to concentrate on the final two presentations. "Thanks a lot . . . thanks much . . . you're all too kind . . . please, please . . .

"I would like all of you to give an Olympic salute to our silver medalist, Akira Okuda; come up to accept your award."

Akira Okuda understands few English words and speaks even fewer and yet, he is overwhelmed with the proceedings. The energy resulting from the ceremony is unlike anything he has witnessed. Okuda accepts his belt buckle, bowing in deference to the man in charge. *"Thank you, Norman-san. You are too kind. Thank you."*

Sproul prevents the Japanese runner from departing. "Please wait one moment. I have something I would like to say to you and Pavin." He speaks slowly to Akira, hoping a few words sink in, and then turns to the audience. "If someone speaks Japanese, please come up here. We need a translator."

A young Asian woman in her twenties arrives on stage. The three individuals exchange proper salutations.

Sproul then returns his attention to the audience. "Olympic Champion. Western States Champion. Both have a nice ring, don't they. Let's give a champion his due . . . Girolamo Pavin, come on up!"

Pavin recognizes his name and simultaneously feels a pinch on his buttocks, care of his fiancée. He beckons her to come with him. "*Please Sabrina, your English is much better than mine.*" Girolamo tugs gently on the gold medal which he has strapped around his fiancée's neck. The Italian senses her concession when she reluctantly agrees. The two walk hand in hand toward the stage, both sporting chic sunglasses.

"Nice meeting you. Can you speak English? Sproul asks the young woman beside the gold medalist.

With a delicate smile Sabrina replies, "Yes, a little."

Taking the robust, bronze Cougar Trophy from the adjacent table, Sproul presents the most coveted award in ultrarunning. "I am pleased and happy to present the Cougar Trophy to the champion of this Olympic edition of the Western States Trail Run, Girolamo Pavin."

The crowd, once again, applauds feverishly.

Pavin is awestruck. He hears Sabrina's interpretation, but he's not listening. The Italian sees his name engraved on the trophy - recognizes the name of the trail, the date and the Olympic rings inscribed below his name. He gulps, attempting to restrain the inevitable. His eyes moisten and a tear spills onto his cheek.

"*Be strong my love. Courage now. Remember, no tears, you promised.*" Sabrina stops speaking and steps backward; she can't even hear herself think, let alone translate.

Girolamo Pavin kisses the bronze cougar and then hoists the trophy into the air for all to see.

The ovation continues.

Norman lifts the Robie Cup, and then points at Girolamo Pavin's name already engraved on the side of the trophy. His is the eleventh recorded below the large silver chalice.

The Italian recognizes only one other name on the trophy – the American whom he had past just after crossing the bridge called No

Hands. *"Thank you, Sir. But, you are too kind."* He wipes a tear from his cheek with the back of his hand.

Sproul motions for Okuda to come forward. He practically shouts at the two women to translate the best they can. Speaking into the microphone he requests the attention of the audience one last time, "Please, please. I just have one more thing to say . . .

"Many people asked me to predict the outcome this race. And many of you recall I predicted Washington had the best chance to win, since Nate lives and trains here, and I believe that experience on the trail is irreplaceable." Sproul admonishes himself. "Well, I was disproved yesterday. Two newcomers arrived here and proved that anyone can win this race. These two men have shown true grit and determination. They, like all the other runners, have taught us all an invaluable lesson." Sproul stops his reflection momentarily. "That anyone of us is capable of doing far more than what we once thought possible. What's the cliché? Oh yeah; we're all better than we think we are and we can do much more than we think we can." Sproul waves and offers another broad smile.

Turning he hears the final comments of the women translating to each respective competitor. He shakes Okuda's hand and then Girolamo's a final time proclaiming, "You two are truly remarkable. Congratulations."

High energy music is playing on the stadium's sound system. Blue Oyster Cult's, "Don't Fear the Reaper" is blasting through the midmorning air. Some are mingling, some are dancing; others exchange handshakes and hugs; all are congratulating one another. The celebration continues . . .

*   *   *

As with any significant event in a person's life, one salient outcome is omnipresent among all the competitors. Each runner left a piece of himself on the Western States Trail the day before, and each runner takes a piece of the trail with him. And the piece taken will persist through a lifetime, regardless of race, religion or nationality. Whether the man walks a trail in the Snowy Mountains of Southeastern Australia, or backpacks between the refuges found in the Dolomites of Southern Austria, or treks across the footpaths of the Central Himalaya, each runner will always remember the day he crossed the mountains and foothills of the Western Sierra Nevada in one day's time. And no matter which path, whether figurative or literal, the runner chooses to follow during his life time, he has learned much about himself and what he is capable of accomplishing.

To quote Rudyard Kipling regarding boys becoming men: "If you can fill the unforgiving minute with sixty seconds' worth of a distance run, yours is the earth and everything that's in it." For these men who defied both time and distance, their unforgiving day was filled with twenty-four hours of an incredible endurance run none would soon forget. And for that single day when the world watched, the planet was rightly theirs.

Their destiny partially fulfilled, each man will draw strength from the mountains and the experiences held deep within.

Chapter 21 - Squaw Valley, California
7 February 2004

"Daddy, when are we going on the sled? You said you would take me and . . ."

"I know Little One. We're going very soon. I just want to show you something - something Daddy did long ago." The American has his daughter's tiny hand in his. The two are walking across a spacious parking lot filled with SUVs, jeeps and other all-wheel drive vehicles. He looks down into his youngest daughter's, hazel-brown eyes and sees frustration. Her fawn hair is tied neatly into two pig-tails. "Don't worry, it won't take long."

"Okay Daddy, but remember, you promised."

People mill about the ski lodge, looking more like models than weekend skiers. Taken from the pages of Vogue or Gentlemen's Quarterly, they dress to impress the opposite gender . . . or the same, if sexual preference precludes their disposition. Gortex suits, large fiberglass boots and fashionable accessories illustrate their wish to demonstrate their current position within the social strata.

A digital recording of Evanescescence's, "My Immortal" plays over an audio system in which the music sounds superb. The fidelity is so good; the musicians could be playing live on the veranda of the ski lodge.

Light flurries of snow fall from gray skies. A ten to twelve foot snow base greets the skiers and mounds of snow are piled everywhere around the walk ways. Winter recreation is in fifth gear.

The American wears a pair of faded blue jeans and an insulated metro jacket. His once thick, long reddish-brown hair has long since thinned, and faded to gray. His hair is trimmed and his face clean-shaven. He's twenty pounds heavier than when he raced, yet still appears youthful in his canter. The two individuals approach a large boulder with a bronze plaque emplaced into the stone.

People engaged in conversations or imbibing spirits are oblivious to their presence.

"Can you read that?" The American stands behind his daughter and points to the plaque in front of them. A flawless snow flake clings to her cheek and then quickly melts.

"Sure Daddy. Miss Johnson says I'm a good reader."

A proud father replies, "So I've heard."

"Wh . . . Whest . . . ern Sta . . . Western States . . . End . . . ur . . . ance Run"

"Very good, Little One, continue." Deep within his own blue eyes, he sees a little girl whose innocence and sweetness are adorable.

"Daddy, this is the race you did a long time ago, isn't it?"

Goosebumps surface on the back and shoulders of the five-time Western States Champion. "Yes, it is. Go on, keep reading." The man begins to reminisce when he reaches to touch the Olympic rings engraved at the bottom of the plaque.

"This pla . . . aqu is ded i c . . ."

Nathan Washington thinks not of the five Cougar Trophies that garnish his fireplace mantle, or the Olympic bronze medal that adorns an adjacent wall, nor the sterling belt buckle fastened to a leather belt on his waistline. Instead, he recollects the race he was supposed to win. A time when the world came to his race, and people from all corners of the world watched and wondered in amazement as men engaged themselves in a fierce struggle against nature's harshest elements. The Olympic race had raged on for hours – from sunrise till sunset and for some, practically another sunrise. A race that pitted . . .

"Daddy, what's this word mean? Rugd?"

"You mean rugged, right?"

"Oh, rugged, that means really rough."

Washington nods, "You're almost done. Keep going."

Few of the men from the 1984 Olympics had ever returned. The Canadian, Jones was one. Badillo another. Even the zealous Irishman, Horgan had returned in attempt to win. All would significantly improve, but none would ever be crowned Western States Champion. In fact, the only foreign name ever engraved on the Robie Cup was the Italian's. Washington had lost contact with nearly everyone from the 1984 race, except J. P. who would occasionally surprise him with a phone call or a visit.

280

How close he had come to greatness. A myriad of times Nathan had thought, one more push to the finish line, one more burst of energy, and Olympic glory achieved. Over the years the scenario had been played many times in his mind, and only in his dreams he had visualized success. Awakened from his reverie like many times before . . .

The daughter looks up and finds a blank stare on her father's face. "Daddy, are you okay?" After a brief pause she adds, "Let's go find Mommy."

Snapped out of another daydream Daddy replies, "That's a good idea; let's go find Mommy." Washington gazes upward at the snow covered mountains and knows these mountains have befriended him . . . on more than one occasion. And deep inside, he is thankful, shouldering no regret about what he had or had not accomplished.

The Atari's progressive version of the tune "Boys of Summer" resonates through an open courtyard. The American immediately recognizes the lyrics and murmurs, "I like Henley's original version better."

"What did you say, Daddy?"

Smiling, he gently clutches his daughter's hand. "Nothing, nothing of importance, Little One." The two stroll to the parking lot from which they had arrived, amidst the winter's grandeur of the monolithic Sierra Nevada.

EPILOGUE

The robust male easily lifted his friend and tossed him into the water. The splash and subsequent noise captured the attention of the few endemic birds and mammals that remained close to the watering hole, watching the two hominids frolic in the shallows of the lake. The smaller one swam to his friend and tackled him gamely; the heavier one's weight buoyed by waist deep water. The larger one, surprised by the strength of his friend and his ability to swim underwater, stumbled to find good footing. Momentarily, the two young men forgot about their hunger and thirst, forgot about predation and survival. They simply had fun splashing, wrestling and acting as juveniles . . . for a time.

The smaller male, a year older and a year wiser, had run away from his buddy over the last quarter mile of the race. As hard as the younger male tried to withstand the surge of his opponent, he could not muster the energy or skill to keep pace. Muscles inevitably binding, he watched helplessly as the lesser male's back became more distant until invariably, the other disappeared into the shallows of the lake. Shortly thereafter, but which seemed for a long time, the victor jumped straight up into the air, initially causing apparent consternation as to what the winner had encountered when he entered the murky water. However, upon turning the lesser male exulted, grinning ear to ear and chattering like a hyena. When the larger male arrived less than a minute later, both individuals breathed heavily, spent from the two mile race. And that's when the robust male, after assisting the smaller one to his feet, had hoisted him into the air and hurled him like a large stone.

Closer inspections of the lake's banks revealed edible grasses, bulbs and tubers to the delight of the trespassers. In addition, minnows, crickets and worms were readily consumed. The auspicious day had indeed paid dividends to the two juveniles. They had encroached on the animals and plants living in the riparian habitat, reaping its rewards. But since the two were nomadic by nature, they would depart by days end leaving the habitat to its original caretakers. Both males approached reproductive maturity, and nature compelled them to continue their quest – a quest for the survival of their species.

Above the rocky crag from which they came loomed a large thunderhead cloud. Its enormous gray mass darkened the skies creating an ominous sight – the portent of a savanna tempest. It was late afternoon when the lesser male caught sight of an incendiary flash followed by more tendrils of incandescence. He pointed at the streaks of dazzling white light emanating from the thunderhead as deep groans of thunder resonated into the basin. They were scared of nature's wrath and decided the time had come to move on. Hastened by the approaching squall, each quickly wrapped food stuffs into large green leaves which were easily portable. The land opposite the thunderhead was flat and the horizon revealed wide open space, beckoning them to explore a new territory. The two young men began to jog . . .

Acknowledgements and Postscript

As an author, trying to recollect all the people to whom I have spoken, interviewed and/or communicated is a daunting task to say the least. Simply put, there are too many to list here and to be truthful, too many I've forgotten. But nonetheless, there are a few who assisted me in my endeavor to complete this work of fiction, and I would be remiss not to mention their names. First and foremost, Dr. Roberta Reynolds of the College of San Mateo was instrumental in helping me learn to write clearly and skillfully. Without her, this novel would have been nothing more than a pipedream. In addition, her students often offered incisive and sometimes harsh criticism regarding the manuscript. Without their contribution, progress would have been tediously slow, and my writing would not have been nearly as good. The three years of attending Dr. Reynolds' classes helped give me purpose and direction. Dr. Scott Bennett of Georgian Court University offered sound advice and insight regarding some of the historical aspects of the novel dating through the 1980's. Yvonne Sullivan, my editor, spent numerous hours reading, correcting and ultimately, polishing the script, preparing it for publication. Zoltan Chulay provided valuable comments regarding certain aspects of the narrative and character development. Michelle Wilkinson assisted in preparing the cover pages and formatting the text for print. Each aforementioned individual kindly offered their expertise to aid and assist the author, bringing this novel to the reality of publication.

Thank you very much.

Two great influences that positively impacted my life were running and travel. During the 1980's I made the most of my opportunity to travel, train and race. Every holiday brought a new place, new culture and most often, a different language. I reveled in thought of visiting new lands and meeting new people, and I always brought my running shoes with me. Regardless of location I always took the time to run, preferably on trails. The new people I met offered a different testimony, describing their lifestyles, families and cultures. Without question, these individuals I met along the path called life taught me many meaningful lessons, providing a global perspective on issues facing humanity. The bottom line: we as a species, though quite sophisticated, are as diverse as the animal and plant kingdoms combined. If you do not agree with me, then just compare the male and female sexes of <u>Homo</u> <u>sapiens</u>. I rest my case!

In terms of running – running gave me strength. And that strength carried over to other aspects of my life – both personal and professional. This book is a reflection on the strength of which I speak. Few people believed that I could persevere and complete the task of writing <u>100 Miles to Destiny, a Novel on Running</u>. The naysayer or two who told me this project was beyond my means did not know my obstinate persona. Just imagine telling a person who runs 100 mile endurance runs that he/she can't do something; now isn't that ludicrous. I will paraphrase the quote by Nietzsche used earlier in this book: What doesn't kill you – defines you. And like each of the 100 mile endurance runs I completed in the past, this book, despite being a work of fiction, defines me.

Twenty-one years ago in a small cottage near Moncrivello, Italia I sat at an antique wooden kitchen table and began writing notes about an Olympic 100 mile endurance run on the Western States Trail. I still have the original thirty-five pages of hand written material. A marriage, kids, a divorce and yes, even running prevented me from pursuing this endeavor to write "the great American novel." Later, much later, in January of 2001 I took the monumental first step. I enrolled in a writing class at a local junior college and began my personal quest to bring this novel to fruition. Six years later I sit in my office typing on a keyboard the postscript, finally and ultimately, bringing the book to closure. No question, academically, intellectually, creatively, it is the greatest accomplishment of my life. I can honestly declare that no matter how successful (or unsuccessful) the book becomes, I will take the experience with me forever and smile knowing I completed one of my life-long goals.

I am not sure if this story will inspire someone to run 100 miles or write a book about running the distance. Regardless, for me personally, the experience of writing has been an awakening, a renaissance in my life and I know I have greatly benefited from its trials and tribulations. I read a statement not too long ago on an inspirational poster that sums-up my feelings about running and writing: What the mind can conceive and believe, we can achieve.

One final thought regarding the outcome of the novel: Many individuals who read this book may wonder - why an Italian? Why not an East African or other nationality? Aside from personal and historical reasons I care not to elaborate; Race results of the 1980's reveal that Italian nationals won the New York City Marathon three times, plus Italians had fine performances in other international races, culminating with Gelindo Bordin's Olympic gold in Seoul in 1988. Incidentally, Bordin also won Boston in 1990. Alberto Cova successfully defended his ten kilometer gold medal of the Moscow Games with another golden finish in Los Angeles. Don't be misled; Italy has produced some great distance runners over the last twenty-five years. If you do not believe me, just look at the results of the marathon in Athens, 2004.

Cool runnings (Jamaican for Happy Trails),
W. B. M$^{\underline{c}}$.
San Mateo, CA
USA
e-mail: wmccarthy@serrahs.com